Daughter of Valor

Emily Mims

www.BOROUGHSPUBLISHINGGROUP.com

DAUGHTER OF VALOR
Copyright © 2015 Emily Wright Mims

ISBN 978-1941260-99-9

To the men and women of the United States military

With special thanks to our wounded warriors

ACKNOWLEDGMENTS

As with all my work, I did not write this book in a vacuum, but instead had valuable input from several outstanding sources. I would like to thank both my agent, Tina Tsallas, and my editor, Jill Limber, for their always spot-on suggestions on how to make my story a better one. And I would especially like to thank Captain Brian Mims, United States Army, for answering all of mom's questions about all things military, from how a firefight goes down to how a grenade works and what a Special Forces nickname might be. This book could not have been written without his help, and any mistakes I've made are not Brian's but are mine and mine alone. Hooyah!

CONTENTS

DAUGHTER OF VALOR

Chapter One

Al Anbar Province, Western Iraq

The dry desert wind blew through the early morning haze, kicking up licks of dust and sand that sent a reddish cloud rolling through the vicious-looking barbed-wire fence and icing the squat bunkers and scattered military vehicles with a fine layer of red powder. Captain Holly Riley leaned on the hood of a scratched and dented-up armored Humvee and squinted into the brilliant orange of a desert sunrise. "When do you think the general and the congressmen will get here, sir?"

"Any minute now," Colonel Melton laughed. "I've never seen anyone so eager to go for a joyride with the brass."

"You bet I'm ready to get off this base for a few hours. I'm turning into a fobbit." She despised the "stay safe on base" moniker.

"Tough," Colonel Melton said, trying to keep the laughter out of his voice. "It's your job to be a fobbit on this base. You're the best damned XO I've ever had."

A small smile touched Holly's mouth. "Thanks, sir."

Col. Melton hid a smile that was part amusement, part affection for his young executive officer. It would be good for her to get away from the base for a few hours. Besides, he was not about to deny his boss and the congressmen the company of a sharp and knowledgeable soldier on the fast track to general who just happened to be a beautiful young woman. Even in the DCUs and full body armor Holly Riley was striking, with long auburn hair she wore in a no-nonsense topknot, exquisite cheekbones, and a long aquiline nose. Full lips quick to smile and sparkling golden-brown eyes emphasized what Col. Melton already knew: Holly Riley loved being in the Army, loved being part of the action, and even loved dealing with the tough questions she was bound to face this morning from the congressional delegation.

Her helmet secure on her head, her 9 mm pistol holstered and M4 carbine rifle over her shoulder, Holly waited impatiently until they heard the roar of a Blackhawk helicopter sweeping over the desert. On cue, an armored SUV pulled up driven by Corporal Valdez. "Anything in particular you want me to stress, sir?" Holly asked quietly as the chopper settled noisily on the landing pad.

"Just the usual," Col. Melton said. "Violence is down, cooperation with the Iraqi Security Forces is up, so on and so forth. Sheppard and Acosta will be easy but that old fart Rutledge from North Dakota can be a pain, so lay it on thick with him."

Holly tried not to laugh but failed. "Yes, sir," she said as the chopper's engines whined to a stop and five figures emerged from the cockpit. Holly recognized General Kelley and cameraman Chet Greely. Salutes and "How do you do's" were exchanged all around and Holly ushered them toward the armored SUV. General Kelley put the congressmen and Chet in the back and motioned Holly to sit in the front. Chet immediately started shooting video as the gates to the FOB swung open and the SUV with two escort vehicles headed down the dusty, pitted path that passed for a highway. Corporal Valdez turned his attention to the surrounding countryside, his machine gun cutting from one side to the other as he scanned the rolling desert for any threat.

Congressman Rutledge looked around at the bleak sandy landscape with something close to disdain. "So what is it we're supposed to have accomplished in this God-forsaken hellhole lately?" he demanded.

Holly turned around in the seat as best she could and on the fifteen-mile drive to Husyibah she described the progress that had been made during the long years of war and occupation.

As they entered the village, one of hundreds scattered along the Euphrates River and consisting of mostly squat dusty buildings and parched walkways, it appeared deserted except for a hungry-looking yellow dog scrounging in the fetid garbage outside one of the buildings.

"Why are we stopping here?" Congressman Rutledge asked curtly as the SUV pulled to a stop. "Shouldn't we be getting back to camp?"

General Kelley shot Rutledge a dirty look as a wizened old man emerged from one of the buildings. "We have been granted a rare privilege," General Kelley quietly told the congressman. "Sheik Abad has offered to sit down with you and give you his perspective on our role here and what we've accomplished."

Holly hoped her surprise didn't show; such a meeting was rare and she had not known it was on the agenda.

General Kelley got out of the SUV and motioned for the congressmen to follow. At Holly's direction, the escort vehicles immediately began pulling security on the entire area.

The old sheik, his white robes billowing around him in the desert wind, greeted General Kelley. "As-salamu alaykum and welcome to my village," he said with a perfect British accent, including the congressmen in his greeting.

"Wa alaykumu s-salam, Sheik Abad," General Kelley said. "We are honored to be here." They exchanged more words of greeting and the old man motioned for the general and congressmen to enter the dilapidated old house.

Holly watched the men disappear into the dwelling and wished she could be inside. She would bet a month's pay old Rutledge would have his eyes opened in the next hour or so.

Sure enough, Harry Rutledge's expression was thoughtful as the delegation came out into the bright sunlight. Thanking the sheik for his hospitality, they climbed into the SUV and General Kelley began driving back to the FOB. Holly turned to the congressmen, saying nothing but with a question in her eyes.

"So they prefer the White Devils to Al Qaida," Max Sheppard said thoughtfully.

"Not all of them," Holly admitted. "But a lot of them do."

"Enough to have turned things mostly our way," General Kelley said. "I think—"

"WATCH OUT!" Corporal Valdez roared from the gunner's hole as a flash of light and heat enveloped the vehicle.

The SUV bucked and rose from the pavement, the driver's side crumpling as the explosion blew out the entire left side of the armored truck. Holly stifled a scream as the SUV flew across the road, the screeching and tearing of metal assaulting her ears as the vehicle tumbled down the pavement, its hapless passengers tossed around like so many rag dolls as it pitched and rolled and finally came to a stop on its side a good twenty yards from where the IED, an explosively formed penetrator, had gone off. Pain tore through Holly's knee as she coughed and gagged the stench of sulfur and blood.

We've been hit, she thought dazedly as she tried to blink away the dust. *We caught a damned IED with a load of VIPs in the truck.*

Holly grimaced in pain as she twisted her head around. She felt rather than heard Corporal Valdez moaning on top of her. "Corporal, can you move?" she asked as she tried to squirm out from under him. "See if you can kick open the damned door."

Corporal Valdez groaned. "I think my leg's broken. I can't kick anything."

"Then let me crawl over you," Holly said. She twisted around and gasped at the sight of Chet lying beneath her, now missing the left side of his head. "Aw, hell," she murmured under her breath as she scrambled off the dead man.

Ignoring her own injured leg, she squirmed out from under Corporal Valdez and with her good leg pushed open the SUV door. She could hear movement in the back of the SUV and painfully pulled herself to where she could see into the front seat of the vehicle. One look told her that General Kelley was dead. The congressmen were still alive, but Sheppard and Acosta both had significant injuries. Holly grabbed the radio in the console and thumbed it on. "This is Captain Riley. We were hit by an IED and need a quick reaction force now!"

"We have you on GPS," a disembodied voice on the radio said. "Apaches inbound to your location. ETA one zero minutes. Out."

Ignoring the pain in her mangled leg, Holly backed out of the Humvee and as gently as she could pulled Valdez from the battered vehicle. She looked to her front and saw the lead escort vehicle was toast—completely destroyed by the explosion. She dropped Valdez down behind the overturned vehicle and was reaching for the nearest congressman when a shot rang out and dinged against the front of the SUV. She swore and dove behind the car. "What the hell?" she snapped as another bullet winged the truck.

"It's a fucking ambush, Captain," Valdez snapped as a third bullet dinged the SUV. "They're shooting from over there." Immediately the gunner in the undamaged rear escort vehicle opened up with heavy machine gun fire on the nearby shack. A single, much louder shot from a Russian-made rifle rang out from the shack and the gunner's head viciously snapped back and his body slumped down in the vehicle.

So they have a sniper with them, Holly thought as she crawled to the edge of the downed vehicle. Squinting into the smoke and dust, she could see the barrel of a rusty AK47 assault rifle peeking around the corner of a dilapidated shack in the center of a cluster of ramshackle buildings about fifty yards away. Swearing, she tossed Valdez her M4 rifle. "Cover me. I've got to get the men out before one of them gets shot," she ignored the pain that was making her eyes water.

Holly straightened cautiously and climbed back into the SUV. The white-faced congressmen flinched when Valdez set off a burst of rifle fire. "Unbuckle your seat belts and see if you can move this direction," Holly said soothingly as she reached for the nearest man. The congressmen, one at a time, made their way through the torn metal and dead bodies toward Holly, who half guided and half pulled one man after another down out of the SUV and behind it to relative safety. Holly emerged last with the general's undamaged M4 rifle as well as her pistol and took a position on the other side of the vehicle. A rifle barrel poked out from behind a second building and Valdez shot off another round.

A hooded figure poked his head around the corner of another of the shacks and Holly promptly fired, grimacing wickedly when the figure lurched backward and fell. "Good going, Captain," Valdez murmured as he got off another round at yet another of their attackers.

"Captain, do you have another weapon?" Harry Rutledge asked.

Holly nodded and handed him the general's rifle. As she crawled toward Valdez, the unwelcome odor of leaking diesel fuel teased her nostrils and she spotted a growing puddle of moisture in the otherwise dry sand. "Hells bells, the damn gas tank's ruptured. One spark from a bullet and we're toast."

"Yes, ma'am," Valdez murmured weakly.

Holly glanced around, looking for alternate cover. The rear escort vehicle was too far to try to run to and desert stretched unbroken behind them. The only cover she spotted that might remotely give them alternate shelter was a shallow ditch about twenty yards away. If they could get to the ditch, they might be able to hold off the insurgents until the response team arrived. She jerked her head in the direction of the ditch. "We go there," she said. "I'll get them over there and you cover."

Ignoring the pain in her own leg, Holly helped a shaky Max Sheppard to his feet. Valdez and Rutledge peppered the shacks unmercifully as Holly half-carried first Sheppard and then Acosta to the shallow ditch. "Your turn, Mr. Rutledge," Holly said as she slid back behind the SUV. "And then you can cover me while I help the corporal."

Harry Rutledge looked down at Holly's blood-covered DCUs. "You can barely walk on that leg of yours," he said baldly. "Besides, that boy probably weighs over two hundred pounds. I'll carry him."

Holly looked at the big-boned corporal and nodded her head. She sank down in the dirt and pushed another clip into the rifle, feeling it snap into place. Rutledge squatted down behind Valdez and awkwardly hoisted him to his feet. Holly leaned around the vehicle with her M4 as Rutledge and the corporal left the cover of the SUV and started painfully across the exposed highway. Immediately rifle barrels appeared from behind the shacks but quickly disappeared when Holly sprayed the walls with a liberal burst of fire. She continued to fire round after round toward the crumbling buildings. As the bullets shredded the rotting wood she glanced toward the white-headed congressman and the injured young soldier as they made what felt like glacial progress across the exposed highway. *Please, please get to the ditch before I run out of ammunition,* she breathed as she continued to pepper the dilapidated old buildings.

Finally Rutledge and Valdez disappeared into the blowing sand. Just then Holly felt rather than heard the distant *whomp whomp* of the approaching Apache attack helicopters. *Oh, thank God, now these little al-Qaida bastards are going to pay!* Holly thought as Rutledge poked his head up and motioned to her. She shook her head, motioning to the approaching helicopters, and turned around just in time to see one of the insurgents step out from behind a wall with a rocket-propelled grenade launcher on his shoulder and take aim at the SUV. *Shit no, an RPG,* Holly thought frantically as she scrambled out from behind the wreck. She rolled and jumped up, stumbling on her bad leg and losing precious seconds. Lurching and hobbling, she made her way across the open space as Rutledge sprayed the insurgents.

Please, please let me make it, she thought as she dragged herself as fast as she could toward the ditch and safety. Her mind raced frantically as she felt rather than heard the RPG slam into the SUV behind her.

The force of the impact lifted her off her feet into the air, had her flopping helplessly as she flew upward and spun crazily in the hot desert air. A burning sensation screamed down her left arm and new pain bloomed in her injured leg.

She gasped and uttered a wordless howl as her battered body, still airborne, tumbled end over end through the hot desert morning. Needles of agony burned through her as she reached the apex of her flight. Then gravity began its work, speeding her toward the dusty road. She landed face down on the hot Iraqi highway.

In the awful deafening silence, Captain Holly Riley could feel no more.

Chapter Two

Fourteen months later

The rat-tat-tat of automatic weapons fire filled the air as Major Jimmy Adamcik raced down the Baghdad sidewalk. The stench of explosives teased his nostrils as he and the troops in his command ran toward the courtyard of an old villa, deserted now but for the American soldiers holed up on the roof taking potshots at the insurgents shooting from a stronghold on the next block.

I'd love to get those bastards, Jimmy thought as he struggled to keep up with the much younger soldiers in his unit. They had attacked a convoy and taken out a Humvee full of infantrymen. Jimmy and the men with him were out for blood, and his heart pounded as they covered the last yards to their destination and poured into the palm-lined courtyard.

The privates standing guard, big, hand-picked kids, waved them on with barely a glance. Privates Barnes and Donahue, a couple of cheeky giants from the same part of central Texas as Jimmy, grinned wickedly as Jimmy and his soldiers ran through the courtyard to the winding stairs in the stately old home. Jimmy sprinted up the stairs as fast as he could and burst onto the roof, where he found a small group of soldiers behind the rooftop wall shooting at the ragtag group of fighters returning fire.

"Bout time you got here, Major," said Captain Peterson. "Find anything in the door-to-door?"

"Not a damned thing," Jimmy admitted as he took his place next to Captain Peterson on the wall and aimed his rifle toward the concrete fence. "Those houses were clean as a whistle."

"Maybe we have them cornered," Captain Peterson said. He saw a head pop up above the concrete and fired off a round.

More heads popped up and a hail of bullets sprayed the villa. The soldiers ducked behind the wall as bullets rained down on the old stone walls, splintering the walls and raining puffs of powdered brick. Before the volley had even slowed the Americans were returning fire, sweeping back and forth as they continuously sent round after round toward the fence.

"Shee-it!" Sergeant Washington crowed when a bullet passed within an inch of his head. He scrambled to the wall and sent a round toward the fence. "Hoo-ah! I got one of the bastards!"

"Good going, Washington," Jimmy said as he pumped his fist in the air. Maybe if they could get a few more of them it wouldn't be so bad when they had to leave the relative safety of the villa and take out the rest.

Jimmy hoped to take a few of the younger, more frightened insurgents alive; they would be the most likely to break under interrogation and talk.

More volleys of gunfire were exchanged before the street grew momentarily quiet. The soldiers looked at one another, tension shimmering in the hot Iraqi sun as they peered into the next block. Jimmy's nostrils flared in the heat as he and his men waited for long, tense moments, but the insurgents did nothing. Then a light sound wafted through the air, a sound that did not belong on the war-shredded street below them—the sound of a child's gentle laughter.

The soldiers drew themselves up and peered over the wall. "Shit, it's a little kid," Sergeant Washington said. "By himself out there. Somebody's got to go get him."

Jimmy peered over the roof. Sure enough, a little boy of not more than two or three wandered down the street, talking to himself. "Where the hell did he come from?" Jimmy asked as the child wandered toward the villa. "Those houses we checked were deserted."

"Kid sure picked a sorry place to play," Captain Peterson said. "Are we gonna go get him?"

"Give it a minute. See if the mother shows up," Jimmy said as the child came closer to the courtyard entrance. They watched for long minutes but no adult appeared to see to the child's safety. Jimmy was about to order one of the sergeants to go downstairs and investigate when the privates standing guard spilled into the street and surrounded the child. At that moment Jimmy spotted a figure rising from the behind the concrete wall with a detonator in his hand. "No, get back, it's a trap!" Jimmy screamed as a deafening flash of orange flame exploded from the street and the screams of the dying sounded in his ears...

"No, get back, it's a trap!" Jimmy screamed as he bolted upright in his bed. Sweat poured down his naked chest as he took huge gulps of air and the fishy odor of the lake water took the place of the metallic tang of explosives. He slowly left the streets of Baghdad and returned to his house on the lake and his life as a small-town lawyer in Verde, Texas. It had been years since he had walked the dusty streets of that war-ravaged city but the blasts of weapons and the screams of the dying and the blood and the gore were as fresh in his mind as they had been when he had gone house-to-house that morning.

Jimmy got to his feet and with shaking hands pulled open the curtains to the sliding glass door that opened onto a small balcony overlooking Lake Templeton. A brisk May breeze fluttered the curtains and kicked up waves and a bright half-moon lit the churning water of the lake. Jimmy stood at the window for long minutes, willing the tension in his body to dissipate and his heart to stop pounding. He was not in Iraq anymore. He was not even in the reserves anymore. He was back home now, a small-town lawyer with a house on the lake doing his best to raise his little girl by himself. So why was a part of him still trying to fight a war?

Jimmy glanced at the alarm clock on what used to be Lauren's side of the bed and groaned. It was almost five and he knew there was no way he was going to get any more sleep. Besides, it was not sleep that he craved after the dreams, it was a cigarette. Lauren would have objected, but God bless her soul, she was no longer here to badger him. He rooted around in the night stand and finally found an old lighter and the remnants of a pack. Pulling on a T-shirt from the pile of unfolded laundry on Lauren's loveseat, he loped down the stairs and pushed open the sliding glass doors to the wooden deck built out over the sloping lot that led down to the water. The wind was cool on his bare legs as he flopped down on a lounger and put the cigarette to his lips. As the nicotine worked its soothing magic, Jimmy let himself think about the nightmares that had haunted him on and off since his tours. They had started on his first tour and gotten worse with each trip back, but hell, everybody had the shakes over there. He had assumed they would go away once he was back home for good with Lauren. But coming home to Lauren had involved another kind of nightmare, the kind where his young and beautiful wife was dying of cancer before his eyes. The nightmares about Baghdad had not gone away, but when he woke up, thrashing and in a sweat, Lauren's loving arms would be there to hold him and soothe the demons. Jimmy begged her not to tell and she had taken his secret with her to her grave. Now his secret was his own again and Jimmy was damned determined it was going to stay that way.

Jimmy finished his cigarette and propped his feet on the railing, letting the music of the moving water soothe him. He had grown up on the shores of this lake and its rhythms were as natural to him as the sound of his own breath. The family ranch, up the road a few miles, bordered the upper shores of this huge man-made reservoir. He had spent many happy hours fishing its muddy shores or swimming off the dock at his best friend Jack Briscoe's farmhouse. He would have built Lauren a home on the lakeshore of the ranch property but she liked it better here on the main body of the lake in a little community of mostly vacation homes and retirement houses, so he had paid a ridiculous amount of money for the last two shoreline lots and pissed off everybody but the Verde County tax assessor by building her the house of her dreams, the house where he was now raising their daughter without her.

A pinprick of light caught Jimmy's eye and he stared at the soft glow coming from the dock over at the old Riley house. Someone else was outside smoking a cigarette in the early hours of morning— probably one of the extended Riley clan. Rileys had been in these parts almost as long as Adamciks, and various members of the Riley family had owned houses here in Heaven's Point since the little community was built. Ben Riley, younger brother to the local judge, owned the two-bedroom off-water right across the street. But the little two-story on the water belonged to Ben's oldest daughter, and Jimmy figured the occupant of the dock was probably her. She was now out of rehab at Brooke Army Medical Center after having being blown up in some kind of cluster-fuck outside Ramadi. Talk about a raw deal for the woman, but at least she was still alive, and that sure wasn't true of every soldier who had gone over there. He had seen a little coming and going around her house but had not yet met the seemingly reclusive woman and saw no particular reason to go out of his way to do so. He watched silently as whoever it was finished the cigarette and went back inside the house.

Jimmy pulled himself out of the lounger. The gray light of early dawn glowed gently in the eastern sky and Jimmy didn't think his neighbors would appreciate his being out on the deck in his boxers and T-shirt. He started the coffeemaker and took a longer-than-usual shower, letting the hot water pour over his still-tense back and shoulders, before finding clean boxers and another clean T-shirt in the unfolded laundry on the love seat. He fished his last dress shirt off the hanger and stuffed a pile of dirty shirts into the large laundry duffel; time for another run to the cleaners. He shoved a couple of pairs of dress pants and a sport coat in the duffel with the shirts and dropped it over the hall railing and was about to go wake Carrie when her tousled head poked around the door of her room. "You get mad when I throw stuff down the stairs," she groused.

Jimmy grinned down into the little face that was a feminine replica of his own. "Sorry, kid. Rank has its privileges. Come on; let's get you a bath and some clothes."

"I want to wear my new pink dress," Carrie announced as they trooped into the bathroom.

"But if you wear your new dress you won't be able to go outside and play in Miss Carmela's sandbox," Jimmy replied.

Carrie thought a minute. "Can I wear the pink shorts then?"

"Pink shorts it is," Jimmy agreed. He gave Carrie a quick bath and shampooed her short curly locks. He dressed her and nuked a breakfast sausage sandwich for her and while she ate caught a little of the Austin news.

"Are you going to get married again?" Carrie asked suddenly.

Jimmy choked on a sip of coffee. "What makes you ask a thing like that?"

"Miss Carmela was talking to Miss Caroline and she said you were still a"—Carrie paused and thought a minute—"Hot? Oh, yeah, hottie, and that you ought to find you a new wife. She said she thought you ought to marry Miss Misty."

Jimmy fought back a grin. "And what did Miss Caroline say?"

"Well, she laughed. And then she said something about that fire going out a long time ago and that you and Miss Misty were just friends now."

"Well, you know, Carrie, it's just not that easy for Daddy to meet nice ladies. Verde's pretty small and I'm awfully busy." *And I'm hoping to be a whole lot busier in the next few months.* "Anyway, I'm not getting married again anytime soon. Okay?"

"Sure." Carrie hopped up from the table and went in search of her backpack. Jimmy sighed and ran his fingers through his curling dark hair. A woman in his life? Hell, he couldn't even find someone to keep Carrie for the next couple of months while Carmela and her family took a much-needed sabbatical to Mexico. Carmela left tomorrow and if he didn't find anyone between now and then he would have to take Carrie to the office with him.

Besides, he thought after he loaded Carrie into the car seat in the back of the Navigator and sped down the two-lane, farm-to-market road that would take him into Verde, he just wasn't ready to jump back into the dating scene. Even though Lauren had been gone over a year and he had known long before that he was going to lose her, he'd loved her for years, and a part of him still did. Besides, if he spent the next months pursuing his lifelong dream of running for public office, there would not be room in his life for much of anything else.

Jimmy dropped Carrie off at Carmela's and headed toward the main square of downtown Verde. He parked in his usual spot outside his glass-front office, where he had hopefully posted a "Help Wanted" sign in the window, and headed to the small café next door. He smiled to himself—a sparkling white Lexus and a dust-covered red pickup truck sat in two of the spaces in front of the café. He was about to talk to the two people in the world whose opinion he respected the most and see if they thought he had a snowball's chance in hell of winning an election. Jimmy spotted his mother and his best friend Jack Briscoe drinking coffee while Jack's three-year-old son, Ryan, wolfed down one of Gus's huge buttermilk pancakes. "Jack, if I'd known you were bringing Ryan I'd have brought Carrie with me," Jimmy said as he leaned down and kissed his mother on the cheek. "Hi, Mom."

"Hi, yourself," Janelle Adamcik said as she cast a motherly eye over her only son. "I wish you had brought Carrie."

"Actually, bringing Ryan was a last-minute change of plans," Jack said ruefully. "Caroline isn't feeling so good this morning and didn't want to have to cook."

"Yeah," Ryan piped up, his bright blue eyes dancing. "She called Daddy a horny bastard and said it was his doing. Then she *barfed*. In the *potty*."

Jack turned bright red and a couple of teenagers at the next table snickered. Jimmy's left eyebrow shot up and he looked at Jack wickedly as he made a show of counting on his fingers. "She did, huh? Want to bet the news that the high school principal got the town doctor pregnant in Hawaii over spring break will be all over Verde by noon?"

"So will the 'horny bastard' part," Jack muttered. "Here, Ryan, eat a piece of bacon."

Ryan chewed the bacon contentedly. "So are you all really having another one, Jack?" Janelle asked wistfully. "That is so wonderful."

"And we're delighted except for the morning sickness. Caroline was going to watch Ryan in the morning and keep her office open a little later in the day, and now I don't know if that's going to be an option. What about you? Who's going to watch Carrie for you?"

"Damned if I know," Jimmy admitted. "I'm so desperate I have a help-wanted sign in the office window."

Janelle's mouth tightened. "I told you I could come and stay with her."

"I know, Mom, and I may have to take you up on it once you get that bill rammed through the Senate. But not until the vote."

"And the schools need the money that bill would send our way," Jack said. "I'll keep Carrie myself before I let you pull your mom out of Austin."

"You wouldn't make that offer if I lobbied for the banking industry, would you?" Janelle teased. "Okay, enough small talk. When you called you said you wanted to run an idea by Jack and me and obviously your day care problems aren't it. So what is so important that the email king wants to talk to us both in person?"

Tamping down his sudden nervousness, Jimmy looked first to Jack and then to Janelle. "Do you think I would have a snowball's chance in hell if I ran for Congress? Apparently the rumor that Tom Craig has decided not to run for re-election is more than just a rumor, and there's no heir apparent. The field's wide open." He paused. "Am I kidding myself? Or could I do something like that and win?"

At that moment Jimmy's favorite redheaded waitress came to the table with a cup of coffee for Jimmy. Lisa Simmons took her role as part owner of the cafe very seriously if her We aim to please button was any indication. "Now that Jimmy's here, what would you folks like for breakfast?"

Janelle ordered biscuits and Jack and Jimmy got the works. "So you want to run for Congress," Jack said thoughtfully. "I wondered when that Adamcik political gene was going to manifest itself."

"It's about time," Janelle said calmly. "By the time he was your age your father had run for office three times and won twice."

"And you've run for Town Council three times and won," Jack pointed out. "You're not a total stranger to the political process."

"Are you prepared to put in the time?" Janelle asked. "You'll have to deal with both campaigning and fundraising. What about Carrie?"

"Janelle, don't worry about Carrie. Caroline and I are just down the road," Jack said. "Look, Jimmy, maybe it's a long shot but if this is something you want to do, you know Caroline and I will do everything possible to help you. Can you win? I don't know. But I do know you put a lot of your hopes and dreams on hold when Lauren got sick, and if you don't get them back out and go for them you'll someday wish you had."

"I appreciate that," Jimmy said. "Mom, what do you think?"

"I think that as long as you understand the commitment it will take and are willing to make that commitment, you ought to go for it. You know I'll do everything in my power to help you. And you need to talk to Judge Riley. He would be good for some honest input," Janelle said.

"Call Misty," Jack said. "She moved to Austin to be closer to the political scene. This would be right up her alley."

"You think we can pry her out of the big city to come help me in this little burg?" Jimmy laughed.

"She'll come for a campaign," Janelle said. "Jack's right. Call her."

Lisa brought their plates and they made quick work of their breakfasts, but Jimmy lingered for another cup of coffee after Jack and Janelle's departure. His mother and his closest friend had both given him their seal of approval. They didn't know if he could win, but they both had given him a thumbs-up on the idea of running. Next step—talk to Judge Riley and get his take on it.

* * *

Chucky gripped his coffee cup in his hands and stared at the back of Jimmy Adamcik's head, wondering what Adamcik and his companions were talking about and smiling to himself as he imagined what an armor-piercing bullet would do to Adamcik's unprotected skull.

Be like blowing a hole in a watermelon, he thought as Adamcik finished the rest of his coffee and signaled for the check. *Or maybe a quick swipe of blade across that damned elegant neck. Wipe that self-satisfied smile off that bastard's face.*

It would be so easy, Chucky thought. Catch him some night out there on the deck smoking. Sneak up, cut his throat, and fade into the dark. Quick, clean, anonymous. Just like all the kills his Special Forces team had done. It would be a piece of cake. And besides, the bastard deserved it. If it hadn't been for him—Chucky took a deep breath and let waves of rage roll over him as the waitress approached Adamcik with his change. It was Adamcik's fault, all of it. It was all his fault and he deserved to die.

But that would be too easy, Chucky thought as he watched Jimmy smile at the waitress and hand her some money. And no challenge at all. No, Jimmy Adamcik needed to squirm, to suffer, to lay awake in his bed terrified. Killing him outright would be too easy. Besides, Chucky had gone to a lot of trouble to integrate himself into this God-awful little community of idiots and rubes; if he just murdered Adamcik and disappeared, all that effort would be for naught. No, he would wait and bide his time while he figured out just how to make Adamcik miserable. And after Adamcik had been brought to his knees, then Chucky would do his worst.

* * *

The brisk wind ruffled Jimmy's hair as he unlocked the front door of the long, narrow building, well over a hundred years old, which housed his modest office. The big window looked out on the courthouse and most of the time Jimmy worked from one of the two front desks and his secretary from the other, using the back office for private meetings with clients. Jimmy booted up his desktop and was deep into preparing for the Armbruster divorce case later that morning when an earsplitting roar blasted his eardrums and a maroon Miata skidded into the handicapped parking space. *Inconsiderate little brat,* Jimmy thought as a blue-jeaned teenage girl slid out of the little car and sauntered down the street. *Where's Rory Keller and his ticket book when you need him?* He turned back to the papers and had almost finished his work when he noticed the girl coming out of the courthouse and jay-walking across the street to the Miata, but instead of getting in the car she stopped to read the sign in Jimmy's window. Jimmy watched, curious, as she paused for a moment and then in that peculiar strutting gait walked down the sidewalk and opened Jimmy's door. To Jimmy's surprise the teenager was in fact a young woman, a most attractive but grim-faced woman who seemed somehow familiar. He quickly slid his professional face in place. "May I help you?" he asked.

The woman gestured to the sign. "I wanted to ask about the sign in the window. My uncle said to talk to you."

Jimmy looked the woman up and down. This babe and his precious little girl? *No way.* "Uh, the job's been filled."

"But my uncle said—"

"I said the job's been filled," Jimmy said firmly.

"Fine." The woman shrugged and opened the door.

"Uh, miss." The woman turned back around and Jimmy pointed to the Miata. "The next time you want to impress a potential employer you might want to start by not stealing the handicapped parking place. That's for people who need it."

The woman stood for a moment, looking stunned, then reached into her pocket and held up a blue handicapped placard. "They tend to get stolen off of convertibles. And I will *certainly* keep your advice in mind the next time I ask a rude and pompous asshole for a job. Have a nice day." She slammed the door behind her so hard the plate glass window shook.

What the hell? Jimmy asked himself as he stood and watched her angry retreat. Was that a saunter or a limp? She was almost to the car when she looked up at a window in the courthouse and pointed to his office before making a thumbs-down sign and scrambling awkwardly into the car. His mind racing, Jimmy searched his memory and groaned out loud when he remembered seeing her several years ago with Wily Riley at the Labor Day picnic. "Jimmy Adamcik, you are a fucking idiot!" he said aloud as the woman roared away. Good God damn. Not only had he been needlessly cruel to someone who was every bit entitled to the handicapped space, but if that lady was who he thought she was, the uncle who had sent her over here was none other than Judge Willis Riley himself. And he had just insulted not only the favorite niece of the man whose support he needed so badly, but he had royally dissed the closest thing Verde had to a bona-fide hometown hero.

* * *

So much for Uncle Willis's brainchild, Holly thought bitterly as she roared down the two-lane, farm-to-market road that would take her back to Heaven's Point, her bad knee aching and her weakened left hand struggling to grip the steering wheel of the Miata. The snot-nosed lawyer had taken one look at her and blown her out the door. Not that she could have done much in a law office anyway, she thought as she glanced down at her useless fingers with disgust. It had taken her months of effort to be able to make the weakest of fists and the mangled nerves in her neck and running down her arm would never tell her fingers to type an email or play a piano or bugle again, nor would she ever blast down the highway on the maroon Harley she had recently sold to her brother. After the second surgery on the nerves in her back and arm had done more harm than good, her father had instructed the doctors at Brooke Army Medical Center just to leave her arm alone. Her mother had protested, of course, and according to her Uncle Willis the two of them ended up in a very public shouting match in the hospital lobby.

Not that she had any memory of those weeks. The injury to her head pretty much wiped out the months both leading up to and after the attack in Iraq, leaving her with a steel plate, a permanent six-month gap in her memory, difficulty putting people's names with their faces, and blinding migraines. Damn it all, anyway, she thought angrily as she rounded a curve in the road.

The May sunshine was bright and the wind ruffled the wildflowers dotting the roads, but Holly was immune to the charms of the Texas Hill Country. No, as beautiful as the rugged hills and flower-strewn roadsides were, as picturesque as the lakes and the spot-dappled fawns and does scampering across the pastures, Holly was not happy to be in Heaven's Point. Where she *wanted* to be was anywhere the Army wanted to send her, but thanks to a couple of dipshit congressmen and an insurgent with an RPG she would never again get on a plane headed for an overseas deployment, never don her body armor and get into a Humvee, never feel the adrenaline rush of battle. *That* was what made her so mad, Holly thought as she flew down the road past Jack Briscoe's south pasture. She could have stood the gimpy leg, the useless hand, the damn plate in her head if only she could have stayed in the Army. They had made her out to be such a hero and awarded her the Silver Star and then they had just cut her loose. That was the loss. Not the use of her hand or the weakness in her leg; it was the loss of her beloved career that made her so crazy.

And that military career was all she had ever really wanted, Holly thought as the Miata ate up the country road. She needed the excitement, the high she got from being in the thick of battle. Holly had welcomed the proximity to the action and lived for the adrenaline buzz. And now she was at an absolute loss as to what she wanted to do with the rest of her life. She had no job skills besides being a soldier, but her disability check was not enough to live on and she would have to find something to do and find it soon. It was a hell of a note. She had gone from being on the fast track to general to getting blown off by a two-bit, small-town lawyer.

Holly's phone rang as she pulled into Heaven's Point. She parked in front of the community swimming beach and cursed out loud as her useless fingers tried to hold and answer the phone. The message had already gone to her voice mail but she relaxed when she saw the number: Cathy Armbruster, a fellow wounded warrior, was a double amputee and understood the problem all too well. "Just wanted you to know the hearing's over and I'm a free woman. Am drowning my sorrows tonight with Christi and Tommy Joe. Bye."

Holly threw her phone on the car seat. At least she had Cathy and Tommy Joe and the rest of her soldiers, she thought as she turned her face into the stiff breeze blowing off the water and smiled as she thought of the little group of men and women who thought of her living room and her fishing dock as a second home. Although Holly's injuries had certainly been serious enough, some of her friends were overcoming injuries that made hers look minor. Holly found herself being a friend, a den mother, and a staunch cheerleader for this little group of survivors and for the other groups modeled on hers that she was helping organize. Going to bat for them, especially when they couldn't go to bat for themselves, had quickly become her cause in life and she was becoming more and more determined to get wounded veterans the financial, physical, and emotional support they needed. And her work had another, equally important benefit.

Getting involved with them and their needs had helped her, too, giving her a reason to get up in the morning, pulling her out of the well of self-pity that had threatened to drown her.

And she could still fish, she thought as she left the beach and parked in front of the tiny two-story cottage she was now calling home. She spotted Hal Jackson, another of her wounded warriors, down at the end of her fishing dock with his pole in the water and his service dog, Raven, by his side. She ambled down to the end of the dock. "How's it going, Hal? Having any luck this morning?"

Hal smiled shyly and pointed toward the bucket of fish. "I c-caught th-three," he stammered as he shook Holly's hand with a weak grip. Hal coped with the after-effects of an intracranial hematoma that included seizures and severe limitations to his reading and language comprehension. He was doing odd jobs on a neighboring ranch to fill his days.

Holly leaned over and looked in the bucket. "Nice big ones, too," she said admiringly to Hal. "Give me a minute and I'll be out to join you."

"Th-that's all right, I'm l-leaving in a m-minute," Hall stammered. "T-too hot."

Holly agreed with him about it being hot but she still wanted to fish. Once inside her cabin, she stripped off her hot shirt and clambered awkwardly up the stairs to her loft bedroom. Ignoring the flashing light on her answering machine and the "you have mail" icon on her laptop, Holly headed for the tiny bathroom. Leaning over the basin, she splashed water on her heated face and stared at herself in the mirror. She was thin, much thinner than she had been before the attack, and the dazzling smile that had been her trademark was pretty much history. She had to give the plastic surgeons at Brooke Army Medical Center credit—they put her face back together with such skill that outwardly at least she looked pretty much the same as she always had. It was her attitude, not her injuries, that had robbed her of her sparkling looks and dazzling smile.

In this heat she missed wearing her signature topknot, but putting her hair on top of her head required the use of both hands and she didn't have that, so she found a headband and just pushed her hair away from her face.

Holly snagged an old T-shirt and grabbed her fishing pole and tackle box and was on her way out the door when her landline rang.

She started not to answer but the caller might be Uncle Willis and the last thing she wanted to do was worry him, so she dutifully picked up the receiver and made a face at the sound of her mother's social-director voice. "Holly, dear, I've been trying to get hold of you all morning," Nadine said brightly. "Dell and I are going to be in Mason tonight at a mayoral fundraiser. I know this is last minute, but would you like to drive up and have dinner with us?"

Holly thought a minute. "What's his position on disabled veterans?"

"Whose position?" Nadine asked.

"The mayoral candidate, of course." Holly didn't try to hide her exasperation.

"Don't know and don't care," Nadine said shortly. "He's pro-business and very sympathetic to the oil industry. That's what's important to west Texas, hon." *Not you and your wounded soldiers.*

"Then I think I'll pass," Holly said dryly. "You can pour crude oil on your salads and money on him without my intruding on your evening."

There was a moment of silence. "Never mind. I just wanted to see if you're doing all right," Nadine said finally.

Holly took a deep breath. "Mom, I'm fine, honestly I am. I just don't want to waste my time if the man's not interested in helping with my cause."

"Then promise to come up and see us soon."

Holly mentally crossed her fingers. "Sure, Mom. Soon. Or you could come here."

"And stay where? In Ben and Patsy's tacky little cabin?" It was all Holly could do not to laugh at the ice in Nadine's voice. "I'll pass, thank you."

"Okay, Mom. I'll talk to you this weekend." Holly hung up without waiting for her mother's farewell and headed for the end of her floating fishing dock. Nadine just didn't understand, Holly reminded herself as she fumbled to put her favorite lure on the fishing pole. To Nadine politics was a chess game of power and influence, intrigue, and excitement, and Holly often suspected half the reason Nadine married Dell Hightower after Griff and Sullivan's father walked out on her was because Dell was a lobbyist for the oil industry and had the same love of all things political that Nadine did. Holly reminded herself that it was the political process itself, not any cause in particular, that fueled Nadine's passion, and that Dell as a paid lobbyist had to put the interests of the oil industry first. She just wished that her mother's indifference to her soldiers and their plight didn't hurt so much.

Hal had left and Holly sat down on one of the two folding chairs at the end of the dock and cast her lure into the water. She let the lure sink for a minute and then slowly, *slowly* reeled it in. It was a good thing the lure needed to move slowly through the water, because with her numb fingers she wouldn't have been able to reel it in any faster, and she honestly didn't know if she had the strength to reel in a fish if she got one on the line. But that didn't matter. Fishing just made her happy.

It was the nose-twanging essence of a really wonderful hamburger that alerted her that she was not alone. She finished winding the reel and turned slowly, wondering if she were only imagining the aroma of one of Gus's thick, juicy burgers, but the greasy brown sack was real and so was the tall, dark-haired man holding it. He looked at her uncertainly and cleared his throat. "I was a real shit to you this morning. I'm sorry."

"Yes, you were," Holly said shortly. "I deserve that damned spot."

"You do. But if it's any consolation, your injuries aren't apparent at all. I honestly had no idea anything was wrong." He held out the sack. "One of these is for you."

Holly stared wordlessly at her uninvited visitor. This morning, she had been the one standing and Jimmy Adamcik had been seated, so he had not seemed so big to her. But now she could see just how tall he really was. He stood a good three or four inches over six feet and had the broad shoulders and the long arms and legs of a clotheshorse. *He would be dynamite in the sack,* Holly thought involuntarily as the feminine side of her sat up and took another look.

His expensive shirt and slacks hung elegantly and gold cufflinks winked at his wrists. His face was too long and his nose was too big for him to be truly handsome, but the combination of prominent cheekbones and dark eyes was arresting, and the upward thrust of his left eyebrow gave him a faintly saturnine appearance. His wavy hair, neatly combed but in need of a trim, curled around the strong column of his neck and there was certain sensuality in his casual yet elegant pose.

Yes, Jimmy Adamcik was definitely a dynamite-in-the-sack kind of guy, and Holly was surprised to feel a sudden, visceral level of attraction. Painfully aware of her sweaty T-shirt and worn jeans, Holly continued to stare at him as he sat down in the second folding chair and opened the sack.

"Peace offering?" he asked as he handed her a hamburger. "Your uncle said they were your favorite."

Holly took the hamburger, careful that her fingers not brush up against his. "So you figured out who I was and decided to make nice to Judge Riley's niece with an apology and lunch." She took a bite of the burger and almost swooned. "Good going. This will definitely get you out of the doghouse with me. But I don't know about Uncle Willis. He just might hold out for the pork chops."

"Actually, being favorite Riley kin had nothing to do with it," Jimmy admitted with a rueful grin that made Holly's heart skip a beat. "Although I'll have you know my heart was in my throat when I went to ask the judge where I could find you."

"What did Uncle Willis say?" Holly asked as she tried and failed to stifle a smile.

"He said not to worry about it; you most likely had fun calling me an asshole," Jimmy laughed. "He said you probably loved the rude and pompous part."

"I did," Holly admitted as Jimmy took a carton of fries from the sack.

"And the hamburger is a bribe, pure and simple. That job is not taken, Captain Riley, far from it. And I'll buy you one of Gus's hamburgers every day for the rest of your life if you'll help me out."

"It's just Holly these days, Mr. Adamcik."

"Then it's just Jimmy."

Holly's smile faded as she stared out at the water. "Well then, Jimmy. I appreciate the burger but in all honesty I would be very little use to you in that office. I can't type my way out of a paper bag anymore and I would never be able to keep your clients' names straight. In fact, I wouldn't put it past Uncle Willis to put you up to coming out here just to make me feel better."

Jimmy let out a low whistle. "If you think either Wily Riley or me is that nice you need to get to know lawyers a little better. Although he did say that you're uniquely qualified for this job, having half raised not one but two sets of much younger siblings.

And this offer is not about you or making you feel better." He reached up and ran his fingers through his neatly combed hair. "Holly, I'm at the end of my rope. Carmela Guajardo runs the only day care in town and she's leaving tomorrow for two months. Every parent in town is hustling to make arrangements." He turned to face Holly. "The 'Help Wanted' sign in the window is for someone to look after my four–and-a-half-year-old daughter until Carmela gets back. If I can't find someone by tomorrow morning I'll have to take her with me to the office and God knows what I'll do on days I have court." He stopped and took a breath. "It would only be temporary and I feel a little silly offering it to someone with your qualifications, but…" He looked at her and shrugged. "What do you say?"

Holly looked over at him, puzzled. "Why can't her mother keep her?"

A shadow crossed Jimmy's face. "Lauren died almost a year and a half ago."

Holly whipped around and stared at Jimmy. "Lauren Puckett?" Jimmy nodded. "Aw, *no*. She was the best cheerleader ever. I wanted to grow up and be just like her." Holly paused a minute. "What happened?"

"Cancer," Jimmy said. "I'm surprised Judge Riley didn't tell you."

"I'm sure he did, but I don't remember," Holly said. She hesitated for a moment. "Look, since this job involves the care of a small child there is something else you need to know. In addition to this"—she waved her bad hand—"and this"—she gestured to her weak leg—"I have a metal plate in my head. I have memory lapses and I have a horrible time putting names with faces. And I get migraines." She looked back out over the water. "And as for half raising my siblings, I was a loving older sister. Nothing more. Surely you can do better than me. Couldn't one of her grandmothers help out?"

"Not really. Mom's in the middle of getting a major education bill passed in Austin—she's a lobbyist. And Ida Puckett? Ida does well to manage Carrie's sleepovers." He waited for a beat. "Nope, if you can't come to Carrie's and my rescue my lively, lovely daughter will be doomed to spend the next two months playing with her dollies in the back of my office or going to court and listening to the good judge blister her daddy's ears for no good reason."

Holly laughed ruefully and held up her hand. It was probably the best offer she was going to get for employment and she couldn't afford to turn it down. "All right, all right, you've made your case. No child should have to listen to Willis Riley tirades." She tapped her head gently. "This doesn't bother you?"

"No, and as far as the other, a loving older sister will suit Carrie's needs just fine. Deal?"

Holly nodded and Jimmy held out his hand. Almost tentatively Holly extended hers, a tingling awareness of the warmth of his hand shooting up her arm as Jimmy engulfed her fingers in a firm yet gentle grip. They shook solemnly and Jimmy named a price that Holly thought was high, but she had bills to pay and she accepted it gratefully. "So where do you live?" she asked as they both stood up.

"The big one. Over there." He pointed to the large ranch next to the swimming beach.

"So you're the other early morning smoker," Holly said. Jimmy looked startled for a moment. "Don't worry, your secret's safe with me. I'm not even trying to quit." She looked up at Jimmy thoughtfully. "Why do I feel like I have just fallen victim to a master in the art of persuasion?"

Jimmy grinned down at her wickedly. "Because you have, just-Holly Riley. You really and truly have."

Chapter Three

Holly downed the last of her coffee and for the hundredth time asked herself what she had gotten herself into. Could she handle a four-year-old on a daily basis? And could she handle being around the four-year-old's sensual, appealing daddy on a daily basis without making a fool of herself? But she thought about another day of sitting on the dock fishing and the anemic balance in her checkbook and decided that spending the day with Carrie would be just fine, so she locked her door and walked the short distance to Jimmy's two-story lakefront.

She, along with everyone else on the Point, had roundly cursed the owner of the pricy monstrosity when her tax bill came due, but she had to admit the beautifully designed house was an attractive addition to the little community. Unlike most lakefront houses, the street side of the house was as thoughtfully designed as the lake side, with a wide front porch and cheerfully shuttered windows upstairs and down. A two-car garage housed an expensive fishing boat and a jet ski, and a boat shed along the side of the house sheltered a party boat and an old pickup truck. A gray Navigator sat in the driveway and a pink tricycle graced the front porch. Sweet, Holly thought with admiration. She loved her own little place, but a house like this? The stuff of dreams.

The blinds in a downstairs window fluttered and as Holly crossed the front porch she could hear light, quick footsteps running across the floor. The front door flew open and a dark-haired little girl with a face that was almost comically like Jimmy's stared up at her. "Hi, I'm Carrie." She smiled as she extended her hand. "How do you do?"

Wow, somebody has taught this child some manners, Holly thought as she shook the little girl's hand. "I'm Miss Holly. I'm very glad to meet you." She stepped into a large foyer as Jimmy came down the stairs carrying a laundry basket. He was dressed in pressed dress slacks and a white T-shirt and had a tie looped around his neck, and Holly fought not to stare at the sleek, solid muscles in his arms and shoulders the skin-tight T-shirt did nothing to hide. He skillfully juggled his briefcase and a basket piled high with laundry. "Morning," Holly said. "Lovely child. Lovely manners."

"Better than her old man's, huh?" Jimmy asked, his wicked grin adding to his sensual appeal. "Her grandmother's doing an awesome job. Come on back. Carrie and I can give you the nickel tour."

Even his back and butt were sexy, Holly thought as she followed Jimmy into the huge, beautifully appointed family room that occupied most of the lower floor of the house. The wooden pieces of furniture were sleek and dark and elegantly simple, and an expensive leather sofa and chairs were grouped in front of a natural stone fireplace flanked on one side by bookshelves and on the other by an armoire housing an upscale entertainment system. The family room flowed naturally into a huge kitchen and breakfast area and a sliding glass door, and a floor-to-ceiling bank of windows looked out onto a large multi-level wooden deck and dock and the lake just beyond.

Even the clutter and the dust and the obvious signs of neglect could not dim the charm of the house. "Oh, my God," Holly breathed. "In my next life I get this place."

Jimmy looked around. "For two cents you could have it right now." He put the basket on the kitchen counter. "Thanks for being early. I need to go by the cleaners for a shirt on my way to work."

Holly felt Carrie tug on her fingers. "Daddy can't iron," she said. "He burned my pink dress but bought me a new one."

Holly's lips twitched. "That's okay; my daddy can't iron either."

Carrie looked at Holly curiously. "Did your daddy burn your dress after your mommy died?"

Holly glanced toward Jimmy and was not particularly surprised to see a shadow cross his face. "My mommy's still alive," she said gently. "But she burned one once."

"Oh." Carrie let go of Holly's hand and headed for the kitchen.

"Sorry about that," Jimmy murmured.

"Believe me, that's nothing," Holly said. "My parents were divorced and remarried. You should have heard the questions I came up with." She felt a wave of compassion for the little girl and knew this would be an easy child to love. She turned to Jimmy, all business. "Now, if you would, please give me a run-down of Carrie's schedule, what she eats, what she likes to do, do's and don'ts, where her swimming gear is, and anything else I need to know," Holly said crisply. "And then I'm sure you'll need to be on your way."

"Yes, Captain Riley!" Eyes dancing, Jimmy popped Holly a swift salute and laughed out loud when she blushed, but he promptly complied with her request and left her the keys to the truck. He told her to call him if she had any questions and left Carrie with a hug and a kiss that was touching in its tenderness.

Holly and Carrie wandered back into the kitchen and Carrie stared mournfully at the bowl of soggy cereal and glass of juice on the kitchen table. "I let it get soft," the little girl said as she spooned up the limp morsels.

"How about a fresh bowl?" Holly asked as she whisked the soggy bowl out from in front of Carrie and poured another. Holly put her hands on her hips and shook her head as she surveyed the counters overflowing with groceries that had not been put away and the unwashed dishes in the dishwasher and sink. Her gaze traveled beyond the kitchen to the dusty family room piled high with newspapers and glassware and empty soda cans. This will not do, she said to herself as she thought of her spotless little cottage down the way. "Carrie, where does your daddy keep the garbage bags?" she asked.

Carrie hopped up and led Holly to the large utility room. "Up there," she said as she pointed out a cabinet. "What are we going to do today?"

Holly's eyes twinkled as she looked down at the little girl. "How would you like to start by playing 'Clean the Barracks'?" she asked as she found a box of garbage bags and a broom and dustpan. "I used to play this when I was in the Army."

"I never played that with Daddy," Carrie said as she followed Holly back into the kitchen.

"I can tell," Holly said. "We can start by you finding all the empty Coke cans and putting them in this sack. Can you do that?"

"You betcha!" Carrie said as she happily took the sack and started finding cans.

Eight hours later Holly looked around the downstairs with a sense of satisfaction. It had been slow going, with her left arm so useless and her balance still difficult, but she and Carrie had done it—the 'barracks" were finally cleaned. The dust and clutter was gone, the counters were clear, and the floors were swept and vacuumed. She had rummaged around in the freezer and found a pot roast that was not too badly freezer-burned for the slow cooker, and

Carrie, her hair still damp from the shower after a short trip to the beach, was happily coloring in her Dora coloring book. Holly sank down in the luxurious sofa and was flipping through the channels looking for the evening news when the front door opened.

Carrie jumped up in a flash and barreled across the floor. "Dad-dee!" she cried as she jumped into his arms. "Wow, I had the bestest time with Miss Holly!" she said as she clung to his neck. "She's super!"

Jimmy held onto Carrie and swung her around a time or two before putting her down. "I bet she's super! What did you do all day, honeybun?"

"Lots of things," Carrie enthused. "First we played 'Clean the Barracks' and Miss Holly played 'Find supper in the freezer.' We made hot dogs for lunch and she put butter on the hot dog buns. That was so good! She read me a couple of Dora stories and we went to the beach and made a sand castle. Tomorrow she'll bring her suit and go in the water with me. And we're going to play 'Clean the Barracks' upstairs."

Jimmy sniffed the air and followed his nose into the family room. "Are you sure this is the same house I left you in this morning, honeybun? And what's that smell coming out of the kitchen?" He looked through the glass top of the slow cooker to the roast and vegetables nestled inside. "Good lord, there's enough in there to feed an army." He looked over at Holly. "My hat goes off to you and then some. I didn't expect you to tackle the barracks, too."

"Self-defense," Holly admitted. "If I'm going to work here for the next couple of months, I have to have it neat." Tiredly she pushed herself up off the sofa. "There's a made-up salad in the fridge to go with the roast. I'll see you in the morning."

"Where are you going?" Jimmy asked. "Surely you're going to stay and help Carrie and I eat that wonderful-smelling roast."

"No, I—"

"Yes, I insist. You're tired and there is no way you're going home and cooking again for yourself when there's more than enough for all of us."

Holly hesitated. Damn, if she didn't want to stay for a while longer and enjoy the company of this charismatic man and his delightful daughter. She looked at Jimmy and grinned lopsidedly. "You're just as bossy as Uncle Willis."

"Yeah, but I'm a whole lot cuter," Jimmy said. "I take it that's a yes. You sit back down and I'll set the table and get the drinks."

Holly followed Jimmy into the kitchen and sat at the table while he got knives and forks and poured milk for Carrie. "Tea or beer?" he asked.

"One of those Coronas would be heaven," Holly said.

Was it accidental or had the warm, almost sensual brush of his fingers against hers been deliberate as she took the open bottle of Corona from his hand?

Holly wiped Carrie's hands with a paper towel while Jimmy served up the roast. "If I'd thought of it in time we could have eaten out on the deck," he said as he slid into the seat across from Holly.

Holly looked out the window. "We may as well be outside now, with these windows looking out on the water. My view is nice but not this dazzling."

Jimmy tasted a piece of his roast. "This is absolutely wonderful!" he said as he cut several small bites for Carrie. Holly smiled her thanks.

"Yes, Miss Holly, it's as good as the hot dogs!" Carrie added.

Holly and Jimmy laughed. "Great view or no, I've always liked that little house of yours," Jimmy volunteered. "When did you buy it?"

Holly thought a minute. "Maybe four years ago. I needed a tax break after my divorce."

"Didn't realize you'd been married."

Holly shrugged. "We stupidly thought we could be married to each other and the Army, too. Nathan realized it would never work and wanted us to both get out. I wasn't willing, so he found himself a little nurse who was ready to give up the Army and settle down. Last I heard they were on their second baby."

"Ouch. Do I detect a dollop of bitterness there?" Jimmy asked.

Holly looked over at him, surprised. "Not about that, no. I made my decision and Nathan made his and I wish him well. My career in the Army meant more to me than Nathan did. More than anything did. I would kill to have it back." Holly stabbed a piece of roast. "And if you think you detect a little bitterness about now you just might have it right."

"You miss it?" Jimmy asked quietly.

Holly looked across the table. "I loved everything about it, even that damned red desert sand. If I could I'd be on the next plane to Afghanistan so fast it would make your head swim."

Jimmy made no attempt to hide his horror. "Even after you damn near got killed?"

Holly nodded. "That career was my whole life. It's like I've had the rug jerked out from under me."

"Daddy went to Iraq," Carrie piped up suddenly. "He was a major."

"You were?" Holly asked eagerly. "When were you over there?"

Jimmy shrugged. "I did several tours, actually. With my reserve unit—no big deal. By the way, has your Uncle Willis said anything to you about the Memorial Day picnic we have every year? I'm sure he'll want you to go."

Several tours in Iraq? No big deal? Holly looked over at Jimmy with new eyes. With his elegant civilian clothing and the longish hair she would never have pegged him for a fellow military officer. He had changed the subject so swiftly it was clearly not a topic that the former reservist cared to discuss. Holly couldn't help but wonder why. "I think Uncle Willis did say something about the picnic a few days ago. I'm going with some of my soldiers."

"Good," Jimmy said. "It's usually quite a shindig. I'm planning to use the occasion to announce my candidacy for Congress."

"You're going to what?" Holly asked as a smile stole across her lips.

"What's Congress?" Carrie asked.

"It's a part of the government that daddy wants to get elected to," Jimmy said gently. "I want to run for Congress. I talked to Judge Riley this afternoon and basically got his thumbs up. Why the smile, Holly?"

"Because you would be the perfect candidate to look after our interests in Congress," Holly said eagerly.

"Whose interests in Congress?" Jimmy asked, puzzled.

"The wounded veterans, of course," Holly replied. "You're a veteran, you've been to war, and you know the shape a lot of us have come home in." She took a sip of her beer. "Those soldiers I'm going to the picnic with? All members of a support group I organized when I moved here. My injuries are a piece of cake compared to how some of these people came home. We take care of one another, of course, but there's a lot even the best-intentioned friends just can't do. They—*we*—need more support in our corner. Public support. Financial support. Political support."

Jimmy looked at her curiously. "I thought there were already a lot of programs out there for wounded veterans."

"There are some," Holly conceded. "But not enough. That's where you would come in. You would be a voice for the heroes. And they *are* heroes."

Jimmy's eyes danced with amusement. "Whoa, slow down. I have to win both the primary and the general election first. And before I can win either of those I have to raise money. A lot of money, according to Judge Riley."

And Nadine could do that for him. Nadine and her oil industry buddies could—and probably would—raise enough money to finance a young, charismatic candidate's run for Congress. But at what price? "Yes, it will take a lot of money," she agreed slowly. "A lot of driving. And a lot of smiling and shaking hands."

"I know. It's a huge district and I'll probably wear out the Navigator." Jimmy leaned forward, his earlier amusement gone. "Holly, I want this so badly I can taste it. I've got politics in my blood. I was planning a run for state senate after my last tour in Iraq but Lauren got sick and that buggy went in the ditch. I've put it off and put it off and now's my chance, and I am going to do this thing."

Holly nodded as she stared into the light glowing in Jimmy Adamcik's eyes. She had seen that look before; this wasn't just a lark with him. Jimmy Adamcik had fire in his belly and he had the drive and the desire to make this thing work. "Then go for it," she said softly. "Because you'll never be happy if you don't. And I could certainly help some with Carrie."

"I would appreciate that very much," Jimmy said as he glanced down at Holly's empty plate. "Would you like more roast? Carrie? How about you?"

They made inconsequential small talk for the rest of the meal. Holly offered to help clean up but Jimmy shooed her out the door, insisting that she had done more than enough. As Holly gathered up her things, Carrie came and put her arms around Holly's legs in a huge hug. Holly fought to keep her balance and carefully leaned down to return Carrie's hug. "See you in the morning, okay?"

Jimmy and Carrie stood on the front porch until Holly was almost to her house. What a nice little girl, she thought wistfully as she let herself in her tiny cottage. *And her hunky daddy ain't bad, either*, a little voice reminded Holly as she gathered up her fishing pole and headed for the end of the dock. The rangy lawyer definitely had sex appeal in spades. And he was nice, too. In spite of a little arrogance, Jimmy Adamcik was probably the most sincerely appealing man that had come her way in a long time. And a fat lot of good that was going to do her now, Holly thought resentfully as she limped across the floor. That man could have any woman he wanted. He wasn't going to be interested in a woman with a useless arm, a gimpy leg, and a piece of metal in her head.

Holly slammed the door behind her and stomped to the end of the dock. Yes, Jimmy Adamcik was definitely a hunk and she was definitely attracted to him, and unfortunately that was as far as it was going to go.

* * *

Jimmy pulled himself out of the water and climbed the stairs to the lower level of the deck. The sun had set about a half an hour earlier and the western sky was fading from the deep purple of late dusk to the inky black of night. He grabbed the towel hanging on the rail and sat down in the lounger and for the second time in as many days found himself spying on the lone occupant of the dock in front of Holly Riley's house. *She's thinking about the Army*, he thought as Holly cast her line into the water. He would bet Carrie's college fund that Holly was thinking about the places she would never again go and the wars she would never again fight. Go figure. He came home without a scratch and he still had nightmares. She gets blown almost to hell and she wants to go back.

Jimmy went inside and poured himself two generous fingers of Scotch. It was a crying shame she'd been hurt so badly, he thought as he sipped the smooth whiskey. She limped with every step she took and she really couldn't do much of anything with that hand. In fact, he had been astounded at how much she had accomplished in his house.

From the fit of her clothes and the sharp angle of her cheekbones he guessed that she had probably lost quite a bit of weight. At least she hadn't lost her looks, he thought as he went over in his mind the exquisite bone structure in her face and the golden brown eyes that lit up the room when she smiled. Nor had she lost her sex appeal, he thought as he remembered the way her waist curved down to her swaying hips and shapely backside. He'd gotten a glimpse of her creamy breasts encased in a lacy, nearly nothing bra.

Jimmy wondered what she had been like before the attack. Judge Riley had used many adjectives over the years to describe his favorite niece—fireball, delight, ray of sunshine were three that came to mind. Jimmy thought those personality traits had stayed intact, if the warmth Holly showed his daughter and the passion lighting her face when she talked about "her soldiers" was anything to go by. But there were elements of discontent, too, and Jimmy was fairly certain that those would not have been there before.

For the first time since Lauren's death he felt himself attracted to a woman—and this worried him. It worried him a lot.

Jimmy wandered in the house and after pouring himself another finger of Scotch headed for a quick shower. As he began to feel the numbing effect of the whiskey, he threw back the covers and lay down on his bed, falling quickly into a deep oblivious slumber.

He was in Fallujah again, running through the streets, the sound of rockets and RPGs shrieking in his ears as he rounded a corner. "Get back, GET BACK!" the young sergeant yelled, sweat running down his face as he ran toward Jimmy. Jimmy stumbled backward but not fast enough. The explosion caught the sergeant in the square of the back, lifting him into the air and turning his body into a fine mist of pink-tinted flesh that splattered the street, the sidewalk, and the front of Jimmy's uniform. "Aw, Jesus NO," Jimmy cried as he stared at the pieces that had once been a young man…

"Aw, NO, Jesus, NO!" Jimmy cried as he felt tiny hands shaking his arm. What the hell? He bolted upright in bed and stared down into the terrified little face looking up at him. Oh my God, he thought in horror. His screaming had woken Carrie.

Jimmy reached down and with trembling arms picked up the frightened child. "Carrie, are you all right, sweetheart?" he asked as he pushed the curls from her puckered forehead.

A lone tear ran down Carrie's face. "You scared me, Daddy. You were yelling about 'no' and 'Jesus' and you looked mad about something."

"Daddy was just having a bad dream," Jimmy said, hoping Carrie could not hear the quiver in his voice. "You know how you have bad dreams sometime? Well, sometimes daddies have bad dreams, too."

Carrie thought a minute. "But you're a grownup, Daddy. Grownups don't have bad dreams."

Damned if that's so. "Oh, but sometimes we do," Jimmy said quietly. "It's okay, honeybun. I'll be all right." He gave Carrie a big hug. "Let me take you back to your bed."

"Daddy, you're shaking," Carrie said solemnly. "I know! When I have a bad dream you stay with me. I can stay with you until you feel better." Without being asked she crawled under the covers and reached out her hand and placed it on his chest. "Isn't that better?"

"Yes, honeybun, it really is," Jimmy said softly. Carrie drifted quickly back into slumber and Jimmy lay quietly beside her, chagrined to think that he needed the comfort of a four-year-old child to chase away his nightmares. The dreams were getting worse, he admitted to himself as he watched his daughter sleeping. And somehow he was going to have to learn to cope with them by himself. There was no way anyone else on the face of this Earth was ever going to find out about the nightmares, because if they did, the dreams of a lifetime could go up in smoke.

* * *

Jimmy loped down the stairs two at a time. His campaign committee wasn't due to arrive for another half hour, but Judge Riley's beat-up old pickup truck was in the driveway already. Carrie was parked in front of her favorite Toy Story movie and the spread Holly thoughtfully prepared for his meeting had only to be put out on the dining room table. Jimmy smoothed his hair with his fingers and opened the door to Judge Riley. "Come in," he said, smiling warmly at the wizened little judge. "Holly has left us well-prepared in the way of food for the meeting. She said rule numbers one, two, and three were to keep all participants in an election campaign fed."

The judge laughed as he bustled through the open front door. "She learned that from her mother," Judge Riley said. "I'll bet Holly made some of her mother's famous finger sandwiches." He looked around expectantly. "Where is she?"

"Holly? Probably back at her own place getting ready for her support group meeting," Jimmy said as he led Judge Riley into the kitchen. "She made enough for two meetings and I helped her get half of it back to her place."

Judge Riley's face fell almost comically. "I was hoping to see her tonight. How is she doing with Carrie?"

"She's great," Jimmy enthused. "Carrie loves staying with her. And bless Holly's heart, she cleans up this pigsty and has dinner on the table every night even though I told her that was above and beyond." He lifted the cooler lid and gestured to the variety of drinks in the ice. "What would you like?"

Judge Riley reached in for a bottle of water. "And how is Holly doing otherwise? Is she making any friends here on the Point?"

"I certainly think so," Jimmy said as he opened a package of paper plates. "I saw her visiting with Angie Baxter down on the beach the other night. But the people she really seems to have bonded with are the men and women in her support group. She talks about them all the time and is hosting them tonight, or I think she would have been here."

"I'm glad she has those folks. She's doing a lot of good and it's good for her, too." Judge Riley eyed Jimmy thoughtfully. "I still wish she was going to be here tonight. If you could get her involved in your campaign she would be a uniquely qualified committee member," he said as Jimmy put out a plate of sandwiches. "She learned so much from her mom," Judge Riley added as he snagged one of the sandwiches. "These suckers have probably raised more money than all the rubber chicken in west Texas."

Jimmy looked at the judge with puzzlement. "Just who is her mother, anyway?"

It was Judge Riley's turn to look surprised. "Nadine Hightower. Holly didn't tell you?"

Nadine Hightower? Jimmy's jaw dropped. Nadine Hightower was the doyenne of all things political in pretty much all of west Texas. She and her husband Dell had their fingers on, or in, just about every election from Interstate 35 to the New Mexico border and if you were serious about winning an election, Nadine was the woman to see. "No, she didn't say a word," he said, annoyed. "Even when I sat here and ran on about how I needed money for the campaign."

Judge Riley sighed as he took the plastic wrap off the bowl of dip. "I don't know why that surprises me. Holly and her mother don't particularly get along. Holly grew up seeing the seamier side of politics and developed a bit of a disdain for it, and now she's aggravated that her mother has no interest in anything but the oil industry and refuses to take on the plight of wounded soldiers. Nadine's unwilling to do anything that might possibly alienate her fattest wallets." He paused a minute. "Who all do you have lined up to work on your campaign committee?"

"Mom, of course, and Jack and Caroline Briscoe—Jack's helped with all three council elections and Caroline's a fast study. And if I can persuade her to do it, I'd like Misty Martinez to be my campaign manager."

Judge Riley's lips twitched. "That hotshot lawyer out of Dallas? Didn't you used to be sweet on her?"

"Long ago and far away," Jimmy admitted. "She's in Austin now and itching to get involved in a campaign. I'm hoping she'll say yes."

Judge Riley nodded. "You have the people, then. You just need the money."

Jimmy nodded. "And a lot of it, I understand."

"Okay, here's the thing. I can put you in touch with Nadine," Judge Riley said. "And I am sure she and her cronies will be interested. But their support, if they decide to lend it to you, will come with certain expectations. I'm not saying you shouldn't accept their support," the judge continued when Jimmy started to protest. "I'm just saying to be prepared-they are going to have certain demands and you had by God better be ready to accept them."

"Or?" Jimmy asked quietly.

"Their support will evaporate like spit in Hades, and your campaign will be down the tube."

"Well, hell," Jimmy murmured.

Judge Riley grinned wickedly. "Welcome to politics, Jimmy."

* * *

Holly hummed tunelessly as she one-handedly spread a cheerful tablecloth over the small table in her dining alcove. If any more members joined the support group and she would have to find another place for them to meet, she thought as she looked around the tiny living and dining room. Holly considered moving the meeting to the beach but it was still over ninety and her friends didn't seem to mind wedging themselves in, so the living room it was.

Holly set out the food and put out paper plates and cups. She looked ruefully at the bottles of sweet red wine in the door of her refrigerator; she had already put together the rest of the ingredients for Nadine's famous Sangria but the wine would have to wait for someone with two good hands to open it. Or at least one more hand to lend to the cause, she thought as an old yellow Corvette pulled into the driveway and Cathy Armbruster shoved the car door open. Cathy placed her good foot on the driveway and with surprising grace swung her prosthetic leg out. With only a little unsteadiness she walked to the front door.

Holly flung open the door and enveloped the tall brunette in a huge hug. "Damn, you're doing good these days," Holly enthused as Cathy flung her left arm around Holly and squeezed her tightly. "You're walking almost as well as I am, and I got to keep both of mine." She motioned for Cathy to follow her into the kitchen and took the wine from the refrigerator.

"I wish I was doing as well with the arm," Cathy said, taking the wine bottle from Holly. "I'm just not as motivated." She held the wine bottle tightly down on the counter while Holly twisted the corkscrew into the cork. Together they braced the bottle with their weaker limbs and with their good hands they pressed in unison on the bottle opener, expertly pulling out the cork. Cathy smiled lopsidedly, the patchwork of skin grafts on the right side of her once-pretty face puckering around her mouth and eyes. "Adamcik's a good lawyer. I pretty much got everything—except the husband, of course." Cathy looked wistfully at Holly. "And someday I would really like one of those again. Do you think there's hope for a woman like me?"

Holly looked down at her own damaged leg and useless arm. "Damned if I know," she admitted. "Speaking of, here come the lovebirds."

Cathy and Holly walked out on the front porch as an older model crew-cab pickup parked on the street. A tiny blonde sporting a spanking-new engagement ring hopped out of the passenger side and by the time the driver's side door was open she had a lightweight wheelchair out of the back. A redheaded, freckle-faced young man with huge, powerful shoulders skillfully swung himself from the truck to the wheelchair. "Look, ma, no chauffeur," he crowed as he spun the wheelchair in a tight circle. "I passed the driver's test last week. Tommy Joe Reece is back on the road!"

"Aw, geez, the roads won't be safe ever again," Holly laughed as Cathy made a raspberry sound. "Tommy Joe, Christi, get in here out of the heat."

The couple gratefully ducked into the house. "Yeah, and you should see the gas bill he's running up," Christi groused. "But I did find me a really pretty wedding dress in Austin last night."

"Come with me, Tommy," Cathy said as she took Tommy's hand. "Holly and I need some help opening the rest of the wine."

Holly waited until Cathy and Tommy Joe disappeared into the kitchen. "How's he doing, really?" she asked quietly. "And how's it going with—you know?"

Christi's smile faded a little. "He still has his moments. As for the other, he'll never be that horny cowboy I fell in love with, but a few pills and a few toys and a certain amount of imagination goes a long way. Besides, I'd rather have what I have with Tommy Joe than the sweatiest hot monkey sex with somebody else, and thankfully I've finally gotten that through his thick skull, at least most of the time."

"And that in and of itself is a miracle," Holly said, her already considerable esteem for Christi going up several more notches. "Here comes the rest of the gang. My God, will you look at Beto's new wheels! Awesome, dude." Beto Flores swung out of the cab of a new, fire-engine red pickup truck and expertly made his way up the sidewalk. He had been injured early in the war and had been on his prosthetic legs for years but was still struggling with flashbacks and nightmares.

"Changed jobs since I saw you last," he said proudly as he held the door for Armando Fuentes, Armando's wife, Inez, and their four-year-old daughter, Maggie. "I quit the job as night security at the nursing home and went back to law enforcement for real. Night dispatcher for the San Saba County Sheriff's Department. It's about the only thing they're willing to let me do at this point but it beats sitting on my butt at the nurses' station watching people make asses of themselves on reality TV."

"Now you're sitting on your butt taking calls and listening to people make asses of themselves for real," Armando teased as he awkwardly made his way across the floor and eased down onto the sofa, handing his arm braces to his daughter to lean against the wall. "And it won't be long before they let you back out on patrol. Congrats. How's it going, Hal?" he asked as he reached out to shake Hal Jackson's hand.

"Uh, g-good. Really, g-good," Hal said. "I-I've been f-fishing off Holly's d-dock. Y-you, Otis?" he stammered.

"Hanging in there, man." Otis Hibler lowered his ample girth onto the sofa, his long gray beard resting on his fleshy chest. Otis had only recently rejoined the land of the living after years of hiding out on his family ranch, untreated PTSD dating back to Vietnam turning him into a virtual hermit.

The group helped themselves to Holly's spread and spent a few minutes catching up. Beto's job change was widely applauded. Hal said he was afraid he was about to lose his job on a local ranch due to a seizure in a pasture full of cows. Cathy admitted that her job search was not going well and said that she feared the bad facial scarring and the prostheses were off-putting. Holly admitted that she still didn't have a clue what she even wanted to do and Tommy Joe complained that he had plenty of work to do around the ranch and that it was damned hard to do it from a wheelchair, even with Christi's help. Armando reported that although a number of restaurant managers had complimented his resume, they had openly questioned his ability to function in a restaurant kitchen with two arm braces. "I thought handicapped people were supposed to have protection from discrimination under the law," he said with a touch of bitterness. "I thought they had to at least give us a chance."

"Actually, no," Holly said. "When I asked Uncle Willis he said that a potential employer has no obligation to hire anyone that he or she doesn't think could do the job. The burden of proof is on us—we have to show them that we can." Her eyes snapped with excitement as she looked around the group. "Is now the time?" she asked.

"The time for what?" Armando asked as the rest of the group nodded.

Christi jumped off Tommy Joe's lap and took the stairs two at a time, returning momentarily with two big gaily wrapped packages she handed to Armando. "This is from all of us," she said softly as the rest of the group looked on expectantly. "Cathy's idea and Holly was the one to pick them out. We passed the hat while you weren't looking. Go ahead," she urged Armando when he just stared at the packages. "Open them."

With trembling hands Armando tore at the paper on the larger of the two packages and unwrapped a restaurant-sized stockpot. Wordlessly he stared at the pot for a moment before tackling the second package and un-wrapping a large, flat baking pan. "This is the size pan I used to use to cook enchiladas," he said softly.

"And will again," Holly said confidently. "Armando, these are for you to use on your next job interview. Don't just go in and argue your case. Fix a big pot of your famous rice and a pan of enchiladas and take it and show them what you're capable of. *Show* them that, crutches or no, you can still function in a restaurant kitchen."

Tears gathered in Armando's eyes and spilled down his reconstructed cheekbones. "I-I don't know what to say," he whispered. "Thank you so much."

Inez jumped up and wrapped Holly in a huge hug, nearly knocking her down. "Gracias, oh my God thank you all!" she said as she went around the room hugging everyone. "What a wonderful idea. Prove it to them. A demonstration. Armando, why didn't we think of that?"

"And of course we're going to want a demonstration, too," Tommy Joe teased. "Gotta make sure those enchiladas are just right."

Armando and Inez thanked everyone again and Inez took them out to the car. "Guys, fill up your plates again," Holly urged the group. "I have some really good news I want to share with you."

The group hit the table for a second helping. "I don't know if you noticed the cars parked down the street when you drove up, but Jimmy Adamcik's campaign committee is meeting tonight for the first time. Jimmy plans to run for Congress."

"I know him," Cathy said. "He handled my divorce. Damn nice guy and didn't take me to the cleaners."

"Nice m-man," Hal added. "Nice n-neighbor."

"Harold's boy? Otis asked. "Is he old enough to run for Congress? He's just a kid."

"Nah, he's plenty old to be a congressman," Tommy Joe assured Otis. "Anyway, why is this such good news for us?"

"Jimmy's a combat veteran," Holly said. "Did several tours in Iraq with the reserves and saw it all up close and personal. He's going to be a lot more interested in our cause than somebody who hasn't been there and done that. I promise you, if Jimmy's elected, when he gets to Washington he'll be on our side."

Chapter Four

Holly looked critically at herself in the mirror as she stroked a touch of mascara on her pale eyelashes and shrugged off the guilt she felt for being glad that she was still pretty when so many others weren't. Well, mostly pretty, she thought as she tugged on a pair of white capris that stopped just below the last of the scars that graced her left leg and knee. She ran a brush through her hair and, cursing the useless fingers she could not use to put her hair up in a topknot, awkwardly pushed it back with a headband. She dabbed on a generous dollop of lip gloss that matched her pink T-shirt and was halfway down the stairs when she heard Cathy's Camaro in the driveway. "Coming!" she called out as she threw her wallet and keys and a couple of bottled waters into a straw bag.

Holly locked her door and slipped into Cathy's car where Cathy was holding a plastic bottle with her prosthesis and looking disgustedly at the water splashed down her shirt. "Son of a bitch, I guess I should have just used the real one," she said as she moved the bottle to her real hand and drank. "But the occupational therapist keeps harping on how I need to practice with the damn thing." She finished the water and threw the bottle over her shoulder into the back seat. "For two cents I'd get rid of this ugly damned thing and get the Army to make me one of those good-looking fakes. You know, the ones that just hang there. Can't do anything with them but at least they look good."

"Yep, they issued me one of those," Holly said dryly. "Can't do a damn thing with it but it sure looks great."

Cathy looked over at Holly's arm and they both burst out laughing. "Just shut up and drive," Holly said. "And don't worry about the water. As hot as it is, it'll be dry by the time we get there."

"You're probably right," Cathy said. "Anybody else from the group coming?"

"Hal and Beto and Tommy Joe and Christi. So how's the job search coming?"

As they rolled down the highway Cathy filled Holly in on the latest of her job interviews and said she thought that her best bet was a job with a Burnet doctor. Holly tried to listen but could feel her apprehension growing as they got closer to Verde. What if she couldn't remember someone's name and hurt their feelings? Holly's good hand clenched into a fist and the knot in her stomach was definitely getting bigger. Not even the sight of the pretty little town spread out in front of them, with its quaint-looking businesses and church spires and the tall bridge spanning the Verde River was enough to calm Holly's nerves. She felt rather than saw Cathy glance over at her as she put on the blinker. "Hey, girlfriend, it's okay," Cathy said soothingly. "I know everybody in Verde. I won't let you fall on your face."

Holly shot a grateful look in Cathy's direction. "Thanks."

They crossed the bridge and followed the road that ran parallel to the river. From the parking lot Holly could see a covered pavilion set back from the river and what looked like a permanent grandstand with a podium and a portable sound system, all decorated with bunting in red, white, and blue. On one side the smoke from a huge barbeque pit permeated the air with the tantalizing aroma of smoked brisket and sausage. A few yards away a handler was leading a couple of ponies into a small ring. Someone had brought in a small Ferris wheel on a semi and a five-piece band was already setting up under the pavilion. And not too far beyond, the Verde River flowed lazily through the park, its green water moving quietly and smoothly within its banks. In spite of her nervousness Holly had to smile. If this wasn't quintessential small-town America, she didn't know what was.

Tommy Joe and Christi pulled in right behind Cathy and Beto after them, and the five of them exchanged gossip as they collected water bottles and locked their cars. They had barely reached the pavilion when Carrie spotted them and streaked across the floor with a little blond boy on her heels. "Holly! You're here!" she said as she barreled into Holly and almost knocked her down. Cathy grabbed Holly from behind and tried to steady her but her prosthetic leg slipped out from under her and the two of them tumbled right into Tommy Joe's lap. *Well, that's one way to get the attention of a crowd,* Holly thought as she and Cathy scrambled to get up and dozens of eyes turned in their direction.

But it was hard to be upset with a child who was glad to see her. Holly ignored the stares as she awkwardly knelt down to Carrie's level. "Yes, I'm here. And I'll bet this is Ryan," she said to the little blond boy staring in wonder at Cathy's prostheses. "Want to meet my friends?"

Ryan nodded. "What is that?" he asked as he reached out with one finger and gingerly touched Cathy's artificial arm.

"Miss Cathy has a special arm," Holly said gently as Cathy made the pincers open and shut. "And her leg's special. Mr. Beto's legs are special, too."

Ryan looked up at Cathy and grinned. "Wow, Miss Cathy, that's cool!"

"Would that everybody reacted like that," Holly murmured as Cathy and Beto demonstrated their artificial arms and legs to the fascinated children.

A good-looking man about Jimmy's age with honey-brown hair and broad shoulders and a tiny blonde woman swooped down on their group. "I am so sorry," the woman said to Holly. "I turned my back for ten seconds and the next thing I knew…"

"Aw, don't worry about it, Caroline," the man laughed. "Tommy Joe here didn't mind a lap full of pretty women. Did you, Tommy?"

"Loved every second of it." Tommy Joe smiled and grasped the man's hand. "Coach B, good to see you again." He smiled slyly. "Heard you had a great trip to Hawaii."

"Tommy Joe!" Christi whacked Tommy on the shoulder as the couple both blushed furiously. "Holly, have you met the Briscoes?"

The man offered his hand. "Jack Briscoe. We actually met you awhile back."

Holly started to apologize but the tiny woman with Ryan's face offered her hand and it all clicked. "Sure, I remember meeting both of you. It's one of the last clear memories before the amnesia kicks in. It's good to see you again. And congratulations on the new baby." Introductions were exchanged and before Holly quite knew what had happened Caroline Briscoe had maneuvered their entire group to the long wooden picnic table where Jimmy sat with a tall, pretty woman with the high, chiseled cheekbones of her Hispanic heritage. She sprang up and offered her hand. "Hi, I'm Misty Martinez," she said. "I'll bet you're Holly. Nice to meet you."

Misty, Holly told herself. She deliberately used Misty's name twice as she introduced her friends. Beto's eyes widened and Tommy Joe gave Misty an appreciative checking out as Jimmy stood and looped his arm around Misty's shoulders. "Misty's going to be my campaign manager," he said proudly. "She's been promising to help me run for office since we went to law school together."

Bet that ain't all they did together, Holly though as a blade of jealousy lanced through her midsection. But as she glanced over at Cathy her own feelings died at the misery in Cathy's eyes as Beto and Tommy Joe openly admired Misty Martinez. Holly gave Cathy's face a surreptitious once-over. Yes, Cathy had once been every bit as beautiful as Misty, which made her scarring just that much sadder.

Misty gave Jimmy a quick hug. "It's about time you ran, *querido.*" She turned to the others. "He's going to announce his candidacy and Jack's going to introduce him. Everybody, I hate to be rude but I need Jack and Jimmy for a last-minute look at their speeches."

"Why don't the three of us find something for the kids to do?" Holly suggested to Cathy and Caroline as Beto and Tommy and Christi headed toward the concession stand.

The women nodded. Holly and Cathy spent a pleasant hour with Caroline Briscoe and the lively children, then joined Misty and the men in the barbeque line and enjoyed heaping plates of slow-cooked brisket and pork sausage with all the trimmings. As the start of the program drew near, a television crew from an Austin affiliate station pulled up and Jimmy's forehead puckered in a faint frown. "What about San Angelo and Midland?" he asked Misty.

"It's covered," Misty said quickly. "This crew will send their story to all their west Texas stations." Good going, Misty, Holly thought. Misty might be new at this but she'd done her homework.

They all wished Jimmy luck as he and Jack headed for the grandstand. Holly and Cathy sat down beside Tommy Joe and Christi close to the front of the pavilion and Holly got out a small spiral pad and a pencil. "To take notes," she said when Tommy Joe raised an eyebrow. As Jimmy took his seat with the rest of the dignitaries Holly spotted a familiar figure slip unobtrusively into a folding chair in the back of the pavilion. She just couldn't stay away, Holly thought with exasperation. Nadine couldn't be bothered to make the drive from San Angelo to see her own daughter, but a congressional candidate? You better believe it.

The emcee introduced the dignitaries and the mayor made a short speech. Jack Briscoe, relaxed and comfortable speaking to a crowd, gave Jimmy a ringing endorsement that was touching in its sincerity. Then Jimmy stepped forward to the podium and began to speak, explaining his desire to serve in Congress and asking his hometown for their votes and their support. He had their attention, she thought admiringly as the people of Verde watched and listened. He related to them on a visceral level and spoke with fervor and passion, and the crowd roared their approval when he asked for their support.

And yet something was missing. Holly went over her notes as the crowd surged to its feet in support of Jimmy's candidacy. Yes, he had mentioned a few concerns—education and the economy, mostly—but the speech had been carefully crafted to give few specifics and a lot of vague generalities that could be interpreted any number of ways. What did Jimmy Adamcik stand for, really? Charm and charisma alone would not win Jimmy an election-he needed to stand for something.

The cheering stopped and Jimmy opened the floor for questions. An old farmer leaped to his feet. "What are you going to say when that dang Congress wants to raise my taxes?" he demanded belligerently.

"I'm going to remind them that if they raise your taxes they'll be raising their own as well," Jimmy said, his eyes dancing and the crowd laughing a little. "Seriously, Walton, I would have to think long and hard before I would support anything that would put any more financial burden on the small businessman."

Good answer, Holly said as she leaped to her feet. *Now let's see how he answers mine.* "As you know from the time you spent in the fight against terrorism, there are a number of your fellow countrymen and women, myself included, who have paid a higher than average price for the freedoms we all enjoy. What do you see yourself doing as a congressman to help the country's veterans on their road to recovery?"

Jimmy looked down at Holly and her soldiers. "First of all, Captain Riley, I want to thank you and the men and women with you today for your selfless service to our country. I, along with everyone here, owe you a debt of gratitude." He began to clap and Holly and her group were treated to a spontaneous standing ovation. Jimmy waited for the crowd to quiet down. "And I want you to know that I always will support the American veterans in any and every way possible with every vote I cast. Next question?"

That's it? Holly asked herself, astonished, as an older woman asked Jimmy a question about public education. Holly sat back down and hoped her stunned disappointment did not show. So much for thinking Jimmy would support her cause; he spouted the same platitudes everyone else did. She looked over at Cathy, who shrugged her shoulders.

Jimmy took a few more questions and asked again for their support, and when the program ended Jack and Caroline and a tall, elegant woman with beautifully cut silver hair were swamped with people volunteering to help with the campaign. Holly and Cathy made a pit stop in the restroom and by the time they returned the crowd had thinned considerably, but Holly spotted Hal Jackson and Angie Baxter in the handful of volunteers still signing up. "Good to see you, Angie. Hal, how are you? We missed you earlier."

Hal looked a little embarrassed. "I was t-trying to put a coat of p-paint on the eaves and h-had a"—he stopped and groped for the word.

"Seizure?" Cathy asked gently.

"That's tough," Holly said. "But I do love what you've done with the house." Hal was renting an old cottage on the other side of the Point. "And how about you, Angie? How's business?"

"Why, it's coming right along," Angie said with enthusiasm in a deep southern accent that was not typical of central Texas. A short, pretty woman with auburn hair almost the same color as Holly's, she was either amazingly well preserved or the youngest woman ever to have a son in college.

"Aren't you the little pink and green shop just outside the Point?" Cathy asked.

"That's me. I make soaps and organic lotions and cosmetics. Do come by."

Angie and Hal got in the volunteer line as Jimmy and Misty walked over. "Well, how'd I do?" he asked.

"Uh, fine," Holly stammered, hoping Jimmy wouldn't press her further.

"You really had their attention," Cathy added.

"Of course he had their attention! You did wonderfully," Misty enthused. Her eyes widened as she looked across the pavilion.

"Good Lord, is that who I think it is?" she asked as Nadine paid for a Coke from the concession stand and started toward their table.

"The famous Nadine Hightower? The doyenne of west Texas politics? Sure is," Holly said with resignation. "Come on. I'll do the intros."

Holly watched her mother slowly make her way across the pavilion, stopping to speak and shake hands and air-kiss with the charm of a queen. As always, her salon-blonde hair was perfectly groomed, her makeup job was flawless and her trim figure was clad in a simple but wonderfully cut pants suit. Holly could almost hear the wheels turning in her mother's head as Nadine smiled and gestured toward them. Had Nadine found him worthy of her attention, or would she make a polite introduction and swift exit?

"Holly, dear," Nadine said as she descended on their little group. She embraced Holly then stepped back and looked at her critically. "You're looking better. Not so peaked. I guess working for your little cause agrees with you. Now introduce me to these people."

Little cause, my ass, Holly thought as her mind went blank. Names? Oh, my God. She shot a panicked look at Cathy who quickly extended her real hand. "I'm Cathy Armbruster," she said smoothly. "I'm so glad to meet you. Holly's done *so* much for me and the other soldiers in the support groups. She's making an enormous impact with that little old cause of hers." *Good going, Cathy,* Holly thought in spite of her panic.

As Nadine's eyes narrowed, Cathy gestured to Jimmy, who quickly introduced himself, and Holly felt herself calming as the rest of the group followed suit. Cathy and Beto excused themselves, leaving Nadine and Holly standing with Jimmy and Misty and the silver-haired woman Holly had noticed earlier. "It's good to see you again, Nadine," the woman said before turning to Holly. "I'm Janelle Adamcik and you must be Carrie's 'the mostest-fun-I've-ever-had' Holly. I didn't realize you were Nadine's daughter."

"Holly, you should have said something to them," Nadine said briskly as Holly felt her face turning red. "So, Janelle, when are we going to steal you away from the teachers' union and put you to work for the oil industry?"

"About as soon as you trade in your petroleum deregulation for salary legislation," Janelle laughed.

The women exchanged a bit of conversation before Nadine took Jimmy's arm and steered him and Misty away from the group. "I need a few minutes with the candidate if that's all right."

Holly watched her mother from across the pavilion and tried to tamp down the resentment. "She is a bit intense, isn't she?" Janelle asked quietly as she put a gentle hand on Holly's arm.

"She hasn't bothered to come up here and see me since I got out of rehab," Holly said shortly. "But you say the word 'election' and she drives two and a half hours at the drop of a hat and then has to put down the work I'm doing with the soldiers right in front of two of them."

"One of whom gave it right back to her, didn't she?" Janelle laughed. "Your mama does not like being crossed."

"Yes, and if something like my work with the soldiers is not important to her, then it's just not important at all. Her candidates learn that one *real* quick."

An odd expression crossed Janelle's face and she was about to say something when an older couple flanked by a man about Jimmy's age marched up to them. "What in the hell does Jimmy think he's doing, running for office?" the woman demanded. "It's bad enough he's leaving Carrie with a cripple every day, and now he's planning to run all over hell and gone campaigning with his wife barely in her grave."

"Now mom, I told you not to start fussing about this," the younger man said. "Lauren's been gone for over a year and it's time for Jimmy to move on."

"Hello, Bruce, Ida. Good to see you, Randy. Yes, it's definitely time for Jimmy to go on with his life," Janelle said crisply. "He's always wanted to run for a major office and all of us who love him have encouraged him to do so."

"And what about leaving Carrie every day with a damned cripple?"

Holly smiled impudently and stuck out her hand. "Hi, I'm Holly Riley, the cripple in question. I may limp some and my left arm's not worth shit, but I can fix lunch and pick up a little and build a hell of a sand castle. And crippled though I am, I can still move faster than a four-year-old if I have to."

The woman turned beet red. "Never mind," Bruce snapped as he took the woman by the elbow and led her away.

"The Pucketts," Janelle said tiredly. "Carrie's other grandparents."

"Mrs. Adamcik, Miss Riley, I'm sorry," Randy said. "They have resented poor Jimmy since Lauren died and then mom got jealous when Carrie said that Miss Riley was the most fun she'd ever had. You know mom."

"Yes, I know Ida," Janelle said. "Randy, did I see you in the volunteer line?"

"Yep, unlike mom and dad I think Jimmy's candidacy is a great thing and I'd like to help him," Randy said. "I offered the services of my advertising firm."

"Why, that's wonderful!" Janelle said, looking surprised. "Thank you."

Randy wandered off and Janelle turned to Holly. "Wonders never cease," she told Holly quietly. "He used to be almost blind with jealousy where Jimmy was concerned."

At that moment Nadine and Jimmy crossed the pavilion together and Nadine took Holly's arm. "Holly dear, I'm going to have to leave in a minute or two. I have a fundraiser later this evening. Walk me to my car and tell me how you're doing."

They walked toward the parking lot. "I'm doing fine, Mom, honestly," Holly said. "The job with Jimmy's daughter is something pleasant to do during the day, and my work with the soldiers is making a big difference in people's lives, even if you can't see that."

"Touché," Nadine said. "Holly, I didn't mean to put down your work with your soldiers. I gathered from Cathy's pointed little barb that you've helped them a lot. But you have to remember that they are an important but *small* group of people. Dell's and my work for the oil industry doesn't just put money in rich people's pockets. The entire economy of west Texas is dependent on that industry." Holly nodded; Nadine had a point, as much as Holly hated to admit it. "You need to come see us," Nadine continued as she unlocked the Escalade. "Griff and Sullivan are home for the summer and would love to see you."

"I'll do that, Mom," Holly said. "Be safe." Holly watched as the big car pulled out of the parking lot and wandered back to the pavilion. Fumbling with her telephone, Cathy limped across the pavilion with an anxious expression on her face. "Holly, my mother's rushing my grandmother to the hospital in Austin and I need to meet her there—is there any way you can get home under your own steam?"

"Absolutely," Holly assured Cathy. "Give your grandma my love."

Cathy pivoted so quickly she almost fell and hobbled toward her car. Holly looked around and spotted three or four Heaven's Point residents she could catch a ride with. She ambled toward Jimmy and sheriff's deputy Rory Keller, who was holding hands with Lisa Simmons, the tall, redheaded waitress from the café. "Rory and Lisa were just telling me their good news," Jimmy said as Lisa proudly extended her left hand to show off a small but pretty diamond solitaire.

"How beautiful!" Holly said warmly. "Congratulations. When's the big day?"

"Sometime in the fall," Lisa said as she turned to Jimmy. "You'll sing, of course?"

"Be delighted," Jimmy said.

"And what about the organ?" Rory asked. "Maybe Holly could play for us."

Holly felt a fist of hurt punch hard into her gut. "Rory, I can't play a wedding anymore, remember?" she said tightly.

Rory's face turned fiery red and Lisa shot him a dirty look. "I-I'm so sorry," he stammered. "It's just—hell, you do so well, Holly, I honestly forget."

"And I will take that as the highest compliment you could pay me," Holly said as she reached out and squeezed the young man's hand and made herself smile at him. "Say, I've lost my ride. Anybody heading back to the Point any time soon?"

"We are," Jack Briscoe said as he and Caroline came up behind Jimmy, Ryan asleep on his shoulder. "Caroline's nauseated and wants to get home before she starts throwing up again."

Caroline gave Jack a go-to-hell look and Holly couldn't help but laugh. She followed the couple to a brand-new Expedition and Jack strapped the sleeping child in his car seat while Holly struggled to crawl in beside him. "No, I've got it," she said when Jack moved to take her arm. "But thanks."

"Actually, you did that quite nicely," Caroline said as she hopped in the front seat beside Jack. "And your buddies Cathy and

Beto are amazing. Beto could almost run a marathon and Cathy's seems to be learning to use her new leg well also."

"It's good to see Beto moving so well," Jack said as he backed out of the parking space. "He was a dynamite receiver when I coached him." A shadow crossed Jack's face. "The one that kills me is Tommy. He not only played football and ran track, he was a damn good roper. He competed in every amateur rodeo in a two-hundred-mile radius."

"He still has his old cow pony," Holly said. "At least, I think that's the 'Muffin' he's always talking about."

"Does your bad leg bother you a lot?" Caroline asked as Jack took the turnoff that would take them to the Heaven's Point highway.

"If I'm up on it a lot like I was today," Holly admitted. "And I did overdo it. But I wasn't about to sneak out early, especially after mom showed up and Cathy dissed her so royally." Holly's eyes danced and she giggled out loud.

Jack raised his eyebrow and Caroline turned around in the seat, her eyes wide. "What happened?"

"It was priceless. Mom made the mistake of referring to my work with the injured soldiers as my 'little cause' and Cathy told her off." Holly laughed again. "Mom has, shall we say, tunnel vision when it comes to what is and isn't an *important* issue in a campaign. If it doesn't promote the good of the oil industry or the economy of west Texas then she's not interested."

Jack and Caroline looked at one another as a light appeared to come on. "That explains it, then," Jack said to Caroline.

"Explains what?" Holly asked.

"Explains why Judge Riley told Jimmy to give a rousing speech but to stay away from anything too specific," Caroline said. "Gave him a list, even, of topics to avoid. We were surprised because Jimmy's always had very passionate views about some hot-button issues, education and the environment in particular, but apparently he and Misty took the judge at his word and stayed away from the no-no list."

Holly gritted her teeth as she started to steam. "And I guess the welfare of the injured American veterans was on the list, wasn't it?" she asked hotly.

Jack thought a minute. "Fifth one down."

"That wimpy son of a bitch!" Holly snapped. "He didn't even know for sure that Mom would show up and he's already tailoring his campaign to suck up to the great Nadine Hightower. No wonder he spouted platitudes."

Jack and Caroline looked across the seat at one another. "Uh, oh, I guess we should have kept our mouths shut," Caroline murmured.

Holly flicked her hand in front of her. "Uncle Willis would have eventually said something or I would have put two and two together. I'm not surprised. Nadine's war machine has a lot more clout than one little group of gimpy soldiers." She blinked angrily as she felt tears stinging her eyes. "I just thought that, after serving over there, maybe he would understand. That maybe just once a politician would give us more than lip service and might honestly help us a little. Joke's on me, isn't it?"

* * *

Jimmy grabbed a pack of cigarettes and a lighter and locked the front door behind him as he stepped out into the warm evening. He'd set his iPad up in Carrie's room and had his smart phone synched as a baby monitor. She was sound asleep, worn out from the long day at the picnic, and he was only going down the street to Holly's place for a little while—at least, he hoped it would just be for a little while.

Jack had called him earlier, embarrassed that apparently he and Caroline had told Holly that Jimmy had purposely soft-pedaled any mention of specific issues, in particular the whole-hearted support of the injured combat veterans, and that Holly was furious at the lack of support. And he absolutely, positively couldn't afford to run off his daughter's most-fun-ever babysitter.

Jimmy started to ring the bell but headed for the dock when he heard a splash and a terse curse word. "Fucking bastard, I worked thirty minutes to catch you!" Holly snapped as she reared back her bad leg and kicked her bait, bucket and all, into the water. "Son of a bitch, that hurt!" she said as she came back down on the leg and stumbled a bit.

Jimmy let out a low whistle. "Damn, I hate to think what you could do with your good leg. I gather your fish got away."

Holly whirled around and glowered at him. "Your mother-in-law is a real bitch."

Jimmy shrugged. "Tell me something I don't know."

"Okay, then," Holly said. "My mother is a dictatorial, power-hungry tyrant who could give a rat's ass about anything but her God-damned oil lobby. And you're a chicken-shit kiss-up with the integrity of a politician. No, wait. You *are* a politician. Never mind."

Jimmy bit his lip to keep from laughing. "Tell me what you really think."

"Oh, shut up," Holly said crossly as Jimmy dug the cigarettes out his pocket and held them out to her. "Wait. Where's Carrie?"

He held up his phone so she could see the streaming live video of his sleeping daughter.

She nodded then launched back into her tirade. "I am pissed at you, Jimmy. Royally pissed." Holly jerked a cigarette from the pack and he took another as she sat down in her folding chair. "You of all people ought to know what Cathy and Beto and Tommy and all the rest have sacrificed. You were over there and watched them get carried out on stretchers and in body bags. You ought to be ready with unconditional support. Instead, we get a standing ovation and the same platitudes just so you can kiss up to Queen Nadine."

Jimmy flopped down in the folding chair next to Holly's. He lit both cigarettes and leaned back. "Okay, let's imagine a redo. I come out there and start detailing my political agenda. I stand up and loudly advocate teacher pay raises, environmental accountability for big business, high-dollar assistance programs for all of our veterans, not just the injured ones, and so on and so forth. What will your mother do?"

"Get in the Escalade and high-tail it back to San Angelo," Holly said. "And what would be so wrong with that?"

Jimmy looked at Holly unbelievingly. "When were you born, late last night or early this morning? Do you have any idea the kind of money Nadine has available at the snap of her fingers?"

Holly shrugged. "There's other money out there besides Nadine's." She looked up at the sky and blew out a plume of smoke. "Jimmy, I know you probably thought any number of unkind things about me when you found out Nadine Hightower is my mother and I hadn't said anything. But this is exactly the scenario I was trying to avoid. You've barely begun your campaign and she hasn't offered you a plug nickel and you're already dancing to her tune. You're walking her walk and talking her talk. And the fact that you think you need her money doesn't impress me."

"The fact that you're ignoring political reality doesn't impress me much, either," Jimmy said coolly as Holly turned a baleful eye in his direction. "The bottom line is while I support every man and woman who served in the United States Military and am prepared to vote their way every chance I get, I damn well can't afford to alienate the money Nadine's contacts can bring into a campaign. So yes, I may soften some of my sharp edges and candy some of my positions. That's politics." He turned to her and grasped her hand, the unexpected touch of his fingers sending a little zing up her arm. "Holly, please understand how damned important it is to me to make this run. Maybe I'm naïve, but I honestly think if I were elected that I could make a difference. And I have to have financial backing."

Holly sighed as she looked down at their entwined hands and then over at Jimmy. "That's probably the most honest statement you've made all day, and believe it or not I can understand just how badly you do want to run. I'm just not sure you understand exactly how much Nadine and her contributors will expect out of you."

Jimmy let go of her hand and sat back. "Well, I have a chance to find out. Nadine invited me to drive up to San Angelo next Saturday and sit down with some potential backers. These men and women are not particularly pleased with any of the other candidates out there and she would like for them to meet me. I'd like you and Carrie to come with me. I know you and your mom have your differences, but she acted like she'd like to see you, and a home-cooked meal couldn't be all that bad. And honestly, I'd like the company."

"Whatever. Maybe Griff or Sullivan will be there. We can take Carrie to the movies or something while you wheel and deal. Oh, and just so you don't blow it with Mom. Do not in any way, shape, or form let on how much you like and admire Uncle Willis and do not under any circumstances say *anything* nice about my father," Holly said. "Mom and Dad absolutely despise one another and she doesn't have much use for Uncle Willis either."

"Mind if I ask why?"

Holly shrugged. "Dad got my stepmother—Patsy Harrington, of the San Antonio Harrington dynasty—pregnant with my brother Russ while mom was pregnant with me. He divorced Mom to marry Patsy the minute I was born, so Mom made sure he saw almost nothing of me. Then when I was five, Mom fell in the bottle and got a DUI with me in the car. Uncle Willis got wind of it and Daddy and Patsy got custody of me. They wouldn't let me spend any time with mom until her second husband, Griffin Graham—you know, chairman of Graham drilling—threatened to bankrupt Patsy's father's law firm if the custody agreement wasn't amended, and to this day my parents can't stand each other." Holly smiled ruefully. "I was just the tennis ball."

Jimmy whistled under his breath. "And Judge Riley goes ballistic over custody battles. So what do I say to the backers?"

"Let your conscience be your guide."

Jimmy chuckled as he took Holly's hand again and rose, bringing her with him. Holly watched, mesmerized, as he leaned in closer to her. "You're a sweetheart, Holly Riley," he said softly as he touched her lips with his own.

He only meant for it to be a tender kiss, a gentle kiss between friends, but as his lips met the softness of hers and he inhaled the fresh scent of her skin and hair a flare of desire hit him right in the groin. What the hell? Jimmy wondered as his mouth tightened on hers, forcing her lips open and stealing his tongue inside the sweet depths of her mouth.

He had been fully aware he was attracted to her, had known he wanted to kiss her, but he had not expected this explosion of raw unadulterated lust as his lips plundered hers. He felt Holly momentarily stiffen in his arms, but when she did not push him away he snaked his arms around her waist, drawing her closer to him.

She reached up and wrapped her good arm around his neck, pulling him even closer as her tongue slipped out from between her teeth and fought a duel with his. Jimmy's head spun as the blood pounded in his ears and rushed to the lower portion of his body, swelling his manhood until it was pressed uncomfortably against the rough denim of his jeans. Holly's body quivered against his at the sensual onslaught. He could feel her nipples harden beneath the soft cotton of her T-shirt and felt the catch in her breath as he flattened his hands against her back below her waist.

Her uninjured arm was strong and warm and felt oh-so-right as Holly moaned softly in his arms. Sweet, so sweet and so sensual and so nice, he thought as they clung together for long moments, his body pressed against the softness of hers as he kissed her and touched her and made love to her with his mouth. Holly responded in kind, holding him and returning his kisses with a passion that at least equaled his own. So long, he thought as he held Holly close. It had been so long since a woman had come apart in his arms.

Breathless, Jimmy finally lifted his lips from hers and stared down at her dazed and thoroughly kissed face. "Holy hell, did you see that coming?" he asked, his voice a broken croak. Holly shook her head. "Well, neither did I," Jimmy admitted as he bent down to feather gentle kisses along the sides of her mouth. "But I'm sure as shootin' not knocking it."

Holly nodded and stood on her tiptoes to reach his lips. If anything, their second kiss was more passionate than the first. Jimmy trembled as Holly feathered her fingers up into his soft hair, her good hand surprisingly strong as she caressed the back of his head. Their bodies plastered together, they clung to one another for long moments, oblivious to the slap of the waves against Holly's dock or the fiery splendor of sunset bathing them in its glow, aware only of one another as they kissed and touched and caressed, both starved for the other's touch. Holly's fingers dug into his hair and Jimmy's hands dropped to cup Holly's soft bottom. Finally Holly pulled away slightly and shook her head. "No more," she said softly.

Jimmy's eyebrow shot up as he looked down at her passion-swollen lips. "Don't like it?" he asked softly.

Holly laughed ruefully. "I like it too much," she said as she slipped from his arms and fled as though the hounds of hell were after her, leaving a stunned Jimmy staring at her back door and wondering what the hell hit him.

* * *

My, oh my, this is getting interesting, Chucky thought with delight as he watched Jimmy and Holly cling to one another at the end of her dock. The last rays of the setting sun bathed the couple in a crimson glow and Chucky moved further back into the shadows lest one of the nosy old geezers that populated the Point spot him watching the show. Not that anyone would notice him, with the spectacle that bastard Adamcik and the Army bitch were making of themselves. Chucky put down the binoculars and folded his arms as the bitch broke off the kiss and disappeared into the house and Adamcik stood there with his tongue hanging to his knees.

Show appeared to be over, at least for now. But if the way they were clinging to one another was any indication, Chucky would bet his old M16 that Adamcik and the Army bitch would be doing the mattress tango at some point in the fairly near future.

Chucky waited patiently and as the light faded and the stars winked on an idea wove itself together in his head. What if he used the Army bitch and her bunch of gimps to discredit the run for Congress that the asshole announced this afternoon? What if he had a little fun with them and somehow associated the wreckage with Adamcik's campaign? Yes, his ultimate target was the bastard Adamcik, delivering the payback Adamcik so richly deserved, but he wasn't all that fond of the gimps either. Bunch of useless, broken, whiny wimps, every one of them. As collateral damage they would be perfect.

So now he had a plan, Chucky thought as he slapped at a mosquito feasting on his neck. Go after the gimps and use that to ruin the Adamcik campaign. Then go after the bitch. And then go after Adamcik himself and make the bastard pay for what he did.

It would be so much fun.

Chapter Five

Holly sat quietly in the passenger seat and stared out at the darkness of the rugged ranchland outside San Angelo. The highway they traveled was dark and quiet and the moonless sky was awash with a blanket of stars blazing in the deep ebony sky. The faint sounds of Carrie's movie on the built-in viewer were the only sounds in the peaceful darkness.

Jimmy appeared deep in thought as he drove, and Holly realized the headache she had fought all afternoon at the movies and later during her mother's dinner was turning into a full-fledged migraine. Content with the silence between them, they were past Eden before Holly reached over and laid her hand on Jimmy's forearm. "How did it go in there this afternoon?" she asked. "With Purcell Reynolds and the others." Nadine had lined up some of the most influential movers and shakers in west Texas and Jimmy had spent over two hours with them at her dining room table.

"They offered me their full-fledged support," Jimmy said tersely.

"But?" Holly prompted.

"They want me to drop education and put my environmental concerns on the back burner if not completely off the stove when it comes to petroleum exploration. Hells bells, those are the two issues that mean the most to me. And you and every other veteran in this nation gets...let's see...'lip service will do just fine.'" Jimmy ran his hand down the side of his face. "They don't give a damn about what I stand for. They just want to further their own agenda."

Holly sighed. "What do you think I've been trying to tell you? Did you really think any of them were going to give a damn who you are or what you stand for? You hit the nail on the head. All they care about is furthering their own agenda. Having their own private puppet in Congress would be a hell of a nice way to do that."

Jimmy's mouth tightened. "I wouldn't be anybody's private puppet."

"If you expected to last for more than one term you would be," Holly said. "The last two congressmen have very much danced to those people's tune."

"Then fine. You tell me how to win either election without their support."

"Don't take a dime of their money. Raise your own."

"Damn it, Holly, I don't know if I can!" Jimmy snapped. "I haven't exactly been inundated with donations. And mom and I sure don't have the kind of personal fortune that Alex Navarro has."

Holly groaned. "Alex Navarro's running? Oh my God. No wonder they want you beholden to them. The Navarros are billionaires. His dad can and will finance the campaign and if Alex wins he'll tell them where they can stick it and smile while he's doing it."

"Now do you see the problem?" Jimmy asked tiredly. "If I'm serious about running I have no choice but to take their help."

"Well, you can get out there and at least try to raise your own money, can't you? You might very well be able to come up with the cash," Holly countered as a wave of pain broke over her. She groaned and gripped the sides of her head. "Oh, God almighty, that hurts. Can we have this argument another time?"

Jimmy glanced over at her pain-twisted face. "One of your headaches?" he asked. "Do you have anything for it?"

"I didn't think to bring the pills."

"Should we stop in Mason and try to get some Tylenol?" he asked.

"Wouldn't do any good. Just get me home."

Jimmy hit the gas and the Navigator ate up the miles. They had nearly reached the turnoff that would take them to Verde when Holly's cell phone rang. "Leave it," Jimmy said gruffly as he glanced over at Holly's ashen face.

Holly looked down at the number. "It's Christi Bailey. I'll tell her to call me tomorrow."

Holly answered the phone and even from across the car Jimmy could hear the hysteria in the young woman's voice. "Christi, Christi, slow down," Holly said crisply into the phone. "Take a deep breath and tell me what's wrong. Okay, I understand. The barn's burning and the animals are trapped inside. Have you called 911? You have? Okay, then use a hose if you think it will help but please don't do anything to put yourself or Tommy in danger. Those animals can be replaced. You and Tommy can't. I'll be there as quickly as I can." She closed the telephone. "Damn, of all times for this. Can you get us out to the Reeces'?" Jimmy started to protest but instead took the turnoff that would take them to the Reece ranch on the other side of Verde.

They could see the fire from the road. The volunteer fire department was already on the scene, doing what little they could to contain the flames that were voraciously consuming the ramshackle old barn, and several firefighters were busy putting out the sparks that threatened the equally run-down farmhouse. Holly recognized Rory Keller's rangy silhouette on the farmhouse porch talking to the soot-smudged, pajama-clad young couple watching as the firefighters put up a valiant but hopeless battle, and another deputy was in the cruiser on the police radio. Jimmy parked behind the cruiser and each of them took a wide-eyed Carrie's hand as they made their way to the front porch.

Tommy looked up at Holly and Jimmy, his eyes dull with shock and pain. "Muffin was in there. I couldn't get her out. The door was nailed shut." He took a deep breath. "Beauregard was in there, too. Best breeding bull I ever had." He took another breath and looked up at the ceiling. "*Son of a bitch!*" he cried suddenly as he clutched the arms of his wheelchair. "Is this fucking universe *ever* going to cut me a break?" He reached out to Christi and wrapped his arms around her waist as violent sobs tore through his body.

Tears poured down Christi's face as she looked at Holly. "Tommy thinks he could have saved them if he'd been able to walk," she said brokenly. "He thinks they died because he couldn't break them out from the chair." She turned anguished eyes on Jimmy and Rory. "Who would do such a thing? Who would nail the door shut and torch a barn and leave two innocent animals to die?"

Yes, and who would target a paraplegic soldier's barn and animals in the first place? Holly thought angrily as Tommy sobbed. Jimmy hoisted Carrie up on his shoulder and they watched the old barn burn. When the worst was over and the hoses had soaked what was left, Harvey Watson, captain of the volunteer fire brigade, trudged tiredly to the front porch. "Barn is a total loss," he said unnecessarily. "But the sparks are out and any danger to the house has been averted. Rory, you or Lester needs to call Austin and get the arson boys out here. We could still smell the gasoline that was used to fuel it."

One of the younger firefighters trotted up to the porch and pointed back over his shoulder. "I don't know if it means anything or not, but when I was trying to aim the hose I tripped over some kind of sign. Couldn't read it in the dark. Miss Bailey, did you have a little sign on a post over there?"

Christi shook her head as Rory snapped on a pair of latex gloves. Taking the young firefighter with him, Rory returned momentarily carrying a cardboard sign on a wooden stake. He laid the sign face up on the porch and held a flashlight up to the cardboard. "What the hell?" Jimmy exclaimed when the 'Adamcik for Congress' slogan appeared through the soot marks.

"Daddy, isn't that one of your signs?" Carrie asked.

They all stared down at the smoky sign. "That *wasn't* out there when I went out to feed the animals this evening," Christi said firmly. She turned to Jimmy and blushed when he raised his eyebrow a little. "I-I didn't mean it like that," she stammered, red-faced. "I just meant that somebody else put the sign out there after I was in the barn tonight."

Rory looked back down at the sign. "Tommy Joe?"

Tommy Joe sniffed. "No, I don't know where it came from either," he said slowly.

"Then I'm going to take it in and treat it as evidence," Rory said as he gathered up the sign. He looked over at the ruined barn. "Damn, Tommy Joe, I'm sorry. Do you have insurance?"

Tommy Joe shrugged. "Not enough. Besides, no damned policy in the world's gonna bring back Muffin." Another round of tears welled up in the boy's eyes. "Jesus, Mary and Joseph, why in hell did I have to be in this *fucking* chair? On my feet I could have saved them."

"Tommy Joe, I seriously doubt that," Harvey Watson said as he leaned against the porch railing. "I worked arson for the Austin fire department for twenty years. That fire was set in such a way that the most able-bodied man in Verde County couldn't have gotten them out in time, especially with the door nailed shut. Quit beating yourself up." He straightened and headed tiredly for the fire truck.

"What a crock," Tommy said bitterly as the firefighters climbed into the truck. "Feed the crip bullshit to make him feel better."

Holly and Christi exchanged a look over the top of Tommy's head. Holly awkwardly knelt down in front of Tommy and put on her best Captain-Riley face. "Tommy Joe, look at me," she said in her most authoritative tone. "Look at me, Tommy," she demanded as the young man raised tear-stained eyes to meet hers. "Harvey Watson is not a liar and he and everyone else around here have too much respect for you to feed you a line of bull. If the man says you couldn't have done anything, then you couldn't have. Got that, soldier?"

Tommy looked at her for a moment before snapping a salute. "That's better," Holly said quietly. "Tommy, the barn and the bull can be replaced and believe it or not you will learn to love another horse. Just be glad it wasn't you or Christi." Jimmy offered her his arm as she struggled to stand up. "I'll be back out to check on you tomorrow." She gave Tommy a quick hug and let Jimmy help her down the porch stairs.

Christi followed Jimmy and Holly out in the yard. "He was doing so well," she said as more tears welled in her eyes. "This is bound to set him back."

Holly enfolded Christi in a hug. "We won't let that happen, all right?"

Christi nodded and started back toward the house. "I never heard you talk like that," Carrie said in wonder. "Like you talked to Tommy."

"She was being Captain Riley," Jimmy murmured to his daughter. "She's really good at it."

Holly clung to Jimmy's arm as the sickening aura of the migraine engulfed her even more viciously than before. Her legs started to buckle as Jimmy effortlessly swept her up into the Navigator. "Impressive demonstration of mind over matter," he said as he buckled Carrie into her seat. "You must have been one hell of an officer."

"General Patton, Mother Theresa and Combat Barbie all rolled into one," Holly murmured dryly. "Did I lie to that boy, Jimmy? Could he have saved those animals if he hadn't been in that chair?"

"Who knows?" Jimmy said tiredly as he pulled out onto the highway. "The important thing is that Tommy thinks he could have. Shit. Who would do that to a paraplegic soldier who couldn't defend himself?"

Holly held onto her pounding head. "I just can't believe it." She groaned as she turned her head in Jimmy's direction. "And where did that campaign sign come from?"

Jimmy blew out his breath. "We're giving them out all over town. The question is, who the hell put it there and why?"

Chapter Six

Holly moaned and gripped the sides of her head as the combination of the severe migraine and the horror of what she'd just seen at the Reece ranch sent waves of pain ripping through her head. "God, this has to be the worst one of these I've ever had," she groaned as Jimmy raced down the highway.

"We'll be there in a few minutes," Jimmy said soothingly. Holly tried to make it but the nausea was too much and Jimmy had to stop on the road into Heaven's Point so she could throw up. By the time they got to the house Holly was almost screaming from pain. "Will you wait until I'm in the house before you leave?" she asked.

"Give me your house keys and tell me where you keep your pills and your nightie," Jimmy said. "No way are you staying by yourself tonight as sick as you are."

"That's not necessary," Holly said. "I'll be fine—oh, God," she said as she rolled out of the Navigator and threw up again.

Jimmy reappeared a few minutes later carrying her tote and wordlessly they drove to his place. Jimmy carried his sleeping daughter to bed first and quickly returned for Holly, ignoring her protests and sweeping her into his arms. "Put your good arm around my neck," he whispered as he kicked the Navigator door shut. Jimmy's chest felt hard and warm and it was all Holly could do not to snuggle closer. Her body tingled with awareness as Jimmy carried her in the house and up the flight of stairs and into the pretty bedroom next to his own. He laid her down and disappeared, only to return momentarily with her tote and a glass of water. "I found these in your bathroom cabinet," he said as he showed her a bottle of medication. "Is this the right stuff?"

Holly nodded. "I usually need two."

Jimmy shook out the last two pills and Holly washed them down with the water. Jimmy fished out Holly's satin sleeping shirt. "Can you manage?" He asked as he handed it to her.

"I'll be fine," Holly assured him.

"I'll leave this door open and mine, too. Call me if you need anything." He turned out the overhead light but left a small lamp burning on the nightstand.

So damn nice, Holly thought as she shrugged out of her clothes. *So damn sexy and so damn nice.* He didn't have to take her out to the Reece ranch nor did he have to take care of her tonight, and he had done both. Holly gently laid her pounding head on the pillow. Poor Tommy. His barn and his bull and his old cow pony all gone. Why would anyone do that to Tommy Joe? And why on Earth was there an 'Adamcik for Congress' sign posted at the scene of destruction?

* * *

Damn, another soldier is having a nightmare, Holly thought as the sound of screams penetrated the dense fog of sleep. Should she get up or let one of the sergeants handle it? She waited for a beat but as the screaming worsened Holly opened her eyes and found herself not in a field tent outside Baghdad but in Jimmy Adamcik's guest room, and the man in the middle of night terrors was Jimmy Adamcik himself. Oh my God, Holly thought as she stumbled out of bed and made a beeline for the next room.

The drapes were open and the light of the not-quite-full moon shone in on the man twisting and turning in the tangled bedclothes. "Damn it no, don't, it's a trap!" he cried out in his sleep. Clad only in boxers, his lean, muscular body gleamed in the dim moonlight as he thrashed and punched his fists into the mattress. Sweat poured down his face and dampened the thick hair that covered his chest. Under other circumstances Holly might have stopped to admire Jimmy's trim hips and beautifully sculpted body, but right now she had to somehow awaken him without getting herself hurt in the process. And she could very easily be hurt if this was a full-blown flashback. Because Jimmy's nightmare wasn't just another run-of-the-mill bad dream. Jimmy had PTSD.

Holly eased herself onto the bed beside Jimmy and took his shoulders in her hands. "Jimmy, wake up," she said gently as she massaged his shoulders, her left hand not firm but still conveying a comforting touch. "Wake up, Jimmy," she said over and over as he twisted and tried to pull away from her. "You're not there anymore. You're here, you're home, and it's okay now." For long minutes she rubbed his shoulders and arms and spoke gently as he relived some wartime horror, but finally his eyes snapped open.

"What are you doing here?" he whispered brokenly, his eyes wild and haunted.

"You were screaming in your sleep," Holly said gently as she released his shoulders. "You were having a nightmare. You weren't coming out of it so I woke you up."

"Shit." Jimmy ran his trembling fingers through his tousled hair and leaned back against the padded headboard. "Baghdad again." He looked over at the clock and groaned. "Damn, it's only four-thirty. I'll be up the rest of the night."

"It's too early to get up," Holly said as she reached out and touched his bare chest, hard and trembling beneath her fingers. "You're soaked and you're starting to get chilled." She went to the bathroom for a towel and while he dried his chest and arms she found him a clean T-shirt.

Jimmy's hands were still shaking as he pulled the T-shirt over his head. "I'm sorry I woke you. How's the head?"

"Better but not great," Holly admitted. "Why don't you lie back down and try to get a little more sleep? You can't have had more than a couple or three hours."

"It's pointless. I haven't been able to go back to sleep after one of these things since Lauren died."

"That's because you had her to go back to sleep with," Holly said softly. "Lay down, Jimmy. I can finish the night in here." She slid under the covers beside Jimmy. He hesitated for a moment before sliding down beside her and pulling the sheet up to his waist. Holly reached out and rested her hand on his chest. "Sleep now, Jimmy," she said soothingly as she felt the tension slowly draining from his body. "It will seem better in the morning."

Jimmy put his hand over hers. "Thanks, Holly." He smiled just a little as she replied with a soft snore.

* * *

Holly sighed and snuggled into the warm masculine body spooned up against her. A strong arm was thrown across her waist and soft breath tickled her neck. What a nice way to wake up, she thought as she opened her eyes just a smidgen and looked around Jimmy's peaceful bedroom. Jimmy was still awake when she had drifted back to sleep, but if the even breathing of the man who held her close was anything to go by, slumber had overtaken him again and somehow they had ended up cuddled together under the silky sheets. Holly could not even remember the last time she had awakened in a man's arms. Even though she knew she should slip out of bed she lay still and savored the warmth and the closeness. Jimmy slept on, his arm draped across her waist, his knee poking into the back of her leg, and the hard thrust of his morning erection telling her that even asleep Jimmy was aware that he held a woman in his arms. When Holly thought she heard Carrie rustling around she eased herself across the bed and sat up. She felt Jimmy stir and looked over her shoulder to find his eyes wide open. "Where are you going? I was enjoying that," he said as he smiled sleepily at her. His arm snaked out and snared Holly around the neck, pulling her down to him.

"So was I," Holly admitted as she blushed.

"And I would enjoy a good-morning kiss even more," Jimmy said as he pulled Holly closer. "Good morning, Holly," he said as he captured her lips with his, his kiss at first gentle and then demanding as he bore Holly down into the sheets. Holly reached around with her good arm and ran it down Jimmy's back, his hard muscles bunching under the demanding touch of her fingers.

In spite of the lingering effects of the headache Holly felt the blood rush to her midsection and her nipples harden. Jimmy's kiss was long and lingering and thorough but eventually he raised his head and scooted away. "I wish we could continue this but I hear Carrie. Thanks for coming in here last night," Jimmy said. "It took a while but I did fall back to sleep. Head better?"

"I'm almost there. How long have you had PTSD?" Holly asked as she stood up and wandered over to the window.

Holly felt rather than saw Jimmy stiffen. "What do you mean, PTSD?" he demanded as his eyes narrowed. "I don't have PTSD. I just have a nightmare now and then."

Holly whirled around and stared at Jimmy in astonishment. "What do you mean, you don't have PTSD? What do you call last night?"

Jimmy rolled out of bed and glowered at Holly. "I call last night a fucking nightmare. I don't call it PTSD."

"Oh." Holly pointed down at her bad knee. "And I guess this was just a fucking boo-boo. Jimmy, you can call it or not call it anything you want to, but PTSD is PTSD. It took me ten minutes to get you awake. That's not just a run of the mill nightmare." Her face gentled. "It's no shame, Jimmy. PTSD has happened to some of the strongest men and women I've ever known."

"And when did you start practicing psychiatry?" Jimmy demanded.

Holly folded her arms in front of her. "It doesn't take a shrink. I saw a boatload of it in Iraq and even more in the hospital." She stopped and took a breath. "What I saw last night was a vivid reliving of whatever hell you went through in Baghdad, and that, Jimmy, constitutes PTSD."

"A bad dream in and of itself is not a sign of PTSD," Jimmy ground out.

"All right. Let's talk about some of the others," Holly said. "Do you have horrible dreams where you can't wake up? Do you still go hunting, or do the sound of gunfire and the sight of blood turn you off these days? Are you jumpy? Do you flinch at the sound of a car backfiring? Do you still like Rambo movies or are you picking your entertainment in the comedy section?"

Jimmy's eyes widened briefly before his face froze in an implacable mask. "If any of that's going on, and I'm not saying that it is, it's nobody's damn business but my own," he ground out.

"It's a medical condition you need to deal with," Holly shot back.

Jimmy's temper snapped. "God damn it woman, I *do not* have PTSD!" he roared. "And I am not going to ruin a run for Congress because my touchy-feely neighbor thinks I'm a nutcase and wants me to run to a shrink. And you damn well better not tell anybody; do you hear me?"

Holly stood up toe to toe with Jimmy. "I don't blab," she said hotly. "But *you* damn well better listen. I know what PTSD looks like and you have it. And I'll bet a year's worth of disability checks that yours is escalating. What are you going to do when you wake Carrie up with your screaming?" She saw him flinch. "Oh my God, it's already happened, hasn't it?" Holly breathed. "Jimmy, you could hurt her!"

"Damn it, I would never hurt my daughter!" He was opening his mouth to say more when the doorbell rang. "Oh, hell, I forgot. Caroline Briscoe wanted to take Carrie out to the ranch for the day."

"We'll finish this later," Holly said as she beat a hasty retreat to the guest bedroom and pulled on the clean jeans and T-shirt that Jimmy had so thoughtfully packed for her. What should she do? Jimmy had full-blown PTSD—a pretty severe case of it if that nightmare was any indication—and the worst case of denial she had ever encountered. What if the depression continued to escalate? Would that put Carrie in danger? What about her promise not to tell? And who would she tell, anyway?

Holly ran her fingers through her hair and was coming down the stairs with her tote when Carrie pulled open the front door for Caroline and Ryan. Caroline's eyes widened when she spotted Holly. "Morning," Holly said, hoping she sounded nonchalant. "I came back from San Angelo with the migraine from hell and the fire out at the Reece place just made it worse, and Jimmy was kind enough to put me up in his guest room."

"Yeah, the fire was huge and Tommy and Christi cried," Carrie said. "And then daddy had to stop the car so Holly could throw up."

Caroline was instantly all concern. "Do you have any meds for that?"

"Yes, but I took them all last night." Holly dug her medicine bottle out of her tote. "I really wish I'd gone ahead and made you my physician of record. I'm going to need a new scrip."

Caroline took the bottle and pulled a prescription pad out of her handbag. "I can write it for you." Caroline scribbled on the pad and handed the prescription to Holly. "Carrie, is your daddy awake yet?" Caroline asked.

"He must be. He and Holly were yelling at each other in his bedroom when I woke up."

* * *

Jimmy pulled on a pair of cutoffs and rubbed his hand down his unshaven face. His eyes were bloodshot and his face was drawn and he hated going down the stairs to face the infuriated Holly and the too-perceptive Caroline Briscoe, but if he didn't get down there quickly Holly might say something to Caroline about the nightmare. He ran a toothbrush over his teeth and loped down the stairs just in time to hear Carrie announce that he and Holly had been not only in his room together but yelling about something. His mind raced for an explanation. "Holly, I didn't mean to fight with you about your mother and the committee," he said, hoping she would take the hint.

Holly was no fool. "I told you what you were getting into when you went to San Angelo," she said as Caroline looked from Jimmy to Holly and back to Jimmy. "Thanks for taking care of me last night." She turned to Caroline. "I appreciate the prescription. I'll have the doctors at BAMC send you my records. Good to see you again, Ryan. See you tomorrow, Carrie." She winced as she opened the front door. "Damn, it's bright out here," she grumbled as she shut the door behind her.

Caroline's lips twitched as she caught Jimmy's expression. "Arguing about Nadine, huh? Good save."

Jimmy glowered at Caroline. "She was sick. She went to sleep on my bed. That's all."

Caroline's eyebrows rose. "Jimmy, I am well aware that nothing interesting whatsoever happened in your bed last night. I know what the morning after a good night before looks like and poor Holly sure didn't look like that. For that matter, you don't look so great, either. Are you all right?"

"Just tired, that's all," Jimmy said quickly, hoping Caroline wouldn't press the issue. "And unfortunately, our argument over Nadine is all too real. Come have a cup of coffee with me and I'll tell you about the fire at Tommy Joe's and the meeting in San Angelo. Carrie, why don't you and Ryan go upstairs and play while Miss Caroline and I have a cup of coffee?"

The kids darted upstairs and thankfully Caroline left well enough alone, and while he made coffee Jimmy filled her in on the fire and the meeting in San Angelo. "So it boils down to this," Jimmy admitted as he handed Caroline a steaming cup of coffee and sat down at the kitchen table across from her. "The only reason they're interested in me at all is that I'm the only one they think might beat Alex Navarro in the primary, but if I want their financial support it's their way or the highway. To hell with anything but their business interests. Holly's upset because they don't give a damn about the welfare of wounded veterans. They're opposed to anything that would raise their taxes one damn dime."

"What was Mrs. Hightower's take on it?" Caroline asked.

"I think her exact words were 'Welcome to world of big-time politics.' Holly thinks I at least ought to try to raise the money myself before I become beholden to the barracudas," Jimmy said. "That's what we argued about."

Caroline eyed Jimmy thoughtfully. "What do you think, Jimmy?"

Jimmy hooked his legs around the back of his chair. "I don't know what to think. Of course I would love to support Holly and all the others like her. You know how I feel about education and the environment. But Caroline, you can't imagine the money those people have at their disposal. I'm going to need a lot of money if I have to go up against Alex Navarro and I'm just not sure I can raise it by myself."

Caroline thought for a minute. "You know, I mean no disrespect to Mrs. Hightower, but if I were you I think I would listen to Holly. She's been around enough politics to have something of a feel for things. And you said yourself that you won't be able to accomplish what you want to if you have to dance to these people's tune."

"I think the word Holly used was 'puppet.'"

"Well, there you are." Caroline drank the last of her coffee. "Can Carrie stay until after supper? Ryan is getting so bored he's driving Jack and me crazy. I can hardly wait for Carmela to come home."

"Sure, keep her as long as you like," Jimmy said. "Holly packed her a dress for Sunday School."

Caroline left with the children and Jimmy poured himself another cup of coffee and carried it out to the deck. Holly was wrong, he assured himself as he sipped his coffee and watched a boat tow a pair of skiers across the lake. He didn't have PTSD; he just had a nightmare or two now and again. He didn't particularly want to go hunting anymore, but he had never been that fond of it in the first place. He jumped when a car backfired, but so did everybody. And he never had liked Rambo movies anyway. He was all right. He had to be, because the alternative could cost him his dream.

* * *

What a totally terrible a day, Holly thought as she dropped Cathy off in front of her house. First she'd had the fight with Jimmy, and then she and Cathy had driven out to the Reece Ranch, where their words of encouragement had fallen on deaf ears as Tommy stared morosely out the window at the wet ashes that were all that remained of his barn. "He's back to square one," Christi admitted to Holly as she cried in the kitchen. "I tried to talk to him but all he'll say is that he's stuck in that chair for the rest of his life and that nothing is going to change that." And then on the way home one of Cathy's friends texted her that an announcement of her ex-husband's engagement had appeared in the San Antonio society pages. Holly roundly cursed Darryl as she watched a teary-eyed Cathy, still not quite steady on her feet, limp up the sidewalk and fumble in her handbag for her key.

And what about Jimmy? Holly stomped on the accelerator and flew down the highway. No matter what his protests, the man had PTSD and needed to get help with it. Damn it all, she thought as her bad knee almost buckled getting out of the car. She poured herself a big glass of herbal tea and sat down to see if any interesting emails had come her way. Spotting a recent one from her ex-husband, she opened it and stared with disbelieving eyes at Nathan's terse message for long moments. "Good God damn it, *no,*" she finally cried as she stood up and kicked a plastic wastebasket across the room, scattering paper scraps from one end of her living room to the other. "Not Sean. Oh please God, why did it have to be Sean?" she cried. "Damn it, no! Why did we all have to lose so much?!" she wailed as for long moments she screamed her rage and pummeled the wall with her fists. Finally spent, she collapsed on the sofa and curled up in a ball of despair and for once just let the tears fall.

Chapter Seven

Jimmy peeked out the sliding glass door at Holly's still-vacant dock and wondered if she planned on her daily fishing session. He'd had most of the day to think about their argument this morning and, although he didn't have PTSD, he was sure she had spoken with only the best of intentions and he had rewarded her concern with an uncalled-for display of temper. He owed her an apology and had planned on taking her a cold drink when she came out to fish, but since most of the day was gone and she still had not appeared he was going to have to walk over and ring her doorbell if he wanted a chance to talk to her.

He knocked on Holly's door and wondered what kind of reception to expect. Anger, maybe? Or exasperation? What he did not expect was to be greeted by a teary-eyed Holly, her nose red and her eyes swollen. "What do you want?" she asked tiredly as she gazed at him through watery eyes.

"I came over to apologize for my big mouth. I seem to be making a habit of it with you." He looked at Holly and his face softened. "What happened, Holly? Is there anything I can do?" Holly shook her head. "Are you going to let me in? Something has to be pretty wrong."

Holly nodded and stepped back wordlessly. Jimmy stepped into her tiny foyer and followed her into the small living room. Except for an overturned trash can and a scattering of paper scraps and magazine coupons on the carpet, the little room was absolutely pristine. There was a casual yet stylish sofa and matching chair and a flat-screen TV mounted on the opposite wall. The TV screen had an image of a group of soldiers frozen in Pause who on closer inspection weren't soldiers at all, but a bunch of college kids in old-style BDUs with Texas A&M insignias on their shoulders. When Jimmy took another look at the kid on the far right he recognized Holly under an outrageous amount of camouflage paint. Holly sat down on the sofa and Jimmy eased in beside her. "Okay, Holly. Tell me what's going on."

"Everything," Holly said quietly. "Cathy and I went back out to see Tommy Joe and Christi this afternoon. Tommy's really down. He kept on talking about how he had to listen to his horse die and how he has to sit in that wheelchair for the rest of his life and there wasn't much we could say, because you know what, Jimmy? He does. Then Cathy got a text that Asshole Armbruster already announcing his engagement to another woman." She stopped and swallowed. "And then when I got back home I found an email from my ex-husband." Holly gripped the remote tightly and gestured to the image on the screen. "See the cadet two over from me? The one with red hair and that silly grin?"

Jimmy nodded, knowing what was coming and dreading it. "What happened to him?"

"Taliban ambush. He was one of five." Holly swallowed again and started to tear up. "His name was Sean Mallory. He was the best man when Nathan and I married." She reached up with her bad hand and made a feeble attempt to swipe her tear-stained face. "He was getting married when his deployment was over. He's the third one to die out of my company in the Corps of Cadets. And then I've lost five I served with while I was stationed in Korea and at Fort Bragg. That makes eight friends who've come home in a box. Damn it to hell, it sucks."

"That it does," Jimmy said softly. "Play me a little of your tape. It might help to see your friend in happier days."

Holly hit the play button and together they watched her video. The first few minutes were of the cadets horsing around on an ROTC training exercise and then the old video switched to a segment of the A&M band marching across the campus. Jimmy quickly spotted Holly on the very edge of the row, marching in the old-fashioned uniform and knee-high riding boots that were worn so proudly by the seniors. Holly's steps were sharp and crisp, her hair was swept back from her face in a flattering twist under her uniform hat, and her eyes sparkled. "Daddy shot those for me. That was our last football game of the season."

"You looked great," Jimmy said honestly.

"Can't do that anymore," Holly said shortly as she watched her image on the screen. "I couldn't march like that if I had to and I sure can't play a bugle. I can't even fix my hair like that." Angrily she stabbed the remote and let the tape fast-forward through the marching band segment, stopping at what appeared to be a party. She was sitting at a keyboard and Sean and a serious-faced young man were standing behind her. Holly's fingers flew over the keys as the three of them sang a ribald version of a Garth Brooks classic. The boys couldn't sing their way out of a paper bag but Holly had a ringing soprano that was surprisingly beautiful. "I can't do that anymore, either," she said bitterly.

"Why not? Were your vocal cords hurt in Iraq?" Jimmy asked steadily.

Holly shot him a dirty look. "I don't sing; I play the piano. Or I did."

"Your singing voice is superb. Better than mine by a long shot and I've done a lot of singing in my time."

"Whoopee," Holly said sullenly. "Anything else you'd like to add?"

Jimmy's mind raced. If he wasn't mistaken, Holly was in the middle of a serious pity party. How was he going to handle this? He stared at Holly thoughtfully. "I suppose it wouldn't do a bit of good to remind you of all that you have that Sean and some of the soldiers in your support group don't, would it?"

"Not particularly," Holly admitted. "Yes, I know I'm better off than Cathy or Tommy or Armando and I'm sure as hell of a lot better off than Sean. But honestly, Jimmy? Do you know what I would give to go for a run? To ride a Harley? To tear up a keyboard or even type a damned email? To put my hair up? To remember somebody's name? To do the work that I loved?" She shifted on the sofa. "Damn it, I've gone from being on the fast track to general to not even having a real job. Try facing that one every morning. I do try to remember that I'm better off than some of the others, honestly I do. I hurt like a son of a bitch for them and cry bitter tears for the ones who've gone. But damn it, don't I get to grieve for the parts of *me* that are gone forever?"

Jimmy sat quietly. "I suppose so, if they're really gone forever. But are they really all that gone? You say you can't run anymore. Why not swim? No Harley? That cute little convertible's probably just as much fun. And I heard you sing on the damned tape, Holly. If you want to make music, sing." He reached out and took Holly's hand. "And aren't you doing work that you love when you go to bat for one of your wounded warriors?"

"Because swimming's for old ladies and a Miata's still a car and *I want to play the piano.* And as much as I love helping my friends, it's no substitute for a real career and it sure as hell can't hold a candle to a good firefight. You just don't get it, do you? " Holly asked. "They're substitutions. Pale imitations of the real thing. And that pretty much sums it all up, Jimmy. Cathy and Tommy and Beto and me—we're pale imitations of the people we once were, and we're living pale imitations of the lives we once had."

"But those pale imitations beat old nothing, and frankly, Holly, that's what Sean has now, old nothing," Jimmy replied firmly as Holly's eyes went round. "You've cried this afternoon for all you've lost and you have every right to. But at least you and your wounded warriors have life, even if it isn't the ones you all thought you were going to have." Jimmy looked unflinchingly into Holly's eyes. "Lauren cried, too, Holly, when she realized she would never know Carrie as an adult or see me with gray hair or have some kid at school say 'you taught my mother.'" He paused a minute to let that sink in. "Sean and Lauren will never go fishing again, never sip coffee while they watch the sun come up, never feel a child's arms around their neck," he said more gently as he eased closer to her. "They will never get put out with their mother or argue politics or give a pep talk to a fellow soldier who's down." He stared into her eyes as he leaned closer to her. "They won't ever get to do this," he whispered as he touched his lips to hers. "Or this," he whispered as he nuzzled her cheek. "Or this," he said as he claimed her lips in a deep, passionate embrace.

Jimmy groaned as Holly opened her lips to his, giving him entrance to the warm sweetness of her mouth. Sweet, so sweet, he thought; this woman felt like heaven in his arms, but then he'd known she would. His hands grasped her shoulders, pulling her closer as he devoured her lips with his own. Blood rushed to his head and his groin as he inhaled the warm sweetness of the hair tumbling around her face. Oh, sweet Jesus, why did this woman make him feel the way she did? He felt Holly's arms creep around his waist, her weak hand tentative, her good one clutching him tightly as she opened her lips fully and let him plunder the sweetness of her mouth. Warm, he thought, warm and soft and everything a man ever wanted in his arms. He felt her breasts stiffen under the thin tank top as his fingers crept down to softly caress the tight tip beneath the silky fabric. So sweet, he thought as his finger tortured first one of the hard little nubs and then the other. So beautiful, he thought as his fingers worked their erotic magic on the warm, wanton woman in his arms.

Without breaking the kiss, Jimmy bore Holly down on the long sofa, snuggling his body in next to hers, their legs tangled together and the evidence of his arousal hard against her hip. Jimmy made no attempt to hide his arousal from her; he wanted—no, *needed*—for her to know just how much he responded to her silken touch. Her softness beneath him, Jimmy and Holly shared one long, sweet bone-melting kiss after another, her breasts crushed against the rock hardness of his chest, her fingers wrapped around him as he caressed her with his lips and his eyes and his hands. "Beautiful, so beautiful," Jimmy murmured as he nibbled at her earlobe and ran his soft lips down her cheek to the sensitive skin on her neck. Jimmy's heart pounded and his breathing snagged as he felt the tension rising in both their bodies, the primal awareness of one another and what this was about to explode into.

Jimmy groaned as Holly arched even closer to him, clutching wildly at the fabric of his shirt. "Sweet, you're like kissing heaven," Jimmy whispered as his hand reached up and clutched Holly's head. He threaded his hands into her hair, his fingers encountering what felt like a ridged scar running down the side of her head.

Holly froze and Jimmy's fingers stilled. "What's the matter?" he asked as Holly struggled to pull away from him.

Holly shook her head and Jimmy moved back to let her sit up. "That's where the metal plate is," she said. She slid off the sofa and sat a foot away on the carpet.

"I figured as much," Jimmy said evenly as he fought to catch his breath. "Holly, it's nothing."

"It is to me," she replied. She drew her knees up and looped her arms around her legs. "Jimmy, it would be the easiest thing in the world for me to fall into bed with you this afternoon. I'm upset about Tommy Joe and hurting over Sean and in the middle of feeling sorry for myself, and you're by far the most appealing man who's come my way in a damn long time. But it would be a pity fuck and we both know it."

A spurt of anger shot through Jimmy, killing the lust buzz. Was that what she really thought was going on? He deliberately arched his eyebrow as he stared down at her. "Maybe I don't want a pity-the-lonely-widower fuck either. Works two ways, you know." He stood up and hoisted her to her feet. "Now, are you going to be all right?" he asked.

Holly looked at him uncertainly. "I don't have much choice in the matter, do I?"

"Now, that's more like it," Jimmy said. He grinned wickedly as he deliberately let his gaze travel downward. "By the way, you have great legs, Combat Barbie," he said with a wink.

Holly's face turned crimson. "Oh, you," she said, rolling her eyes. "Here, I'll see you out."

Jimmy stepped out onto Holly's front porch, turned around, and pulled her out for one more quick kiss. "See you tomorrow," he said as he turned on his heel. He could feel Holly's eyes on him as he set off in the deep gloom of late dusk. Deep in thought, he walked past his house and wandered toward the beach, where he sat down on the concrete retaining wall and stared out at the water. Wrapped up in helping others, Holly so seldom dwelt on her own losses that it was easy to forget just how much her life had been altered. Even though outwardly things didn't seem all that different, the fact that the Army wouldn't take her back spoke volumes. He hadn't realized until today just how badly she missed playing the piano or that she couldn't do something as simple as putting her hair up, nor had he given much thought of how devastated she must feel over the loss of her career. And if her life had been so drastically affected, what must it be like for the others? For the Armbruster girl, struggling to adjust to her injuries and the desertion of her husband at the same time? Or Tommy Joe, the one-time athlete confined to a wheelchair for the rest of his life?

Jimmy stared into the lapping waves. He'd already done what he could for Cathy Armbruster, but he thought about Holly and Tommy Joe. Holly? What were some of the things she could still do that would restore some of the self-esteem that her injuries and losing her career had cost her? And what about Tommy Joe? If Holly's self-esteem had taken a beating, Tommy's must be just about DOA. Jimmy mulled over the options. There had to be something out there, he thought as his nimble brain sorted through the possibilities. Something for Holly and something for the Reece boy to give them back some of what life had so cruelly snatched away from them.

* * *

They're at it again, Chucky thought with cold satisfaction as he watched Jimmy plant a hard good-bye kiss on Holly's swollen mouth. Were they doing the dirty yet? Nah, they both looked too frustrated for that, but Chucky would bet his next homemade IED that there had been one hell of a make-out session, if the blush on Holly's cheeks and the tightness in Jimmy's jaw were anything to go by. Won't be long, Chucky thought as he smiled evilly. Those two would be doing the mattress tango before too much more time went by. And then he would take them down, Chucky thought as he clenched his fist. She wasn't worthy of life, and it would be the payback Adamcik so richly deserved for what he was responsible for.

But not tonight. With a silent sigh, Chucky slipped from his hiding place in the shadows and made his way across the little community to where his car was parked. It was too soon, he admitted to himself as he drove to the place he thought of as his sanctuary. Although the relationship was definitely going places, the bitch and that bastard Adamcik were not involved to the point that Adamcik would be that deeply affected by anything befalling her. Better to wait until Adamcik and the bitch were much, much closer. And then Chucky would strike—and strike hard. Besides, there were others who needed a visit from Chucky first, he thought as he eyed the deadly bomb coming together on the rickety folding table.

* * *

Holly gently touched her lips with her forefinger as she watched Jimmy disappear into the deep gray dusk. Venus was already shining brightly in the west and in just a matter of minutes the night sky would glitter with the bright canopy of summer stars—stars that Sean would never see again. But she would see them, and Tommy and Cathy would see them, and all the rest of the members of her brave little band would, too. This new life was worth living, she assured herself as she stared out into the night. Jimmy was right. Her life was different than she expected it to be, but at least she had it.

And where would they be right now if she hadn't called a halt? She pulled the front door closed behind her and sat down on the top step of her porch. Would they have made it all the way to her bed, or would they be sprawled across her couch, naked as jaybirds, taking each other on the ride of a lifetime? Too bad she had backed out, she thought as she roundly cursed her cowardice. Making love with Jimmy would have been something else.

Holly stared into the deepening gloom. What was that? Her spidey sense, the almost uncanny knowledge that danger awaited her, went on high alert. She had learned in Iraq to trust her spidey sense and it had saved her life more than once. But why would her she go on alert here in Heaven's Point, halfway across the world from the field of battle? She whipped around, staring into the darkness across the road. Was that something in the thick stand of trees in her neighbor's yard? Had the shadow pattern changed? Was there something—no, someone—out there who meant to do her harm?

* * *

Holly stood in Caroline Briscoe's kitchen watching Carrie and Ryan play in the back yard with Ryan's new puppy. Jimmy had called her around noon and asked if she would like to accompany them out to the Briscoe ranch this afternoon so Jimmy could help Jack round up a young bull he was selling to Tommy Joe. Jimmy had been most insistent, so the three of them piled into Jimmy's truck and came here to the Briscoe place.

"Great-looking house," she said approvingly to Caroline, glancing around at the brightly painted red and white kitchen. "Jimmy said it used to be a mess. Bet you didn't wait for the wedding to get started on it, did you?"

Caroline laughed out loud. "You better believe I didn't," she laughed as she poured two big glasses of iced tea. "I've worked on it like you wouldn't believe." She peeked out the window. "Here he comes," she said. "Come on out. I wouldn't miss this for the world."

"Here who comes? Miss what for the world?" Holly asked as she followed Caroline back out on the porch, where Tommy Joe sat with Christi. Caroline pointed toward the north, where a beautiful black horse and rider herded an obstinate-looking young bull across the pasture. Holly watched with the others as the horse and rider skillfully guided the bull toward a pen where Tommy Joe's trailer was parked in front of a chute. Holly wondered at the admiration in Caroline's eyes as the rider bounced toward them—he didn't seem like that skilled a horseman to her. But as he drew closer Holly noted the back support on the saddle at about the same time she spotted the straps holding his legs in place as he herded the bull into the pen, where Jack and Jimmy waited to guide the bull up the chute and into Tommy's trailer. Holly's mouth flew open and she decided to add her admiration to that of Jimmy and Caroline. "Sweet," she murmured as she peeked down at the astonishment on Tommy's face.

The men got the bull loaded and wandered over to the porch, the stranger still on his horse. Jimmy reached over the porch rail and grasped the man's outstretched hand. "Duncan, long time no see," he said warmly as the men shook hands. "Come down off your high horse and meet these good folks."

"Still a wiseass," Duncan said as he handed the reins to Jimmy and untied his legs. With grace borne of long practice he slid off the horse and into the wheelchair Caroline had waiting for him, and with only a little help from Jimmy he popped his wheelchair up onto the porch and held out his hand to Tommy Joe. "Duncan Royal," he said as Tommy reached out to shake hands.

"Tommy Joe Reece." Eyes still wide, Tommy eyed the man in the wheelchair and the horse tethered to the porch rail. "How the hell did you learn to do that?"

"It was either that or give up ranching," Duncan said easily. "And you two must be Christi and Holly."

Christi nodded as Holly held out her hand. "I'm Holly Riley and I have a support group for wounded warriors and we are *so* going to talk before you leave here."

"It's a date," Duncan said. "Come on; let's go meet the newest addition to the Reece ranch."

Holly grasped Jimmy's hand as the others surged off the porch to surround Tommy's trailer. "Where in the world did you find that man and why didn't you say anything sooner?"

"Because I didn't know sooner," Jimmy admitted. "Duncan went to Texas Tech with Jack and me and in all honesty I'd lost track of him. When I said something last week to Jack about Tommy he told me that Duncan was riding after a similar injury and offered to get them together. Duncan makes part of his living now training horses and their handicapped riders and could probably teach Tommy to ride well enough to do his ranch work. So you see, Holly, Tommy isn't stuck in a damned wheelchair for the rest of his life, not if he doesn't want to be."

Holly wasn't prepared for the onslaught of tears rushing to her eyes. "Oh my God, that's wonderful," she said as she determinedly gulped back her emotion. "He and Christi will be so happy. Holly reached out and squeezed Jimmy's arm. "Thank you. Yes, you did do something," she said when Jimmy started to protest. "You cared enough to say something to Jack which got the ball rolling."

Soon they were all crowded around Caroline's huge kitchen table feasting on her famous fried chicken and mashed potatoes. Tommy and Holly peppered Duncan with question after question and learned that Duncan worked with all manner of handicapped riders. "I could have you riding well enough to work from a horse in a matter of a couple of weeks," Duncan said to Tommy as Caroline sent the platter of chicken around for seconds. "It would be a matter of training the horse, too, and I'm continually amazed at how well the animals catch on. And I would absolutely love to work with any of the other members of your support group who want to ride," he added to Holly.

"I will certainly pass that offer along," Holly assured him.

"I could work—really work—again," Tommy said, his face lighting up. "You have no idea hard it is to ranch from a wheelchair."

"At least you have work," Holly pointed out. "A lot of wounded vets don't."

"That's a shame," Duncan agreed. "Do you have a job, Holly?"

Holly shrugged. "Not really. I was career military. That's all I ever trained for and all I really ever wanted to do. Now I have no idea what I could do for a living."

Jack eyed Holly thoughtfully. "Ever do any instructing in the military? Were you good at it? Did you like it?"

"Yes, yes, and I guess so," Holly replied.

"Then why in the world aren't you looking at being a teacher?" Jack asked.

"Me? And fifteen-year-olds?" Holly asked. "Are you kidding?"

"Why not?" Jimmy asked. "Those fifteen-year-olds of Jack's are not so different from those eighteen-year-old privates you had quaking in their boots."

"At least give it some thought," Jack urged. "We're always hurting for good teachers."

"I'll do that," Holly said.

"How did you get hurt, Mr. Duncan?" Carrie piped up suddenly. "Are you a hero like Miss Holly and Mr. Tommy?"

"No, child, I owe mine to a drunk driver," Duncan said, his eyes kind. "I'm not a hero like these two."

"I'm no hero," Tommy piped up. "Wrong place, wrong time, good tango sniper. Now Holly, she got a Silver Star along with her Purple Heart."

"I'm impressed," Duncan said.

"Jimmy, isn't that the one you got on your second tour?" Jack asked.

A Silver Star? Jimmy earned a Silver Star? Holly whipped around but froze at the closed-off expression on Jimmy's face. "It was no big deal," he said dismissively. "Right place, right time."

And he doesn't want to talk about it. Once again he had sidestepped talking about his military career, this time to the point of dismissing one of the highest honors the Army could bestow. Why? Was his reluctance to talk just modesty, or had earning the Silver Star also earned him the painful dreams he still relived in the dark of the night?

* * *

Jimmy followed Holly up the sidewalk and waited patiently while she fumbled with her lock in the dark. Caroline's impromptu invitation for Carrie to spend the night left him with the evening free—an evening he and Holly could spend together, talking and kissing and maybe, just maybe taking their friendship to a different level altogether. He had noticed the way Holly sneaked hungry looks at him all week when she thought he wasn't looking; not that he hadn't done his share of admiring the goods, he thought as he pictured Holly's long legs in her skimpy shorts or the alluring jut of her breasts in a sexy tank top. Hell, she even made combat boots look hot, he thought as he followed her into her tiny house. "Got anything to drink?" he asked.

"Beer, wine; take your pick." Holly sat down on the sofa and started unlacing her boots. "If you want a real drink the liquor's in the corner cabinet."

"Beer's fine. Want one?"

Holly gave Jimmy a thumbs-up and he opened two of Holly's favorite microbrews. "Thanks," she said as Jimmy sat down. She eased off the second boot and took a grateful swallow of the beer. "Isn't Duncan Royal something else? He gave me his card and I just might go out to his place sometime."

"Swapping your steel horse for a real horse?" Jimmy teased.

Holly shrugged. "I sold the Harley to Russ after I was hurt. It was A&M maroon and he wanted it."

"A maroon Harley? God help!" Jimmy held his throat and made gagging noises. "What is it about Aggies and maroon wheels? Nadine said that one of the twins is looking to buy a maroon pickup."

"She did?" Holly eyed Jimmy sharply. "When did you talk to Nadine?"

It was Jimmy's turn to shrug. "We've spoken a couple of times this week."

"She didn't mention it to me," Holly said a little too casually. "What did you talk about?"

"What do you think we talked about? My accepting their help. Specifically, just what my accepting their help would entail and how much compromising I would be expected to do if they do help me. Nadine was kind enough to clarify some points I was unsure of."

Holly tensed. "I thought you'd decided to decline their offer and raise the money yourself."

Jimmy's eyebrow flew up almost to his hairline. "Have I said any such thing?" he asked mildly. He reached over and took Holly's hand. "I have every intention of trying to raise the money without them, but I certainly haven't given Nadine and her friends a definite 'no' and I have no intention of doing so. Besides, who wants to talk about Nadine and money?" He lifted their joined hands and nibbled Holly's fingers. "Carrie's not here and you and I started something last Sunday that I would very much like to continue."

Holly tugged her hand away from Jimmy's mouth. "Please don't try to sidetrack the conversation. I thought you had decided to forego Nadine's money and were going to raise it on your own."

Jimmy shrugged and let go of Holly's hand. "You knew damn well I hadn't told them no."

"No, I didn't," Holly said. "Stupid me. When you came over and apologized for yelling at me I thought you were apologizing for the argument over Nadine and the money. I guess you were apologizing for the other fight."

"That's right," Jimmy said. "Now, can we please not worry about Nadine and money tonight? I'm a whole lot more interested in us kissing and touching and holding one another and maybe, just maybe ending up in either your bed or mine tonight."

Holly scooted away from Jimmy. "But what about my soldiers?" she asked tightly. "If you use Nadine and her cronies to raise campaign money you can't support the soldiers."

Jimmy's mouth tightened. "And if I accept Nadine's help and don't support your pet cause we don't kiss or make love? Is that your game?"

"What makes you think it's a game to me, Jimmy?" Holly asked, aghast. "My work with the soldiers is just about the most important thing in my life. And no, I'm not feeling particularly romantic at the moment. It's a little hard when you think I'm playing some kind of game."

"And maybe I don't like your attitude much, either," Jimmy shot back. "Correct me if I'm wrong, but the message I'm getting is that if I want you and me—*us*—to go any further, I better be ready to push your cause, and to hell with Nadine and the resources she could bring to a campaign that badly needs it."

Holly thought a minute. "Actually, you're getting the right message. Jimmy, I like you and I'm attracted to you and I'd love a smokin' hot affair with you, but my work with my soldiers means everything to me, and I can't with any good conscience take our relationship one bit further if I…they…*we* don't have your support."

"So if I support your cause to get you in the bed, which one of us does that make the whore?" Jimmy snapped.

"I don't know, but I know which one of us is the whore if Nadine's money gets involved," Holly shot back angrily. "Damn it to hell, Jimmy, *please* don't sell out to the bastards in San Angelo. *Please.*"

Jimmy stood up and stalked to the front door. "Holly, I haven't accepted their help yet, and I won't if I don't have to. But if I can't raise the money alone I will by God take their help and their conditions because *I want to win the election.* And I will be damned if I let anything get in the way of that, including a smokin' hot affair with you."

"Thank you so much for clarifying that for me," Holly said icily. "It makes me feel so good to know just where my soldiers and I rate. Have a good evening."

"Holly, I—oh, to hell with it," Jimmy snapped as he walked out and slammed the door. He looked at his watch. It was still relatively early and since he would not be spending it getting to know Holly a lot better, he may as well pay a visit to the local watering hole, toss back a few, and play some pool. Damn, he thought as he pulled out of Heaven's Point onto the highway. How in the hell had their potentially romantic evening deteriorated into a shouting match over campaign financing? And why did Holly insist upon making their relationship contingent on his supporting her cause? He should have been more diplomatic, he thought as he slowed down to keep from hitting a doe and her fawn. He had seen the hurt in Holly's eyes at his smoking hot affair crack. But he had only spoken the truth. He did intend to win the election and nothing—*nothing* was going to get in the way of that, including Holly Riley and her misguided idealism.

* * *

Holly dumped out the rest of her beer and threw the bottle into the full trash bucket. "Damn Jimmy Adamcik anyway," she snapped as she yanked the plastic liner out of the bucket. If it weren't for his pigheadedness over taking Nadine's money they would be in each other's arms right now, kissing and caressing each other and probably becoming lovers. But no, he not only was still flirting with taking Nadine's support he had told her in no uncertain terms just where a relationship with her ranked on his list of priorities.

"Well, if he feels like that he can take a relationship with me and shove it," she said hotly as she carried the sack of garbage outside. If he valued a relationship with her so little, then so be it.

Holly was halfway back to the house when she felt that familiar prickle on the back of her neck. She whipped around, staring deeply into the gloom as she searched the inky darkness for some sign that she wasn't alone. She watched for long minutes—was that just a hint of movement in the Mackey's yard? Was that a shadow in Ben Riley's backyard? *Was someone out there watching her?*

Chapter Eight

Holly stood with her good arm around a sobbing Hal Jackson as they both stared down at the dying dog sprawled on Hal's driveway. "W-what's the matter with him?" Hal stuttered brokenly.

Holly shook her head as another seizure gripped the dog. "I don't know, Hal." She knelt down and sucked in her breath at the faint odor of almonds. "But I'm afraid he was poisoned." She got out her phone and punched in 911. "Is Rory or any of the other deputies anywhere near the Point? Hal Jackson's service dog is having seizures. It smells like cyanide." She cringed as Hal cried out and fell to his knees. "No, it's not an emergency. The dog just died." Holly hung up the phone and knelt down beside Hal. "Hal, I am so sorry," she whispered as Hal gathered up the animal and rocked back and forth in the early morning breeze. "He was a damn fine animal." *And a valuable investment that has been willfully destroyed,* she thought angrily.

"W-why would someb-body want to hurt Raven? He never barked or made any n-noise."

"I don't know, Hal," Holly admitted.

Angie Baxter jogged around the corner and, spotting them on the driveway, made a beeline for Holly and Hal. "Oh, no, did something happen to Raven?" she asked.

Holly was thankful to see Rory's cruiser coming around the corner. "H-holly thinks poison."

Rory got out of the cruiser and motioned them back so he could examine the dog. "Damn, it does smell like cyanide. I'm going to call the CSU boys in. Is that your campaign sign, Hal?"

"S-sure, all the v-volunteers have them," Hal said.

Rory hit speed dial and explained the situation. "No, damn it, the dog wasn't just a pet," he snapped. "He was an extremely expensive service animal and this needs to be treated as a felony." He turned to Hal. "Hal, what was Raven worth in dollars and cents?"

Hal blinked and turned to Holly. "Over ten thousand," she said tersely.

Rory relayed the information and finally punched off his phone. "The poison specialists from Austin will be here within the hour. In the meantime, show me Raven's food and water bowls."

Hal motioned for them to follow him around the house. "I-I normally fed him inside, b-but it was nice last night and h-he wanted out so I-I moved his w-water bowl." He let them in a small fenced back yard and pointed out a large aluminum bowl. "Th-there."

Rory's eyes narrowed as he knelt and found an Adamcik for Congress brochure under the bowl. Holly felt her heart drop to her feet. "Hal, did you put this brochure under the bowl?"

"N-no," Hal stammered, staring at the brochure like it was a snake.

"I heard something," Angie chimed in suddenly. "Early this morning. It woke me up."

"What exactly did you hear?" Rory asked sharply.

"I'm not sure," Angie admitted. "By the time I was awake it was already gone."

"What time, Angie?" Rory pressed.

"Alarm clock read five-fifteen. I know it's not much."

"It's a start," Rory said quietly. He looked across the fence into the yard next door to Angie. "I'll talk to the neighbors and see if any of the old timers were up by then. Maybe some of them heard or saw something." He clapped Hal on the shoulder. "I'm so damn sorry, Hal."

Hal nodded wordlessly and Holly watched as the stricken man disappeared into his tiny cabin. "I'll call Jimmy," Rory volunteered. "He needs to know what happened this morning."

"What did happen this morning?" Holly said.

"Well, unless you believe in coincidences, for the second time someone went after a soldier in your support group and left behind an artifact from the Adamcik campaign."

"But why?" Holly asked in bewilderment. "Why would somebody do a thing like that?"

Rory shrugged. "I'll be damned if I know."

* * *

Holly's thoughts were not pleasant as she turned off on the farm to market road that would take her into Heaven's Point. She had spent most of the day with Hal while the poison specialists carried out their gruesome chores and then helped Hal bury the dog in her Uncle Willis's pasture. But Holly had more than Hal's troubles on her mind. She was again at loose ends with no plans for her immediate future; her job taking care of Carrie would be over next week and her bank account was running low. As promised, she had given Jack's suggestion of teaching school some serious consideration. She had done plenty of instructing in the military, but what would she teach in a civilian high school? Her degree was in psychology and her experience was in combat support. She would have to ask Jack Briscoe if he had any ideas—hopefully she would see him at the Fourth of July picnic tomorrow.

And then there was Jimmy, she thought resentfully. Since their falling out almost a month ago he had pretty much stayed away from her and her from him, and as much as she hated admitting it to herself, she missed him. She knew from a couple of brief comments from her mother that he had not yet taken Nadine and her friends up on their offer of help and from a cryptic comment by Judge Riley that he was trying to raise his own money and not doing too well. She had wondered more than once what would have happened if they had become lovers and she found out afterward that he had not ruled out taking Nadine's help. Would she have been able to separate sex and politics or would the result have been that much worse?

The sun was just dropping down beneath the western horizon when Holly pulled into Heaven's Point. She parked in her driveway and sighed when she spotted Jimmy waiting for her on the front porch with a sack of groceries. Great—she was hot and sweaty and smelled like dead dog and Jimmy looked like he stepped out of *GQ*. "I figured you had a crappy day," he said as he followed Holly into the house. "I brought something for supper if you haven't eaten."

"No, I haven't and I'm starved," Holly admitted, hoping her surprise didn't show. "That was thoughtful. Thanks."

Jimmy set the bag down on the counter. "This will take a few minutes," he said. "You have time for a shower if you like."

Holly took a quick shower and made her way to the kitchen as Jimmy stirred together a macaroni and cheese mix to go with a grocery store chicken and bagged salad. "My mom took Carrie for a girls' night out in Marble Falls and is staying with me and Carrie tonight so she can do the picnic with us tomorrow. This is about the extent of my cooking talent, except for barbequing." He set a plate of food in front of Holly and dished up another for himself.

They ate mostly in silence. "So what did they decide happened to Raven?" Jimmy asked finally.

"Cyanide in his water bowl," Holly said. "Rory is most interested in your campaign brochure being left at a second crime scene. He says the sixty-four–thousand-dollar question is who these attacks are aimed at. Does somebody hate you that badly?"

Jimmy's eyebrow shot up almost to his hairline. "And what makes me the ultimate target? It's members of your group who are being targeted for attack," Jimmy countered smoothly.

"Then why leave your signs behind at the scene?' Holly replied equally smoothly.

Jimmy ran a frustrated hand through his hair. "Damned if I know." He paused for a minute. "I think you should seriously reconsider this support group thing," he said quietly.

"Why?" Holly asked as she put their dirty plates in the sink and sank down onto the sofa.

"Because your wounded warriors have been attacked twice now. Your group is particularly vulnerable."

Holly bristled. "We're also combat-trained veterans. Besides, what the hell is it to you?"

"Jesus, Holly, don't be an imbecile," Jimmy said gruffly as he sat down and pulled her closer to him. "You think I don't care if anything happens to you? You think my daughter doesn't care?" He framed her face with his large, gentle hands and his lips descended on hers.

"Jimmy, I—" Holly's halfhearted protest was smothered by Jimmy's insistent lips. She froze for a minute under the sensual assault before meeting his passion with passion of her own. Tender yet demanding, Jimmy feasted on Holly as his tongue caressed her with familiar yet exciting intimacy. Oh, she had missed him, she thought as her tongue snaked out and fought a duel with his, touching and teasing and torturing both herself and the man in her arms. She had missed him so much. Jimmy held her face immobile in his big, gentle hands as he explored her mouth at leisure and then nibbled on her lower lip, his lips moist and his teeth gentle as he continued his sensual exploration of her face.

Tendrils of desire curled through Holly as the fingers of her strong hand clutched the fabric of Jimmy's shirt, slowly pulling it out of his jeans and permitting her access to his hard, warm, muscular back, the quivering tension she felt there telling her just how affected he was by her. She touched him and stroked him greedily, inwardly cursing the weakness in her left arm that would not permit her to hold him and stroke him and touch him with both of her hands.

So sweet, she thought as his lips trailed down the side of her jaw and onto her neck, where he whispered feather-light kisses down the side of her neck to where the V of her T-shirt revealed just a hint of creamy cleavage. So sweet and so sexy. Holly felt her nipples harden as Jimmy caressed first one swollen nub and then the other through the thin T-shirt and lacy bra that barely concealed her breasts. Heaven, sheer heaven, Holly thought as she felt the heat rushing between her legs. With a single motion Jimmy yanked her T-shirt over her head and popped open her bra, baring her round breasts to his greedy eyes. "God in heaven, you are so beautiful," Jimmy whispered as he bore Holly down into the sofa cushions and indulged in a leisurely exploration of first one nipple and then the other as Holly writhed beneath him. "And you taste so damn wonderful."

Lost in a haze, Holly writhed and shivered under Jimmy's sensual ministrations as he nipped and nibbled and tasted and touched her for long minutes. Her fingers returned the favor, running up and down Jimmy's back and around to the hard, warm muscles of his shoulders and chest, finding and caressing one of his small nipples hidden in the thick springy hair covering his upper chest. She felt him rise for a moment and whip off his shirt, leaning back down to kiss her lips as the hair on his chest teased and tantalized her already sensitive nipples. Grinning wolfishly, he nibbled a trail down her body, stopping to again tease first one breast and then the other and then trailing further, stopping only when he reached the waistband of her jeans. Unable to deny him anything, Holly arched toward him, offering herself to do whatever his desire, but rather than unzip her jeans he sat up, arching one eyebrow and looking at her quizzically. "What do you want to do?" he asked solemnly. "Do we finish this now or are your principles still standing in the way?"

"What?" Holly stared up at him, still lost in a fog of sensual desire. "Why did you stop? I'm certainly not saying no."

"But you haven't said yes, either," Jimmy said as he reached down and tickled one of her nipples with his tongue. "And I don't want you coming back and saying I seduced you. So what's it going to be, Holly? Do we finish or do I put my shirt back on and take your leave?"

Holly looked at him unbelievingly for a couple of long minutes. "You could have had me, you know," she said hotly as she sat up and threw Jimmy's shirt at him. She pulled her T-shirt back on and glowered at him from across the sofa.

"Maybe I didn't want you that way," Jimmy admitted as he pulled on his own shirt. "Seduced and willing and mad as hell later. I haven't made up my mind about accepting help from Nadine and you haven't changed your mind about help for your soldiers, and no matter how great the sex was we'd still have that bone of contention between us."

"You're damn right we would," Holly snapped.

"And there we are," Jimmy said. "It's foolish, don't you think, to let our political differences stand in the way of something as good as what we could have together?" he asked as he headed out the front door. "Let me know if you change your mind."

"Damn your hide, Jimmy Adamcik!" Holly ground out as she threw a couch pillow at the front door. "Damn you for being right," she added more softly as she touched her still-tingling lips. Yes, he could have taken her in a haze of mindless sensuality and both of them would have loved it. But with nothing changed between them, the aftertaste would have been bitingly, painfully bitter.

* * *

Jimmy swore and slapped at the Off button on the alarm clock. He had been hours getting to sleep and then another nightmare hit about two, and Jimmy wished there was some way he could just go back to sleep. But the rest of the officers of the homeowners' association were elderly and couldn't lift the mesquite logs or the barbeque pit's heavy grate, so Jimmy pushed himself up out of the bed and started the coffeemaker before he took a quick shower and dressed in old work clothes. The door to the guest room was closed and Jimmy breathed a sigh of relief that his nightmare had not awakened his mother. The last thing he wanted was for Janelle to find out about the dreams. He was afraid she would jump to the same conclusion Holly had, and Janelle would be a lot harder to put off than Holly had been.

Jimmy took a mug of coffee out on the deck. Holly had not mentioned the nightmares again and Jimmy was grateful to her for that, and he cursed himself for a fool for not seducing her last night and giving them both what they wanted so badly. But she would have been furious this morning and any hope he had for more than just a physical relationship with Holly would have been doomed. And he wanted more from Holly Riley than just a good time in bed. He wanted a real relationship with her. That made Jimmy cautious. He had seen the painful aftermath when Jack tried to push Caroline into a relationship she wasn't ready for, and he didn't want the same kind of misunderstandingto happen with Holly. No, as much as he wanted Holly Riley in his arms and his bed, he would wait it out, patiently, he hoped, until the lady was willing to put aside their political differences and build a real relationship with him.

Holly stood in her underwear and looked critically at her legs—specifically, her left leg—in the full-length mirror. She hated for the scars to show, but it was already as hot as a two-dollar pistol outside and if she wore long pants she would roast. She bit her lip and was about to put on a pair of jeans anyway when her front door opened and a familiar voice called her name. "Holly? Where are you? Are you decent?"

"Up here, Emily, and only if you're alone," Holly called as Emily Riley took the stairs two at a time and launched herself into Holly's open arms. "How's summer school going?" Holly asked as her redheaded sister stepped back and eyed her critically.

"Fine, and just who are you planning to seduce in that getup from Victoria's Secret?" Emily asked as she took in Holly's lacy, barely-there underwear.

Holly felt her face warm as yesterday evening's encounter flashed before her eyes. "I just got tired of those god-awful hospital clothes," she said. She held out her leg to Emily. "What do you think? Can I get away with shorts?"

Emily looked carefully at Holly's leg. "I've seen worse on jocks after they've blown a knee."

"Shorts it is, then," Holly said. "So tell me all about school."

Emily flopped down on the foot of Holly's bed and while Holly dressed and did her face Emily chattered about her coursework at

A&M and her lack of a love life. Unlike the rest of the good-looking Riley/Graham tangle of siblings, Emily took too much after Ben Riley to ever be more than pleasantly attractive, but Ben and Patsy had instilled a sense of worth in Emily that transcended her lack of physical beauty. Her struggles with juvenile diabetes had inspired an interest in medical research, and Holly reflected idly that Emily had a better idea of what she wanted in life at the ripe old age of nineteen than Holly did at thirty.

The Riley sisters carried folding chairs down to the beach where a crowd was beginning to gather for the homeowners' meeting. Holly spotted her father and stepmother and, to her surprise, her brother Russ. She let out a little squeal of delight and launched herself at Russ, forgetting her bad knee that promptly gave out and landed her in a heap in her brother's lap. "Russ! When did you get here? Why didn't you say something, Emily?"

"I didn't know. Shove over and let me give him a hug." Emily leaned down and joined Holly in hugging Russ. "So when did you get back?"

"I was wheels down at zero-two-hundred last night," Russ said. "I drove in this morning."

"How long are you home for this time?" Holly demanded.

Russ shrugged. "I'm not sure."

Holly started to ask more but her father reached out his hand and helped her from Russ's lap. "Come here, both of you girls. Patsy and I need hugs, too."

Holly hugged her father with enthusiasm and then turned to Patsy, who opened her arms and hugged Holly with the same love she gave her own children. Whatever the issues plaguing her husband and his ex-wife, Patsy Riley had been wonderful to the frightened five-year-old who had come through her door so many years ago and had done her best to let Holly know she was loved the same as Russ and later Emily. And Holly loved Patsy back. A woman of simple tastes in spite of her old-money roots, Patsy lived mostly in jeans and shorts and liked to cook and loved nothing more than to come with Ben to the cabin and spend the afternoon fishing. Her graying hair was cut simply and she had become gently rounded over the years. Her children adored her and Ben loved her dearly, and in spite of the fact that Patsy had taken Nadine's place in her father's life Holly could see why.

Patsy stepped back and studied Holly critically. "You look wonderful," she said finally as she blinked back tears. "You don't know how happy that makes me. Where are your support group buddies today?"

"Hal's helping Jimmy barbeque, Cathy's not coming, and I guess Tommy Joe and Christi are late."

Holly and Emily unfolded their chairs as the president of the homeowners' association called the meeting to order, and for the next hour Holly fought not to laugh out loud as everything from raising the association dues to the misuse of golf carts on the Point was roundly debated in the closest thing to true democracy that Holly had ever witnessed. Holly was surprised that Jimmy was neither present on the podium nor part of the discussion until she spotted him standing with Hal next to the huge barbeque pit, his face grimy with soot and sweat pouring down his pinched features. *Damn,* Holly thought. He looked just like he had the morning after the nightmare and Holly knew as sure as the sun shone that he'd had another one.

The meeting was almost over when an old car with an A&M sticker on the bumper pulled up in the parking lot and a group of college boys commandeered the one remaining picnic table. Emily's eyes lit up and she leaned toward Holly. "Friends of mine," she said as she made a beeline for the boys. Holly promised herself that she would walk over and meet Emily's friends, but just as the meeting adjourned she spotted Nadine's Escalade pull up. She tried to make her way across the park to waylay Nadine but the Briscoes and Ryan picked just that moment to come over and meet Russ. By the time greetings and introductions were over Nadine was just a few feet away and Holly had no choice but to motion her over.

"Holly, dear, how are you?" she asked as she gave Holly a hug. "Have you regained any of the use of your arm? I so wish we'd gone ahead and tried again," she added.

Way to go, mom, Holly thought impatiently. *Bring up the sorest spot you can.* She made an outward show of shrugging her shoulders. "The jury's still out."

"Damned arm looks fine to me," Ben said darkly. Russ's lips twitched and Patsy looked put out. "So where is our candidate?" Nadine asked as she turned to Jack and Caroline. "How do you guys think the campaign is going?"

Jack and Caroline ushered Nadine toward the barbeque pit. Ben muttered something under his breath as he and Patsy headed off in the other direction. "That went well," Russ said, his eyes dancing.

Holly shot him a go-to-hell look. "How would you like it if your parents acted that way in front of God and everybody?"

"Last time I checked, one of them was. Holly, you may as well give up. They're not going to change and you may as well get over it," he said.

"You're right. So, how long are you home for this time?" Holly asked.

Russ glanced toward his parents and lowered his voice. "I'm not sure. I've met somebody new."

"So what else is new? You meet somebody new all the time. At least three or four a year. Why else do they call you Randy Rusty Riley?" Holly said. "And why the lowered voice?"

"Because this time is a little different," Russ said. "So, is it my imagination or is that your esteemed candidate buddy coming over to say hello? Should I give him my don't-fuck-with-my-sister-I-am-a-combat-soldier speech?"

"He did some time in Baghdad, too," Holly said quietly, watching Russ's opinion of Jimmy ratchet up a notch or two. "Jimmy, come meet my brother Russ."

Jimmy introduced himself and looked from Holly to Russ. "I'm trying to decide if the two of you look alike," he said.

"We don't," they said in unison.

A piercing whistle cut through the air from the table where Emily sat with her friends. "I think that little redhead over there is calling us," Jimmy laughed as Emily motioned them over.

They ambled over to where Emily sat with her companions. Two of the boys were bareheaded and dressed in shorts, but the third, a big, broad-shouldered young man with his face turned toward Emily, had on jeans and long sleeves and wore a baseball cap pulled low on his face. Jimmy clapped one of the boys on the back and shook the hand of the other. "Benny, Wade, how are you doing?" he asked as the good-looking young men stood up.

"We're good, man," Benny said as he pumped Jimmy's hand.

"Had a great year," Wade seconded. "And you must be Holly Riley. You're even prettier than mom said."

"This is Angie Baxter's son," Jimmy said. "And Rory's brother."

"We brought our new roommate," Benny said. "Jason, get over here and meet everybody."

The young man turned from Emily and stood up and in spite of all Holly had seen during her months in the hospital it was all she could do not to flinch. Jason had some of the worst burn scars she had ever seen. Nothing was left of his face but a mass of twisted scar tissue, his hair and ears were gone and Holly could only guess at the devastation that lay beneath the long-sleeved shirt and jeans. Only his eyes, a bright, intelligent blue, were unaffected. He smiled politely at Holly and Russ, but when he turned to Jimmy his eyes widened and he smiled as much as his face would let him. "Major Adamcik! How are you, sir?"

Jimmy stared in shock at the young man as his face turned pale. "Private Donahue?" he asked, his voice thick. "Jason Donahue?"

"You do remember me. I wasn't sure you would."

Jason held out his hand and Jimmy took it gently. "Of course I remember you. I didn't think you'd make it. I'm so glad you did." He turned to Holly and Russ. "Jason served under me in Baghdad." He turned back to Jason and although he hid it well Holly sensed he found being around Jason painful. "So how do you know these clowns?"

"Roommates," Jason said. "And Emily, who is so not a clown, lives next door."

They all made small talk until Jimmy excused himself to return to the barbeque pit. Holly sat down and gestured for Jason to sit beside her. "So how long were you in BAMC?" she asked. "I was eight months getting out."

"Almost three years," Jason said. "And months of outpatient after that. I was already a junior when I got hurt and I'm just now getting my degree."

"Job?" Holly asked.

"No luck yet," Jason said. "Nobody wants to look at this ugly mug. How about you?"

"Pretty mug, no job skill," Holly admitted.

"Jason has a degree in marketing," Emily said. "He wants to go into sales." She squared her shoulders. "I think you should keep looking. Somebody's going to give you a chance if you'd just let them," she added tartly as she stood up and walked off.

Holly looked at Jason in confusion. "Did I miss something?"

Benny and Wade rolled their eyes. "She has the hots for him big time, but our interesting-looking friend here is too stupid to ask her out."

"No, she doesn't," Jason said quietly. "She just feels sorry for me."

Holly took a deep breath. "And you think she's offering you a pity fuck. What's the matter, guys? Never heard the word before?" she laughed when Russ and all three of the boys looked at her in shock.

Jason looked a little embarrassed. "Well, isn't she?"

"Jesus, Holly, did you have to put it like that? Jason, she's not offering you any kind of fuck," Russ snapped. "Emily's not like that."

"No, she isn't," Holly agreed firmly. "Okay, Jason, it's like this. Those god-awful scars are your new reality, just like a metal skull and a crappy hand and sorry knee are mine. Now, you can accept them and go on with your life, including your love life, or you can throw in the towel and sit on the sidelines for the rest of eternity." She leaned toward Jason. "I know Emily and she isn't offering you anything out of pity, if the look on her face when she stalked off was anything to go by. She's into the real you. Now get up off your duff and go ask my sister out."

Jason looked pole-axed and Wade and Benny laughed out loud. "Why, Miss Riley, I think I will," Jason said softly as he hopped up and spotted Emily across the park.

"Wow, you're something else," Benny said admiringly as they watched Jason weave through the crowd. "We've been trying to get through to him for months."

Holly thumped gently on the plate in her head. "Yes, but I have credentials you don't."

"And she's used to giving orders and she has definite opinions on pity fucks," Jimmy said as he slid into the space vacated by Jason. "Sorry, Holly, I didn't mean to startle you."

"I'm not that bossy," Holly insisted, her face flaming as she thought of their passionate embraces of the night before. "How much did you overhear?"

"The whole thing. And I didn't know you knew that word, either," Jimmy said, his eyes dancing when Holly blushed furiously. Jimmy turned to Wade and Benny. "Seriously, how is he doing?"

Benny thought a minute. "Other than looking like hell over a good bit of his body, not bad at all."

"I'm sure it took a toll on him, but he's doing pretty much okay," Wade added. "We've asked him what happened over there, but he absolutely refuses to talk about it."

"He's got good reason not to," Jimmy said tersely as his fingers tightened on the table. "For his sake, just leave it alone."

Angie Baxter came toward them with a big smile on her face. She reached out and pulled Wade into a huge hug. "I just now spotted you," she said chidingly. "Why didn't you come by the house earlier?"

"Yeah, Wade, if I had a hot babe like that one at home I'd go by the house big time," Russ piped up.

Angie and Wade both shot Russ a go-to-hell look and the rest of them burst out laughing. "Russ, the 'hot babe' here is Wade's mom, Angie," Holly said. "Angie, this reprobate is my brother Russ."

Russ looked from Wade to Angie and back. "Your *mother*?" he asked unbelievingly.

"Delighted to make your acquaintance," Angie said, icicles dripping from her voice. "Benny, good to see you again."

"Yes, it is," Jimmy said as his gaze drifted across the park and fell on Jason Donahue. He stood up abruptly. "Holly, the main reason I came back over here was to tell you that Jack has the hots to talk to you when you have a minute. I'll catch you all later."

Holly watched Jimmy head back toward his house, his shoulders tense and his face pinched. *He was there,* she thought. Jimmy was there the day Jason Donahue was burned so badly and had probably been part of whatever happened to him. And Holly would bet a year's worth of fish bait that Jason Donahue appeared on a regular basis in Jimmy's tortured dreams.

* * *

Holly spotted Jack Briscoe with Ryan and Carrie splashing in the waves and sat down under a shade tree to wait for them to come out of the water. When they finally emerged, Jack toweled off and motioned Holly to an unoccupied picnic table. "I need your help," he said without preamble as he pulled his T-shirt over his head. "The teacher who agreed to teach our new ROTC program resigned yesterday. I want you to take his place."

Holly blinked. "Just like that?" she asked.

"Just like that," Jack said. "You said your job skills didn't match anything in the civilian world. Well, now they do. These kids want to learn everything they can about the Army and you can teach them that. You would be great at it, Holly."

"Wouldn't I need a bunch of education courses or something?"

Jack leaned forward. "Just between you and me, those courses aren't worth a damn thing. We're doing a lot of alternative certification these days, which is a polite way of saying on-the-job training. We could have you in the certification process before school starts."

"Could you tell me more of the particulars?" Holly asked.

Jack nodded and in the next few minutes he outlined her responsibilities and compensation. The salary and benefits were adequate, and the challenge—and it would be a challenge—of introducing one hundred-plus teenagers to military customs and discipline frankly intrigued her. She thought about the young men and women she had instructed over the years—American soldiers and Iraqi militia alike—and wondered if teaching in the high school would really be so different. Was this the something that would fill the void that leaving the Army had left in her?

Jack finished his spiel and leaned back. "Well, how about it?" he asked.

"How soon do I have to let you know?" Holly asked.

"The sooner the better, but I can hold off a week or two," Jack said.

"All right then. Let me consider it."

"Fair enough. Thanks."

Jack threw up his hand to someone behind her and for the second time that day Jimmy slid in beside her on a picnic bench. He'd had a shower and the pinched look was gone from his face. "The band leader asked me to sing a song or two with them," he said to Holly. "I told him I would if you would."

"Mighty free with my singing, aren't you?" Holly groused.

"Aw, come on." Jimmy half-dragged Holly to the bandstand and they chose a couple of old country and western standbys they both knew the words to. Holly stepped up to the microphone and Jimmy sidled up to her, the guitarist played a short intro, and before she knew it she and Jimmy were belting out an old Reba McIntire hit, Jimmy's baritone harmony weaving surprisingly well around her soaring soprano. Caught up in the singing, Holly forgot her audience and was completely surprised by the enthusiastic round of applause that followed the song. Egged on by the crowd, Holly and Jimmy sang three more, and Holly's face was wreathed in a smile as she and Jimmy thanked the bandleader for including them in his performance. "That was great!" Holly said as she and Jimmy left the bandstand.

"I'm glad you liked it," Jimmy said, a look of satisfaction on his face. "I told you that you could still make music." He glanced across the park and his eyes widened. "Uh oh, looks like the competition's just shown up," he said as a dark-haired, handsome young man helped a pregnant blonde out of a Lexus SUV.

Holly's head snapped up as Nadine made a beeline for the couple. "Alex Navarro," she observed. "Mom wouldn't be high-tailing over there otherwise."

"Nothing like bearding the lion in his den," Jimmy said as he took Holly's hand. "Let's go say hello."

They met the Navarros halfway across the park. "Jimmy, long time no see," Alex said smoothly as he and Jimmy shook hands. "This is my wife, Leigh Anne, and you must be Captain Riley. I've heard about your work with the wounded soldiers."

"It's just Holly these days," Holly said as Alex met her gaze. He had it down pat, she thought as he made just the right amount of eye contact and shook her hand with the perfect touch.

Holly turned to Leigh Anne and was treated to a warm, megawatt smile. "Alex and I are so hoping you plan at some point to help start a group in the Midland area," she said. "The need is great and no one has stepped up to the plate."

"I'll put it on my list," Holly said.

"Jimmy, would you be interested in a public debate or two a little closer to the election?" Alex asked. "I think we owe it to the voters to let them get to know us and I don't know of a better way to do it."

"I absolutely would," Jimmy said. He whipped out his wallet and jotted down a phone number on his business card. "Misty Martinez is managing my campaign—I added her cell. Have your manager call her and they can set something up."

"Will do. Good to see you both." Alex took Leigh Anne's hand and they waded fearlessly into the crowd. Jimmy and Holly watched silently as Alex and Leigh Anne skillfully worked the picnic, relaxed and charming but not spending too much time with any one group until they came to the picnic table where Jason Donahue and Emily were sitting with Tommy Joe and Christi. They sat down and were soon in a lively conversation with the young people.

"I would give my right arm to know what they're talking about," Holly murmured as laughter burst from the group.

Jimmy shrugged. "Go on over. Nothing's stopping you."

"I wouldn't do that to you in front of everybody," Holly said shortly. "Emily or Tommy Joe can fill me in."

Alex and Leigh Anne spent another thirty minutes at the picnic, their smiles warm and genuine as they bid their farewells. Holly made her way to her sister and friends. "Well, what did you think of him?" Holly asked as they watched the Navarro SUV drive away.

"He was good," Emily said frankly. "Very good."

"He had a lot of ideas for helping veterans like Jason and me," Tommy said. "I like that."

"Yes, he actually acted like he gave a damn," Jason said. "By the way, Tommy tried to hustle me for the Heaven's Point group, Holly, but I'd rather you help me set up one of my own in College Station."

"I'd love to," Holly said. "Emily knows where to find me."

Jason and Emily said their good-byes and Holly followed them out to the parking lot. Jimmy looked around, relieved to see Nadine sitting at a picnic bench with a couple he didn't know. She spotted him coming toward her and motioned him over. "I was just talking with the van Cleaves about Alex Navarro." Nadine's lips thinned. "West Texas simply can't afford to have that man in Congress."

Jimmy took a deep breath. "I agree," he said. "So are you and your associates in San Angelo still interested in backing a Verde lawyer for Congress?"

Nadine looked at the van Cleaves and nodded. "We were hoping you'd be over here to tell us that," she said. "Glad to have you on board."

They shook hands all around. *God, I hope this is the right thing,* Jimmy thought. But what other choice did he have? Alex Navarro was a pro, a retail politician who had charm and money to burn. *Holly, I'm sorry,* he thought as she caught his eye from across the park and gave him a go-to-hell look. He was sorry he'd disappointed her, but he needed Nadine's support, and if he had to deal with the devil, well, deal with the devil he would.

Holly put cold sodas and brisket sandwiches in a cooler and headed back to the beach, where families continued to linger in the late afternoon sunshine. She was still aggravated with Jimmy for accepting the assistance of Nadine and her cronies but not aggravated enough to refuse the leftover brisket he offered her. She hated the thought of him tailoring his campaign to fit her mother's expectations, but after seeing Alex Navarro in action this afternoon she could understand it. Alex had clearly left a swath of fans in his wake and with that kind of charisma and the money he had at his disposal Jimmy was going to need a lot of help to beat him. She spotted Jimmy and the Briscoes sitting at a picnic table on the far side of the park and whistled to get their attention.

Jimmy jumped up and loped across the park. "Was there enough brisket to make a sandwich for everybody?" he asked as he relieved her of the heavy basket.

"Yes and I have brisket for several more meals," Holly said. "Thanks."

Jimmy peered down at her. "Am I still in the doghouse?"

"Arf, arf," Holly said tartly. "Oh, I guess I understand. Alex Navarro's a force to be reckoned with. Even Emily, who has the political experience of an asparagus spear, could see that he was good." She laid a hand on his arm. "Just don't let them dictate everything."

Holly and Caroline put out the sandwiches and the Briscoes joined Jimmy and Holly for the light picnic supper. As the sun went down over the water a huge flat-bottomed barge pulled around the point and anchored itself about fifty yards out. "Oh, good, the Baptist Church must be sponsoring a fireworks show again," Caroline said with enthusiasm. "The one last year was spectacular."

"Why out over the water?" Holly asked.

"Safer," Jimmy said shortly.

The sun slid below the horizon and the sky darkened. Jimmy didn't have much to contribute to the conversation and Holly attributed that to fatigue until she glanced toward him and saw that the pinched expression had returned to his features. *Uh oh,* she thought as the first of the Roman candles rose with a loud pop. Holly reached for Jimmy's hand and went up on her tiptoes as the second rocket went off. "Don't stay," she whispered as another round of popping had Jimmy squeezing her hand for dear life. "Go home. I'll watch Carrie."

Jimmy shook his head and sat down on the picnic table but when another round of explosives shot up into the air with a resounding boom, Jimmy let go of her hand and stood up. "Guys, I'm really beat," he said to Jack and Caroline. "That four a.m. booty call. Will you help Holly watch Carrie?"

The Briscoes promised to help keep an eye on Carrie and wished Jimmy good night. Holly made a point not to watch Jimmy leave, instead giving her full attention to the surprisingly spectacular display. When the fireworks from the boat ended, Jack and Caroline and some of the residents of the Point set off smaller ones on the wet, sandy beach, and it was well past ten when Holly finally took Carrie home. She looked in on Jimmy and was pleased to hear soft snores coming from his bed. Thank goodness, he appeared to be sleeping peacefully.

Holly gave Carrie a bath and dressed her in her summer pajamas, but after a couple of rounds of sugar and caffeine the child was wired. Bowing to the inevitable, Holly found a brand-new DVD and made popcorn for the two of them. Carrie talked and bounced and wiggled through the entire DVD and Holly was about to despair of her ever going to sleep when the little girl dropped off suddenly during the closing credits. "Thank goodness," Holly breathed as she lifted the child in her good arm and struggled up the stairs. With a sigh of relief Holly laid Carrie down on top of the covers and turned out the light. She took a few minutes to clean up the corn popper and was about to walk out the front door when she heard a blood-curdling yell. "Oh, my God," Holly breathed as she stumbled up the stairs as fast as her bad leg would carry her. Another nightmare, and if the scream that had just come out of Jimmy was anything to go by, this one was a real lulu.

Holly threw open Jimmy's door to find him thrashing in the bedcovers, his bare chest covered with sweat and stark terror on his face. "Jimmy," she said soothingly as she approached him with caution. "Jimmy, wake up. Wake up, Jimmy, it's all right."

Holly reached down and tentatively touched the side of Jimmy's face. He sat up suddenly, his eyes open but unfocused as he grabbed her arm and threw her away from him. "No, get out of here, it's a trap!" he moaned as he stared unseeingly into the dark.

Shaken, Holly approached him again. "Jimmy, wake up," she said softly as she tried to reach out to him.

Jimmy stood swaying and pushed Holly away from him roughly, sending her into the doorjamb with enough force to make her see stars. "Get away from me, damn it! It's not safe!" He collapsed back onto the bed, shaking uncontrollably as Holly painfully pushed herself away from the door and stared at him in horror. "Go on, get out of here!" he moaned as he rocked back and forth.

Holly shook as her mind raced. She wasn't about to touch him again and risk getting hurt even worse and she wasn't going to be able to reach him by talking to him. Jimmy was a danger to himself and to others right now and even with all the experience she'd had in Baghdad, she was in over her head and she knew it.

Holly heard Carrie cry out and realized in horror that Carrie was standing in Jimmy's open door with tears running down her face. "I saw Daddy push you," she said as she stared at her father.

Carrie started toward Jimmy but Holly scooped her up and whisked her down the stairs. "Carrie, Daddy's very sick right now," Holly said soothingly. "We need to leave him alone for a few minutes."

"When I'm sick Daddy takes me to see Miss Caroline."

Out of the mouth of babes, Holly thought. "Do you know Miss Caroline's phone number?"

"I think it's by the phone in the kitchen," Carrie said.

Holly grabbed Carrie's hand and practically ran to the kitchen. With trembling fingers she dialed the Briscoes' landline. Jack's sleepy voice answered. "Jack, it's Holly Riley. I need to talk to Caroline. Jimmy's having the flashback from hell and I can't wake him."

"*Flashback?* What the hell??" Jack demanded.

"Just come," Holly pleaded as Jimmy let loose upstairs with another blood-curdling yell.

Holly unlocked the front door and sat on the sofa with her arms around a terrified Carrie. It seemed like an eternity but in fact was less than ten minutes before Caroline Briscoe pushed through the door with her medical bag with Jack on her heels carrying a sleeping Ryan. Caroline skidded to a stop in front of Holly and Carrie. "What in God's name happened to your face?" she demanded as she knelt in front of the two of them.

"Daddy pushed Holly," Carrie said solemnly. "He told her to get away, it wasn't safe, and then he pushed her into the door."

At that point Jimmy let out another scream that made them all flinch. "Go tend to him," Holly said urgently. "I'm fine."

Jack laid Ryan down on the sofa and took the stairs two at a time, Caroline right behind him. She heard Jimmy's door open and the screaming start again. "No, get back, it's a trap!" Jimmy cried over and over. Holly could hear what sounded like a scuffle and a sharp curse from Jack.

Jimmy let loose with a bellow of anger. "What the hell was that?" he demanded.

Holly could hear both Caroline and Jack speaking to him in soothing tones for a few minutes. She sat with Carrie on her lap and rubbed the frightened little girl's back until Carrie drifted back to sleep. She laid the child on the other end of the sofa from Ryan and with trembling fingers found Jimmy's cigarettes in his desk drawer. She was about to step out on the deck and light up when Jack and Caroline came tiredly down the stairs. Their clothes were rumpled and Jack had a fresh bruise on his cheekbone. "Did he push you, too?" Holly asked.

"No, he slugged me. Kept calling me a 'Qaida bastard,'" Jack said. "Caroline had to sedate him."

"I gave him enough to put a horse to sleep," Caroline said. "He'll be out until morning." She looked at the cigarettes in Holly's hand. "I'm prescribing something a hell of a lot stronger for you and Jack than nicotine. Where's Jimmy's whiskey?"

Holly motioned to the cabinet by the sink and Jack poured a stiff drink for her and himself. Caroline made Jack and Holly cold compresses and the three of them sat down at the kitchen table. "I told him he had PTSD," Holly said as she downed half the whiskey. "He wouldn't believe me."

Holly could see Caroline swiftly connecting the dots. "That morning after your migraine," she said. "That's what you were fighting about in his bedroom."

"I was able to bring him out of it that night," Holly said. "Usually if you talk to them gently and maybe touch them it will wake them up."

"That only works if it's a nightmare," Caroline said. "This was a full-blown flashback. Those are different."

"Amen to that," Holly said as she touched her bruised cheek gingerly. She turned anguished eyes on Jack and Caroline. "I tried to tell him he needed help and he blew up. Insisted it was just a few nightmares and that he wasn't about to risk his candidacy because his"—she thought a minute—"touchy-feely neighbor thought he needed a shrink. And he made me promise I'd keep my mouth shut."

"I wonder what triggered it," Caroline said. "The fireworks, maybe?"

"Seeing Jason Donahue again. That friend of Wade and Benny's, the boy with those god-awful burn scars, served under Jimmy in Iraq and Jimmy nearly fainted when he realized who the boy was. I'm pretty sure that whatever happened to that kid is what Jimmy's dreaming about."

Jack whistled under his breath. "Yep, seeing that boy and then the fireworks—that would do it. I wonder how long this has been going on."

"Long enough that he's woken Carrie at least once," Holly said. "What would have happened if Carrie had gone to bed when she should have and I hadn't been here? He could have hurt her!"

"Yes, he certainly could have," Caroline said grimly as she looked at Jack. "I think Jimmy needs a come-to-Jesus talk from me tomorrow morning."

"You're welcome to him once I get done. Holly, thank you for calling us. I'm sorry you got hurt."

Holly shrugged. "I'll live. Do you need for me to add my two cents in the morning?"

"No, the ass chewing he's going to get would be better coming from us," Jack said.

"What you could do, if you don't mind, is let both the kids sleep at your place tonight and stay with you in the morning until we're through over here," Caroline said. "It's going to get loud and rude and we may have to say some things to him that Carrie shouldn't have to hear."

"Works for me," Holly said as she drained the whiskey. "Thanks, guys. I hope Jimmy appreciates just how good a friend he has in both of you."

Caroline reached over and gave Holly a hug. "He's got just as good a friend in you," she said softly. "And we are so glad."

Jack picked up both sleeping children and carried them down the now-quiet street toward Holly's house. Damn it, she could feel it again, she thought as she unlocked her front door. Somebody was out there watching her. Holly whipped around in the dark, scanning the inky yards across the street and beyond the beach, searching in vain for any sign of movement in the shadows. Swearing to herself, she opened the door for Jack and motioned for him to lay the children down on her wide sofa, and after he was gone she checked both doors three times to be sure they were locked. *Damn you, whoever you are*, she thought to herself as she poured herself another shot of whiskey. *What are you doing? Which of my soldiers is next? And who are you really mad at—my soldiers or Jimmy Adamcik?*

* * *

Chucky stuck his finger in his mouth to keep from laughing out loud when Holly whipped around and peered into the dark. She knew he was out here, he thought as she unlocked the door for Jack Briscoe and the Briscoe and Adamcik brats, both of whom were sound asleep. But why were the adults still up? Why was Holly keeping the children overnight at her place? And why had Adamcik had been off his game for most of the day? He had definitely not been his usual chipper self that morning and had high-tailed it out of there the minute the fireworks started, and now he's having a midnight visit from the doctor. Chucky waited for the better part of an hour, growing more curious than ever when the lights went off at the Adamcik house and the Briscoe SUV stayed in the driveway. Something serious was going on over there, and Chucky would give his eyeteeth to know what.

Chucky itched to slip under the cover of darkness to the Adamcik house for a quick look-see through the open drapes—but that was taking a chance, and he wasn't to the point where he could take foolish chances. As it was, he almost got caught today and it was only a quick exit down a side street that had saved this mission. No, he had too much to do and too much mayhem to create to take chances now. He would save any recklessness for later, when it got to the point where he had nothing to lose.

Chapter Nine

Jimmy swore softly as he felt himself slowly coming up from the depths of a hellish and terrifying slumber. The dream had come again, the ear-splitting boom of the explosion and the shrieks of the soldiers as they lay burned and dying. As he always did, Jimmy screamed and cursed and yelled for them to get back and as always the soldiers kept coming, closer and closer until the bomb ripped them into pieces.

Last night's dream had been terrifyingly vivid, the fire brighter and the stench more powerful and the screams louder, but to his puzzlement Jimmy had no memory of waking up in terror. Forcing the dream from his thoughts, he turned over and grasped the extra pillow and was about to shut his eyes when he heard a soft snore coming from his recliner. He opened his eyes to find Jack Briscoe asleep in the chair, his clothing rumpled and a fresh bruise on his cheek. What in the world? He sat up quickly and nausea hit him so badly he barely made it to the bathroom. Leaning over the toilet, he retched and heaved for what seemed like forever.

Jack poked his head in the door and immediately wet a washcloth and handed it to him. Jimmy wiped his face and his neck and gratefully took the arm that Jack offered. On trembling legs he made it across the room to sit down on the side of his bed. "Why are you here?" he croaked.

"I'll explain in a minute." Jack opened the bedroom door and called down the stairs. "He's awake, Caroline." He turned around to Jimmy. "Coffee?"

"I don't think so," Jimmy said. "But I will have a cigarette if you don't mind," he added as he fumbled around in the nightstand drawer, finally unearthing a pack of cigarettes.

Jack sat back down and in a minute Caroline marched into the room and plopped down in Lauren's chair. Jimmy took a deep drag on the cigarette. "Why are you both here?" he asked warily as he looked from Jack to Caroline. Neither of them appeared to be very happy with him. "Is Carrie all right?"

"She spent the night at Holly's," Caroline said. "We had to get her out of here."

"What—why?" Jimmy asked.

"How much do you remember about last night?" Jack asked.

Jimmy's mind raced. "Uh, I came home early and went to sleep. I think I heard Holly bring Carrie home but I'm not sure."

"And then what?" Caroline prompted.

"Nothing. I woke up feeling like hell and found Jack asleep in the chair."

Jack's lips thinned. "Cut the bullshit, Jimmy, and tell me the truth."

Caroline turned to Jack. "He really may not remember." She turned to Jimmy. "Or then again he may." She nailed him with a stare that would take paint off the wall. "Now, I want the truth, the whole truth, and nothing but. *What do you remember about last night?*"

Jimmy looked at their grim faces and the fresh bruise on Jack's cheek and started to get a really bad feeling. "All I remember about last night was a nightmare about the war. What happened?"

"You had the flashback from hell and Holly called us after you knocked her into the doorjamb." Jack fingered his bruise. "She has the matching one of these. Why the hell didn't you tell me you have PTSD?"

"Because I don't," Jimmy snapped. "Holly shouldn't have told you that. I just have a few nightmares. That's all."

"Nightmares? You call last night 'just a nightmare'? Jimmy, are you out of your ever-loving mind?" Caroline snapped.

"Good lord, Jimmy, you sent a woman flying across the room and called me a Qaida bastard and slugged me. I outweigh you a good forty pounds and it was all I could do to hold you down while Caroline pumped chill juice into you. Never mind that your four-year-old daughter was witness to the whole thing. And that was *just a fucking nightmare?*"

"You never came out of it," Caroline said. "That's why I made Jack spend the night in your room. I'm no expert on flashbacks and I wasn't sure what to expect this morning." Her jaw tightened. "You were a dangerous man last night, Jimmy. If Holly hadn't been here you could have injured or killed your daughter."

Jimmy swallowed. "I would never do anything to hurt Carrie," he said stiffly.

"Would you shove Holly into a door or slug Jack?" Caroline shot back. "Jimmy, you weren't in control last night. Your eyes were open but you were seeing Baghdad."

"Why in the hell didn't you say something, Jimmy?" Jack demanded. "I'm your best friend. You could have told me."

"And I'm your doctor," Caroline reminded him. "I need to know something like that."

"Damn it, I didn't want you to know," Jimmy said brokenly. "I didn't want anyone to know how weak I am." He buried his face in his hands. "You don't know how it feels to be at the mercy of a bunch of God-damned dreams."

Jack and Caroline looked at one another. "Oh, but I do," Caroline said softly. "Jimmy, ever since Ryan was kidnapped and Aaron was murdered, if I have to treat a gunshot wound I have a nightmare that night. I even warn Jack so he can help me deal." Caroline's first husband was murdered and Ryan snatched from her as an infant, and it had taken her over a year to be reunited with her child.

"Lauren used to do that for me," Jimmy said. "So what did you do about it?"

"I got professional help," Caroline said. "Just like you're going to do. This week. And the first step is to admit to yourself, and to those around you, that you have PTSD."

Jimmy was quiet a minute. "I'll admit it to myself," he said slowly. "And to you, and Jack, and Holly. But it stops there. I'm not telling the world."

"Janelle?" Jack asked.

"No," Jimmy said firmly. "It will only worry her."

"What about the campaign?" Jack asked cautiously. "Don't the voters deserve the truth?"

"If I go public it will cost me the campaign," Jimmy said. "I have the same right to medical privacy that any other citizen does."

"Yes, you do," Caroline agreed unexpectedly. "And you have our promise that we'll keep our mouths shut. And in exchange I want your promise that you'll seek help immediately. I'm starting you on meds this morning and tomorrow I'm calling a PTSD specialist in Austin and making you an appointment."

"I don't want to go to a shrink. Can't you treat me?" Jimmy asked.

"No, I can't," Caroline said firmly. "You're going to an expert in PTSD."

Jimmy looked from Jack to Caroline. "I'm sorry about last night, guys. And thanks."

"You don't have to apologize to us," Jack said quietly. "Or thank us. But you do need to thank Holly for last night. She took the brunt of it and instead of running out of here she got you help. You owe that lady a big one."

Jimmy nodded. "I know." He buried his head in his hands. "I'll talk to her tonight. God, I am mortified. What am I going to say to her?"

"I wouldn't worry too much about that," Caroline said. "Of all the people in your life, Jimmy, she is probably going to understand the best."

* * *

Holly shook the soggy remnants of a bowl of cereal into the garbage. After Patsy's big noontime meal she could have skipped supper altogether, but her stomach still burned from the whiskey and the fear from the night before and the cereal helped. Caroline and Jack had been late in the morning picking up Carrie and Ryan, and Jack said they were taking Carrie for the day. Caroline said that the talk with Jimmy went better than expected, but Holly still wondered what he would have to say to her now that she had been forced to rat him out. But maybe it was for the best; whatever his feelings toward her, now that Jack and Caroline knew about the PTSD he would have to deal with the problem.

Holly was halfway through a brand-new historical romance when she heard a knock on her front door and was not surprised to find Jimmy standing on her front porch looking like he would rather be just about anywhere else. "Come on in," Holly said. "I have iced tea made up."

Jimmy followed her into her miniscule kitchen and accepted a glass of tea. He caught her chin and turned her face from one side to the other. "What does it look like under the makeup?" he demanded.

"The cold compress took care of the worst of it," Holly said. "Jack's is worse." She smiled slightly in spite of herself. "You must have one hell of a right hook."

Jimmy didn't so much as crack a smile. "So how in the hell do I apologize for last night?"

"You admit to yourself that you have a problem and you seek treatment," Holly said.

Jimmy took a deep breath and took a bottle of pills out of his pocket. "Caroline gave me these to tide me over until I can get to a PTSD specialist in Austin," he said. "I'm going sometime this week, even if I have to get a court date postponed."

Holly nodded. "That's more like it," she said as she took Jimmy by the hand and led him to the sofa. "It's no shame to have PTSD. Some of the strongest men I served with got hit with it."

"But not everyone gets it. You don't have it. You were hurt, even, and you don't have it."

"I also have a six-month gap in my memory," Holly reminded him. "It's hard to be traumatized by something you can't remember." She reached for her glass of tea. "What do you think set you off so badly? Jason? Or the fireworks?"

Jimmy shrugged. "Both, probably. I was in so much combat over there I have a lot of bad dreams, but the one I dream most often is the day Jason was hurt. It was right at the beginning of it all," Jimmy said, more to himself than to her. "The regime had fallen and Baghdad was chaos—but you know all that." Holly nodded. "Anyway, we had just gone house to house looking for the tangos that'd taken out a Humvee full of men and thought we had them cornered on the next block. We were on the roof of a deserted house and there were a bunch of privates standing guard downstairs when this little kid not more than two or three comes wandering down the damn street by himself. Of course, the guards all go spilling out to check on the little kid." Jimmy coughed and cleared his throat. "I saw the SOB hold up the detonator. I screamed at the guards to get back, it was a trap, but they either didn't hear me or they didn't think—" Jimmy gulped and brushed the tears out of his eyes. "Those sons of bitches had wired that beautiful little boy with explosives. They blew him up along with five of my soldiers. Two of those young men died on the spot and the third bled out ten minutes later. The other two—my God, if you think Jason looks bad now you should have seen him that day. I'm honestly surprised they were able to save him." He knuckled more tears out of his eyes. "The medics took away the two that were still alive and we gathered up what was left of the others. We were out of body bags so we put them in garbage can liners. And here I am, years later, reliving it nightmare after nightmare after nightmare."

Holly sat silent a minute. "Jimmy, in all my years in the service, I never saw anything that horrific," she said quietly. "That would give anyone PTSD." She thought a minute. "Was this the Silver Star?"

"Nah," Jimmy said. "That was later. When I pulled a couple of guys out of a burning Humvee while the insurgents shot at us. I spent the rest of my tours trying to make up for what happened to Jason and the others."

"And you still blame yourself for what happened," Holly said thoughtfully. "Survivor's guilt. I get that one, too, sometimes. I'm sorry it's been so hard on you."

Jimmy shrugged. "It was a lot harder on Jason and the dead ones."

"Maybe yes, maybe no," Holly said. She turned to Jimmy and held his face between her hands. "I'm going to suggest something and you're probably going to resist but I'm going to suggest it anyway. You need to be part of a support group. If not mine, someone's."

"Are you out of your mind?" Jimmy asked as he pulled away and stood up. "Do you have any idea what that would do to my chances of getting elected?"

"Damn it, does everything in your life have to be about getting elected?" Holly snapped. "What about your mental health?"

Jimmy sat back down and took Holly's hand. "Holly, do you have any idea how much I would love to sit down with your group and talk? But I can't. I won't risk the election. I told you I'm getting professional help from a doctor who has to honor doctor-patient privilege. That has to be enough."

"All right," Holly said slowly. "If you make damn sure to go through with it."

"With the Briscoes on my ass? Are you kidding?"

Holly laughed softly. "Good." She paused a minute. "Are you going to be all right? Do you—? Would you—? Would it help to…do you want to—?" Holly broke off and blushed furiously. "And it wouldn't be pity," she added fiercely. "I want to make love with you for my sake as much as I do for yours. To hell with politics. Let's just do it."

Jimmy leaned forward and kissed Holly gently on the lips. "Talk about timing," he said ruefully. "I finally have you where I want you and I'm so chilled out with the medicine it would be an assault with a dead weapon." He leaned forward and kissed Holly hard on the lips. "Will you take a rain check? Come with me to Dallas or San Antonio next weekend?"

Holly shook her head in frustration. "Our timing really does suck. I called BAMC this afternoon and made an appointment for another surgery on my arm next Thursday. I'll be out of commission for at least two weeks, maybe three."

Jimmy looked at Holly in surprise. "Why? I thought you'd decided enough was enough."

"I had, but there are just too many things I can't do any more." She gestured to her bad arm. "I'm tired of this useless son of a bitch and am going to give it one more shot. Besides, I called Jack this afternoon and took the teaching job, and if I'm going to function in a classroom I need whatever use the surgeons can restore to it."

"Well, okay then," Jimmy said. He leaned back and looked at Holly. "You do know that every boy in that room is going to be looking at you in your Army uniform and dreaming about how you look out of it, don't you?"

Holly's eyes danced. "Don't worry; the teenagers in Verde can't be any hornier than the soldiers in Baghdad. I know how to deal with Combat Barbie Riley syndrome."

"I sure hope so!" Jimmy laughed out loud and kissed Holly again.

* * *

Holly stared nervously out the window of the Navigator as Jimmy took the expressway exit and sped down the road leading into the back of Fort Sam Houston and the new, state-of-the-art Brooke Army Medical Center. The huge hospital housed probably the best burn treatment center in the entire world and had additional wings and personnel to treat and rehabilitate soldiers with lost limbs and various injuries. Considering the shape she had been in when she had first come through its doors Holly knew that she had a lot to be grateful for, but that did not make the prospect of returning for yet another surgery any less daunting. She glanced over at Jimmy as she pointed out the entrance ahead. "I made this drive so often when I was outpatient I could do it in my sleep," she said.

"This traffic is terrible," Jimmy complained.

"Austin and Dallas are worse," Holly teased.

"Tell me about it," Jimmy said. "It was so bad in Austin yesterday I'm tempted not to go back."

"You can't do that," Holly said quickly. "You have to get treatment." She glanced over at Jimmy. "How was it?"

Jimmy shrugged. "Man knows his stuff."

And from the set look on his face that was all he was going to say, Holly thought as Jimmy pulled up to the entrance gate to Fort Sam Houston. They both showed their IDs and Holly pointed out a parking lot, and Jimmy wheeled Holly's carry-on across the blisteringly hot asphalt and up the imposing walk into the sleek, modern building. They had just stepped into the wide, spacious lobby when a young man and woman approached and brandished their press cards. "Captain Riley? Imogene Ganshaw and Doug Doyle, *San Angelo Tribune*. We're here doing a story on the wounded veterans and couldn't believe our luck when the PR department said you were scheduled to check in this afternoon. Could we trouble you for a moment or two of your time?"

"Sure," Holly said. "And it's just Miss Riley or Holly these days." She gestured toward an adjacent waiting room.

Imogene took a couple of quick shots of Holly and turned her camera toward Jimmy. "Mr. Adamcik, I apologize for not recognizing you right off."

"Then take my picture and put it in the paper," Jimmy quipped. "We need to remedy that."

Doug and Imogene laughed and Imogene turned to Holly. "How do you feel about the medical care you received after your injuries in Iraq?" she asked.

"It was excellent. I'm doing great considering the shape I was in when they wheeled me in here."

"Then why are you just now having the surgery on your arm?" Doug chimed in. "Was there a waiting list or something?"

"Oh, nothing like that," Holly said. "I am going to state for the record, and please get this word for word, that the medical care I got here at BAMC could not have been any better. This place is absolutely the best. Today's surgery is a third attempt to correct the rather severe nerve damage that has cost me most of the use of my left hand, and the only reason I haven't had it earlier was that I was tired of the hospital. Now that I'm going back to work I need it to be as functional as I can get it."

"You were injured pretty severely," Imogene Ganshaw said thoughtfully. "How difficult has your recovery been?"

"It's been a hard road," Holly said. "So much of our healing goes beyond just the physical injuries. Sometimes we need more than just medical care, and that's where support groups come in."

"Yes, the PR liaison said you have become quite the activist," Imogene said.

"I wouldn't say that," Holly said. "We just get together from time to time to lend one another support."

"What kind of support?" Doug asked.

"Moral support. Practical support. And knowing where to go for help when you need it support. Sometimes it can be as simple as a couple of restaurant pans. One of our members, Armando Fuentes, was having no luck convincing a restaurant manager he could handle himself in a commercial kitchen on braces until we bought him a couple of pans and he took prepared food into his next interview. He landed that job."

"What about the political arena?" Imogene asked as she looked from Holly to Jimmy.

"As a congressional candidate, where do you fit into Miss Riley's agenda?" Doug asked Jimmy.

Gotcha! Holly thought as she could feel Jimmy's mind racing. "Naturally, I support everything Holly is doing," Jimmy said smoothly. "She and the members of her group have done wonders for one another."

"But what are your plans, should you be elected, to help Miss Riley further the cause?" Imogene persisted. "Do you have any particular projects or programs in mind?"

"More and better training programs," Jimmy said. "More effective counseling for soldiers like Holly who can no longer go back to their former careers. Quicker access to medical and psychiatric treatment provided by the VA—a six-week waiting period for a suicidal veteran is unconscionable. And perhaps public support for private and grassroots initiatives such as Holly's."

Holly tried not to let her astonishment at Jimmy's comments show. So he had given their cause some thought and his ideas were good. But the question remained: would he feel free to work for the implementation of those ideas if he was under the thumbs of Nadine and her cronies, or would he have to knuckle under and support their agenda if he wanted to stay in office?

* * *

Jimmy ran his hand down his face and wished for the umpteenth time that he'd accepted Patsy Riley's offer of a guest room for the night. But he had a court date in Burnet tomorrow mid-morning, so after he had gotten Holly settled in he had gotten back in the car and started home. Thankfully his next few days were flexible and he would be able to make the trip back to San Antonio whenever Holly was discharged. A rueful smile touched Jimmy's lips as he remembered Holly's swiftly disguised surprise at his comments this afternoon. What had she expected him to say under the circumstances? That he planned to throw the wounded veterans under the bus? And the sad part was that he firmly believed in every idea he had thrown out to Imogene and Doug, but political reality being what it was, he would probably never be able to implement a one of them, even if by some miracle he managed to beat Alex Navarro.

Jimmy's cell phone rang and he spotted Nadine's number. "Yes, I got Holly to San Antonio and she's checked in. She's fine."

"I'm not calling about Holly," Nadine snapped. "Purcell Reynolds just called. The comments you made to those damned reporters is already on the *Tribune* website and will be on the front page in the morning. The committee's furious."

"Nadine, what was I supposed to say?" Jimmy asked, exasperated. "I'm sitting there in the lobby of an Army hospital beside a wounded war hero—*your* wounded war hero daughter—and I'm supposed to say what? Tough luck, they knew what they were getting into when they joined the Army? Or hey, we'll do what we can, but they shouldn't expect much because we don't want to spend the money?"

"What's wrong with a few vague platitudes that sound good?" Nadine shot back. "Damn it, Jimmy, don't make it sound like you plan to go in and spend a small fortune. Platitudes. Vague platitudes. No expensive-sounding proposals and no promises. Got that?"

Nadine disconnected before Jimmy could answer. Jimmy gripped his phone, resisting the urge to throw it across the car. That was the deal he had made, he reminded himself. A deal he had to make even if it was beginning to make him feel uneasy. He was taking their money, so he would have to support their party line. Damn it anyway, he thought as he remembered the way Holly's eyes shone when she talked about her work with the soldiers. They really needed an ally in the political system if they were going to get the support they needed and deserved. It was too bad that even if he won the election he would not be able to be the friend in Congress that they needed so much.

* * *

Chucky sipped his morning coffee and stared at the headline in the San Angelo paper. "Adamcik on Veterans' Side" blazed across the top of the paper above a color photograph of Adamcik and the bitch sitting in what looked like a hospital lobby. "So, we just love the gimpy bastards now, do we?" he said as he eagerly read the first couple of paragraphs of the article. "How sad for them. Let's see, who's going to get it this time?" he said gleefully as he bit off a chunk of toast. It was too soon to target the bitch herself, but what about the fat old man with the Santa beard? Or—

No, no, no, this is perfect, Chucky thought as the name "Armando Fuentes" jumped out at him. Chucky shoved the rest of his toast into his mouth and paid a quick trip to the Internet, which after a speedy search yielded up Fuentes's address, phone number, and Facebook page. Oh, the things people post online, Chucky thought as he jotted down the date and time of little Maggie's birthday party. Quick in and out while they partied at the park and then…*boom*! Chuckie snickered as he glanced at the homemade bomb in the corner and the Adamcik for Congress sign next to it. Time for another little delivery.

Chapter Ten

Holly eased across the bed and slowly raised herself into a sitting position. Her back and neck were stiff and sore and her fingers were numb, but at least the anesthesia had worn off and her mind was clear. She pulled on her robe and slid into her backless slippers and was about to tackle a walk in the hall when a civilian in khaki pants and a polo shirt stuck his head in. "Miss Riley? Sam Ramirez, Austin arson squad. Could I have a word with you?" He flashed his shield and pulled up a chair. "We spoke to a Mr. James Adamcik over the phone last night and he told us where we could reach you." The detective's eyes sobered. "Are you acquainted with Armando and Inez Fuentes?"

Holly's eyes widened as she quickly connected the dots. "Oh, no. They put his name in the paper and something happened. You said you were arson, didn't you?"

"The Fuentes house was bombed yesterday afternoon during the little girl's birthday party. Thankfully no one was home at the time. An Adamcik for Congress sign was in the yard."

"Oh, my God," Holly breathed. "How bad?"

"Between the bomb and the ensuing fire they pretty much lost everything," Ramirez said.

Holly turned anguished eyes on the detective. "Is it because of me? Did my talking about Armando get his house bombed?"

"We don't know," Ramirez said. "The only lead we have is the campaign sign, which I understand is the third time an Adamcik campaign artifact has been left at the scene of an attack on one of your soldiers. I realize you're just out of surgery, but I still need to know everything that has happened so far. Mr. Adamcik filled me in on a lot of it but I'd still like to hear it all from you."

Holly nodded and over the next twenty minutes she told Inspector Ramirez everything that had happened. When he had finished with his questions Inspector Ramirez leaned back in his chair and looked over his notes. "I just have one question and it's about the campaign signs—more specifically, why Mr. Adamcik's campaign material would be left at the scene of the crimes. Just what is Mr. Adamcik's connection to your support group?"

"That's what has everyone so baffled," Holly admitted. "He has no direct connection to the support group members. His only connection to them is his friendship with me."

"Definitely odd," Inspector Ramirez agreed. "It looks like we have three connected crimes in two jurisdictions, which is of course going to complicate matters when it comes to the investigations," he admitted as Holly picked at the bed sheet. "It would be my guess then that it's somebody local, especially if you think you're being watched. It originates in Verde but has now followed your group to Austin."

"This terrifies me," Holly admitted as the inspector packed away the notepad. "More than fighting a war ever did."

"It probably should," Ramirez said frankly. "In a war, even in a messy war like Iraq, you know who your enemies are. This is a nameless, faceless enemy who could be anybody and has already shown that his sphere isn't limited to Verde." He shook Holly's hand again. "Thank you for your time. Please watch your back, Miss Riley."

"I will," Holly said dully as she slid down in the bed and pulled the covers up to her nose. Damn, she thought as a lone tear trickled down her face. Armando and Inez hadn't had that coming, and neither had Tommy Joe or Hal. Why, oh why had she mentioned Armando by name in the interview? What part did Jimmy Adamcik play in all this? Was Jimmy the ultimate target or was it her soldiers? Just how far was this unknown assailant willing to go? And what could she and her soldiers do to protect themselves?

* * *

Holly took a deep breath and unlocked the door to the ladies' lounge, where she had spent the last thirty minutes by herself having a good old-fashioned cry. She had gotten up early and driven into San Antonio, and after a friendly young physician's assistant removed her stitches she spent the morning in the therapy rooms, performing test after test to see what she could and couldn't do with her hand. And as the morning progressed Holly had become more and more disappointed. Yes, some mobility had been restored. She would be able to carry a plate to the sink and put a tablecloth on a table with both hands, and she could probably ride a Harley again.

With the right hair clips she might even be able to put her hair up. But typing an email or a letter? Probably not, and she could out and out forget the piano and organ. Determined not to let her disappointment show, Holly held herself together until she could find an empty lounge, where she sat down on the vinyl sofa and let herself have a good crying session. She had tried and the doctors had tried and if she would never play the piano or organ again, then so be it.

Holly wandered out to her car and found some eye drops in the glove compartment. She called Patsy's landline, hoping to hijack her stepmother for lunch, and was surprised when her father snapped a terse "Hello.". "Daddy? What are you doing home in the middle of the day?"

"Driving to Killeen to get your idiot brother out of the brig. We're leaving as soon as Patsy finishes packing."

"Brig? What is Russ doing in the brig?" Holly demanded.

"He got himself in hot water over some damned woman he's been sleeping with," Ben said. "Do you know anything about it?"

"No, he was very closed-mouth about the whole thing," Holly said. "So why is he in trouble?"

"She was married and in his chain of command. JAG friend of mine said he can probably get the charges dropped but his military career's toast," Ben said acerbically.

"Well I guess I won't be stealing Patsy away for lunch," Holly said. "I was going to cry on her shoulder a little."

"Uh oh," Ben said. "Surgery results not what you hoped? I'm sorry, hon."

"Me too, but you and Patsy have more pressing concerns this afternoon than my crappy arm," Holly said. "Give Russ my love and tell him to start thinking with his other head." She laughed as her father sputtered indignantly. "Bye, Daddy." Lord, the messes we make for ourselves, Holly thought as she headed out the gates of Fort Sam and got on I-35, deciding that a little retail therapy at the outlet malls in San Marcos just might a nice way to spend the rest of her day.

* * *

Holly rounded the curve in the farm-to-market road and took the turn that would lead her into Heaven's Point. She had not spent much at the malls but she had thoroughly enjoyed window-shopping. Tired out by the long day, she was tempted to go home and shut her door, but she had promised Jimmy and Carrie that she would have dinner with them and she was not about to disappoint. She was almost to the gate of Heaven's Point when she spotted Angie Baxter's cheerful little shop. Although it was probably past closing, Angie's van was still parked in front and the Open sign was on, and on impulse Holly whipped into the parking lot. The delightful little store brimmed with fanciful jewelry and whimsical accessories and Angie's handmade soaps and perfumes and sweet-smelling lotions. There seemed to be no one manning the shop but Holly could hear a radio playing softly and she could smell a delectable fragrance— lavender and roses, maybe?—coming from the back. One wall was taken up entirely by bottles and jars of cosmetics and another was stocked with men's products, including something labeled "Dirt Soap." "That's for the hunters," Angie said as she came out of the workroom. "So the deer can't smell them."

"Wow, you nailed the dirt smell perfectly," Holly said admiringly as she sniffed the bar once more. "This place is neat."

"Thank you," Angie said proudly. "Other than Wade, this shop's the best thing I've ever done."

"I've met Wade and I'd say you're right," Holly said.

"Thank you." Angie made no attempt to hide her pride in her son. "Is there anything in particular I can help you with?"

Holly looked around at the huge collection of fashion accessories. "I want to wear my hair up again, only my hand still isn't what it ought to be and I can't quite style it. Have you got some kind of gizmo I could use to get it up in a topknot?"

Angie thought a minute. "Actually, I have two or three," she said. She quickly located a couple of clips and scrunchies. "There's a mirror. Why don't you experiment with these while I go pour this batch of soap in the molds? Won't take me but a minute."

Angie disappeared and Holly got her brush out of her handbag. She leaned over at the waist and, using her hands and Angie's clips, managed to get her hair into a respectable topknot. She tried out all the clips and scrunchies, and by the time Angie returned Holly had also found three soaps she really liked and added them to her pile.

"Your soaps are fabulous," Holly enthused as Angie wrote up a ticket. "But do you get enough business out here in the country to stay afloat?"

"Actually, ninety percent of my business is over the Internet," Angie said. "I have almost more business than I can handle." Her eyes sparkled. "I'm making enough to help Wade with his college expenses and for the first time can actually pay for health insurance. Doc Briscoe practically did a happy dance." Angie put Holly's purchases in a bag. "Is there anything else I can do for you?" she asked.

Holly looked thoughtfully over at the wall of cosmetics. "Do you carry or could you develop some kind of concealing foundation?"

"Why? You don't need to conceal anything," Angie said. "Oh, I bet you're thinking of Cathy Armbruster. Sure, I could put together something. I'm not saying that we could cover everything but I could sure take the redness and the uneven coloration out." She paused a minute. "Has anybody figured out what's going on with your soldiers?"

Holly shook her head. "Not a damned thing. It's so frustrating and scary too. Several times I've felt like somebody was watching me there at the house. Why?"

"Well, besides something waking me up the night Raven was poisoned, a couple of times late at night I felt like somebody was outside my house, too," Angie said slowly. "You know how you have that feeling?"

Holly reached out and grasped Angie's hand. "The next time you feel something, will you call me, please?"

The women exchanged phone numbers and Angie promised to call. Holly was thoughtful as she drove home. Angie was about as solid and sensible as they came, and if she had sensed something… Holly could feel the beginnings of a headache coming on and willed her anxious thoughts away. The last thing she wanted tonight was another migraine.

Holly hurried into the house with her purchases and made quick work of changing her clothes and putting her hair up. She arrived at Jimmy's just as he and Carrie were driving up with a huge sack of food that smelled delicious. "I didn't want to suffer through my own cooking and didn't know if you would feel like it," Jimmy said as

Holly leaned down for a big hug from Carrie. "Nadine said you were getting your stitches out. Why didn't you tell me you were going into San Antonio today? I would have juggled things and driven you."

"I know that and I appreciate it," Holly said as they trooped into the house. "But I wanted to be alone in case I had occasion to cry."

"Did you cry, Holly?" Carrie asked as Jimmy put the sack of food on the table.

"Yes, Carrie, I sure did," Holly admitted. "I can do more than I could, but I'll never play the piano again, and that was what I was hoping to get back," she added to Jimmy as Carrie ran upstairs to wash her hands.

Jimmy frowned as he poured them each a glass of tea. "I thought you were okay with that. Doesn't singing sort of take the place of the piano?"

"Not really, but that's just the way it is." Holly shrugged as she glanced over toward the staircase. "I didn't want to say anything in front of Carrie. But I was in Angie's this afternoon and she said that a couple of times she felt like there was someone outside her house." She looked at Jimmy curiously. "Have you ever felt like someone was watching you here?"

"No, but this house has no nearby trees or any other kind of shelter for someone to watch from," Jimmy said as he got out some paper plates. "There's no one in Heaven's Point more down-to-earth and sensible than Angie. If she felt like someone was in her backyard, then somebody probably was."

"And that makes me more frightened than ever."

Jimmy reached out with a quick, reassuring hug. "I'm sorry," he said softly.

Dinner was mostly a quiet meal. Holly caught Jimmy looking across at her with something like speculation in his eyes and she wondered if he still believed their coming together as lovers was a given. She put away the leftovers and did what little cleaning the kitchen needed while Jimmy bathed Carrie and put her to bed. She sat down on the sofa, exhausted by the long, emotional day she had put in, and for long moments she let her mind just drift.

She felt rather than saw Jimmy sit down beside her. "Tired?" he asked as she felt his arm go around her and pull her close.

"Tired and disappointed," she said as she opened her eyes and stared up into Jimmy's intense features. "And wondering who in the hell was in Angie's yard."

"How about we think about something else for a few minutes," Jimmy said softly as he slowly and almost tentatively lowered his mouth to hers. Feather-soft, gentle, his lips were coaxing rather than demanding as he oh-so gently and tenderly again made her acquaintance. Holly sat passive for a minute, just savoring the tender sensations that teased and touched her lips and her tongue as Jimmy nipped and nibbled and caressed her lips and her face.

Slowly, gradually, Jimmy increased the pressure and the intensity of his caress, sliding slowly from tender and gentle to firm and demanding as Holly slowly raised her arms—both of them—and clutched the back of his neck as she opened her mouth to his devouring possession. For long minutes their lips and tongues fought a sensual duel as each sought to renew their connection. All thoughts of the day fled and Holly could only feel and sense the man who was taking over her body and her emotions as surely as he possessed her lips. His arms pulled her closer even as he slid down on the couch and pulled her on top of him.

Her breasts flattened against his chest, her stomach against his and their hips grinding together, the evidence of his need for her poking into her crotch, their legs tangling as Jimmy nestled his knees between hers and propped his feet on the arm of the sofa. "God, you feel wonderful on top of me," Jimmy murmured against her face as he feathered kisses down her cheek and onto her jaw.

He ran his hand down her left arm and the hand that was tightly clutching his shoulder. "It feels so good to have both of your arms wrapped around me. But this—" He reached up and loosened the scrunchie that held her topknot in place. "This has got to go." He laid the scrunchie on the coffee table and ran his fingers through the hair now tumbling around her face. "That's better."

"Hey, I like my topknot," Holly protested weakly as the touch of his fingers running through her hair sent chills down her back.

"So do I, just not right now," Jimmy said as he pulled her head down to his and met her lips again with his own. For long moments they shared long, sweet, drugging kisses, their bodies growing more and more aroused as their hands eagerly explored one another, Holly's hands clutching Jimmy's sides and Jimmy running his hands down the curve of her back and possessively caressing her hips and backside. All rational thought gone, Holly let herself go and gave herself over to the passion flowing between them.

Finally Holly raised her head and looked into Jimmy's eyes with a question in her own. "Are we going to carry this to its logical conclusion?" she asked softly.

"Are you ready to admit that we're meant to be lovers?" Jimmy demanded softly. "Are you ready to admit that our coming together is inevitable?"

"Yes," Holly whispered. "I'm afraid so."

"Then we'll be lovers," Jimmy said as he held Holly away from him and sat up. "But not tonight. Our first time isn't going to be on a night when you're exhausted and emotionally wrung out and my daughter's in the next room. I'm going to Dallas this weekend to talk to a potential contributor while Carrie has a weekend with Grammy in Austin. We can spend the rest of the weekend in Fort Worth. Would you like to make a weekend of it?" He reached up with both hands and held Holly's curtain of hair away from her face. "I want it to be special for you."

"I'd like that," Holly said softly.

Jimmy held her face tenderly between his hands as he gave her a long, lingering kiss ripe with promise. "I'll make you glad you said yes," he promised as he kissed her once again before releasing her and handing her the scrunchie. "It's late and you're tired. Come on and I'll walk you home."

Holly felt no unseen eyes peering her way as Jimmy walked her to her door and gave her one last kiss before disappearing into the gloom. So they were going to take their relationship to another level, she thought pensively. She had to admit that it was inevitable that they would. She had been drawn to him since their first encounter in his office and the attraction had only increased as she had gotten to know him. Under other circumstances she would have been dancing with joy that an intelligent, kind, passionate man like Jimmy Adamcik wanted to make her his own. But Jimmy was a politician, so hell-bent on winning an election that he was capable of allying himself with the devil and compromising his own convictions—and hers—to achieve that goal. And could she accept that? Holly wondered as she pulled her nightgown over her head and pulled back the covers. Could she accept that part of Jimmy Adamcik or would she come to despise him for his willingness to deal?

Chapter Eleven

Holly reached into the small cooler at her feet and pulled out a cold bottle of water. Smiling a little, she opened the bottle and handed it to Jimmy. "Show-off," Jimmy said as he took the bottle from her. "You couldn't have done that before they worked on you."

"Yes, it's been kind of nice to have my hand back," she said as she opened a second bottle. "I still wish I could play the piano again."

Jimmy whipped around a slow-moving eighteen-wheeler. "Have you actually sat down at a keyboard and seen what you can do?"

"Nah, I know I can't play a piano anymore, so why depress myself?" Holly asked. She turned to Jimmy and grinned wickedly. "I would much rather think about all the delectable things you and I are going to do to each other between visits to the shops and museums."

Jimmy laughed out loud. Holly felt a shiver of anticipation arrow from her head to her toes as Jimmy picked up her hand and nuzzled it absently while he effortlessly negotiated the heavy traffic. At the same time she wondered if she and Jimmy were making a colossal mistake. She honestly didn't know whether she would be able to put aside their political differences for the sake of their relationship but at this point she wanted him so badly she was willing to take the risk.

Smiling mysteriously, Jimmy handed Holly an unfamiliar address to key into the GPS and soon they were driving into a nondescript Dallas strip center. *What in the world?* Holly wondered as Jimmy took her hand and practically dragged her down the sidewalk and through the burglar-barred door of a small shop. "I know it doesn't look like much on the outside, but they supposedly have the best selection in the state," Jimmy said as he took a business card from his wallet and asked to speak to a salesperson named Cheryl.

A middle-aged black woman introduced herself and took Holly and Jimmy back into to a large showroom where Holly spotted an array of keyboards set up and plugged in to outlets in the floor. "I've set up some of our better instruments for Miss Riley to try out. I'm sure there's one here that will meet her needs."

"What are you doing?" Holly whispered furiously to Jimmy. "I told you I can't play anymore." She turned to the saleswoman. "I'm not sure what this is about, but I can't play a keyboard anymore," she said tightly. "I've lost much of the use of my left hand."

"So have I," Cheryl said easily as she held up a badly mangled left hand and slid onto a stool behind one of the keyboards. "But I can still play using one of these, and with a little practice you can, too. What kind of keyboarding did you do?"

"All kinds," Holly said, her anger fading and curious skepticism taking its place. She watched in fascination as Cheryl hit a few buttons and launched into a keyboard version of the theme from *Rocky*. She played a few bars before hitting more buttons and going into a jazzy blues number. Holly stepped behind Cheryl and watched her hands, particularly her left, as Cheryl finished off the smoky blues number and changed settings again, this time setting up a marching cadence as she launched into "Battle Hymn of the Republic." Cheryl was doing very little with her left hand, just hitting the key of the chord that she wanted, but the machine filled in so completely that only another musician would realize how much the keyboard was actually doing. Another few flicks of the button and suddenly the majestic swells of "Amazing Grace" filled the showroom.

Holly watched and listened in fascination as Cheryl finished the beloved old hymn and stood up from the stool. "Why don't you sit down and let me show you how to use one of these?" Cheryl said.

Holly sat down and Cheryl took a few minutes to explain what the keyboard was capable of and how to set up the machine. Amazed at the capability of the keyboard, Holly started with pop music before switching the keyboard to a marching cadence and going into the "Aggie War Hymn." The fingers of her right hand flying over the keys, Holly was soon lost in the pure joy of making music with the keyboard. It didn't matter if her left hand couldn't fly like her right one could; it could do enough with the little keyboard's magic that she could play again. And that was all that mattered. She switched into church organ mode and tried "Amazing Grace" herself, tears pouring down her cheeks as she played that beautiful old hymn before launching first into "Trumpet Fanfare" and then "Lohengren." When the last of the notes died out, she looked up and was surprised to see tears in both Cheryl's eyes and Jimmy's. "You were wonderful," Cheryl said admiringly as she handed Holly a tissue.

"My God, I had no idea," Jimmy said. "No wonder you missed it so much." He whipped out his cell phone. "Would you be willing to play for Rory and Lisa now? I'll call her if you are."

Holly smiled and started to nod, but took a look at the price tag and made a face. "It depends on how soon they have the wedding scheduled," she said. "It's going to be months before I can afford this thing." She glanced around at the other keyboards. "Do any of these go for less?"

"Not necessary," Jimmy said as he handed Cheryl a debit card. "My treat. Holly needs the best one she can get."

"Jimmy, you can't possibly buy me that expensive a gift," Holly sputtered. "That keyboard costs a small fortune!"

Cheryl quickly disappeared with the debit card. Jimmy put his arm around Holly. "Holly, I can and I will buy you that keyboard," he said softly as the warmth of his body and the gentleness of his tone effectively stilled her protest. "After all you've done for me and my daughter and those soldiers of yours, you deserve it. Besides, I'm buying a second one for Carrie and I hope you'll start teaching her to use it."

Holly leaned even closer to him. "Put that way, I guess I can't say no," she said as Jimmy placed a soft, gentle kiss on her parted lips. "Go ahead and call Lisa. I would love to play her wedding for her."

Lisa was predictably delighted and Holly promised to get together with her soon to plan the music. Jimmy turned Holly around and put his hands on either side of her face and pulled her toward him. This time his kiss was not gentle; it was firm and possessive, the kiss of a man claiming his woman as his own. Holly's hands— both of them—clutched Jimmy tightly as her body responded to the sensuality and possession of his kiss. Holly clung to Jimmy, her mouth opening to his sensuous assault as he plundered her sweetness. She too was staking a claim, branding Jimmy with the passion of her lips and the promise of her body. "How far did you say that hotel is?" she asked breathlessly when Jimmy finally broke free.

"Too damn far, probably," Jimmy murmured as Cheryl bustled back into the room with the paperwork. Jimmy signed for the two keyboards and they loaded them into the back of the Navigator, covering them with a ratty old quilt. The traffic had not let up any while they were in the music store and Holly laughed out loud at Jimmy's impatience as they crawled down the expressway with the rest of the traffic. "Are you looking forward to working at the school?" he asked suddenly. "Do you think it will replace what you had with the Army?"

"I honestly don't know," she said as she reached over and stroked Jimmy's thigh. "I doubt it. And the only thing I'm really looking forward to right now is getting you in that bed in Fort Worth."

"Shameless hussy," Jimmy teased as her hand crept higher up his leg. "Good lord woman; quit that before I wreck the damn car," he said as Holly's fingers skimmed the juncture of his pants legs, sending a jolt of awareness through his body and causing him to spring to attention under her exploring fingers. "I said *stop that,*" he said as she stroked him intimately through the fabric of his slacks.

"Oh, am I doing something wrong?" Holly asked innocently as her fingers explored his hardening manhood through the silky fabric. "Just practicing with my hand, you know. This is something else I couldn't have done before I had the surgery."

Jimmy groaned and Holly laughed out loud as she gave him one more intimate caress. Thankfully the traffic was thinning out some and before too much longer they found their way into downtown Fort Worth. The slanting rays of the late afternoon sun spilled across the historic old blocks of Sundance Square, dappling the gilded angels outside Bass Hall and bathing the shops and restaurants in a mellow glow in the relaxed ambiance of a warm Friday evening. Holly clutched Jimmy's hand as the clerk made quick work of checking them in, but as they headed to their room Holly's anticipation began to fade and apprehension took its place. What if she was a disappointment to Jimmy? She hadn't made love to a man in a long time, long before she was injured, and she was suddenly afraid the reality of a relationship with her would not be all Jimmy expected it to be.

Jimmy held her hand as they walked into their corner room, almost decadent in its opulence, with crimson drapes and a creamy satin spread. Jimmy dropped their bags and drew Holly into his arms, filling her mouth with a long, deep, possessive kiss that had Holly melting. Oh, please don't let me be a disappointment to him, she thought as Jimmy's caressing hands slid slowly down her back to cup her bottom. She looped her arms around his neck and they clung to one another for long minutes as they made love with their mouths and lips and tongues. Holly could feel Jimmy growing hard, his erection straining against her belly as he pulled her even closer. She moaned and threaded her fingers through his hair, but even the warmth of Jimmy's body and the evidence of his arousal could not quench her growing nervousness.

She sensed the moment that Jimmy picked up on her hesitation. He stepped away slowly and put his finger under her chin, lifting her face and looking into her eyes. "Why do I feel you pulling away from me?"

Holly looked into the warmth of his eyes. "I'm nervous," she said honestly. "I haven't done this since before I got hurt and…well…" She stopped and took a deep breath. "I haven't had all that many lovers, but any time I was with a man I always made it a point to give and not just take. I always made damn sure that he was glad he'd come to the party. And with my arm and my leg bunged up I'm not sure I can do that anymore." She paused and swallowed. "I just don't want to disappoint you."

Jimmy laughed softly and shook his head. "And here I was worrying about disappointing you," he said as he leaned down and kissed her ever so gently on the lips. "I'm out of practice, too, you know. I haven't been with a woman since Lauren got too sick for sex and it was just her for years before that. Holly, there is no way in hell you could disappoint me as a lover. And I'm going to do my best not to disappoint you either. Come here." He pulled her across the room and with a single flick of his arm threw open the drapes. The reds and golds of the slowly setting sun poured into the room and bathed them in a romantic amber glow. "This is the most beautiful time of day," Jimmy whispered as he reached for the buttons on Holly's blouse. "I want to see you naked in the light of sunset."

Holly started to protest, but there were no other buildings around anywhere near this high, and they were so far up from the street that there was no way they could be seen by anyone on the sidewalk. A romantic ambiance enveloped both of them as with trembling fingers Jimmy carefully unbuttoned Holly's lacy blouse and pushed it off her shoulders, baring her to the waist but for a lacy wisp of bra. That went next as Jimmy deftly undid the tiny front hook holding the bra to her body, freeing her pink-tipped breasts to the golden light. Holly reached down for her skirt but Jimmy pushed her hands away, unhooking the clasp and lowering the zipper himself, pushing both the skirt and the silk half-slip to the floor, leaving Holly clad only in a lacy thong that did nothing to cover her feminine charms. Sensing that Jimmy wanted to finish unclothing her himself, Holly waited patiently until he had looked his fill. She felt surprisingly wanton as his fingers skimmed the lacy scrap down her legs and off her body, leaving her completely bare in the evening sunlight. "Sweet, so sweet," Jimmy said as he gazed at her womanly curves. "You have your figure back. You were way too thin when I met you."

Holly looked down and shrugged. "I guess Combat Barbie's back after all."

"Yeah," Jimmy said, grinning wickedly as he swiftly unbuttoned his dress shirt. "Combat Barbie. Does things to those DCUs that has the sergeants snapping to all kinds of attention and—oof, what was that for?" he laughed when Holly grabbed a pillow off the bed and whacked him with it.

"Shut up, Combat Ken, and get your clothes off," Holly demanded as she whacked him again with the pillow.

"I'm hurrying, I'm hurrying," Jimmy laughed. He shrugged out of his shirt and practically ripped his undershirt and slacks from his body and kicked out of his shoes. He hesitated for a moment before turning slightly away from Holly and shedding his boxers. Jimmy shy? Holly wondered as his hip hid his full nudity, but then he turned back around and Holly stared with stunned admiration as Jimmy blushed furiously.

"Oh. My. God," Holly breathed as she took in the sight of Jimmy fully aroused. "That's—you have to be—oh, for crying out loud, quit blushing. Just because God loves you more than any other man on the planet."

Jimmy turned even redder. "You're staring."

Holly reached out and pulled him into the sunlight. "So? You stared at me, didn't you? So I get to stare at you. And believe me, you're worth staring at." She reached out and encased Jimmy's erection in her hand. "I get to stare at you and I get to touch you and

I get to kiss you and I get to make you glad you came to the party. That work for you?"

"Absolutely," Jimmy breathed as he grew even larger and harder in Holly's hand. "I want you so bad I can taste it." He reached for his suitcase on the floor. "Let me get some protection."

"I'm on the pill, and considering the lively sex lives we've been enjoying I seriously doubt we have anything else to worry about," Holly observed. "Don't worry about it. Besides, I doubt they make one big enough anyway."

Jimmy blushed again. "Aw, and here I was trying to make like a Boy Scout and be prepared," he teased. "So bare it is."

The romantic spell was long broken, but something stronger and more powerful had taken its place. Desire, raw and animal, surged from Jimmy to Holly and back as he hoisted Holly up and carried her to the bed, where he deposited her unceremoniously in the middle before following her down and covering her naked body with his. Holly arched into Jimmy's body, his magnificent erection surging against her as Jimmy rained kisses down her face and throat, his powerful arms wrapping her tightly against him as he lowered his head and explored one rose-tipped breast, then the other. Holly ran her hands down the length of Jimmy's back and onto his backside, where she touched and stroked him intimately, the muscles of his butt flexing under her caress. Jimmy's lips drifted lower, down to her belly, where he tickled her belly button with his tongue, and even lower, finding first the nest of auburn curls and then the sweetness within.

Holly arched and nearly came up off the bed when he found the core of her sexuality and caressed it intimately with his tongue. "Good God," she breathed as she clutched desperately at the brass bars on the headboard. "Just do it, Jimmy," she pleaded as he drove her upwards, the culminating delight swirling just out of reach. "I want you inside of me when I come."

"Shh; I'm right where I need to be," Jimmy said hoarsely as he continued to torture her with his lips and his tongue. Holly could feel herself climbing higher, a misty haze blocking out everything but the sensations rocking her as Jimmy worked his magic. She cried out as the crest broke over her, spasms of pleasure and release tearing through her body, wave after wave of unimaginable delight as the powerful orgasm tore through her body and left her trembling. Her breathing ragged, Holly gasped for oxygen as Jimmy raised his head and covered her mouth with his. She could taste herself on his lips as he positioned himself and gently parted the folds of her body with his. In contrast to his earlier passion, his entry was slow and gentle as he inch by inch filled her in a way that she had never been filled before, hesitant even as he carefully fitted their bodies together. "I just wanted to be sure I didn't hurt you," he explained when Holly looked at him with a question in her eyes. "That's why I made sure you'd already come once. I had to be sure you were ready for me."

Holly framed his face in her hands and pulled his lips down for a lingering kiss. "I can see why you're careful, but you feel great and I'm not made of spun sugar. Make me glad I came to the party. And I'll make you glad, too." She tightened the muscles of her vagina and fit her sheath even closer around him. Jimmy's eyes widened as the muscles of her stomach and pelvis and feminine channel stroked his penis, alternately tightening and loosening the pressure on him, stimulating his already aroused manhood until he was straining to hold on. Slowly at first, and then with more force, Jimmy began to move over Holly, matching his rhythm to hers as she worked her magic and he worked his. Holly felt herself spiraling upward again, reaching again for the pinnacle as they moved together in tandem, her body on fire as passion, hot and untamed, caught both her and Jimmy in is whirling vortex and spun them wildly. Out of control, Holly moved instinctively, her earlier deliberate movements giving way to a primal response that was neither deliberate nor calculated as Jimmy responded in kind and the two of them spiraled together into a spinning, dizzying pinnacle that seemed to go on forever as spasms of pleasure tore through the two of them, leaving them gasping together in a silken, sensual haze. Jimmy carefully rolled Holly to her side and they lay together side by side, spent, and still joined together as the fiery red sun dipped below the horizon, its final rays bathing them in their sated post-coital exhaustion.

Jimmy kissed her tenderly as he gave in to a soft chuckle. "And you were worried about disappointing me," he said as he feathered gentle kisses down her jawline. "That's almost funny, Holly," he added as he nibbled her ear. "You were so worried about your arm and your leg when you can do whatever that was that you were doing. Where in the hell did you learn to do that, anyway?"

"Would you believe I learned to do *that* in a human sexuality course I took in college?" Holly said. She ran her hand through the thick hair on Jimmy's chest and pulled away from him, sitting up cross-legged and staring down at the body of the man who had just made her own body sing. Even relaxed as he now was, he would be the envy of the locker room, with not an ounce of fat anywhere on his lean, rangy body, well-muscled arms and legs and thick dark chest hair arrowing down his stomach to flare again around that oh-so-magnificent penis. "You," Holly said as she leaned down and planted a kiss in the middle of Jimmy's chest, "are something else." She let her lips crawl lower, down his chest to his stomach, where she drew circles around his navel with her tongue, and as his penis showed signs of stirring she let her lips drift further downward. "Wanna find out what else I learned in that college course?" she asked, grinning wickedly, as she nibbled up the side of his now fully aroused organ and took the tip of his penis into her mouth.

"Absolutely," Jimmy said, almost coming off the bed as Holly took him into her moist pink mouth and started to work some more of her magic on him. He gasped as the pressure built from Holly's ministrations, his body shrouded from view as Holly's auburn hair cascaded around her head and onto his stomach, its erotic touch further fueling his arousal as she worked with her lips and tongue until Jimmy felt himself exploding from her touch, his second orgasm no less satisfying than his first. His passion slaked for the moment, Jimmy pulled Holly back down to the bed and again spread her legs, his fingers and lips assaulting her femininity until she was again whimpering with pleasure as a third orgasm ripped through her body, leaving her boneless as she lay on top of the satin bedspread they had never pulled back. Jimmy slid down beside her and took her hand in his. They lay still beside one another, for the moment spent, as their intense passion gave way to a satisfied glow.

Now that her hunger for Jimmy had been filled, Holly realized that she was hungry for a meal when her stomach rumbled loudly. "Shall I call for room service, or do you want to go down and see what we can find to eat?" Jimmy asked.

Holly jackknifed from the bed and peered out the window. The western sky was left with only the purple glow of a long-faded sunset and below them the neon lights of the shops and restaurants shone with a lively ambiance that promised an evening to remember.

"It looks like a lot of fun down there," she said as she reached for her overnight case. "I can be ready in fifteen minutes."

They found a wonderful Cajun restaurant on the Square, where they ate etouffee and dirty rice and a spicy gumbo that had Holly's eyes watering. Jimmy's expression was relaxed, satisfied even, and Holly knew she probably looked the same way. It wouldn't take a genius to look at the two of them together and figure out how they had spent most of the early evening. And Holly didn't care. She was happy, truly happy for the first time in a long time, and if wild sex with Jimmy was what it took to get her there she didn't mind looking the part. And she made Jimmy happy, too. All she had to do was look across the table.

They wandered around the square, poking into the occasional shop that was still open and finishing the evening with ice cream cones before going back to their hotel room for another spirited bout of lovemaking. Finally spent, they curled up together and Jimmy quickly drifted off to sleep, his even breathing segueing into a soft, comforting snore.

Holly snuggled up under his arm and stared out the window at the not-quite-full moon suspended in the inky sky. Just where were she and Jimmy headed from here? What they had was not just a casual fling or an accidental or spontaneous coming together of two people in the grip of lust. They had, in spite of the very real issues that separated them, chosen to become lovers, and Holly was glad. But she had to wonder if the sex, wonderful as it was, would be enough to bridge the very real chasm that still separated the two of them.

* * *

Jimmy sighed as he glanced over at Holly's tight features as she stared sightlessly out the passenger-side window of the Navigator. He was sorry that their weekend together was ending on a sour note, especially since the rest of it had been so wonderful. They had spent Saturday visiting the museums and shops in downtown Fort Worth and finished the day eating barbeque and boot-scootin' at the historic Stockyards, and he had lost count of how many times they'd come together as lovers. But this morning reality intruded in the form of political supporters Cyrus and Shirley Atkins. After an hour in their company Holly was furious and Jimmy could see why. Holly, thankfully, had kept her displeasure hidden, especially considering the size of the contribution check in his front pocket, but once the Atkins's front door was closed Holly shot him the mother of all go-to-hell looks and hadn't said anything since.

"I know you're pissed," he said tightly as he gunned the Navigator onto the expressway. "And I do appreciate you not letting on in front of the Atkins."

"God damn them and God damn the rest of the greedy bastards like them out there!" Holly exploded. "Did you hear them, Jimmy? School kids are 'a problem' and wounded warriors are 'fat old soldiers too lazy to work'? I wonder how that arrogant bastard would feel if somebody blew off his leg or burned off forty percent of his skin." She turned tear-filled eyes on Jimmy. "Couldn't you at least have defended the veterans, Jimmy? Couldn't you have done at least that much?"

"And piss off a man who's ready to contribute and contribute big to my campaign coffers?" Jimmy snapped. "Damn it, Holly, Atkins just wrote me a check for the legal limit on a campaign contribution! What was I supposed to say? 'Mr. Atkins, you're full of shit about the veterans but hey, I'd still like your money'? Holly, get real. You've seen Navarro in action and you know I need money and lots of it if I'm going to win this." Jimmy could feel his jaw tighten and his teeth grind together.

"Forgive me. My bad," Holly said tonelessly as she stared straight ahead at the teeming Dallas traffic. "I thought—I hoped—oh, hell, never mind."

"Never mind what?" Jimmy demanded. "I was supposed to change my mind and start championing your cause just because we spent the weekend together? That wasn't on the table and you knew it. If you felt that way you never should have come with me this weekend."

"Believe me, I know that," Holly said hotly. "I honestly thought I could keep it separate. I guess I can't. But it's partly your fault, too, you know."

"My fault? How the hell is it my fault? I didn't lie to you and tell you I'd change my mind, did I? And I sure didn't kidnap you and throw you in the car. You made a deliberate decision to go to bed with me."

"But you kept pushing. You said it was inevitable!" Holly snapped back.

"Because, damn it, I thought it was," Jimmy ground out. "I still think it is, if you would get off your soapbox for just a couple of minutes and try to see things from my point of view. You know, the one where I'm trying to raise the money to conduct a congressional campaign?"

"Have you ever thought about trying to see things from my point of view?" Holly shot back. "You know, the one where I'm trying to improve the lives of injured veterans and those veterans and I could use some political support? Besides, it's going to look a little funny if you don't, with a wounded war hero for a girlfriend."

"Nadine has a wounded war hero for a daughter and she doesn't support your cause," Jimmy pointed out.

Holly shrugged. "I'm used to her callousness. I guess I was hoping for better from you."

Jimmy was gathering his thoughts when his cell phone rang and Holly's rang an instant later. Holly opened hers and was surprised to see Rory Keller's number. "Rory, what's up?"

"You and Jimmy need to get back to Verde *now*," Rory said without preamble. "Somebody's posted a video of Armando Fuentes's burning house on Jimmy's website using Jimmy's log-in with a message that Jimmy and his lady friend had better watch their backs. Jack Briscoe and I are already here at the campaign headquarters and the FBI's on their way."

"*What in the holy hell?*" Holly said. She looked over at Jimmy and from the horrified expression on his face she realized that someone, probably Jack Briscoe, was delivering the same message to him. "We're heading back now, Rory," she said quietly. "We'll be there as quickly as we can." Holly snapped her phone shut and waited for Jimmy to do the same.

He spoke softly, obviously giving instructions to whoever was on the line with him, and when he was finished dropped the phone in his pocket. "Son of a bitch," he said dully as he glanced over at Holly. "I gather you just got the same news?" Holly nodded. "I told Jack to get hold of the hosting provider and tell them to take down the damned video. I also told him not to make the Feds wait for a warrant. Misty's going to have a statement ready by the time I get there."

Jimmy drove quietly for a minute before stomping on the gas and letting loose with a string of curse words that shocked even Holly. "Damn it, swear if you want to but slow down!" Holly snapped. "I'd like to get home in one piece."

"Yeah, right," Jimmy said. But he eased up on the gas and looked over at Holly. "I guess we could go back to our argument if you want to, but I'm afraid we both have bigger problems this afternoon than the damn campaign."

"You got that right," Holly admitted as she reached in her bag and got out her sunglasses. "But just because we have a bigger problem right now, that doesn't mean the other's going away."

They made the trip in record time. Jimmy tried to talk to Holly a couple of times but she was uncharacteristically uncommunicative and he could only suppose that she was still angry with him. Or was she quiet because she was frightened? Jimmy glanced over at her and found her staring sightlessly out the window.

The parking lot of Jimmy's campaign headquarters was almost full. Jimmy parked in between two unmarked sedans and he and Holly made their way into the controlled chaos of his normally orderly campaign offices. There was an FBI technician sitting at every one of the desktops, their fingers flying over the keys as they plumbed the mysteries of whatever had been done on the machines.

Jack and Misty and Rory were huddled in one corner talking to an older agent that Jimmy, to his surprise, recognized, and in the other corner Betty Cleburne and Lisa Simmons were seated at a desk with Sheriff Waller. Jimmy took Holly's hand and steered her toward Jack and Misty. "It's good to see you again, Agent Russo," he said as he shook the agent's hand. "Just not under these circumstances." Joe Russo was the FBI agent who had diligently worked to find Ryan Briscoe after he had been kidnapped from Caroline and her late husband Aaron and Jimmy had immense respect for the man.. Jimmy quickly introduced Holly. "Okay, let me see what was posted."

"It's up on that machine over there," Misty said with a shudder.

Jimmy pulled up a second chair for Holly and sat down in front of the desktop. They stared in silence at the video of Armando and Inez's pretty little house being blown to smithereens, the glass in the windows flying outward and spewing flames, with smoke coming through the roof.

The Adamcik for Congress sign had been placed far enough out in the yard that it would not be damaged by the explosion, but was prominently visible in the video. At the bottom of the video a stark message had been posted—"Adamcik—Chucky says you and your lady friend need to watch your backs."

"Who the hell is 'Chucky'?" Jimmy asked. "I don't know anybody who goes by that."

"Whoever Chucky is, he did a good job of the bombing," Holly said thoughtfully.

Jimmy looked at her and then at Russo. "Yes, it does look professional," Russo said quietly. "Probably ex-military. And the placing of the sign says it all."

Jimmy looked up at the ring of concerned faces surrounding him. "It's me, isn't it?" He ran his hand down the side of his face. "Holly isn't the ultimate target. It's me. And it's somebody with ties to my congressional campaign."

Rory nodded. "I'm sorry, Jimmy, but that's sure what it looks like."

Holly looked at Jimmy and shook her head. "Well, Jimmy Adamcik, ain't this your lucky day."

Chapter Twelve

Jimmy left his luggage in the foyer and stumbled tiredly into the kitchen to make himself a sandwich. It was after ten and he hadn't had a bite to eat since breakfast, but the sandwich tasted dry in his mouth and he gave up after a few bites and poured himself a little Scotch instead, mentally thanking his mother for offering to keep Carrie for another night.

He had given Misty's prepared statement to the reporters and answered a few questions. He then spent hours with Joe Russo and Sheriff Waller as they questioned him thoroughly, trying to pinpoint someone who had both an axe to grind with him and ties to his congressional campaign. He answered their questions while his mind tried to wrap itself around the fact that someone close enough to the campaign to gain access to his log-in bore him that much ill will, but try as he might Jimmy could think of no one who should have been that angry with him. But someone was, and, for the life of him, Jimmy had no idea who. The techs finally determined that the posting had not been made at any of the computers there in the building, and maybe when they figured out where it had been posted the Feds would have some clue.

Jimmy propped his feet on his deck railing and stared out at the moon-dappled waves as he sipped the Scotch. It had been a real bitch of a day in spite of waking up with Holly Riley in his arms. And it would be a miracle if that happened again anytime soon, he thought bitterly as he stared down the way at her darkened windows. She had not been at the campaign headquarters when Russo finally finished questioning him. Betty Cleburne said she caught a ride back to the Point with Lisa Simmons. The keyboard was still in the back of the Navigator but he loathed using it as an excuse to see her again today. He'd give it to her sometime in the upcoming week.

Had they made a mistake in becoming lovers? And what kind of danger was she in from the lunatic who was out to get them? Jimmy tossed back another mouthful of Scotch as he remembered the vivid images of the exploding Fuentes house. Even though Jimmy knew he was the ultimate target, the bomber had threatened Holly as well. She already felt like she was being watched and it would be a short leap from watching to doing something to her. But why? Why was his tormenter out to get Holly, too?

Jimmy rubbed the back of his neck as his mind wandered to the sensual intimacies he and Holly had shared during the lovemaking marathon in Fort Worth and he could feel himself growing hard again, just the memory of her sensual caress enough to send the blood flooding to his loins. Cursing his unwanted arousal, he slammed the whiskey tumbler down and stalked to the sliding doors just in time to hear his ringing cell. He started to let it go to voice mail but picked up the phone and cursed to see Nadine's number on the screen. "Hello, Nadine," he said quietly. "What can I do for you?"

"You can tell me what in the hell you're doing to disassociate yourself from that damned video," Nadine demanded. "Purcell called me, he's furious and demanding to know what kind of damage control you're doing."

"Obviously we took it off the Internet," Jimmy said. "And I've already issued a statement. I don't know what more Reynolds expects."

"He expects that the money we're pouring into your campaign isn't wasted because of that video," Nadine said.

"That video is a direct threat to your daughter," Jimmy reminded her. "I did what I could, Nadine, but to tell you the truth I'm more worried about your daughter's safety right now than I am campaign funding and I would think you and Reynolds would be, too."

"Of course I'm worried about her," Nadine said indignantly. "But I'm also concerned about the impact this is going to have on your campaign and I think I have every right to be."

Jimmy took a deep breath and hoped his distaste didn't show. "I'm concerned, too, Nadine," he said. "The Feds and the locals are investigating, and I think the wisest thing I can do is to continue campaigning and raising money. By the way, Cyrus and Shirley Atkins certainly bestowed this morning."

Jimmy could almost hear Nadine perk up on her end. "Well, I figured they would. And if you can get this other issue handled, there will be more contributions like theirs coming your way. I need to go. Have a nice evening."

Sheesh, Jimmy thought as he upended the rest of the Scotch. Talk about *cold*. An innocent family's house was blown up and her own daughter publicly threatened on the Internet and all Nadine and her cronies were worried about was whether their campaign contributions were being wasted. What a bunch, he thought as he trudged up the stairs. No wonder Holly had tried to discourage him from taking their help. He thought of the check Cyrus Atkins had written and it was all he could do not to groan out loud. He had made a deal with them and now they expected him to deliver, and by God he had better do so if he wanted the money to keep on coming.

* * *

He was in Baghdad, running toward the little boy with the explosives strapped to his body, his heart pounding in his throat as he saw Holly and Jason running toward the child. "No, get back, it's a trap!" he yelled, but Holly and Jason kept moving and there was no way he was going to get to them in time. He raised his rifle and took aim at the man with the detonator. Jimmy emptied his rifle into the Iraqi but it did no good; the insurgent pushed the button and Holly and Jason were blown backwards into the street, their faces and arms on fire as they screamed in agony. "No, oh God no!" Jimmy cried as he ran toward their smoking bodies, the seared flesh on their faces blistering and charred.

He ignored the stench of burning skin and hair as he swept Holly into his arms and looked into her ruined features. "You're too late," she wheezed through her mangled throat as Nadine, not Holly, looked up at him. "You're always too late…"

Jimmy bolted upright in the bed, drenched in sweat and trembling from head to foot. He turned on his side and curled himself into the fetal position and lay still for long minutes until he could get the terror and the shaking under control. Should he go in the bathroom and take the tranquilizers Dr. Jacobsen had given him? He slowly raised himself up on one elbow and squinted at the alarm clock and uttered a muffled curse. It was already after four—too late in the night for a pill. Moving like an old man, he raised himself to a sitting position and found the remnants of a pack of cigarettes. As much as he hated to smoke in the house, nicotine was about the only comfort available to him right now.

Or would Holly come if he called her? His shaking fingers hovered over his cell phone. But no, he thought as he reached instead for the lighter. He wasn't going to wake her up at four in the morning because he'd had another dream—no, another PTSD episode. Dr. Jacobsen had stressed that he had to be honest and admit, at least to himself, that he indeed did suffer from PTSD.

So okay, he'd had another dream? Flashback? Jimmy was not sure what to call it and didn't really care. All that mattered was that he had been back in his own private hell. And it didn't take a psychiatrist to decipher the message in that one, he thought as he sucked greedily on the cigarette. He had been too late to save Jason Donahue and Patrick Barnes in Baghdad. It was too late to get out of the arrangement he'd agreed to with Nadine and her cronies. And unless he was very, very lucky, it was about to be too late for his relationship with Holly Riley.

* * *

Chucky sat at the computer in his bedroom and stared at the downloaded images of the blazing Fuentes house and the message to Adamcik. It was down now, he thought as he studied the picture. No matter. He had known when he posted it that the Adamcik campaign would get it removed, but at least there had been time for him to make it home from that nice little anonymous Internet café and download them onto his own laptop. Nice touch, using Adamcik's log-in to post them; Betty Cleburne really was a careless idiot, leaving the door to the back office open all the time. Bet they change the log-in, Chucky thought. That was okay. He had gotten this one and he would get the next one, and the one after that, and keep on getting them as long as he needed them. Because he had every intention of committing more mayhem, and he intended to post pictures every time. Payback's a bitch, isn't it, Adamcik? And Adamcik deserved every bit of the payback Chucky could deliver.

Chucky hummed tunelessly as he sipped his rapidly cooling coffee and watched as the light filtering in the sheer drapes went from gray to pink. He had known better than to try to sleep last night. He was high, not on drugs but on the sheer delight in the blow he had struck. A discreet drive by headquarters yesterday afternoon revealed a parking lot full of cars and a beehive of activity inside, and he could only imagine the horror and the consternation as the Feds and the locals tried in vain to figure out just who their bad boy was. But they wouldn't figure it out this time, and they wouldn't figure it out next time, or the time after that, or the time after that. And that made him so happy. Chucky laughed out loud, the sound maniacal even to his own ears, delighted with the mayhem his little posting had caused Jimmy and Holly and looking forward to the next few weeks and months.

Holly pulled her new Harley into the teacher's parking lot of Regional High School and found the freshly painted parking space labeled "JROTC Instructor." Nice little perk, she thought as she took her backpack and her lunch koozie out of the saddle bag. As she replaced her helmet with her beret and headed toward the main building she wondered for the thousandth time if she was going to be able to live up to the expectations of Jack Briscoe and her students. Yes, she had done plenty of teaching in the Army but this was different, and all the reassurance from Jack and her fellow teachers hadn't convinced her she was going to be all that good at teaching. Still, it felt good to be back in her DCUs and even better to have a job to get up and go to.

Especially since the affair she had started with Jimmy appeared to be dead in the water. She had not seen him but once since the disastrous Sunday when everything had fallen apart for them, and even then he had dropped off the keyboard and left before they had a chance to talk. He was avoiding her and maybe that was a good thing, since all they were likely to do if they did get together was continue their argument. She had spent several long sleepless nights trying to put herself in Jimmy's place but her feelings were still bruised by what she felt was his betrayal, and the threat to her had her checking her doors every half hour and peeking out the curtains and looking over her shoulder. So far her spidey sense hadn't picked up anything amiss but she was still tense and troubled, because there was no way their tormenter was through with his campaign of terror, and she was terrified of what—or who—was next.

Holly was about to take the wide hall that led to the main office when she heard angry voices and a scream coming from a side hall. "Stop it, Markie! It's none of your business!" Doesn't sound good, she thought as she rounded the corner as fast as she could and found a tight cluster of students surrounding a pair of furious-looking boys about to square off and a girl trying to push them apart. Holly glanced around at the kids and groaned inwardly; far from getting any help with this from the kids they were actually egging the boys on, with calls of "Go for it, Markie!" and "Clean his clock, Gabe!"

The only other teacher in sight was a small, very pregnant math teacher who had out her cell phone. Holly's instincts took over and she elbowed her way through the gathering crowd, reaching the boys as the larger of the two made a fist and took an angry swing at the smaller. Calling on long-ago skills she thought she had forgotten, she lowered her head and rammed herself full-force into the larger boy, knocking him into the crowd. She followed him down and took advantage of his surprise and disorientation to whip him over on his stomach and wrench one of his arms backwards until he was immobile. She plopped herself down on his squirming backside and whirled around to face the other combatant, who was coming toward them with his fists raised. Holly reached out with her bad leg and caught his feet, sending him sprawling face-down in the floor. Pain wrenched through her knee but the look of stupefaction on the smaller boy's face was worth it. "Don't even think it," she said evenly as he tried to get to his feet. "I kill."

The boy stared at her as he stumbled backward and landed on his butt. Jack Briscoe reached in, his face grim but his eyes dancing as he took sight of Holly and the boys. He hauled the smaller boy to his feet and handed him over to the vice principal. He held out his hand to Holly, who winced as she put weight on her bad leg. "Are you all right, Captain Riley?" he asked in front of the students.

Holly put on her best professional voice. "Yes, Mr. Briscoe. Army hand-to-hand is useful at times."

Jack reached out and pulled the larger boy to his feet. He turned to Holly. "Thank you so much, Captain Riley. I'll need a referral written on this before you go back to your classroom." He leaned in closer so as not to be heard. "That was seriously something else. I can just see the crowd in the counselor's office signing up for ROTC. Welcome to Regional, Holly."

* * *

Cathy peered at herself closely in the mirror. "My God, Angie, I don't believe it," she whispered as she reached up and gently touched her cheek. "I look like me again."

Angie smiled proudly as she took Cathy's chin and gently turned her face first one way and then the other. "It does look good, doesn't it?"

Holly leaned against the wall, trying to take some of the weight off her aching leg, and beamed happily at the two of them. "You look wonderful, Cathy," she said as she peered critically at Cathy's artfully made-up face. "Angie's outdone herself. You can hardly see any scarring at all with Angie's magic at work."

"That's it!" Angie said as she dropped Cathy's chin and turned around and gave Holly a huge hug. "That's how I'll sell it. 'Angie's Magic.'"

"'Angie's Miracle' might be more like it," Cathy said. "My God, how can I ever thank you?"

"You can wear it every day and tell everybody who put it together for you," Angie said. "And that I do custom formulas." She turned to Holly. "And you can remind them that I do a sheer foundation for those of you who are already gorgeous."

"I sing your praises often," Holly said honestly. "You got another stool? My leg's killing me."

"Sure." Angie pulled out another and Holly sank down gratefully. "How's it going at Regional?"

"Would you believe that fighting a war was less strenuous?" Holly said tiredly. "I was out in the hot sun for most of the day trying to teach them to march in formation. I swear half the kids in Verde have two left feet."

"Scuttlebutt I've heard says that she's good and the kids love it," Cathy volunteered. "Win-win for everybody." She glanced toward the door. "Has the midnight stalker come back?"

Holly shrugged. "Not as far as I know," Angie said. "I haven't heard or seen anything lately."

"But it still has me scared," Holly admitted.

"But not scared enough to disband the support group?" Angie asked.

"Hell, no," Holly and Cathy said in unison. "In fact, we have a meeting tonight," Holly added.

The mood that evening in Holly's living room was cheery in spite of the cloud hanging over the little group's heads. The men greeted Cathy with good-natured wolf whistles and playful passes and Beto couldn't seem to keep his eyes off the glowing young woman. Hal said that he had another dog lined up and Armando said that his house rebuild was finally getting started and that the rental they were living in wasn't too bad. Tommy Joe shyly showed the group a picture taken at Duncan Royal's ranch of himself astride a pretty roan mare. Holly reminded them all that they were still targets and that they needed to watch their backs. "We need to think about what we can do to protect ourselves from this monster. Any ideas?"

Beto shrugged. "I'm armed and you all should be."

"I'm applying for a right to carry permit tomorrow," Cathy said.

"I have mine already," Tommy Joe volunteered. "I just haven't been carrying a gun."

"Well, if I were you I'd start," Otis said. He pulled a small Beretta out of his pocket.

"S-sweet," Hal said. "J-just not my choice." He unearthed a wicked-looking Bowie knife from his boot.

"I'm putting in the security system from hell," Armando said.

"Looks like I'm the one who needs to catch up," Holly said. "So let's everybody by the next meeting have a right-to-carry permit and a decent security system. And we all need to be a little more diligent about our privacy, like being careful what we put on Facebook and Twitter about our comings and goings."

"The Feds think it was a Facebook post that tipped him off we'd be gone that afternoon," Armando added.

"Ouch," Tommy Joe murmured.

"But a big part of the problem as I see it is that the authorities still don't have a clue as to who is doing this or why," Holly said. "All we really know is that it's somebody who has enough of a connection to Jimmy's campaign to get their hands on his log-in."

"Speaking of, how goes the campaign?" Beto asked. "Other than the pictures on the Internet I haven't been keeping up."

Holly shrugged. "It's going. Jimmy's finally beginning to raise enough money to pay for a campaign."

"I heard your mama and her buddies are helping him," Otis said.

"That would be correct," Holly admitted. "No sin in that."

"Well, I for one am just as interested in how things are going with Alex Navarro," Tommy said. "He seems to have a lot of ideas about things that could help us."

"Uh, is that really necessary?" Holly asked quickly. "You've known Jimmy Adamcik all your life."

"We-we don't need to t-talk to anybody else," Hal said. "J-Jimmy's our c-candidate."

"According to his website, Navarro has some mighty fine ideas," Otis popped up.

Holly rolled her eyes. "All political candidates have mighty fine ideas when they're in the middle of a campaign," she said cynically. "The question is what they do with them once they're elected."

"Still doesn't hurt to look into things," Otis said mildly.

"We-We don't need to d-do that," Hal protested. "J-Jimmy's our man."

"Yours, maybe," Beto said. "I'd like to talk to both of them."

"That's a good idea. Why don't you set up something, Holly?" Armando suggested. "Invite them each to a support group meeting. Let us ask them some questions."

"I'd like that," Cathy volunteered. "I know Jimmy would do it. Can we get in touch with Alex Navarro and invite him also?"

"I'm sure we could," Holly said slowly, ignoring the sinking feeling in her gut. "If you're sure you want to."

"Why wouldn't we want to?" Tommy asked.

Because one of the candidates is my erstwhile lover? "No reason. I'll take care of it," Holly said. "I'll ask them to come on separate nights. Extra meeting okay with everybody?"

The group was good with the extra meeting and Holly made a note to herself to contact both campaigns. The topic of the election did not come up again and it was only after the last of the group left that Cathy brought up the campaign. "Well, are you going to call the Navarro campaign and ask him to come?" Cathy asked as she wiped off the kitchen table with a wet rag.

"Don't have much choice, do I?" Holly said shortly. "They asked me to invite him and I said I would."

"Way I see it is that you do have a choice," Cathy said frankly. "You could just tell them you spent the weekend in Dallas with Jimmy and that you aren't going to invite your lover's rival to the meeting."

Holly made a face. "What lover? After the fight we had on the way home and then the Internet fiasco it isn't like he's come through my door since."

"What did you fight about?" Cathy asked.

Holly and Cathy sat down at the table and Holly gave her a rundown of their meeting with the Atkinses. "My bad," she admitted. "I guess I naively expected him to come around to my way of thinking just because we were lovers. He hasn't and he isn't going to."

Cathy drummed a finger on the kitchen table. "I hate to say this, Holly, but of the two of them Jimmy may not be our best bet. It sounds like Alex Navarro may be a whole lot better choice for looking out for the needs of veterans, wounded ones in particular."

"But...but—"

"No, hear me out," Cathy persisted. "Jimmy has made it clear to you that he's not going to let his relationship with you change his political position one iota or jeopardize one penny of potential campaign contributions. You're going to have to do the same, Holly. You can't let your love life interfere in what's best for us."

"Just like that?" Holly asked.

"Yes, just like that. Holly, don't you think you at least ought to hear what Alex Navarro has to say about the needs of veterans? Don't you think you owe it to us—and to yourself—to find out if he just might be better for us in Congress than Jimmy would?"

"Yes," Holly agreed slowly. "I owe it to all of us, don't I?"

Chapter Thirteen

Jimmy leaned on the doorframe and watched Joe Russo pull out of the campaign headquarters parking lot. The Feds had zero, zilch, nada, and although they promised they would figure it out, Jimmy wasn't sure it would be soon enough to save his campaign. And the bastard had threatened both him and Holly, and after the bombing of the Fuenteses' house he had to admit that the threat this Chucky posed was not an idle one. He stifled a curse and walked back through headquarters, where a few volunteers addressed 'Meet the Candidate' postcards and ran them through a postal meter. He wondered how much the postcards were costing and if enough potential voters would show up at the scheduled town hall meetings to justify the cost, but Misty insisted that he needed to start pitching his case to the voters and not just Nadine's moneyed contributors.

And he was going to start that tonight, with an in-depth meeting of the minds with Holly's support group. Holly had called him a couple of days ago and asked if he would sit down with her soldiers for a question-and-answer session. While the votes of a tiny group of financially strapped injured veterans might not seem important to a campaign the size of this one, Jimmy knew that the little group had a whole lot of sympathy and support in the community and that they could sway any number of other voters, so tonight mattered. But so did the money, he thought as he went over the financial statement Jack had left him. There was money coming in all right, but not as much as he needed and almost every bit of it from Nadine's contacts. Damn it, Jimmy thought as he balled up the printout and threw it at the wall. He was becoming more and more indebted to that bunch check by check..

He decided to call it a day and was loading his briefcase when his cell phone rang. He looked down at the screen and sighed inwardly. "What can I do for you, Nadine?" he asked as he continued to one-handedly load up the briefcase.

"I hear that you're meeting with Holly and her group this evening," she said without preamble. "I understand that you need to sit down with them, Jimmy, but for God's sake be damned careful what you say."

"What do you suggest, Nadine? Holly's soldier friends aren't stupid and know a meaningless platitude when they hear one. Navarro's promising the stars and the moon, and if I can't come up with something concrete they're going to throw their support to him."

"Yes, and if you make any expensive-sounding promises that get back to Purcell and the others you can kiss what money you're getting good-bye," Nadine shot back. "Look, Jimmy, you're a politician. You can think of something. And besides, you have Holly in your corner, don't you?"

"I honestly don't know if I do or not, Nadine."

"So take her back to bed!" Nadine snapped.

Jimmy laughed in spite of himself. "Think that will do it?"

"She's a woman and you're hot. Of course it will work." Nadine laughed, too. "But seriously, Jimmy, don't say something that will end up biting you in the butt. Purcell and his friends were fried over the Internet postings and they're nervous enough to pull the plug and we don't want that."

"No, Nadine," Jimmy said tiredly. "We don't want that."

* * *

Holly cut the crusts off the last of the finger sandwiches. "That hand of yours is doing a lot better job these days," Cathy said as she loaded a filter into Holly's coffee machine.

"So's yours," Holly said as she carried the crystal plate loaded with sandwiches to the dining table. "You're finally mastering the fake."

"And with my face back I guess I'm good to go," Cathy said as she opened a pack of napkins. "I owe Angie a big one for the makeup, and her scrunchies aren't bad either."

"So what's next? A new fella?"

Instead of laughing Cathy looked a little embarrassed. "I caught Beto looking at me a couple of times at the last meeting," she said. "Do you think he would be interested?"

"Don't know why not," Holly said. "He's hot and single; you're hot and single."

"And there are some things he would understand," Cathy said softly.

"Yes, there are but you'd have other things in common as well. Like hot monkey sex."

"You mean like you and Jimmy?" Cathy asked slyly.

Holly snorted in disgust. "I hope to hell you can do better than we are," she said. "He still hasn't come back around."

"And neither have you," Cathy pointed out. "So what are you going to do about it?"

"I don't know what I can do. We're already at odds and he's really going to be unhappy when he finds out Alex and Leigh Anne are coming to talk with us next Tuesday."

"What difference should that make? He expects you to understand his position. Why shouldn't he be expected to understand yours?" Cathy asked dryly.

The doorbell saved Holly from having to answer. Jimmy stood on the doorstep, his hair damp from a recent shower. He was freshly shaved, bringing back to Holly a memory of him shaving in Fort Worth clad only in shaving cream. Holly's body tensed at the flood of desire that the memory evoked and she ruthlessly pushed away the mental image.

"Well, are you ready to knock them dead?" she asked as she opened the door and motioned him inside.

Jimmy smiled crookedly. "I'm going to do my best." He ran his knuckles down the side of Holly's face. "We need to talk," he said softly.

"Yes, we do," Holly admitted.

Within fifteen minutes the entire support group was crowded into Holly's tiny living room with snack plates piled high. Holly called for the group's attention. "I think most if not all of you have already met Jimmy, so I'm going to turn the floor over to him. Jimmy, it's all yours."

Jimmy gave the group a brief rundown of his life and why he wanted to serve in Congress. "I honestly think I can make a difference and I'd like the chance to do so." He looked around at the small group. "Maybe you could introduce yourselves and tell me one thing you'd like me to know about being a wounded warrior."

Good move, Holly thought as her soldiers introduced themselves and told Jimmy something they wanted him to know about their lives. He listened carefully and asked the kind of probing questions designed to get someone to open up. And open up they did, sharing their heartaches and frustrations as they described their efforts to build new lives for themselves. And then with a few deft questions Jimmy steered the discussion from their current lives to their wartime experiences and soon the room was moved to both laughter and tears as the soldiers refought old battles, and to Holly's surprise Jimmy opened up about that awful day in Baghdad.

"So how did your experiences in Iraq impact you?" Cathy asked. "How have they influenced your political philosophy?"

"I would like to think it's made me sensitive to the needs of all servicemen and veterans and in particular those who have made the kinds of sacrifices you all have made," Jimmy said. "And as a congressman I would make damn sure that my voting record reflected that."

Now let's see how he handles the nitty-gritty, Holly thought as Jimmy went into warm and fuzzy assurances that the veterans and in particular the wounded veterans could always count on him and that he would always have their back. Jimmy managed to sound strong and convincing while at the same time offering nothing of real substance in the way of concrete plans or real support for any new or innovative programs. When questioned about his ties to Nadine and her supporters, Jimmy managed to make it sound like he was accepting their support on his terms, not theirs, and that he was free to vote in the manner that he chose. He had the I'm-on-your-side spiel down pat and he presented it well. But were her soldiers buying it, or were they reading between the same lines she was?

The questions finally came to an end. Holly sent everyone back to the table for another round of snacks, and, after wolfing down a second helping of finger sandwiches, Jimmy thanked the group for their time and excused himself. Holly followed him out the front door and shut it behind her. "Thank you for coming," she said softly.

Jimmy reached out and grasped her hand. "Come over tonight," he said. "Carrie's grandmother has her for the night." He framed her face with his big hands and planted a swift, hard kiss on her lips. "Bring your things."

Holly nodded wordlessly, anticipation making her entire body tingle. Jimmy kissed her again and set off across the yard. As Holly turned to go back inside, she caught a glimpse of something out of the corner of her eye in the trees across the street and a chill ran down her back. Damn it, was the bastard, whoever it was, out there spying on them again? Or was her imagination working overtime? She peered again into the gloom, again spotting the faintest of movement, and almost collapsed with relief when a doe and her fawn tentatively stepped out of the trees. "Damn it, Bambi, you scared me," she laughed as she opened the front door.

The soldiers were waiting for her in the living room, their faces pensive, and Holly felt her spirits sinking. "Did you enjoy the meeting with Jimmy?" she asked brightly, hoping to put a happy face on the evening.

They were silent for a beat and then Otis reached up and scratched his nearly bald head. "I never heard so much nothing in all my life. I'm sorry, Holly," he said when he saw her stricken expression. "I know he's your boyfriend but for all his slick 'I'm on your side' talk he didn't have one good idea for helping folks like us. And frankly, that disappoints me."

"Otis is right," Tommy Joe piped up. "I felt like I was wheeling through more bullshit than I had in my old barn."

In spite of herself Holly joined the others in laughter. "Come on, Tommy. Jimmy's a politician. You have to expect a little bovine excrement."

"But I was looking for more than that," Beto admitted. "He didn't propose a single new program or idea. Damn it, I got my legs blown off in the service of this country and I want a congressman who's seriously in my corner."

"Frankly, I'm concerned about his ties to that business group out of San Angelo," Armando said. "No disrespect to your mother, Holly, but that bunch is known for their support for the oil industry at all costs and their almost allergic reaction to taxes. Hell, I don't like taxes any more than the next guy but let's face it, the programs that we and those like us need come out of the tax dollar, and as long as Jimmy's accepting their support he's not going to be able to support anything that might cost the taxpayers money."

"Wow, guys, why don't you tell me how you really feel?" Holly asked acidly.

"You-you're n-not being f-fair," Hal stuttered angrily. "You-you know N-N-the o-other guy's rich. Jimmy n-needs m-money."

"Hal, I know he needs their money," Cathy said gently. "Holly, don't you think every one of us feels badly about this? We know you and Jimmy are close, but I think as a group we're just not sure he's going to go to bat for us the way we think he should. And remember, he's made no secret to you that you have to understand where he's coming from on the support from Nadine and her friends. He's just going to have to do some understanding, too."

"Could you guys at least wait until you've talked to Alex and Leigh Anne before you make up your minds?" Holly asked. "I know Alex has some really good sound bites coming out but you've not heard from him in depth yet."

The group looked around at one another. "Of course," Beto and Cathy said almost in unison. "That's the only fair thing to do."

"Thanks," Holly said. "And I'll share your concerns with Jimmy." Not that it would do a damn bit of good as long as Nadine and her buddies had their claws in him, she thought.

The soldiers spent the better part of another hour together before they began to take their leave. Beto was looking at Cathy again, Holly thought with affectionate amusement as the two of them pitched in to help her clean up the kitchen. The man was about as subtle as a sledgehammer, but if the sexy little smiles Cathy was sending his way were any indication she didn't mind a bit. *Why, she's a flirt!* Holly thought with astonishment as Cathy ran her hand down the length of his arm. And a cute one, too. Holly had never seen this side of Cathy before and she found it somehow endearing.

Beto trailed Cathy out the door and, bum knee or no, Holly almost ran up the stairs. She yanked out her overnight bag and threw in a Verde faculty polo shirt and a pair of khakis along with her underwear and a skimpy nightgown. She tossed a few essentials in a gift-with-purchase cosmetic bag and was almost out the door when her phone chimed with Cathy's ringtone. "What's up, you big flirt you!" Holly teased.

"He asked me out on Friday night. We're going to the San Saba-Verde football game and out for a burger afterward," Cathy said.

"Sounds fun," Holly said. "So he likes the new makeup job, does he?"

Cathy was quiet for a minute and Holly heard her sniff. "Not exactly," she said finally, a wobble in her voice. "He said the makeup was nice and all but he didn't really give a damn about that. He said it was the smile; it was the first time he'd really seen me smile."

Holly sucked in a breath. "Cathy, you better not blow this. That man's a keeper."

"Don't I know it," Cathy said. "I guess I better keep smiling."

* * *

Chucky sat motionless deep in the shadows and watched the bitch and the two gimps moving about in the bitch's kitchen. So tonight the bitch and her gimpy group heard from the mighty Jimmy Adamcik, he thought as the airhead with the silly soap shop jogged by in the dark. He wondered if the bitch or the airhead could sense his presence tonight. The bitch was getting more suspicious by the day and the airhead had figured out that someone was in her backyard, too. He didn't want to mess with the airhead, especially since he bought her dirt-smelling soap, but he would do what he had to do to accomplish his mission. If she figured out what was going on he would have to take her out.

So who to hit on next? Maybe these two, he thought as the gimp with no legs walked the girl with the fakes and the screwed-up face to her car. Somehow she wasn't so damned ugly tonight—a trick of the light, or had she found some way to cover up the damage? Wasn't going to matter, once he got through with her. Chucky's hand tightened on the weapon he carried. Quick head shot to the woman while the gimp's standing right there? Easy as pie.

Chucky raised the Walther and took aim at the woman's head. No, too easy, Chucky told himself as they stood by the woman's car, deep in conversation. Slowly, he lowered the pistol, reluctant to give up the almost sensual pleasure of having her head in his sights. She needed to feel more pain than a head-shot would inflict and the bitch needed to watch it happen. Just not yet. He would wait awhile, lull them all into thinking Chucky had gone away. And then he would strike. There would be pictures, he thought as his mouth curled into a snarl of a smile. Pictures posted from the new Adamcik log-in for the entire world to see. The bitch's front door opened and the bitch herself left the house, carrying a small bag with her as she scooted down the deserted street toward the Adamcik house. Oh, ho, the lovers meet again, he thought as his fingers again tightened on the pistol grip. The bitch froze in her tracks and turned to scan the area where he'd hidden. Chucky stood motionless, barely breathing until she turned around and headed toward Adamcik's.

Shit, she was good, Chucky admitted to himself as he remained frozen in place, and in her pre-injury days she would have been a worthy opponent. Now she was a gimp just like the others. And, like the others, he would deal with her.

* * *

Damn it, he was out there, Holly thought as she picked up her pace and moved as quickly as she could toward Jimmy's house. Fear mingled with anger as she felt unseen eyes staring at her in the night. *Who are you?* she asked herself fiercely as she scurried up Jimmy's sidewalk and skidded to a halt at his front door. Who are you and why are you after me? She rapped sharply on Jimmy's front door and waited impatiently for Jimmy to answer. "What's wrong?" Jimmy demanded as Holly almost knocked him over getting inside.

"I swear to God I could feel him watching me," Holly said as she whirled around and locked the front door. "The whole time I was walking over."

Jimmy's mouth tightened. "Do you want me to get a gun and try to find him?"

Holly shook her head slowly. "No, I don't," she said. "He's at least as good as you are, maybe even better, and he has the advantage of surprise. We'll get him another way."

"Are you sure?" Jimmy demanded. "I can get Rory to help."

"He's probably gone by now," Holly said. "Or hell, it might just be the deer I saw earlier." She turned around and put her arms around Jimmy's neck. "I've missed you."

Jimmy lowered his head and nibbled her lips. "I've missed you, too. We were stupid to fight."

"Yes, we were," Holly agreed as Jimmy reached down and swept her into his arms. "Jimmy, what are you doing?"

"Me Rhett, you Scarlet," Jimmy said as he started toward the staircase. "I always wondered just what happened when he got her up those stairs."

"Probably all kinds of interesting things," Holly said as she tightened her arms around Jimmy's neck. "Bet we could figure some of them out."

"Bet we could," Jimmy said as he strode up the wide staircase, barely breathing hard as he carried Holly down the hall and into his bedroom. But rather than depositing her on his bed, he carried her on into the bathroom and stood her beside the huge jetted tub. A bottle of white wine rested in an ice bucket and two glasses waited for them on the counter. With a flick of the wrist Jimmy turned on the spigot and steaming hot water poured out of the gold-plated faucet. "It will be full in a minute," he said as he reached out and pulled her knit T-shirt over her head. "I thought a little spa time might be nice."

"Yes, it would," Holly agreed as she boldly unhooked her bra and let it fall to the floor, baring her completely to the waist. She grinned as she unbuckled Jimmy's belt and pushed his jeans down his hips. "You'll have to get your shirt yourself," she said as she gently palmed his growing erection through his silk boxers. "You're too tall for me to get it."

Jimmy pulled his shirt and T-shirt over his head and finished pushing down his jeans. He toed off his loafers as Holly shimmied out of her jeans and panties and tentatively stuck his hand in the water. "Perfect," he said. He pushed another button and the nearly full tub erupted into a froth of bubbles and foam. "After you," he said as he took Holly's hand and helped her over the side of the tub.

"Ahh, this is heavenly," Holly breathed as she sank down into the water.

Jimmy poured them each a glass of wine and handed one to Holly. He slid in beside Holly and stretched his legs out in front of him. "I don't use this thing often enough," he said as he glanced over at the built-in shower across the room.

"You should use it more often," Holly said as she slid even closer to Jimmy, their legs and hips brushing together under the surface of the water. "I swear the hot water cures just about anything that ails you." She raised her legs and let them float in the water. "This feels good."

"Yes, it does," Jimmy agreed. They lay back together, almost floating, sipping their wine and letting the churning water work its magic. The water lapped around Holly's nipples in a warm, sensual caress as she leaned back against Jimmy's arm and shut her eyes. Almost of its own volition her hand snaked out and stroked Jimmy's stomach, meandering its way down his body and finding Jimmy swelling to her touch. "Ever done it in here?" she asked.

Jimmy shook his head. "Lauren wasn't much for that kind of thing. You?" He swallowed the rest of his wine in one gulp and set his glass on the floor beside the spa.

"Nope. It wasn't even mentioned in that course I took," she said as Jimmy took her half empty wine glass out of her hand and set it on the floor beside his.

"It wasn't? How rude. Guess we'll just have to make it up as we go along," Jimmy teased as he openly admired Holly's naked body outlined under the foaming water. "Let's see, how about this?" he asked as he lifted Holly onto his lap and cradled her breasts in his hands, teasing her sensitive nipples with his thumbs. Tremors shook Holly as she felt his lips nuzzle the back of her neck as their legs tangled together under the water and his insistent erection thrust into her lower back. "How's this?" he teased as one of his hands drifted lower, gently teasing and caressing her midriff and then her stomach, paying special attention to her navel before snaking even lower. Holly gasped as Jimmy's fingers nudged her legs open and he found the sensitive nubbin between her legs. "Wider, Holly," he demanded, his voice a rough growl in her ear. "I want to give you pleasure there."

Holly let her legs fall open, hooking her feet around Jimmy's calves. "But what about you?" she breathed as Jimmy's fingers and the foaming water worked together to spin a magic web for her.

"My turn will come," he said, his breath a sensual caress as his tongue caressed her nape. "Besides, do you have any idea of the pleasure it gives me when you respond like this to my touch? When you come apart in my arms?" he demanded as his fingers touched and teased and coaxed her upward. "Fly for me, Holly. Fly."

"Jimmy, I—I—" Holly gasped as the first orgasm took her by surprise, her body exploding in sensual delight as a tremor shook her from her head to her feet. But Jimmy did not stop there. He waited until the last of the tremors had subsided and began another sensual assault, his fingers returning to caress her between her legs until she was again trembling to his touch. Gasping, soaring, Holly was aware only of the sensations Jimmy was creating in her body, the passion and abandon of the moment, the sensual feel of his body gently cradling hers as he worked magic with his fingers and his mouth. Holly felt herself arching toward his fingers as another climax tore through her, shattering in its strength and intensity as she flew apart in his arms. Spent, she let her body float weightlessly against his as the ebbing tremors subsided. "My God, the things you do to me," she breathed as she bobbed in the foaming caress of the water.

Jimmy's fingers trailed lazily up Holly's body as she spent a minute catching her breath. "Do you know what it does to a man to have a woman as responsive as you are in his arms?" he asked as he flipped Holly over to straddle him. "It's like being king of the world." He pulled her face close to his and covered her mouth in a hot, steamy kiss. Holly melted against him, desire rising again as her tongue fought a sensuous duel with his and they made love with their lips. Jimmy lifted her out of the water just far enough to tickle first one breast and then the other with his tongue, the heat of his mouth tantalizingly sensuous. "You are amazing," he whispered as her breasts swelled under his ministrations.

"I'm not the one who looks like a Greek god," she breathed as she caressed his shoulders and chest, greedily touching his hard, sensuous body, drinking in the feel of him underneath her and hers now to touch and kiss at will. Hard, insistent need engulfed them and, further foreplay forgotten, he put his hands on her hips and guided her onto his straining manhood, impaling her as she draped herself above him.

Her knees along the side of the tub and the buoyancy of the water cushioning her bad knee, Holly took complete control of the moment, rising and falling as the churning water and the strength of Jimmy's hunger spurred her on, desire a whirling vortex that sucked her back into the depths and heights of passion. He thrust upward, taking his rhythm from her as they moved as one with each other and the water that frothed and splashed around them. Their bodies moved together, riding the crest of their mutual desire until first Holly and then Jimmy arched and cried out, urgent cries of release and pleasure as they spiraled into the passionate free-fall of mutual delight as tremor after tremor engulfed them in a pleasure and satisfaction beyond anything else they had experienced before.

Holly leaned forward and laid her head on Jimmy's shoulder. They remained joined together for long moments, too spent by the explosion of passion they had just shared to even pull their bodies apart. "That was awesome," he breathed as she eased herself away and sat back down beside him. "For round one, that is."

Holly leaned away and grinned wickedly at him. "Round one, huh? How many rounds are we going for?"

Jimmy stood up and pulled her up beside him. "As many as we can. God, I've missed you, Holly." He snagged a thick fluffy towel from the rack and draped it around Holly's shoulders. Tenderly, he blotted the water from her body and helped her over the side of the spa. He made quick work of the water on his body with a second towel and took her by the hand and led her to his bed. Her lips parting, Holly gave in to the passion that was again igniting between them. She moaned softly as Jimmy took her mouth in a sweet, drugging kiss, their tongues conducting a thrust and parry as he skillfully brought her to trembling again. "I want you again," he murmured. "I want what we had in Fort Worth. I need to be buried inside you again."

"I need you, too," Holly admitted as they each took a step backward and tumbled into Jimmy's huge bed, the moonlight bathing their bodies in its silvery gleam. "This time is for you," she whispered as she pushed him into the sheets. "And I'll make you so glad you came to the party." She leaned down and smothered his lips in a passionate, possessive kiss that had both of them gasping.

Jimmy's hands played over her body as she continued to kiss and caress him intimately. She had spent the entire weekend in Fort Worth learning to please him and now she brought every bit of that knowledge to their encounter. She touched him as he loved to be touched, first with her hands and then with her mouth as she kissed and suckled and tormented her way down his chest, stopping to pay homage to his surprisingly sensitive nipples, down to his stomach where she blew teasingly into his navel, and on down to the organ that never ceased to amaze her as it swelled again.

She reached out with her pink tongue and teased its tip, laughing as he arched beneath her. "God, woman, you're dynamite," he groaned as he ran his hand up her back and stroked the tender skin of her shoulder.

"So are you," she breathed as her tongue flicked back and forth over the sensitive tip.

Jimmy's hands tangled in her hair as she brought him almost to the brink, but knowing even sweeter things were coming he made no protest when she raised herself and positioned herself above him.

"Ride me, baby," he said as she lowered herself slowly onto his magnificent erection.

Holly gave herself a minute to savor his presence in her body, then she started to move, her body rising and falling as she worked her magic. With one hand, he braced her weak knee and with the other he cupped her mound and forayed into the tight folds of her femininity, finding and caressing the tender nub with his fingers as they spiraled together toward a mutual explosion. They were in that wonderful place between first-time and long-time lovers, where they knew enough to seriously pleasure one another and yet it was still new and fresh for them. They moved together as their weekend together had taught them to do, and when he felt her arch her back and cry out he let loose with his own orgasm, their bodies shuddering together as they rode out the simultaneous conflagration that threatened to consume both of them.

"My God, that was unbelievable," she breathed as he shuddered beneath her.

Their bodies still joined, Jimmy rolled them so that they were side by side facing one another. "Want to try for one more?" he asked with a wicked grin on his face.

"Nah, I'm done," she said as she pushed herself away and sat up. "At least for the time being."

"We could go downstairs for ice cream and start all over again," he said hopefully; evidence of his intent obvious.

Holly looked down and laughed. "But then I have to go to sleep. I have to teach tomorrow."

They pulled on a pair of his pajamas—she wore the top and he the bottoms—and wandered downstairs. he went into the freezer and pulled out a carton. "Rocky Road okay?" he asked as she got bowls and spoons.

"Sure." She handed Jimmy a bowl and served herself a big scoop of ice cream. "I can't believe I'm hungry again," she said idly as she licked the ice cream off her spoon. "As much as I fed everybody this evening."

"So how'd I do?" Jimmy asked a little too casually.

Holly set her spoon down on the table. "Great, until it came time to talk about specific plans to help us," she said slowly. "At that point it fell apart. I'm sorry," she said quickly as his face fell. "Believe me, I'd rather be delivering another message, but I owe you the truth. Jimmy, if you want the support of veterans, specifically wounded veterans, you're going to have to quit with the platitudes and have some specific things in mind that you're willing to commit to, mom and her cronies be damned. Otherwise, they're going to throw their support, insignificant as it may be, to Navarro."

"That's the problem," he groused. "Your soldiers are very significant. Talk about being between a rock and a hard place." He paused a minute. "You realize your mom called me this afternoon. Warned me against making any expensive promises that would alarm her cronies."

"I figured as much," Holly said. "And their support in and of itself is problematic to some." She reached out and grasped his hand. "Let me talk to them some more. I'll do my best to persuade them to throw their support your way." She scooped up a big bite of ice cream and held it out to him. "Now, eat up," she coaxed him teasingly, a seductive smile on her face. "You'll need the energy in a few minutes when we go back up those stairs."

* * *

Jimmy groaned and reached over Holly's sleeping body to slap at the alarm clock before he realized that it was the doorbell not the alarm clock that had awakened him. He muttered a muffled curse word and reached for his pajama bottoms, then uttered a louder curse word when he saw the time. "Holly, up and at 'em," he said as he swatted her lightly on her backside. "We overslept."

She came straight up out of a sound sleep and swore when she saw the time. "Damn! I'm due in class in less than an hour." She leaped out of the bed and grabbed her overnight bag. "Is that the damned doorbell?" she asked as she slammed the bathroom door behind her.

He ran his hands through his hair as the doorbell pealed again then grabbed his pajama top and threw it on as he loped down the stairs and opened the door to Carrie and an impatient-looking Ida Puckett. "Took you long enough," Ida complained as Carrie darted between them and into the house. She eyed Jimmy up and down, taking in the unbuttoned pajama top and heavy-lidded satisfaction that even his abrupt awakening couldn't quite disguise. "Late night?" she asked tartly.

"Late enough," Jimmy said, hoping his irritation didn't show. "Did Carrie have a good time?"

Ida's face did not soften. "Yes, she enjoyed herself very much."

Holly, her hair wet from a hasty shower, hurried down the stairs dressed in her polo shirt and khakis. "Got to run," she said as she went up on her tiptoes and gave Jimmy a quick kiss. "Oh, hello, Mrs. Puckett," she said brightly, ignoring Ida's icy disapproval. "Good to see you again." She darted out the door and hustled down the street as fast as her bad leg would carry her.

Ida turned contemptuous eyes on Jimmy. "Carrying on while Carrie's out of the house?"

Jimmy's eyebrow shot up almost to his hairline. "Would you rather I carried on while Carrie's in the bedroom down the hall?"

Ida's lips tightened. "I'd rather you didn't dishonor my daughter's memory at all," she said coldly. "Lauren's barely in the ground and you're already carrying on with somebody else. That's shameful, Jimmy. Just shameful. Lauren would be appalled."

His face hardened. "Actually, Lauren would be glad for me, Ida. She made me promise her on her deathbed that I would go on with life and get out there and get laid on occasion." He shrugged his shoulders and scratched his bare chest.

Ida gasped audibly. "Well, I never," she huffed as she turned on her heel and stomped down the porch stairs.

He sighed and shook his head. It would be all over town by the end of the day, he thought ruefully as he shut the front door behind him and trudged up the stairs. Ida had the biggest mouth in the county and she was probably already on her cell phone running it. Pretty ROTC teacher caught in the bed of the widowed congressional candidate.

And people were going to talk.

It was one thing to have a weekend fling a hundred and fifty miles away but quite another to get caught carrying on here in Heaven's Point. Jimmy yawned hugely as he shucked off the pajamas and turned on the water in the shower. He supposed he should be worrying about the effect of the gossip on his campaign, and he was certain that he would eventually get around to it. But not this morning. He just felt too damn good to be worrying about anything.

* * *

Holly locked the door to her classroom and wandered tiredly out of the annex, pretending to ignore the peeks and stares as she made her way to the main building. Ida Puckett must have every gossip in Verde County on her speed dial, she thought sourly. Word of Holly's sleepover at Jimmy's had already reached the Verde faculty lounge by noon if the winks and stares and the occasional pumping of a feminine fist were anything to go by, and, by the middle of the afternoon, even the students had gotten word. Thankfully, nobody on campus seemed too upset and if anything she had gone up a notch or two in the students' eyes. But she had not heard from Nadine nor had Cathy or any of her soldiers called, and Holly had no idea what their reaction would be at her very public outing.

Holly made it to her car and was almost home when her cell chimed. It was Nadine's ringtone and Holly almost ignored it, but figured she'd have to have the conversation sometime and may as well get it out of the way—and have a little fun while she was doing it. She let her phone ring a couple more times. "Hello, you have reached the voice mail of Holly Riley. I'm on my way to a torrid assignation with congressional candidate Adamcik and am unable to take your call right now. If you'll leave your name and number I'll call you when we come up for air later this evening. Have a nice day."

Nadine was silent a minute. "I guess it was too much to ask to expect you to take this seriously," she said tartly. "Damn it, Holly, what were you thinking, getting caught in Jimmy's bed like that?"

"I was thinking that I better high-tail it out of there and get to my job on time. Unlike those in your camp, I have more to worry about than a damned congressional campaign."

Nadine made a sound somewhere between a squeal and a shriek. "Damn it, Holly, you could have waited five minutes before you walked out. Do you have any idea of the political repercussions this could have? A couple of my more conservative supporters have already called and complained."

Holly's lips tightened. "It's not like we were a big secret," she said. "Everybody in Verde knew we spent a weekend together."

"Yes, and having a discrete weekend together out of town isn't exactly the same as getting caught together in his bed by his tight-assed mother-in-law, is it?" Nadine fired back. "Maybe Jimmy doesn't realize how it came across; he's a political newbie, but you've been around enough politics to know better. I just hope to hell this doesn't reach out and bite Jimmy in the butt."

"Jimmy's got more to worry about than a few old fuddy-duddies," Holly said. "Thanks to your sage advice, he went over like a lead balloon with the soldiers last night. They want to throw their support to Alex Navarro. It was all I could do to talk them into waiting until they had actually talked with Alex in person."

"Then I guess you'll just have to see that they change their minds," Nadine said firmly.

"I'm not sure if I can," Holly snapped. "Mom, they're not stupid and they know a platitude when they hear one. And they're sick of getting the run-around from politicians who don't think they're worth the tax dollars."

Holly heard Nadine suck in her breath. "I know that," she said quietly. "But money's important, too, Holly. If Jimmy doesn't have the money to run a campaign he's out on his ear, supportive soldiers or no. Look, just do your best to persuade them. That's all I can ask."

"I'll try," Holly said as she sped past Angie's shop and turned into Heaven's Point. She was just pulling into her own driveway when Cathy's Camaro pulled up behind her with Tommy Joe in the passenger seat. *Uh-oh, they sent a delegation*, she thought as she got out of the Miata and helped Cathy unfold Tommy Joe's wheelchair.

Tommy Joe swung himself from the car and into the wheelchair while Holly unlocked the front door. "What can I get you to drink? And does mine need to be alcoholic?" she asked dryly as Cathy shut the front door behind her.

Cathy and Tommy Joe looked at one another. "Depends," Tommy Joe said. He looked Holly straight in the eye. "Heard you spent the night in Adamcik's king-size," he said, his face turning red. "You sure you ought to be doing that?"

Holly nailed him with a hard stare. "And since when did my sex life become any of your business?" she demanded. "Am I out at the farm policing yours?"

Tommy Joe turned even redder. "I'm not sleeping with the congressional candidate I'm trying to persuade all my friends to vote for." He turned embarrassed eyes on Holly. "It was one thing when you and he were just a rumor. Now you're an item and you know that both of you are going to assume that we'll support him just because he's your boyfriend."

Holly looked from Tommy Joe to Cathy. "Is that what you and the soldiers honestly believe?" she asked slowly. "That I would assume any such thing?"

"But you did try to get us to support him," Cathy reminded her gently.

"I did no such thing," Holly said tartly. "All I asked you to do was wait until you've heard from Navarro before making up your minds. And after that, yes, I intend to plead Jimmy's case, but you and the other members of the group are under no obligation to listen to me or agree with me. Now if you will both excuse me, this is the second butt-chewing I've had over this in the last ten minutes and if you don't mind I need to get busy sewing a nice scarlet 'A' to fit over the DCUs on Monday."

"Aw, Holly, we're sorry," Tommy Joe said, hanging his head a little. "You know we didn't mean anything like that. And I like Jimmy Adamcik, I really do, and will vote for him just for introducing me to Duncan Royal. But you have to understand. If Alex Navarro has better ideas and is willing to do more for us than Jimmy Adamcik is, the soldiers are going to support him. Can you understand that and not be mad?"

"Yes, of course I can," Holly assured him. "I can understand that completely."

But could Jimmy?

Chapter Fourteen

Jimmy tapped the bank printouts with a pencil and looked up at Jack Briscoe. "Not so great, is it?" he asked idly as he perused the statement again. "At this rate Navarro's going to be able to spend two dollars for every one of mine."

"And that's just out of his personal checking account," Jack teased. "You haven't had a really healthy infusion of money since the check from that couple in Dallas. Nadine's friends are still coming through but the numbers aren't what she told me you could expect."

"Thanks to that Internet incident," Jimmy said sourly. "Damn, I'd love to know how whoever's doing this got my log-in. Of all the luck"

"Not all your luck's been that bad lately," Jack said dryly. "I actually heard one of the English teachers asking Holly if the rumors about you were true."

"What rumors?" Jimmy demanded.

"Not sure. Something about your manly assets. My faculty doesn't confide that kind of thing in me." Jack's eyes danced with glee as Jimmy turned red. "I must admit that both you and Holly have gone up several notches in the student body's estimation."

"Great. Wonderful. I wish Nadine shared their opinion. She gave both Holly and me hell for getting caught here in Verde." Jimmy shrugged. "At least maybe now that our relationship is so public Holly's soldiers will throw their support in my direction. Speaking of which, I promised Holly I'd pick us up some dinner at the café and I need to get over there and put in my order."

They locked up headquarters and Jack headed home. Jimmy ordered a family meal of Gus's pork chops and swung by Carmela's for Carrie and soon they were pulling into Holly's driveway. "Do you like Holly's bike?" Carrie asked as Jimmy parked behind her new Harley. "She calls it her steel horse."

"I like the real thing better," Jimmy said as he and Carrie walked to Holly's front door.

Holly threw open the door and ushered them inside. "Thanks for bringing supper. I was on my leg all day and it's sore." She leaned down and hugged Carrie. "I've missed you, Carrie."

"You, too," Carrie said as she flung her small arms around Holly's neck.

Jimmy helped Holly to her feet. "Still dealing with all the left feet in the ROTC?"

"No, today was rifle instruction and it went wonderfully," Holly said as she opened the takeout cartons. "Most of the kids around here grew up with a rifle in their hands and for the most part they already know what to do." She spooned Carrie-sized portions on a dinner plate and larger ones for her and Jimmy. "So why don't you both tell me about your day?" she asked as she sank down tiredly.

She was so delightful to be with, Jimmy thought as he and Carrie told Holly about their days. It wasn't just the sex with her, although that was admittedly spectacular. It was the way she smiled at the two of them and was eager to hear about Carrie's day and the way she listened, really listened when he talked about his concerns. He felt his midsection tighten as Holly rose to refill Carrie's glass and she absently ran her hand across the back of his neck, the light touch of her fingers sending a current of awareness down his body. She smiled teasingly at him over his daughter's head, her bewitching expression making tantalizing promises as she gave Carrie back the glass, and Jimmy wondered how soon it would be before he could arrange another sleepover for Carrie.

They chatted about this and that as they cleaned their plates. Holly put on a video for Carrie while she and Jimmy cleared the table and loaded up the leftovers. "There's enough for you and Carrie to make another meal of this," she said as she resealed the takeout containers.

"You want to make a couple of lunches out of it and I'll bring us another dinner from the café tomorrow?" He asked.

"Can't," Holly said. "The support group's coming back over tomorrow. The Navarros are driving down to talk to them."

Jimmy felt himself freeze at the sink. "I didn't realize you still intended to talk to them," he heard himself saying tightly.

Holly looked a little defensive. "Why wouldn't we?" she asked. "I told you last Thursday the group wasn't sold on you. They really want to hear what Alex Navarro has to say."

"Yes, but now things have changed," Jimmy said.

"And exactly how have they done that?" she asked as she put the takeout containers back in the sack.

"Well, mostly that everybody in town knows we're sleeping together," he said. "It's not going to look so good for me, is it, when word gets out that my girlfriend's support group is hosting the other guy. They need to understand that."

Holly's expression froze. "You sure have a lot of expectations, Adamcik."

"Exactly what do you mean by that?" he demanded.

"What do you think I mean?" She snapped. "You expect me and my group to understand that you won't support us because you're afraid of alienating a bunch of tightwad contributors, but you expect *our* support because your big-mouthed mama-in-law caught me in your bed. I've already had a visit from a support group delegation. They're unhappy because they think I'm trying to get them to support you because of our relationship, and they made it damned clear to me that they don't intend to do that and that we better get ready to understand their position."

"In other words, they expect us to keep our relationship separate from our politics," he said slowly.

"So? You've expected that from me all along. Now somebody expects it from you. Think you can handle it?"

Jimmy felt anger and confusion wash over him. "I'm not sure," he admitted finally. "I don't think I should have to."

"Maybe I shouldn't have to, either," she said with exasperation. "Jimmy, back in the summer you made a choice. You decided to accept both the money my mom and her cronies offered and the conditions they laid out for you. Did it ever occur to you that by doing that you were going to alienate some voters? Did it ever occur to you that if you're not willing to support the wounded warriors and Alex Navarro is, *they are going to vote for him,* no matter what you and I are up to?"

Jimmy could feel his face start to burn. "I guess not."

"Well, maybe you better get started."

* * *

Holly bit her lip and peeked out the window, wondering for the umpteenth time if she was doing the right thing hosting the Navarros this evening. She and Jimmy had parted on distinctly chilly terms and she spent the better part of the day wondering if she should move the meeting to Cathy's house. But that would have been cowardly and hypocritical. If Alex's ideas for helping her soldiers were as good as she expected them to be, her soldiers were going to throw their support to him no matter where they held the meeting. And if they did throw their support to Alex, Jimmy was just going to have to understand.

Holly spotted the Navarros' SUV pulling into the driveway. "Come on in," she said as she threw open the front door. "Everybody's here but Hal. We're having a little fun giving Cathy and Beto a hard time. They're dating now and the support group's having a field day with it."

"Yes, romance does seem to be in the air," Alex said teasingly. "Thank you for having us."

Holly could feel herself blushing. "Thank you for coming. Leigh Anne, you're positively glowing."

Leigh Anne ran her hand down her baby bump. "Thanks."

The soldiers and the Navarros served themselves plates of Holly's delicious snacks and were soon seated in a circle in Holly's living room. The members introduced themselves and gave Alex and Leigh Anne a quick summary of where and how they were injured, with the Navarros solemnly taking in every story and sharing quick bios of their own. "I was a member of college ROTC and was looking forward to putting in a few years with the Army after I got my law degree," Alex volunteered. "But then two of my uncles were killed in a plane crash and I had to take my place in the family business. I have always felt like I didn't do my part as an American, and that's a lot of why I'm running for Congress—I want to serve my country and I'd like to see some things done differently."

"What things?" Beto asked.

Alex gave a ten-minute rundown on his positions that had Holly's lips twitching. No wonder Nadine and her tightfisted crowd didn't want Alex Navarro in office. Even though his proposals for educational spending and environmental protection were quite modest they still flew in the face of everything Nadine and her cronies stood for, and if he were to be elected Alex Navarro wouldn't owe Nadine's crowd the time of day. Alex's ideas were appealing and he had the money to get those ideas out there, and for the first time Holly could appreciate the serious bind a candidate like Jimmy with no real wealth of his own would find himself in.

The soldiers had a few general questions for Alex and then Cathy broached the subject that was foremost on their minds. "Obviously, we share the same concerns about education, taxes, and the environment that any other citizen has," she said. "But as wounded combat veterans fighting our way back to a normal life, we're tired of the same old 'thank you for your service to our country' crap and then nothing of substance to go with it."

Like they got from Jimmy, Holly thought.

"Well, I was going to start by thanking you all for your service to our country," Alex said dryly. "I can skip that if you'd rather."

The soldiers laughed. "Seriously, what would you as a congressman be willing to support for us?" Beto asked.

"Any number of things," Alex said. He leaned forward and looked the soldiers in the eye. "You have my word that if I win this thing I will vote for each and every bill that would do anything to support American veterans, whether or not they have been injured in a war. Education, housing, you name it. The vets will get my vote. I don't care what it costs—we can take it out of somebody's big fat pork barrel. Or, God help us, tax somebody."

Like mom's beloved oil companies, Holly thought wickedly.

"Now, as to what I'd do for you specifically. Frankly, I'd start with doing what I could to secure more funding for more and better staffed veterans' treatment facilities, particularly in the area of mental health. I would push for more and better training facilities for soldiers whose injuries cost them their military careers or their civilian job skills. And I would support anything that would direct public funding to private initiatives, such as your support group."

Holly blinked and fought to conceal her surprise. Alex's proposals were almost identical to the ones Jimmy had thrown out to the San Angelo reporters that afternoon at BAMC. But as a congressman Alex would have the freedom to implement those proposals while Jimmy would forever have Nadine and her crowd looking over his shoulder.

Leigh Anne looked over at Alex and he gave her a slight nod. "I have seen up close how the wreckage of war can devastate an entire family," she began. "My young cousin was killed in Iraq and not only did his parents separate for a time but his older brother, also a soldier, had a complete meltdown and has basically disappeared from our lives. I would lend my support to the establishment of nonprofit agencies for support and counseling for families facing a similar loss as well as counseling and support for the families of wounded soldiers, hopefully funded at least in part by federal grant money." She leaned forward, her eyes sparkling. "I write a mean grant proposal."

I bet she does, Holly thought.

"Another initiative that could be at least partially funded through federal money is the designing and building of handicapped-equipped housing as well as the rehabbing of existing homes," Alex broke in. "Leigh Anne's brother's construction company has built a number of these already."

"And I would love to see women like you two ladies and that wonderfully talented woman who designs your makeup doing self-esteem workshops for the women, again at least partially funded by a little grant money," Leigh Anne enthused. She looked over at Cathy. "They were able to fix you up with an arm and a leg but not much in the way of self-confidence, right? That needs to change."

As the conversation continued Holly sat back and watched and listened. The couple had clearly done their homework. Maybe not all of their ideas would fly, but at least they had some concrete proposals. And unless Holly was very much mistaken, their caring and concern was real. Oh, yeah, the group would be throwing their support to Alex, and as much as she cared about Jimmy and hated the damage this was going to do to their relationship, she really couldn't blame them.

It was another hour before Alex and Leigh Anne took their leave. Holly shut the door behind them and turned to the men and women seated in her living room. "Well, what did you think?" she asked quietly.

Her support group looked around at one another before looking uncomfortably at Holly. "Holly, we're sorry," Cathy said finally. "I know you and Jimmy are close, but I feel like Alex would do a better job for us than Jimmy would. He has a better handle on our needs." Holly started to object. "No, that's not it and we both know it," she amended. "I'm sure Jimmy knows just as well as Alex what we need from a congressman. But because of his obligations to your mom and his other supporters, Jimmy's not able to lend us the kind of support we need, and Alex is."

"All right, let me play devil's advocate here for a moment," Holly said slowly. "I will be the first to admit that Alex and Leigh Anne sounded really good tonight. But was Alex telling the truth? Will he in fact do all the things he promised to? At least Jimmy's honest enough not to make promises to you that he can't keep."

"He is, and I sincerely appreciate that about him," Otis said. "But with Alex we at least have a chance of getting the support we need. With Jimmy we know we won't."

"Don't you think you're being a little disloyal?" Holly asked, stung and not trying to hide it. "Most of you have known him for years and he's done some really nice things for some of you."

"Damn it, Holly, do you think this is easy?" Tommy Joe shot back. "Yes, I owe Jimmy big time for introducing me to Duncan Royal and I'll vote for him for that reason alone. But for the rest of the group it still boils down to which man has the freedom to represent our interests in Washington. Alex does and Jimmy doesn't. And until he shakes loose of your mama and those barracudas she runs with, he won't. End of story."

"Holly, would it be possible for Jimmy to end his association with Nadine and her crowd?" Cathy asked quietly. "They're the problem, not Jimmy."

"Not if he wants to raise the money to mount a campaign," Holly said tartly. "Look, I get where you're coming from, and my love life isn't your concern. Do what you have to do."

"Then I guess we better make it known that we support Alex Navarro and recommend that all the other veterans groups do the same," Armando said solemnly. The rest of the group nodded.

"Fine. I'll let Jimmy know," Holly said tersely.

Cathy volunteered to draft a statement and before long Holly's living room was empty. Holly gathered up the trash and shoved it into a garbage sack. God, what was she going to say to Jimmy? She wheeled the garbage bin to the street and trudged toward Jimmy's front door. Should she make a public break with her support group and come out for Jimmy? Would that do any good? Holly wished with all her heart that she and her friends had never gotten involved with the congressional race in the first place, but they had and now it was too late.

Jimmy took one look at Holly's face and ushered her in grimly. "They decided to support Navarro, didn't they?" he demanded tersely.

"I tried to get them to change their minds," she said quietly. "I'm sorry."

"You're *sorry*?" He demanded incredulously. "You and your buddies are going to embarrass the hell out of my campaign and you're *sorry*? May I be so bold as to ask what made them throw their support to Navarro?"

"Jimmy, get real," she shot back. "You have platitudes. He has a plan."

He flinched. "Do they realize the position I'm in with your mother and her buddies?"

"That's part of the problem," she admitted. "They feel like you won't have the freedom to represent their best interests and Navarro will."

"Why didn't you fight them?" He asked. "Why are you just going along with what they're doing to me?"

Holly was silent for a moment. "Because if I weren't involved with you, I would be doing exactly what they are. And as much as I hate to admit it, I think Alex Navarro would be light years better for me and my soldiers than you would."

"Oh, really? Then your buddies can take a hike and you can go with them," he said angrily.

It was Holly's turn to flinch. "If that's how you feel I will most certainly be taking that hike. But first I'm going to tell you to your face that you are a hypocrite of the highest order. Yes, you are," she continued when he started to object. "You expect me to separate my feelings for you from my work with the soldiers. You expect them to understand when you would rather brown-nose my mother and her supporters for their money than support them. And then you act like a spoiled brat when my soldiers throw their support to the candidate who might actually do something for them. That, my friend, is hypocritical."

She jerked open the front door and turned back around. "You know, Jimmy, an election isn't just about money," she said softly. "It's about *votes*. And if you run off all your votes chasing the money, you're going to lose the election, no matter how much money mom's cronies put into your coffers." Tears stinging her eyes, she turned on her heel and left his house, shutting the front door quietly behind her.

* * *

It had been almost two hours since Alex and Leigh Anne climbed into their SUV and drove away and Chucky still shook with anger as he stood watch in the shadows. How could they kiss up to that worthless bunch of gimps? How could they turn their back on everything near and dear to them? *How could she?* Navarro, maybe, he was an opportunistic SOB who put himself and his own welfare first, but Leigh Anne? The depth and breadth of her betrayal took his breath away. The cool lake breeze dried the sweat on his body but did nothing to cool the burning rage in his gut. There was nothing he could do tonight. But sooner or later the traitorous Leigh Anne would pay for her betrayal—Chucky would make damn sure of that.

And in the meantime, what could he do to further unbalance the Adamcik congressional campaign? He watched thoughtfully as Adamcik wheeled his garbage bin to the curb. Now, sometimes garbage was just garbage, but sometimes a sack of garbage could be a treasure trove of juicy, interesting, incriminating information about the household in question.

Chucky stood motionless, secure in his hiding place until the little neighborhood was asleep, then slipped from shadow to shadow until he reached the garbage bin. He quickly snatched the top sack and slipped to his car and soon reached the abandoned double-wide he thought of as his hidey hole. Sitting down at the kitchen table, he untied the strings and eased open the sack, smiling at what looked like office and bathroom trash.

He dumped the sack of trash on the kitchen table and weeded through a wad of junk mail and credit card come-ons. Then he dug deeper, unearthing empty toilet paper rolls and a couple of dirty tissues. Chucky was about to decide his foray into Adamcik's garbage had been a bust when he unearthed an empty prescription bottle with an Austin pharmacy label and the name of one Dr. Hiram Jacobsen. Why was Adamcik driving all the way to Austin when his best friend's wife treated everybody in Verde and there was a pharmacy right on the square?

Chucky powered up the laptop. He first Googled the name of the medication and his eyes widened. It had several uses, the most common being the relief of chronic pain, but it was also used to treat anxiety. Well, what do you know? An evil grin slashed across his face as he then typed in Dr. Jacobsen's name and found an article in a medical journal written by the good doctor himself. Chucky scanned a few pages of the article and returned to the search engine, his absolute glee growing as he found and quickly perused three more articles, all detailing the treatment of PTSD in a variety of post-traumatic situations. Hot damn, he thought as he gave himself a mental high-five. Adamcik had PTSD. The bastard had PTSD and was running for Congress and hadn't said a word about it to anyone.

Closing the laptop, Chucky got a beer out of the frig while he considered his options. He could post a picture of the pill bottle and do a little damage, but if he took a picture of Adamcik at the doctor's office, the impact would be just that much greater. So he would wait and get the picture, he thought as he downed the beer. Because when he dropped this bombshell, he wanted the impact to be maximum.

Chapter Fifteen

Jimmy tipped his chair back and watched his new neighbor Russ Riley stride across the floor of campaign headquarters, his gait cocksure and his uniform hat riding rakishly on his head. The brand-new Verde County deputy might have just been kicked out of the Army on his ass, but gossip had it that he had been a crackerjack investigator with the CID, the Criminal Investigational Command of the Army, and if Riley's self-esteem or confidence had taken a beating by the Army's actions it certainly didn't show. Jimmy raised his hand in welcome and Russ sauntered back. "Good to see you, Riley," Jimmy said. "To what do I owe the honor of this visit? We could always use another volunteer."

Russ grinned. "And piss Holly off? You have to be kidding." Russ's grin faded. "Actually, I'm here in a professional capacity. The sheriff's department has assigned me as the department liaison to the FBI on the investigation of the Internet video posting here and they've also got me working the Reece barn burning and the poisoning of Jackson's dog."

"Jesus, nothing like jumping in with both feet," Jimmy said.

"It's not so bad, really, since it's obviously the same perp involved in all the crimes." Russ got out his electronic pad. "I wanted to share what little, and I do mean little, additional information I found in the background checks and see if anything snaps." He tapped the screen a couple of times. "Most of these good people are as transparent as a pane of glass and I didn't turn up any more on them than the Feds did. Did you know that Misty Martinez's mother and stepfather have long been suspected of aiding political refugees fleeing to the United States?"

"No, I didn't," Jimmy said. "She's never said a word."

"Interesting, but doubtful that it would relate to the investigation." Russ tapped the screen again. "Randy Puckett was arrested during a protest rally in England during his sophomore year in college but charges were dropped a few days later." Russ tapped again. "I took a closer look at Angie Baxter after finding all that stuff about her assault on her ex, but after I read the police report I decided they should have pinned a medal on her. And here's another one the Feds didn't find. Hal Jackson had a run-in with the local authorities when he was off-duty one weekend in Seoul. Got drunk and tied up with another soldier over a drinkee-girl."

"That's odd," Jimmy said. "He told me he didn't drink—couldn't stand the stuff."

Russ shrugged. "As for the rest of your people, it's the usual marriages, divorces, a bankruptcy or two, the occasional arrest for DWI—same stuff the Feds found. I turned up zilch on the close relatives, too. We'll keep digging. There has to be some loose end out there that we can find." He started to stand up but sat back down. "How long do you and my sister plan to be on the outs?"

Jimmy stiffened. "And that would be your business because?"

"Because Holly's about as much fun these days as a bear with a sore paw and I for one am getting thoroughly sick of her." Russ grinned cheekily. "So, when are you going to straighten this mess out so I can stand to be around her again?"

Jimmy's eyebrow shot up. "And why am I the one who's supposed to straighten this mess out? She's the one who stabbed me in the back."

Russ's grin widened. "Funny, I think she feels the same way about you." He shrugged and plunked the western hat on his head. "Thanks for your time. If you think of anything else I'm across the way at mom and dad's place."

Jimmy watched with narrowed eyes as the cocky deputy sauntered to the door. So Holly was missing him, he mused as he idly twirled a ballpoint between his fingers. Well, he was missing her, too. But as long as her group insisted on supporting Alex Navarro for Congress and she supported them in that decision, he and Holly could go right on missing one another.

* * *

Holly pulled the Miata into the handicapped parking space in front of Gus's café. She rose slowly from the driver's seat, her bad knee popping, and limped as quickly as she could into the crowded café, spotting Judge Riley and Russ at a back table. "Sorry I'm late," she said as she slid into the vacant chair across from Russ. "Jason's organizational meeting ran longer than I thought it was going to, and then I made a stop off at the Chevrolet dealership on the way out of town."

"Didn't know you were in the market for a new car," Judge Riley said.

"I'm not. I went by to talk to daddy's old friend Fred Blakely about hiring Jason Donahue as a salesman." Holly's grin faded. "When I got there this afternoon Jason was so down he didn't even want to have his support group meeting and according to Emily, he's been really depressed since he went in to Blakely Chevrolet for a job interview and a little kid screamed and ran away from him. You can imagine what happened to the interview after that. So I went by the dealership to plead his case directly to Mr. Blakely and talked him into giving Jason a shot at Internet sales."

Russ's eyes danced with mischief. "So how did you get him to change his mind? Arm-wrestle him? Threaten to sic the VFW on him?"

Holly grinned wickedly. "I crossed my legs so my scars would show, hiked up my skirt and smiled big." She pushed her chair back a little and demonstrated.

Three teenage boys in a nearby booth whistled. "Don't forget I'm giving you a grade," she reminded them as their faces turned red. She scooted her chair back in. "Seriously, I played on his sympathy and persuaded him that Jason deserved the same chance as any other applicant. After I made my case Mr. Blakely was more than willing to give Jason a chance. Anyway, Jason and Emily are thrilled."

Russ raised an eyebrow. "Jason and Emily, huh? Are they a couple now?"

Holly's grin returned as she remembered the pile of Jason's clothes on the foot of Emily's bed. "I would think so, yes." She sighed wistfully. "I envy them."

Judge Riley closed his menu. "You and Jimmy are still on the outs with one another, I take it? I don't know what's gotten in to that young man."

"I know exactly what's gotten into him. It's called 'campaign fever' and he's had it since mom and her buddies got their claws into him," Holly said tartly. She turned to Russ. "How's the investigation going?"

Russ shrugged. "Slower than I'd like, but I've cracked tough investigative nuts before, and I'll crack this one sooner or later. And if I tell you any more than that I'll have to kill you."

"Got it," Holly said. "And thank goodness, it looks like Lisa's on her way to our table. I don't know about you but I'm starving."

* * *

Chucky stared down at his plate of fried chicken, glad the high-walled booth hid him from the main dining room. He listened keenly as Lisa Simmons took the dinner orders of the bitch and her companions. That snotty asshole thinks he can crack this investigative nut? Somebody ought to take the cocky twerp out and crack his nuts, Chucky thought as he bit into a perfectly fried drumstick.

But, on the other hand, why bother with the deputy? There was much more interesting quarry to be had. The bitch's little sister and her barbequed boyfriend would certainly make interesting targets, and he still planned to catch a picture of Adamcik at the shrink's place. *Such fun.* He would go ahead and add this Jason and Emily to his plans for the next month or two—but they would not be next. He had a couple of other gimps he needed to attend to first.

* * *

Holly climbed into the backseat of Caroline Briscoe's SUV as Cathy clambered into the front. "I guess two out of three isn't bad," Holly said as Caroline got in. It had taken most of the afternoon but Caroline had finally found an elegant cocktail dress that slimmed her baby bump and Cathy an elegant pants suit that mostly hid her prostheses. Only Holly had come up empty-handed. "I swear, I don't remember Homecoming being this big a deal in the San Antonio high school I went to."

"It probably wasn't," Caroline said. "I was really surprised the first time I went to a Verde Homecoming."

"According to Beto, they make just as big a deal of it in San Saba," Cathy said. "I guess I can wear the same outfit to both."

"If mom was speaking to me I'd go raid her closet."

"So what's with Nadine?" Cathy asked. "Still pissed that our 'little group' decided to support Navarro?"

Holly grinned wickedly. "It finally dawned on her that our opinion might actually matter. And then she really got hot under the collar when she called me on it and I asked her to tell me what she and her cronies intended to let Jimmy do for me and mine. She hung up and hasn't called back."

"What about Jimmy?" Cathy asked.

"Haven't heard from him, either," Holly admitted. "And I don't particularly care if I do. Can you imagine? He had the gall to tell Russ I stabbed him in the back, after he refused to commit to doing a single thing for the wounded veterans." She glanced at Caroline. "Oops, I guess I shouldn't have said anything, Caroline. Sorry."

"Sorry for what?" Caroline asked dryly. "Frankly, I find Nadine's demands odious. Besides, since the stink with the video on the Internet, Jimmy's money's about dried up anyway."

"So where's he getting the money to keep campaigning?" Cathy asked.

"A few of Nadine's diehards who are positively terrified of Navarro are still sending a little," Caroline admitted. "But damn few and damned little. Has Russ made any progress with the investigation?"

Holly bit her lip. "No, and it is hell waiting for the next shoe to drop. And you know it will."

"Every one of us is living with one eye on the rearview mirror," Cathy chimed. "It's taking its toll."

"So do you think you and Jack are going to be doing much dancing at Homecoming?" Holly teased as Caroline rubbed her rounded middle.

Caroline looked down and laughed ruefully. "Probably not. But we'll still have fun. How about you guys? Going to be able to dance on those dicey legs of yours?"

"Beto and I have been practicing but we're not doing too well. We ended up in a heap on that nice, soft thick rug in front of my fireplace. And it took us *forever* to get back on our feet."

"Oh, I feel so sorry for you," Holly jeered.

"Seriously, we can dance together just fine," Cathy assured them. "How about you, Holly?"

"I'm a little nervous about it. I haven't gone dancing since I got out of rehab," Holly admitted. "And thanks to Asshole, I don't have anybody to land on the rug with."

Caroline thought a minute. "Tell you what. I'm not offering a rug, mind you, but Jack is one of the best dancers out there. Why don't I send him over tomorrow night after supper and he can take you around the living room a few times so you can see what you can do?"

"I have a better idea. Why don't I cook supper for the three of you and you and Ryan can critique me?" Holly countered.

"Oh, that sounds lovely," Caroline breathed. "A meal I don't have to fix."

Holly smiled. "Then I'll see you at seven."

* * *

Jimmy ran his hand down the five o'clock shadow that covered the lower part of his face and pulled into Heaven's Point. Thank God Janelle had taken Carrie to Austin for a couple of days; he was so tired he was about to drop. He was about to park in his driveway when he spotted a familiar red truck in front of Holly's cabin and headed toward Holly's instead. What was Jack Briscoe's truck doing in front of Holly's place? Was Holly all right? Was Caroline making a house call? He knew it was none of his business, especially with the way things were between them, but Jimmy couldn't have stopped himself if he had tried. He parked next to Jack's pickup and sat for a moment, staring at the muted light behind the drawn shades. At first he could see nothing, but then two figures clinging to one another danced in front of the shades. *No, it couldn't be*, Jimmy's mind screamed. But then they made another pass in front of the window, Jack's broad shoulders unmistakable next to Holly's distinctive topknot.

Without waiting to see more, Jimmy leapt from the Navigator and sprinted for the house. He wrenched open the front door and burst into the living room just as Jack and Holly made another pass toward the windows. Jimmy let out with a bellow of rage and launched himself straight at Jack. "What are you thinking, you two-timing son of a bitch?" he yelled as he wrapped his arms around Jack and jerked him away from Holly. Before Jack could react, he whirled him around and hit Jack full in the face.

"Jimmy, what in the *hell* are you doing?" Holly demanded as she stepped between him and Jack.

Jimmy brushed her aside and started toward Jack. "You cheating bastard, your wife is pregnant." he said as he swung at Jack for the second time.

Jack neatly blocked Jimmy's blow and came back with one of his own, hitting Jimmy in the jaw. Jimmy shook off the punch and lurched toward Jack again. "You idiot," Jack said with contempt as Jimmy lowered his head and plowed it into Jack's chest, knocking him into the sofa. "I'm not cheating on my wife."

"The hell you're not!" Jimmy raged as Jack came off the couch and landed another blow, this one into Jimmy's nose. "You were all over Holly like—*yaggh,*" he choked as an icy deluge landed on his head and ran down his back. He yelped and whirled around to face Caroline Briscoe holding an empty tea pitcher.

"Are you quite finished whipping up on my husband?" she asked, the ice in her voice colder than the tea.

Jimmy looked from Caroline to Holly to Jack. "Oh, shit."

Ryan picked that moment to walk into the living room. "Mr. Jimmy, you're all wet!" "That is the *damned* truth," Jack said as he glared at Jimmy. "Just what I need, to have to go to school tomorrow with a black eye."

"I'll get you a compress," Caroline said. She disappeared into the kitchen and returned with ice wrapped in a towel.

"What about me?" Jimmy asked as Caroline handed Jack the compress.

"You can root hog," Caroline said.

Jimmy got up and came back with a compress of his own. "So I guess I've made a complete ass of myself."

"Yes, you have," Jack agreed tersely. "And this is the second time in three months you've slugged me. I'm getting a little tired of it."

"I'm sorry," Jimmy said grimly. "It's just that I saw the two of you and…have you ever heard the phrase that somebody 'saw red'? Well, I did. I really did see red. I thought you were cheating on Caroline."

Jack and Holly looked at one another. "Great to know what he thinks of our moral values, isn't it, Jack?"

"God damn it, I'm sorry," Jimmy snapped. "But I really thought—"

"Spare me the concern," Caroline broke in. "You were pissed because of Holly, not because of me."

"No, he wasn't," Holly said. "Couldn't be. He told me to take a hike. Hasn't bothered to call or come by."

"Why should I, after your soldiers decided to throw their vote to Navarro and you said you agreed with them." Jimmy said bitterly.

"Only because you're so busy kissing up to Nadine Hightower's political machine you can't be bothered with the likes of us," Holly shot back.

Jack put his fingers between his lips and let out a screeching whistle. "Time out, you two." He put his hands on his hips and looked Jimmy straight in the eye. "Holly hasn't danced since she got hurt and she didn't want to embarrass herself at Homecoming next week, so we went for a spin. I have no romantic designs on her. However, she is one hell of a woman and the next guy who dances with her probably will, so I suggest that you and Holly find a way to resolve your differences before you lose her for good." He looked down at the tea on the living room floor. "And it might not hurt if you got a mop and cleaned up the tea." He took Ryan's hand and held his other out to Caroline. "Shall we?"

"Oh, absolutely," Caroline said. She handed the tea pitcher to Jimmy and picked up her purse. "See you."

Jack followed Caroline out the door and pulled it shut behind them. Jimmy and Holly stood staring at one another. "So what do we do now?" Jimmy asked finally.

Holly looked down at the mess on the floor and shrugged. "You can start by finding a mop."

Chapter Sixteen

Jimmy swung the mop across the last of the tea on Holly's living room floor. "There, that's done," he said tightly as he returned the damp mop to the mop bucket.

"Thank you," she said through stiff lips.

He shrugged. "Least I could do." He walked the mop and bucket to the tiny utility closet. As he headed toward the front door he caught of whiff of Holly's lemony shampoo and it was all he could do to stop himself from reaching out and taking her into his arms. Damn, he had missed her, he thought as his groin tightened and his breath caught. He hadn't realized until now just how badly.

Jimmy reached blindly for the front door before turning and facing Holly, her expression wary but her eyes wide and bright. She felt it, too, he thought as she took an uneven breath. The attraction that always seemed to simmer between them. Still, he had the door half open when she quickly closed the space between them, reached past him and slammed the door. "I didn't stab you in the back," she said bitterly. "And I'd appreciate it in the future if you didn't tell people that I did."

"What would you call it, then?" he demanded and leaned into her as she took a step back, her color high and her nostrils flaring. "Your soldiers threw their support to Navarro and you let them."

"I didn't *let* them do anything," she snapped as she thrust her chin into his face. "They're grown men and women, and they made up their own minds."

"Bull," he said as he took a step toward Holly, forcing her to take another step backward. "You're their leader and they would do just about anything you asked them to. How hard did you try to change their minds?"

"About as hard as you deserved, you egg-sucking kiss-up." she spat at him. "And don't start with me on how you need their money, There are other people you could have gone to for help."

Jimmy grabbed Holly's shoulders and jerked her to him. "You know better than that." he snapped into her upturned face. "I was getting nowhere until Nadine and her bunch stepped in. Damn it, Holly, I had no choice."

"Yes, you did," Holly ground out. "You always have a choice."

"Oh, quit being a naïve little fool, Holly," he ground out as he stared into her irate face. "Naïve and unrealistic and ridiculously idealistic and—God, never mind," he spat out as his control broke and pent-up desire overrode common sense. He bent his head and captured her lips in a grinding, punishing kiss, swinging her around and backing her against the door and trapping her there while he plundered her mouth, his tongue thrusting into her as he poured his frustration and his fury into an embrace of fiery possession.

At first, she pushed ineffectually at his shoulders, but then she too gave in to desire. Her arms tensed and her fingers dug cruelly into his biceps as she arched her body toward his, not in sensual surrender but in an angry sexual challenge, throwing down an unspoken gauntlet goading him onward.

Jimmy could feel her nipples pucker as he raked his fingers down her arms and tightened them around her wrists, yanking her arms over her head and against the door as he continued his sensual assault on her mouth. He pressed his swollen groin tightly against her stomach so that she was left with no doubt as to the state of his arousal.

Anger and frustration and need fueled him as he kissed her with an almost brutal intensity that under other circumstances would have shocked him. But his frustrated desire for Holly overrode even the thinnest veneer of civility, leaving him a slave to his base need to possess and conquer.

* * *

Damn him anyway, Holly thought as Jimmy plundered her lips and mouth unmercifully, sending shock waves of desire coursing down her body to the tips of her toes. Damn him and damn her, too, for wanting this—wanting *him*—so badly. He probably thought in his desire-fueled arrogance that he would conquer her, possess her, put his brand on her and make her his own. But he would not be the victor in this base, primitive duel, she vowed. He was not going to possess her tonight; she would be doing the possessing, not Jimmy. She would do the branding. She'd do the claiming. Arching toward her angry opponent, she met his tongue thrust for thrust, their mouths fighting a tormented duel as the weeks of anger and denial exploded into bitter passion. Lunging forward, she managed to break free of the door, catching him by surprise as she shoved him across the room and tumbled him down beneath her on the sofa, following him down and covering his body with her own where she again met his mouth in a kiss of angry possession and demand. She kissed him again and again, relentless in her assault even as he continued his stranglehold on her arms. Her nipples swelled and she could feel the moist sexual heat between her thighs as her aroused body welcomed the nearness to Jimmy's. Holly breathed in the sensual, musky odor of his desire as it mingled with hers. Oh, she wanted him, she thought as she ground herself against his taut, muscular body, his muscled chest heaving, breath rough in his throat, his arms and hands like steel as he held hers in a vise-like grip. But she was going to have him on her terms. This round would go to her. Even as she felt his thigh forcing itself between hers, she vowed that in the sensual battle between them that tonight she would be the victor.

* * *

She was not going to win this, Jimmy promised himself as she rained down a sensual assault that had his head spinning. *He* would do the possessing tonight, not Holly. Releasing her hands, he grabbed the collar of her T-shirt and ripped it down the middle, exposing her rosy-tipped breasts first to his gaze and then to the sensual possession of his mouth. Gone was the lover who touched and teased and coaxed—this wild man he barely recognized sucked her entire nipple into his mouth and pulled, hard, until she gasped, the roughness of his touch clearly exciting her even as his arrogant possession seemed to inflame her even further.

* * *

Not to be outdone, Holly jerked open his shirt, sending every button flying, and raked her fingernails down his chest and around his sides, leaving the angry marks of her possession on his bare skin. As furious with Jimmy as she was, she reveled in the feel of his strong, muscled body beneath her fingers and the assault of his lips on her bare breasts.

Eager for more, she reached down and with strong and sure movements unbuckled his belt and shoved down his slacks and his underwear, freeing his magnificent manhood into her hand and grasping it possessively in her palm. She looked at him, anger on his face and primitive, unleashed passion in his eyes as he palmed both of her breasts, his fingers firm in their possession as she arched toward him.

Her fingers deft, she stroked the turgid shaft as it grew even more rigid under her firm yet sensual ministrations, her fingers tightening in the dark hair curling at the base as she continued her own sensual assault. Her fingers drifted lower, cupping his testicles as she lightly fingered the sensitive organs, glorying in the power she wielded as his body trembled with desire. Grinning wickedly, she let her fingers drift back to the thick thatch of hair at the base of his penis and gave it a good yank.

His eyes flashing with ire, he jackknifed to a sitting position and stood her up in front of him. His lips tight and his face grim, he unzipped her jeans and yanked them down her body, his hands tangling in the thatch of auburn curls guarding her secrets even as she kicked the jeans and her panties away from her body.

He jerked her toward him and tucked her beneath him even as she maneuvered to be on top. Holly swung her body around and rolled them both off the couch onto the plush area rug, where they twisted and turned, rolling over and over as each of them tried in vain to assume the superior position. She was panting and furious by the time he had her pinned down, her wrists above her head in one hand while he parted her legs with his powerful thigh and with a firm yet deft touch on her most secret spot brought her to a hard, swift climax that left her shaking even as she twisted in helpless fury.

Without letting her out of his control, he bent his head and laved her bared breasts with his tongue as he continued to touch and stroke her intimately. Passion combined with rage as she rose to a second earth-shattering climax, then a third. Without releasing her hands, he slid his body in between her thighs and entered her with one quick, sure thrust, the arrogance of his possession fueling a final surge of ire as she used his body as leverage to whip them over and sit astride him, taking control of their coupling, their hands linked in front of them in a fight for dominance even as she stroked and bucked and rode him in a frantic rhythm until they went up together in an orgasmic firestorm of angry, bruising passion.

Holly heard a high, keening cry that she dimly realized was coming from her own mouth as Jimmy arched upward, perspiration dripping from his face and his body as his back arched and he groaned, his seed pouring into her in powerful jets as his body convulsed beneath her.

Her anger spent, she blinked and stared warily at him as he gazed back at her with an unreadable expression. "Well, who won that one?" she asked tersely as he slowly released his bruising grip on her wrists.

Jimmy shrugged and lifted her off his body. "I'd say it was a draw," he said as he pushed himself into a sitting position. They stared at one another for long moments as they took in the marks their angry coupling had left on their bodies. "Well, fuck," he said finally as he stood up and pulled up the dress slacks that had never completely left his body.

"Yep, that's what it was," she said dully as she looked down at her ruined T-shirt. "And it didn't accomplish a damn thing."

"That's the ever-lovin' truth," he agreed as he shrugged into his buttonless shirt. "And just for the record, Holly. I could have come in here and lied through my teeth to you and your soldiers and told Nadine and her backers not to believe a single one of those promises. But I had enough respect for your soldiers and for you not to do that. So if that makes me an egg-sucking kiss-up, then I'll wear that label with pride." He picked up his car keys off her end table and let himself out of the house.

Holly sat on the rug for long moments. In spite of what they had just said, the sex they had shared tonight had not been meaningless. But it had not been an act of caring, either, she thought despairingly as she finally pushed herself up off the floor and gathered up her jeans and panties. There had been no consideration or tenderness or any desire to please. Yes, they had both reached the summit but even those had been acts of domination and possession, not acts of giving.

But they had both been right about one thing. They had accomplished nothing with the sex but some badly needed physical release. They were no closer to any kind of accord or reconciliation than they had been when Jimmy first burst in the door.

Holly threw the ruined T-shirt in the trash can and ran the shower as hot as she could stand it and stood under it for long minutes, her hot tears mingling with the water cascading down her face. She loved him, she realized with despair. But her love for him did not blind her to his faults or make her willing to excuse his shortcomings. If anything, it made her want to hold him to an even higher standard—a standard that he was either unable or unwilling to meet. He hadn't lied to her and her soldiers and she had to give him credit for that, but neither did he have the courage of his convictions, and for that she held him responsible.

She stood under the pouring water until it began to cool and her tears had stopped flowing. She pulled on a pair of shorts and another T-shirt and curled up in the chair beside her bed. Was she wrong to be disappointed in him? Was he only doing what he had to do? Holly sighed and let the sound of the waves pounding the shore work its soothing magic. Yes, she had fallen in love with Jimmy Adamcik, but she doubted very much that she had a future with him.

* * *

Jimmy unbuckled Carrie's car seat and helped her scramble onto the graveled parking lot of the Verde community center. The lot was almost full and Jimmy spotted Jason Donahue and Emily Riley getting out of a brand-spanking-new Chevrolet. "Daddy, do I look pretty tonight?" Carrie asked eagerly as she smiled up at him.

"God, yes, honeybun," Jimmy said as he swallowed the lump in his throat and bent down to look at his only daughter, her eyes shining, dressed in her new red party dress and with little red roses in her hair. "You're the prettiest girl here, I promise you that."

"I love you, Daddy," she said as she flung her arms around his neck.

"I love you, too, honeybun," he said as he gave her a squeeze. "Now, let's go inside and knock them dead. I hear the band warming up already." Jimmy smiled as Jason and Emily came toward them. "New wheels?" he asked as he and Jason shook hands.

"Nah, it's my demo," Jason said. "Holly persuaded the owner of Blakely Chevrolet to take me on as an online salesman. I owe her one."

"And now he's doing so well Mr. Blakely's threatening to move him to the sales floor, scars or no," Emily chimed in proudly, smiling at Jimmy.

Holly must not have confided in her about their recent encounter, Jimmy thought, or she wouldn't be so friendly.

Emily spotted someone over Jimmy's shoulder and her eyes lit up. "Over here, guys. We just got here."

Jimmy's neck prickled and he turned slowly, knowing without actually seeing her that Holly was in the group. He had not seen or heard from her since the debacle on her living room floor except in hot, stormy dreams. He had started to call her any number of times but something—honesty, maybe, but probably more likely cowardice—stopped him even as he stared at her number on his telephone screen. What could he say to her? He had let her down and he knew it. The breath left his chest. She stood only a few feet away, resplendent in her dress blues even as she stared at him with unreadable eyes. Only the slight flaring of her nostrils revealed that she was not unaffected by their meeting.

"How are you, Holly?" he said, his voice gravel in his throat.

"Fine," she said simply. She looked down and her gaze softened. "You look so pretty tonight, Carrie," she said as she struggled to kneel down to make herself eye level with the child.

Carrie flung her arms around Holly. "So do you, Miss Holly," she said as she hugged Holly around the neck. "You look all official."

Carrie released Holly and she struggled to stand. Jimmy moved to help her but Russ reached her first, his eyes on Jimmy cold. Uh, oh, Russ knew or suspected something. "Cathy, Beto, good to see you," he said quickly before Russ could speak. "Cathy, you look beautiful."

"Thank you," Cathy said tightly, daggers shooting from her eyes. Bet that one knows the whole story, Jimmy thought uncomfortably as Holly and her entourage swept past him to greet Tommy Joe and Christi.

Jimmy took Carrie by the hand and entered the community center, which was gaily decorated for the dance with pumpkins and scarecrows and all the trappings of autumn. He spotted Jack and Caroline on the other side of the room but he wasn't about to forego this ready-made opportunity to politic a little and had only made it partway across the room when a hush fell over the crowd. Holly and her brother stepped in the door with Cathy and Beto, Jason and Emily, and Christi and Tommy Joe. Jimmy felt emotion build in the room as the small group paused on the threshold, the sacrifices each had made evident for all to see.

The crowd was silent for a moment, then as one the people of Verde rose and greeted Holly and her soldiers with a long, rousing ovation, tears running unashamedly down the cheeks of many of the townspeople, and Jimmy felt a lump in his own throat. Finally the roar of the crowd died down and Jimmy made his way over to Jack and Caroline, who looked over at Holly and then up at Jimmy without concealing her exasperation.

"Quite an entrance that little group made," Jack said. "I knew the town held them in high regard, but I didn't realize until now just how deeply the community feels about Holly and her soldiers."

"And you wish I had their support," Jimmy said tightly. "Damn it, Jack, you know what happened. It was either that or lie to them and I don't quite have the lying through my teeth part down pat."

Jack held up his hands placatingly. "I get your point," he replied. "I just wish there was some way to get them on board."

"There is," Caroline said tartly. "Jimmy could support the soldiers and mean it. It's not like Nadine and her friends have been keeping you in style, have they, Jimmy?"

"No, Caroline, but they're about the only support I have," he shot back. "Don't you think I'd like to tell Nadine and her cronies to take their conditions and shove them?"

Jack looked at the two of them and rolled his eyes. "I don't know about you two, but I for one am thoroughly sick of the damned campaign. Could we please, *please*, talk about something else tonight?"

Caroline smiled ruefully and Jimmy nodded. The lights dimmed and with a drum roll Holly's cadets, ramrod straight and marching in perfect cadence, posted the colors and led the crowd in the Pledge of Allegiance. Then the crowd fell silent as Holly stepped to the podium and nodded to the band-leader. Jimmy immediately recognized the opening bars to Lee Greenwood's "I'm Proud to be an American" and a shiver went down his spine as Holly in her golden soprano sang of her love for America. The poignancy was not lost on Jimmy or anyone else in Verde—she had been hurt so badly serving her country and she could still sing about how much she loved it. She was a true patriot if there ever was one.

And what about you? What kind of patriot was he? He wanted to win this election so he could make a difference, but was he going to make a difference if he won by shackling himself to a special-interest group that was so tight-fisted they didn't even want to help the men and women who had been injured protecting *their* freedom? But what choice did he have? Was he the kind of patriot she was? He wasn't sure he wanted to examine the answer to that, as he was beginning to feel more and more like a fraud.

* * *

Holly sipped soothing chamomile tea and stared out her picture window. The first norther of the season had blown in an hour ago, its nippy gusts whipping the water into a churning froth and making an escape to the fishing dock with a cigarette distinctly unappealing, so chamomile tea in front of the big window it was. She propped her legs on the ottoman and willed the melody of the wind and the water to calm the restless agitation that had gripped her since facing Jimmy again tonight. She had planned to give him a wide berth this evening but fate had a different plan and the only reason she had not thrown herself into his arms was sheer willpower. Willpower and not wanting to make a fool of herself.

She finished off the tea and was rinsing out the cup when her cell phone rang. She thought it might be Cathy, but if it was, Holly was going to be seriously disappointed in Beto Flores. She spotted Rory Keller's name and number on the screen and a cold dart of fear shot through her. "What's up, Rory?" she demanded.

"Cathy Armbruster and Beto Flores were attacked at her place a half an hour ago. Brutal bastard knocked Beto out cold and raped Cathy. Beto came to and shot the bastard dead. There were brochures left and there are already pictures and a message from that Chucky person up on Jimmy's website."

"Where are Cathy and Beto now?" Holly's eyes blurred and she nearly gagged in horror. Dear God, after all Cathy had suffered, to be raped just as she was putting her life back together.

"She and Flores are being transported to the emergency room in Burnet. They're asking for you."

"Thanks for the call," Holly said as she snapped off her phone. Damn, damn, damn, she thought as she yanked on a pair of jeans and a polo shirt and raced out to the car. Another attack on her soldiers— two of them this time, she thought as she whipped out of the driveway. And Beto shot Chucky. But if Beto shot Chucky, how could there be pictures posted on Jimmy's website? She spotted Jimmy in his driveway buckling Carrie into her car seat and Russ's taillights racing toward the Heaven's Point entrance and guessed they were both en route to the campaign headquarters. "God, I hope you did shoot him, Beto," she said out loud as she chased her speeding brother out of the subdivision with Jimmy's headlights in her rearview mirror. "I hope the bastard you got was him."

* * *

Jimmy pulled into a parking place in front of his campaign headquarters. His hands had not stopped shaking since Rory's phone call with the news of yet another attack and instructions to get to the campaign headquarters as quickly as he could. He and Russ had broken every speed law and Holly was probably still breaking a few herself on the way to her friends. Fear and a sense of helplessness swept over Jimmy as he envisioned Holly in her tiny convertible out on the highway. What if Chucky was waiting to run her off the road or attack her in the emergency room parking lot? What if he hurt her as he had Cathy Armbruster? *What would he do if something happened to the woman he loved?*

Jimmy unbuckled Carrie and held his sleeping daughter against his shoulder while he fumbled for his office keys.

"Give those to me," Russ demanded as he snapped on a pair of gloves. "Rory called me on the way and said that pictures are already up. Until I know better we're going on the assumption that the pictures were posted here. Jeez, what's this?" he said as he turned and peered at the gaping front door swinging to and fro. "Don't touch anything; he may have left prints on the door. We'll need to process this as a crime scene. Is there another door I can go in?"

Jimmy let Russ in a side door. Russ quickly cleared the scene and within minutes the place was swarming with Verde county deputies, one of whom instructed Jimmy to stay outside. Jimmy put Carrie on the back seat to sleep and watched bleakly as his campaign headquarters was processed. He got out his phone and swore out loud when he found the posted photographs—Beto crumpled in an unconscious heap on the front porch, Cathy with a knife at her throat as she lay pinned beneath her attacker, and Beto shooting Cathy's assailant in the forehead. And yet another chilling message: "Tell the bitch and the cocky asshole deputy that I'm still around. Chucky's getting closer." Who the *hell* was responsible for this? Who was the monster in their midst? And how much longer before he went for Holly?

* * *

Holly sat on the utilitarian sofa in the Burnet Hospital emergency room and watched through a plate-glass window as the sun teased its way over the horizon. Across the room Beto's father sat with Cathy's parents. Holly wondered just how much of the blame for this debacle the three of them laid at her feet.

Beto was being questioned by the Verde County authorities as well as the FBI and there had been a parade of law enforcement officers and medical personnel into and out of the emergency room. Russ had called her about 3 a.m. with the gruesome news that pictures of the attack been posted from a desktop computer at Jimmy's headquarters.

Holly had cursed herself for her morbid curiosity even as she stared in horror at the pictures and message.

Thankfully, the pictures and the message had already removed but the mental image of her terrified friend and the carnage created by Beto's bullet was not going to go away as easily.

An impossibly young-looking dayshift nurse came into the waiting room. "Mr. Flores? The police are through questioning your son and he's asking for you."

Mr. Flores shot up out of the chair and followed the nurse into the emergency room. Cathy's father pointed to Mr. Flores's empty chair and motioned for Holly to come over. "I'm so sorry for what happened to Cathy," Holly murmured softly.

"So are we," Mr. Armbruster said frankly. "But if you're planning to take a guilt trip over it, cancel your reservation. This is the fault of one person and one person only, and that's the SOB who's doing all this."

"I just hope this doesn't ruin what she has with that young man," Mrs. Armbruster fretted. "She's been happier the last few weeks than she has been since she got hurt."

Holly's eyes widened. "I hope so, too," she agreed.

At that moment the young nurse reappeared asking for the Armbrusters. Holly waited for the better part of an hour before they reappeared, both looking less than relieved. "Go on in there and talk to her," Mrs. Armbruster said. "She needs more than we can say to her."

Holly let herself into the emergency room and made her way to Cathy's cubicle. Cathy lay on her side staring dully at the wall. "Go away, Holly," she said softly.

"Not gonna do that," Holly said as she pulled up a chair. She reached out and took Cathy's cold hand in both of hers. "Have they taken care of you?"

"They said I could go home. They said that nothing's physically wrong with me. Can you believe it? I get raped within an inch of my life and they say nothing's wrong."

"Who came out with that little tidbit of wisdom?" Holly asked with disbelief. "I think I'll have a word or two with them."

"Oh, don't bother," Cathy said tiredly. Tears welled in her eyes and she swiped at her face with her prosthesis. "And it was going so wonderfully with Beto. I was going to seduce him, Holly. I had fresh sheets on the bed and eggs and bacon in the fridge. But I guess that's over. Now he'll be out the door so fast it will make your head swim."

"And why the hell would I be out the door so fast it would make Holly's head swim?"

Holly and Cathy both flinched at the sound of Beto's softly angry voice. Holly reached out and grabbed the white-faced young man. "Here, you sit," she ordered as she shoved Beto into her chair. "What are you doing out of the bed? You should be resting."

"Resting? I've been answering questions all night," Beto said tersely. "Now," he said as he turned to Cathy and took her hand. "Why would I be out the door?"

Cathy looked at Beto disbelievingly and pulled her hand away. "I'm dirty," she said. "I'm nasty and I'm used and every time you look at me you're going to see me like that."

Beto reached out and took her hand again. "Cathy, that is the biggest bunch of horseshit I've ever heard. You were *attacked*, for God's sake. You're not dirty, you're traumatized. And how do think I feel? I couldn't do a damn thing until it was too late to help you. I killed a man tonight and I didn't even get the one who was behind it all." He reached up and brushed a tear off his cheek.

"You did get him, Beto. You did get the one who hurt Cathy."

"But the bastard that's behind it all is still out there somewhere." Beto turned back to Cathy and took hold of her chin, turning her to face him. "Look at me and read my lips. What happened last night is not, I repeat, is *not* going to destroy the best thing that's come my way in a long time. Do you understand that?" Holly held her breath, letting it go when Cathy finally nodded. "Now, this is what we're going to do. We're going home together. Doc Briscoe's pulling some strings and getting us both in—tomorrow, hopefully—to see a fancy shrink in Austin who specializes in PTSD and trauma recovery." He leaned over and kissed Cathy softly on the lips. "We'll talk to him and we'll take his advice. Cathy, we're going to get through this. And whenever you think you're ready, we're going to burn up those sheets and eat those eggs and bacon. Does that all work for you?"

Cathy nodded wordlessly as she struggled to sit up. "I honestly thought it was over," she sobbed as Beto cradled her in his arms. "I thought you wouldn't want me anymore."

"Not a chance," Beto said soothingly. Holly slipped a tissue from the box and wiped her own eyes as Beto held Cathy until the sobbing ended

Leaving Cathy in the care of Beto and her parents, Holly tore up the miles to Heaven's Point, hoping to outrun the migraine that was building inside her head. Damn, damn, damn, she thought as she flew past the arches of Templeton Dam, cursing the bright sunlight stabbing her in the eyes. A man was dead. Cathy and Beto were hurt and Cathy's rapist wasn't even Chucky. Russ and the Feds were no closer to catching the bastard. She and Jimmy, along with the rest of her wounded warrior tribe, were apparently sitting ducks for that bastard Chucky.

So what could she and the others do to protect themselves from further harm? Cathy and Beto had both been armed tonight but they were attacked anyway. What other steps could they take? Some of Holly's fellow Army veterans were providing private security; was it time to call in reinforcements? Holly's head pounded and the aura she so dreaded was starting to form. Tomorrow, she promised herself as she rounded the last curve and drove into Heaven's Point. She would call in the experts tomorrow. Today she just needed to go to bed.

* * *

Chucky swallowed the last of his beer and stared at the image on his computer screen of the stranger who had carried out Chucky's dirty work and given his life for the privilege. Stupid prick, Chucky thought as he dropped the empty beer bottle in the trash can by the kitchen table. The dumbass was supposed to have left the gimp dead on the porch. Oh, well. At least he'd managed to get the rape part right. He laughed out loud as he imagined the scene early this morning at campaign headquarters. Adamcik and the asshole deputy must be pissing in their pants, not to mention all the gimps who thought their puny little pistols and their fancy-assed security systems were really going to make any difference. He had wanted to stick around and watch the fun at headquarters but that would have been taking too big a chance.

Not that he wasn't taking plenty of those already. Just recruiting the prick in Austin had been risky enough. And then he had driven the stolen Hyundai all over Verde and broken into Adamcik's headquarters. Last night's plan had been far from foolproof and he could have been caught at any number of points. His actions had definitely gotten riskier. But it didn't really matter; he had only a few more things to accomplish and then it would be Jimmy Adamcik's turn, and at that point Chucky's work would be done— and so would his life. If he carried out his newest plans for Adamcik and the bitch, he too would die. And that was all right. Once his mayhem was finished and Adamcik and the bitch were dead, he wouldn't have that much to live for anyway.

He curled up under the blanket and punched the pillow into a more comfortable shape. So what should he do next? Should he do the predictable thing and attack another gimp? Or should he do something unpredictable? It had taken him awhile, but last week he had finally gotten the pictures of Adamcik that would expose him as the weakling fraud Chucky knew him to be. So what would it be? Another gimp attack, or was it time to drop his little bombshell on Jimmy Adamcik?

Chapter Seventeen

Jimmy sat back and listened patiently to the inevitable Wily Riley tirade condemning divorce-induced greed and hoped that once court was adjourned he would be able to pick Carrie up and go home to a decent weekend of sleep. The nightmares were back in earnest, both the old ones about Iraq and a new set, these featuring Holly crumpled on Cathy's front porch or Holly screaming as a nameless, faceless stranger raped her. Jimmy had done the previously unthinkable this morning and taken an extra dose of medication and now he had the headache from hell. He had a call in to the psychiatrist but hadn't heard back from him and had mentally rearranged the next few days in the event that an additional appointment was needed. He breathed a sigh of relief when Judge Riley finished his dressing down and declared the Bellemer marriage over.

Ducking out of the courtroom, Jimmy headed outside but his hopes for an early start to the weekend ground to a disappointing halt when Russ Riley's cruiser pulled up and the unsmiling deputy disappeared into Jimmy's office. He crossed the street and followed Russ in, motioning the young man past his secretary to his private office in the back. "What can I get you to drink?" Jimmy asked as he opened a small refrigerator.

"I'm fine," Russ replied, his voice and manner clipped.

Suit yourself, Jimmy thought as he found himself a bottle of water and settled back in his chair. "I assume you're here to update me on the attacks last weekend."

"That and to ask a few questions," Russ said tersely. "The dead man at Cathy's place, the one Cathy Armbruster identified as her rapist, was an Austin lowlife named Clarence Briggs. He was a diagnosed sociopath and has spent more time in jail than out of it. He was last seen in the watering hole where his bike was found abandoned. The bartender remembers seeing him talking in a back booth with a stranger but the bar was packed and nobody remembers seeing them leave. Nor does anybody remember anything about the stranger, just that he was medium-sized and apparently had no distinguishing characteristics. We tried a sketch artist with the waitress but her picture is so vague it's nearly meaningless."

Russ turned his pad toward Jimmy and showed him a picture that Jimmy had to agree was useless. "It's almost as though he's had the training to fade into the woodwork," Jimmy said slowly.

Russ shot Jimmy a look. "We've already ascertained that he's probably ex-military where he would have been trained in just that kind of skill. We've gone back over your volunteers again and dug a little more deeply into their military records, but they were medics and file clerks and such. In fact, the only one with any real combat experience is you." He moved his fingers across his pad. "How would you characterize your relationship with Randy Puckett?" he asked.

Jimmy shrugged. "Randy? Years of jealousy and animosity on his part and disgusted disdain on mine. I was shocked when he volunteered to help with the campaign."

"Could you elaborate?" Russ asked.

Jimmy thought a minute. "Randy's always thought I was born with a silver spoon in my mouth. He resented it when I started dating Lauren in high school and hit me in the nose when he found out I was the one who popped her cherry. Got mad again when Lauren divorced his no-good college roommate and took back up with me."

"And how did you feel about him?" Russ prompted.

"I think…thought…hell, I still think that if Randy Puckett put as much time and energy into making something of himself as he puts into envying everyone around him that he'd be a millionaire several times over. Why?"

"Because he has a history with Alex Navarro," Russ said.

Jimmy blinked. "Now, that surprises me," he said. "Randy doesn't resent the hell out of him?"

"Don't know," Russ said frankly. "We know very little about the nature of the relationship, just that they apparently go all the way back to their college years. It was Alex Navarro who bailed Randy out the English jail and Alex's father who waved the magic wand and made the charges against Randy go away."

"So you think that all this may be Randy's way of paying back that debt?" Jimmy asked slowly. "What about his lack of a military background? And for that matter, do you think Alex Navarro and his campaign would be behind the violence Holly's soldiers have been subjected to?"

"I have no idea, but I'm sure as hell going to pursue that line of investigation and see if it takes us anywhere. We can't afford to leave any stone unturned until we get this thing solved." Russ sat back in his chair. "I've spoken at length to Cathy Armbruster and Beto Flores. Thankfully they both seem to be recovering." He paused a minute, his face grim. "The victims are getting closer and closer to my sister. I don't like it."

"You think I do?" Jimmy ground out.

"So why don't you do something?" Russ demanded. "Besides leaving bruises on her during hot monkey sex?"

"Jesus, Riley," Jimmy yelled, his temper snapping. "What do you want me to do? You think I don't lay awake worrying about her alone in that house? You think I *like* having nightmares about her getting raped or murdered? You think I'm not worried sick about the woman *I love*?"

Russ blinked. "So when are you going to let go of your dumb-ass pride and get your rear end down the street and tell her that? Shouldn't she be worth more than a damned congressional election?" Without waiting for an answer, Russ picked up his Stetson and left Jimmy sitting alone at his desk.

He sat for long moments staring at the bluebonnet painting on the wall. Damn it, Russ Riley was right. Jimmy had let his pride and hurt feelings have their way, and instead of acknowledging that Holly's soldiers had a right to their opinions and that she was correct in respecting that he had taken his marbles and gone home. And then he had taken her body in a cold, loveless mating that had left them even further apart. What kind of a fool was he? Was there any way he could repair the damage he had done to their relationship, or had he completely destroyed what they had begun to build together?

Jimmy picked up his phone and promised Caroline Briscoe Sunday dinner in the café if she would pick Carrie up and feed her supper. He swung by the café and had Gus cook up a batch of fried chicken and with his nerves jumping like a broken bed-spring he drove to Heaven's Point. Thankfully both the Miata and the Harley were in Holly's driveway and before he could ring her doorbell he spotted her at the end of the dock. He watched for a moment as she cast her line into the water and slowly and patiently reeled in the bait. The pole bobbed and the line tightened and Holly, her body snapping to full alert, deftly reeled in what proved to be a respectable bass.

She removed the fish and plopped him into an ice chest that had another fish or two inside.

Jimmy wandered down the dock, careful to make enough noise to alert her to his presence. She turned around and her body stiffened and she watched, her expression not particularly welcoming, as he held the sack of chicken out in front of him. "I brought you supper," he said as she eyed the bag. "Unless you'd rather clean and cook the fish."

"Uh, thanks," she said. "The fish will keep until tomorrow."

He handed her the sack and carried the ice chest full of fish back to the house. "How are Cathy and Beto doing?" he asked as she got out knives and forks and a couple of plates.

"Definitely better," she said as he unboxed the chicken, fried okra and corn. "Beto got the stitches out of his head just this morning. Caroline Briscoe sent them to the same psychiatrist you're going to and Cathy's starting to work through what happened to her. And one of my old friends who has gone into the security business is coming to our next support group meeting to talk with us about protecting ourselves."

"I'm glad," Jimmy murmured.

They sat down across from one another and she looked at him, plainly curious and not trying to hide it. "Mind telling me what this is all about?" she asked finally as he pushed the open box of chicken in her direction. "You didn't bring me supper to get an update on Beto and Cathy."

"I want to talk to you and figured the food wouldn't hurt. Want to talk now or after dinner?" he asked.

"Is the conversation going to make me lose my appetite?" she asked.

"I hope not," he said frankly. "Let's eat and then we'll talk."

Holly nodded. They didn't try to make small talk and he could feel the tension building on his part and, he thought, on Holly's part, too, but they both managed to do justice to Gus's fried chicken and were soon sitting in her living room, Jimmy on the sofa and Holly across the room in a chair, staring warily at one another. If he hadn't been so nervous he would have been amused at the way she kept looking first at him and then at the furry rug where they had come together so fiercely.

He sat tongue-tied for long minutes before he finally made himself sit up and look straight into her eyes.

"I'm sorry, Holly. I fucked up badly and I'm sorry. I never should have expected your soldiers, or you for that matter, to endorse my candidacy when I'm not able to offer you the kind of support politically that you're looking for. And I sure shouldn't have sent you out the door." He looked at her unreadable expression and took a deep breath. "Anyway, I know it's asking a lot of forgiveness on your part but if you're willing I want you to take me back."

Holly was quiet for a moment. "I see," she said finally. "If you don't mind my asking, what made you change your mind? You were pretty adamant that as far as you were concerned it was over between us."

Here I go, Jimmy thought, hoping she didn't laugh out loud at him. "How about because I love you," he said simply. "Because I love you and I'm scared for you and I think you're worth more than a damn seat in Congress." He stopped and took a breath. "Because I don't care what you and your soldiers do or how you vote. Damn it, Holly, I don't care if you and your soldiers stand outside the polling place and hand out Navarro brochures. You don't have to agree with me politically." He stretched out his hand toward her. "Just please take me back. Please, Holly, give me another chance."

* * *

Holly trembled as she stared across the room at Jimmy, hardly able to believe what she was hearing. Jimmy loved her. Jimmy wanted her to take him back; he wanted another chance with her. A part of her, the part that was in love with Jimmy, longed to throw herself into his arms, but another part, the part that was all too well acquainted with political reality, kept her firmly rooted in her chair. "I-I want to believe you, Jimmy," she said frankly as she felt tears gathering in her eyes. "And I want to give you that chance more than you'll ever know. But what about the next time our political differences come up? And they're going to. You say that I mean more to you than the election, and God bless you for that. But are you really going to be able to not let the political differences come between us anymore?"

"I'm sure as hell going to try," he said. "What about you? Are you going to be able to go forward with a relationship without our political differences getting in the way?"

Could they really and truly put their political differences aside? Could they deal with those differences and make a relationship work? Holly didn't know, but if he loved her and she loved him they had to give it a shot. She got up out of her chair and sat beside Jimmy on the sofa. "I'm sure as hell going to try," she echoed him as she took his hand in hers. "I do love you. And I'll do everything in my power to make it work for us."

"That's all I can ask," he said as he pulled her toward him. "God, Holly, I've missed you," he said as he held her face between his large hands and looked deeply into her eyes. "I've missed you so much." He pulled her toward him and met her lips gently with his.

It was different this time, she thought as she gave herself over to the tenderness of Jimmy's embrace. It was different, knowing that he loved her and knowing that he knew she loved him. Oh, the passion was still there all right, she as he deepened their kiss and their mutual desire sparked a firestorm of need and want. But there was more, Holly realized as Jimmy's tongue caressed her lips and her mouth and his fingers slipped gently into her hair as he continued to hold her face in a gentle but powerful grip. There was tenderness and caring and *love*, and it was the love that made all the difference. It was love that would see them through the weeks and months ahead, she thought as she slid her arms around Jimmy's chest, cradling him sweetly against her trembling body, her nipples stiffening into hard little peaks as the blood began to pool deep within her body. It was love that would enable them to stand together as a couple when Nadine and her minions and, yes, even Holly's soldiers tried to put a wedge between them. If they made it, and Holly so hoped they would, it was their love that would carry them through.

Jimmy released Holly's lips and began a silky ravishing on the tender skin of her cheeks and forehead. "God, I love the way you feel against me," he murmured as he bore her down into the thick cushions of the sofa and covered her body with his own. For long minutes they kissed and caressed one another, letting the passion between them grow as they let their bodies become reacquainted through layers of clothing, knowing that in due time that clothing would be removed and they would be even closer. Holly's fingers feasted on the strong muscles of Jimmy's back and chest, caressing him lovingly in the same places she had put her angry marks on him the last time they had been together.

Slowly, but with purpose and passion, their clothing slowly disappeared into a heap next to the sofa—his jacket, her blouse, his shirt, her bra, his shoes, her shoes, his slacks, her lacy panties—until she swiftly tugged his boxers down his legs and tossed them aside. She gloried in the feel of his tall, strong beautiful body as they lay together, bare flesh against bare flesh as they drank in the feel of their naked bodies so intimately entwined.

"God, I've missed you," he breathed as he planted long, slow, drugging kisses on her face, capturing her mouth with his even as his burgeoning manhood pressed into the tender flesh of her hip. "I dreamed of you, Holly. I dreamed of you and I reached for you and then I'd wake up and you weren't there."

"At least you could sleep," Holly countered softly. "Some nights I laid up there until two or three in the morning wanting you."

Jimmy glanced down at the fluffy rug beside the sofa. "Even after that?" he asked.

"Especially after that," she admitted.

He pressed his forehead against hers. "I am so not proud of that night," he admitted as he caressed her shoulders and slid one hand down to her pebbling nipple. "I was an animal."

Holly's eyes danced as she stroked his lips with her tongue. "Well, that night was certainly a revelation. No, don't feel that way," she said when his face darkened. "I was just as big an animal as you were, if not worse. In some strange way we both needed that encounter. But," she said as she slid her hands around to caress his muscled backside, "this is so much better."

"Yes, it is," he agreed as he held onto her and rolled them both off the sofa onto the fluffy rug. "Let's re-christen this thing the right way," he said as he sprawled out on the rug on his side with Holly facing him.

This time there was no aggression, no anger, and no attempt at domination as they kissed and touched one another, each touch a loving gift to the other. He pushed Holly over onto her back and bent his head, taking first one nipple into his mouth and then the other, nibbling and kissing and teasing them into sharp peaks of desire.

Holly's breath caught in her throat as, having done his work there, he nibbled lower, slowly coming down the tender skin of her chest and stomach, stopping to pay loving homage to her navel before slipping even lower, past the curling triangle and invading that most secret of places, his tongue finding and teasing the little nubbin of pleasure at her core.

She gasped as his tongue whipped back and forth mercilessly, tender yet insistent as she spun higher and higher, lightning flashing behind her eyes as she drew closer and closer to the ultimate. She broke with a hoarse shout on her lips as tremors of delight radiated outward from her core to her head and her toes and her fingertips.

Jimmy shifted and she gasped as he covered her body with his and entered her with one swift thrust, her taste on his lips as he took possession of her mouth, her body and her soul. With tenderness and passion he moved within her, love and desire in every stroke as together they climbed the mountain, their bodies so in tune that they passed through the sublime portal together.

Holly's release had barely begun when Jimmy came with a powerful thrust that left him deeply buried as his seed poured into her waiting body. Tremors racked them both as they clung together desperately and rode the wave of their mutual delight, long powerful shudders carrying them to a higher sensual level then they had ever experienced together.

They lay together for long moments, waiting for their breathing to slow and their hearts to stop pounding in their chests. Without breaking their connection, Jimmy carefully rolled them to their sides so that they were facing one another and stared deeply into Holly's eyes, his love for her plain on his face. "That was awesome," he said as he cradled her against him. "By God, we have to make this work. We can't just give up on something this wonderful."

"You do realize that mom and my soldiers are not going to be happy we're back together," she said as she gazed into Jimmy's loving face. "We have to...what? Ignore them? Tune them out? Tell them to go to hell?"

"Yes to all of the above," he agreed. "And believe it or not, we have more people rooting for us than you think we do," he added as he swooped in for a short, sweet kiss. "Jack and Caroline want us back together and your little brother told me to do something more than have hot monkey sex with you."

Holly's face turned red. "How did he know about the hot monkey sex?"

"He noticed the bruises. The boy wasn't born yesterday," Jimmy laughed. "Speaking of hot monkey sex," he said as she felt him harden inside of her, "How about a little more of it before I have to go pick up Carrie?"

"You better believe it," she laughed as he rolled on top and pushed her down into the soft rug and made love to her all over again.

* * *

Jimmy propped his long legs on the deck rail in front of him and smiled to himself as he stared out at the lake. The breeze was cool enough to warrant the windbreaker he wore and before long he would be forced to enjoy the view from the sofa or the kitchen table or while curled up in his king-sized bed. He sighed happily— chances were he'd be enjoying the view with one Miss Holly Riley in the easy chair beside him or across the kitchen table or, better yet, curled up beside him in that big lonely bed of his. They wouldn't be able to move in together but her house was a stone's throw away and chauvinistic as it might be, Jimmy couldn't help thinking that the more time Holly spent with him and Carrie, the safer she would be. He had seen the pictures of Beto and Cathy and their attacker and, combat veteran or no, there was no way Holly was a match for this damn Chucky. For that matter, Jimmy wasn't sure he was a match for the monster either, but maybe the two of them together could take him on if they had to.

Jimmy stretched his arms above his head and wondered which camp was going to be more perturbed that he and Holly were back together—Nadine and her money machine or Holly's surprisingly possessive soldiers. But it simply didn't matter what any of them thought. He swung his legs to the deck and ambled in the house. He and Holly were, by God, somehow going to make their relationship work this time, even if it rubbed some folks the wrong way. Even though they had only spoken of the present tonight, he could already envision her wearing his ring, helping him bring up Carrie and having children of her own with him. He wanted the whole enchilada with her and by God he—*they*—were going to get it.

Jimmy stripped down to his underwear and was brushing his teeth when the landline rang. He grabbed the phone and groaned aloud. A call from Misty at this time of night could only be bad. "What's up?" he demanded, swallowing a gob of toothpaste.

"What the hell are you doing sneaking into a PTSD shrink's office and taking happy pills?" Misty demanded, raising her voice over what sounded like a noisy bar in the background.

What in the hell? "Misty, what are you talking about?" Jimmy snapped.

"Another Internet posting," she ground out. "Two pictures, actually. One of you going in the door of a Dr. Hiram Jacobsen and another of an empty prescription bottle of very new, very potent medication with *your name on it.* And another little message: 'Captain Bitch—did you realize you're sleeping with a loose cannon?' Damn it, Jimmy, does this mean what I think it does?"

"You mean are you running the campaign of a nutcase?" Jimmy shot back.

"Well, am I?" Misty asked coldly.

Jimmy felt his heart sinking. "Misty, I've had PTSD since my Iraq tours," he said quietly. "If that makes me a nutcase in your eyes I guess so."

"Aw, Jeez, Jimmy, don't take it like that," Misty said, contrite. "I don't think you're nutcase and neither does anybody else. But don't you think it might have been nice if you'd been forthcoming about it? Don't you think your campaign staff and your volunteers and your contributors and hell, even the voters have a right to know if something like that's going on?"

"No, I don't." It was Jimmy's turn to be cold. "It's a medical condition and according to Caroline Briscoe, I have every right to keep it private. Until now the only three who knew anything were the Briscoes and Holly Riley."

"And Chucky," Misty said.

"Yes, Misty, apparently Chucky is included in that very small circle." *And just how had that son of a bitch managed to join that exclusive little club?* "Okay, I'll put in a call to Russ Riley and you get the pictures down."

"Right," Misty said. "And we need to change hosting providers."

"Like that's going to do any good if one of my volunteers is shoulder surfing," he said. "All right, we'll change companies. See you in the morning."

Misty murmured her goodnights as he hung up the telephone. How had Chucky found out about the PTSD? Had Jack or Caroline or Holly inadvertently let his secret slip? And how would this very public outing of him as having PTSD affect his already troubled campaign? Jimmy's mind spun with too many unanswered questions—questions that he was not going to like the answers to come morning.

* * *

Jimmy sat with Jack and Misty at a table in the back of his campaign headquarters, sipping a cup of coffee and watching impatiently as once more the FBI techies swarmed over the campaign computers like ants over a picnic sandwich. So far the machines were turning up clean and they were no closer to discovering Chucky's identity than they had been before. Jimmy was due at a campaign appearance in Mason and was itching to get on the road but was waiting for Misty to finish some kind of hopefully magic statement about the PTSD for the press. "How long were the pictures actually up before you got them removed?" Jimmy asked his still-irate campaign manager.

"Longer than I want to think about," Misty said as her fingers flew over the laptop. "It was Friday night—who's checking a website then? The only reason I found out about them as soon as I did is that one of my nerdier friends spotted them. The originals are gone but you can bet they've gone viral and that the news people have them by now. Damn it, Jimmy, do you have any idea how bad this is going to go over?"

"Worse than the Fuentes's burning house or Cathy's rape photos?" Jack asked.

"Oh, hell yes this is worse, Jack," Misty snapped. "It's going to look like Jimmy's been lying to everybody—which, come to think of it, he has, hasn't he? And you can bet the Navarro camp will use it to go on the offensive."

"Damn it, it's not like I cheated on my wife or lied about campaign funding. PTSD is a medical condition and I had every right to keep it private. Both Caroline and Dr. Jacobsen said it was nobody's business but mine and there are plenty of people out there who are going to understand, especially if you spin it just right."

"And then there will be those who will not agree with that analysis of the situation," Misty said with frost in her voice. "Me being one of them."

"And I'll bet there's another one of those folks marching in the door right now," Jack said sardonically.

Nadine Hightower shoved open the front door and marched into the room. "So what's this about PTSD?" she demanded as she nailed Jimmy with a glare. "And why do I have to find out about it this morning in the God damned newspaper?" She slammed down the front page of the *San Angelo Tribune* in front of Jimmy.

Jimmy stared down at the newspaper, horrified but at this point not really sure why. The paper had run both Internet pictures under a headline that screamed "Congressional Candidate a PTSD Patient?" "I guess the question mark was to head off a lawsuit," he said ironically. He looked up at Nadine. "You come all this way to yell at me? You could have done that just as well over the phone."

"No, I came to spend a couple of hours with Holly before I'm due at a fundraiser in Austin," Nadine snapped. "Who by the way is smiling like a fool and singing 'I Will Always Love You' at the top of her lungs in the damn shower. Good God, Jimmy, on top of lying about the PTSD and everything else, did you have to take back up with her after her little group gave you the heave-ho? Your supporters are not going to be amused."

"Neither are her soldiers," Jimmy said mildly.

"Hey, man, did she take you back?" Jack asked. "Good going, Adamcik."

Nadine shot Jack a glare as Russ Riley crossed the room and pulled out the last chair at the table. "They really didn't think it was going to be one of these computers this time and they were right," Russ said. "They tracked it to an Internet café in San Angelo and it wasn't even done with your log-in. Do your volunteers ever share their log-ins with one another?"

Jimmy and Jack and Misty all looked at one another and shrugged. "I guess so," Misty said. "Why?"

"Because they found the log-in that was used to post the pictures in your computers as well, mostly linked to work done on your advertising," Russ said. "And the Internet café where the pictures were posted is two blocks from Randy Puckett's condo. So either Randy Puckett's in this up to his ass, or Chucky has gone to a lot of trouble to make it look like he is."

Chapter Eighteen

Jimmy sat down in the easy chair in his family room across from Holly and Carrie, who were curled up on the sofa together so Holly could read Carrie a bedtime story. He sipped his Scotch with a sense of contentment he realized was probably temporary but was nevertheless very real and welcome. It was good to have Holly back in his life, her smile warm and her arms welcoming and at least for now under his roof where he knew she was safe.

She had managed to send her disapproving mother on to Austin and used his kitchen to cook him and Carrie a pot of stew, and a sexy wink over ice cream promised him more in the way of sweetness once Carrie had gone to bed. They would have to be discreet and, at this point, there would probably not be any mornings where he would wake up with her, but after the election and this mess with Chucky was dealt with, Jimmy had every intention of making Holly a permanent part of his life.

But first he had to get the election and the Chucky business behind him, he thought tiredly as he wandered over to the computer and went trolling for news stories. The legitimate press was being careful not to make outrageous allegations but still the implication was there-Can a congressman with PTSD do the job? And the less-than-legitimate press was having the expected field day. And as Misty predicted, the Navarro camp had gone on the offensive. Surprisingly, Nadine had backed down about Jimmy's silence when Jimmy pointed out that, PTSD or no, he had agreed to the San Angelo group's conditions and that Alex Navarro had not. But more troubling to Jimmy was the issue of how Chucky, whoever he was, had gotten hold of the pill bottle and taken his picture in front of Dr. Jacobsen's office. According to Misty, Joe Russo and Russ Riley were in San Angelo questioning Randy Puckett, but Jimmy simply could not picture Randy Puckett torching a barn or blowing up a house or masterminding the rape. But if not Randy, then who?

Jimmy smiled to himself as Holly shut the story-book and stood up with Carrie's hand in hers. "It's bedtime, honeybun," she said to the sleepy child. "Want me or daddy to tuck you in?"

"You," Carrie said, smiling. "I missed you, Miss Holly. Mr. Jack told Miss Caroline that you and Daddy kissed and made up and

I'm glad. Then Mr. Jack said something about Daddy's sheets smoking and Miss Caroline laughed. Why would Daddy's sheets smoke, Miss Holly?"

Holly's lips twitched. "Care to get that one?" she asked Jimmy.

"Actually, Carrie, I don't have any idea what Mr. Jack was talking about," Jimmy managed to say without cracking a smile. "Come kiss Daddy good-night."

Carrie gave Jimmy a kiss and she and Holly disappeared up the stairs. He continued to surf the various news stories, his spirits sinking with each additional unflattering article. Holly was just coming back downstairs with a come-hither smile on her face when the doorbell sounded.

"Oh, joy. Who the hell could it be? It's almost ten." He peered out the window and spotted Russ Riley's cruiser. "Your brother's here," he called out as he opened the door to the weary-looking deputy.

"Sorry to interrupt," Russ said, his tired eyes snapping to attention when he spotted Holly on the stairs. "I'll make this quick so you two can get back to your evening." He looked at Holly with a question in his eyes.

"He took your advice," she told Russ quietly as she took Jimmy's hand.

"About damn time." Russ nodded once and followed them into the family room. "I wish the news out of San Angelo was better, or at least more definitive than it is."

Jimmy and Holly's smiles faded. "So what did you find out from Randy Puckett?" Jimmy asked. "Is he Chucky or part of what's going on?"

Russ grimaced. "Not even close. We—Russo and I—questioned the SOB for the better part of four hours and then questioned some others. It took a while because Puckett didn't want to talk, but when he finally opened up he's alibied for every incident. Jimmy, he's pissed as hell and said to tell you that you could take your campaign and shove it."

"Considering the way he's always felt about me, I can't say I'm too surprised," Jimmy said. "I was shocked that he volunteered in the first place."

Holly looked from Jimmy to Russ. "I don't understand. I know there was bad blood in the past but why is he so angry now? Surely he understands that with the pictures being posted two blocks from his house using his log-in, the authorities had to question him."

"Because to establish a good many of his alibis, Puckett had to admit that he's having a hot and heavy affair with a middle-school football coach," Russ said.

Jimmy and Holly looked at one another in surprise. "I had no idea," she breathed.

"Neither did anybody else in Verde," Jimmy said.

"Anyway, it really didn't help when the San Angelo PD picked up his boyfriend and a couple of other men who are not openly gay, including a Baptist minister, to confirm two of his alibis," Russ continued. "Those poor bastards could very easily end up losing their jobs and they're blaming Puckett, who is in turn blaming you."

"Well, damn," Jimmy said heavily. "I sure as hell never meant to do that to the man. So is Randy at least cleared of the Chucky business?"

"Yes, he's cleared. Completely."

"What about the connection to Alex Navarro?" Jimmy asked.

"He hasn't seen or heard from Alex Navarro in years, and he said that the only reason he was working for you was that Navarro is richer and more spoiled than you are."

"Another dead end," Holly murmured.

"Afraid so, which puts us no closer to identifying Chucky than we were before," Russ admitted. "The obvious question is how Chucky got hold of one of your prescription bottles. How do you handle this prescription, Jimmy? Do you have to take it with you or does it stay here at the house?"

"The medicine stays in my bathroom cabinet unless I have to go out of town, and when I travel I store it in my toiletries kit. And no, I haven't had any of it go missing since it was prescribed."

"What do you do with the empty bottles?" Russ asked.

"I toss them in the trash," Jimmy said. "And then I put it out in the garbage bin and the same commercial garbage disposal company that picks up everybody else's trash on the Point picks up mine, where it is compacted on the spot."

"So basically the only time Chucky would have access to a prescription bottle of yours would be if he broke into your house and took one, which we know has not happened, or if Chucky had access to your garbage," Russ said thoughtfully. "And if he has access to your garbage, then he most likely is located here on the Point."

"I thought we already knew that," Holly said impatiently.

"No, we suspected that, but other than you and Angie thinking someone was out there we had nothing. Now I think we do. Someone from off the Point would have been noticed, but a resident? It would take less than fifteen seconds to grab a sack and throw it in the car."

"So where does that get us?" Jimmy asked. "A good half of the people who live out here are volunteering in the campaign."

"It means we can narrow the search a little, anyway," Russ said. "And that both of you had really better start watching your backs, big time. Holly, have you thought about getting out of town for a few weeks? Maybe staying with Dad and Mom or going to your own mother's house?"

Holly shook her head. "Why? He could find me just as easily at Dad and Patsy's or Mom and Dell's. Besides, I have a job and a fellow here in Verde. My security-techie friend is coming to the next support group meeting. Maybe you could come, too and give us some insight?"

"Okay, then." Russ stood up and planted a kiss in the middle of Holly's forehead. "Be safe, big sister." He shook Jimmy's hand. "That goes for you, too, Adamcik. And both of you remember that I'm just across the way and Rory's two blocks over. I know you're both trained warriors," he added when Jimmy and Holly both started to protest. "But this guy? In another league altogether, apparently."

"That certainly seems to be so," Jimmy admitted. He let the young man out and turned back to Holly, who opened her arms and met his lips in a hot, sweet kiss. Yes, he loved this woman, Jimmy thought as he swept Holly off her feet and carried her up the staircase to his bedroom. And as he laid her on his bed and covered her body with his own, he promised himself that he would keep her safe from their nameless, faceless enemy, or that he would die trying.

* * *

Chucky whistled under his breath as he sped down the four-lane highway that would lead him toward Bryan-College Station and his latest quarry. In years past the drive would have been pretty, with pine trees soaring toward the sky and dappled sunlight falling on the soft roadside grass, but since the wildfires that had ripped through the area a couple of years ago the drive was sere and ugly. The experts all confidently predicted the eventual regrowth of the pine forest, but he was not convinced that would happen. In all honesty he didn't care. He did not plan to be around to see the forest when it came back. There would be tonight's attack and one more that he planned to survive. And then Adamcik and his bitch would be dealt with, and if the last and final mayhem went according to plan, Chucky would die along with them. And before they died he would have the deep pleasure of explaining to Adamcik and the bitch just what he had done and why he had to die.

But first there was the excitement he had planned for tonight, he thought as he parked his car in the deserted alley behind the aging duplex. He put on a pair of latex gloves and checked the items he had brought with him—a short jimmy stick, the loaded syringe and of course the "Adamcik for Congress" brochure—one last time. Chucky licked his lips in anticipation. This attack was the closest yet to his ultimate prey and a deep pleasure to carry out, as the message it would send would shake Adamcik and his bitch down to their bones.

* * *

Holly slapped at the alarm on her bedside table. Damn it, what was it doing going off at three on a Sunday morning? She slapped at it a second time before her sleep-fuddled brain registered the fact that it was her cell phone that had awakened her. Not good. She leapt from the bed and read the number displayed with a sense of dread. "What's wrong now, Russ?" she ground out. "What's happened?"

Holly could hear Russ take a deep breath. "It's Emily. Emily and Jason. The son of a bitch beat Jason to within an inch of his life and pumped Emily full of insulin. She's barely alive. And Jason had one of the brochures thrown on top of him. We've got to get to College Station. Now."

Chapter Nineteen

Holly stood at the foot of Emily's bed in the ICU of the College Station hospital and blinked back tears. Emily lay unmoving, her face deathly pale and only the slight rise and fall of the sheet giving any sign that she had somehow survived an immense shot of insulin. Although the doctors were confident Emily would survive the actual attack they were not as certain that she would come out of the assault entirely unscathed. It had taken the EMS team a few minutes to figure out what Chucky had done to her and several precious minutes more for them to get a glucose IV running. What would be the effect of that delay? Was Emily going to be all right, or would her spectacularly intelligent mind be affected by the sugar deprivation? Holly reached up and swiped tears from her face. "This is all my fault."

"No, it isn't," a gruff voice snapped as a gnarled hand patted her arm. "Holly, this isn't your fault at all."

Holly jumped a little. "Uncle Willis, I didn't know you were here," she said as she reached out and clung to his hand. "Russ contact you?"

"Yes, he called me before he lit out of town. Asked me to make a few calls. Your dad and Patsy are right outside of town and that FBI agent should be here any minute now. Jimmy's already here-for once the Pucketts could be helpful and took Carrie for him. And you need to stop blaming yourself, Holly. The attack on Emily and her young man was not your fault in any way, shape, or form."

"But I feel like it is," Holly admitted. "Everybody who's been hurt has had some connection to me and it keeps getting closer. Last time it was my best friend and this time, for God's sake, it's my little sister!"

"Who we have to have faith is going to be all right," Judge Riley said gently. "Instead of playing the blame game, you need to be spending your energy and your emotions being strong for Emily. And for Jason."

"That's for damned sure," Holly agreed.

A perky nurse with corkscrew curls poked her head in Emily's cubicle. "I'm going to have to ask you to leave," she said briskly. "Emily's doctor needs a few minutes with her, and her parents are in the waiting room. Oh, and Mr. Adamcik's asking for you, Miss Riley, and a couple of people who look an awfully lot like law enforcement are waiting with your brother."

Holly followed her tired-looking uncle out of Emily's cubicle. "Is there any way I can look in on Jason Donahue before I leave?" she asked Emily's nurse as Judge Riley left the ICU.

"Third cubicle down," the nurse said.

Holly found Jason's cubicle and peeked inside, wincing at the sight of the welts and bruises marring Jason's already delicate skin. He, too, was unconscious and his breathing was labored, but his arms and legs were moving a little under the sheet. "Hang in there, buddy," Holly said as fresh tears welled up in her eyes. She swiped at her tears and turned, nearly bumping into a tense-looking middle-aged couple in the narrow cubicle. The woman had Jason's bright blue eyes and the man was tall and big-boned. "Hello, I'm Holly," she murmured as she tried to move around the couple. "Let me get out of your way."

The man immediately put his hand on her forearm. "No, don't run off," he said quickly. "You're Emily's sister. The one who helped Jason get that new job of his. Jason can't stop singing your praises and we so appreciate all you've done for him." He took her hands in his. "We're Edgar and Nicole Donahue."

"Holly Riley." Holly turned around and the three of them looked at Jason. "He's restless."

"The doctor said he's got broken ribs," Nicole said. "And a concussion, but that he's most likely going to be fine."

"Oh, thank God," Holly breathed.

"What about your sister?" Edgar asked.

"Jury's still out," Holly admitted. "We don't know how long her brain went without enough glucose."

Nicole twisted her hands together in front of her. "That girl has to be all right," she said anxiously. "Jason asked me for his grandmother's ring. He wants to ask Emily to marry him." She turned anguished eyes toward Holly. "After all he's been through, he deserves happiness with her, doesn't he?"

Holly nodded. "He certainly does, Mrs. Donahue. And she couldn't find a better man if she tried. Give him my best when he comes around."

The Donahues nodded. Holly found her way back to the ICU waiting room, which had seemed so large when just she and Russ occupied it earlier and now seemed almost too small with the Rileys clustered at one end and Jimmy with Russ and the other law enforcement officers at the other—plus Wade and Benny asleep on sofas in the back. Holly joined Jimmy and the clutch of officers. "We caught a break tonight," Russ told Holly. "Wade and Benny interrupted Chucky's attack. If they hadn't both Emily and Jason would be dead."

"Thank God," Holly breathed. "I'm guessing that pictures were posted?"

"Yes. Oddly enough, they were posted from a used car lot on the outskirts of Bastrop using Betty Cleburne's log-in," Russ said.

"Betty Cleburne's log-in? It still goes straight back to the campaign volunteers," Jimmy said quietly.

"Who in the hell *is* this SOB?" Holly said bitterly. "Who in the hell is he and what have Jimmy and I done to piss him off so badly?"

* * *

Jimmy reached out and grasped Holly's clammy hand. The officers looked around at one another, obviously at a loss, before Russ reached out his arms and Holly fell sobbing into them. "She's going to be all right, Holly," Russ said quietly, crying a little himself. "She's strong and a fighter. She has to be all right."

Holly nodded. "Yes, she does. Mrs. Donahue said Jason's planning to ask her to marry him."

Jimmy felt his lips twitch as Russ pulled away from Holly. "Jason's asking her to what?" Russ demanded. "What do we know about him? Jimmy, didn't he serve under you?"

"I'd let Carrie marry him in a heartbeat," Jimmy said. "Really, Russ, he's a fine young man and would make your sister a wonderful husband."

Jimmy felt a firm hand on his shoulder. "My son thanks you for the endorsement." A tired but relieved-looking older couple stood to one side. "Jason's awake and asking to talk to someone about last night. And we saw some commotion around Emily's cubicle also."

Russ and Holly took off running toward Emily's bedside. Jimmy and the law officers all started toward Jason's bed when an older, fierce-looking nurse stepped into their path. "Two and only two can go back at one time," she said. She looked disdainfully at the crowd around Emily's bed.

Russo and a College Station officer stepped forward. Jimmy turned around and was almost out of the ICU when Agent Russo caught up with him. "Jason said he needs you there," he said.

"Did he say why?"

Russo shook his head. As Jimmy stepped into Jason's cubicle, Holly gave him a big thumbs-up from Emily's bedside. Jason's eyes were open and he looked at Jimmy anxiously. "Any word on Emily?" he demanded. "Mom and Dad said she was not in a good way."

Jimmy let himself smile. "Well, if the thumbs-up Holly just gave me is any indication, I'd say that's changed."

Jason visibly relaxed onto his pillow. "Thank God," he breathed. "What did he do to her?"

"Massive shot of insulin," Russo said. "If your friends hadn't driven up with that pizza she would be dead. And in all honesty, he'd have probably beaten you to death."

"Thank God for the cavalry," Jason murmured. He turned toward Jimmy, wincing as he did so. "There was something familiar about his voice. And then what he said to me was just plain weird. He said it was as much for me as it was for you and the bitch. That's what he calls Holly, right? That's why I wanted you to hear this, too."

Both law officers whipped out their notebooks. "All right, Mr. Donahue, we need for you to tell us everything he did or said from the moment you entered the apartment until the moment he left. What he did and what he said. Word for word, if you can."

Jason thought a minute. "We had been to a movie. Emily went in ahead of me while I checked the mileage on my demo. When I finally did go in I found Emily on the sofa and even in the dark I could tell she was in a bad way. I said 'What the—'. Then I heard this voice say 'What the, my ass.'" Jason again stopped to think. "Then he said 'Take this, you worthless prick. This is as much for you as it is for Adamcik and the bitch.' And then he beat the shit out of me. I tried to fight but he had the stick and to be honest these damn burns took more out of me than I like to let on. Anyway, that was what he said—what he was doing was as much for me as it was for you and Holly. And I swear to God I've heard his voice somewhere before."

Jimmy and the law officers looked at one another. "Where have you heard that voice?" Agent Russo asked. "Think about it for a minute."

Jason lay quietly for a moment. "Was it someone you've met in Verde or Heaven's Point?" Jimmy prompted.

"No, it's not like I've heard it any time recently," Jason said thoughtfully. "It's more like a voice from the past."

"Do you or did you ever know anyone by the name of Chuck or Charles who might be in some way connected to this?" Agent Russo asked. "That nickname means something."

Jason thought a minute. "I've known a lot of men named Charles in my life. But somebody that might be connected? I don't think so."

"Jason, what is your exact relationship with Mr. Adamcik?" The College Station officer piped up.

"Major—Mr. Adamcik was my commanding officer in Iraq until I got hurt. I lost contact with him until by chance I ran into him at the Heaven's Point July Fourth picnic. And I've only seen him once since, at the Verde Homecoming."

"And Miss Riley? Does she go back to your military days also?"

"No, she doesn't," Jason said. "The first I even heard about Holly was when I met Emily and she said that her older sister had also been hurt in Iraq. I met Holly at the same Heaven's Point picnic that I reconnected with Mr. Adamcik."

The police officer looked at Jimmy and Agent Russo. "So there is no point in the past where the three of you connected in any way?" the officer asked.

"No, there isn't," Jimmy said. "I think it's interesting, though, that although Jason's relationship with Holly and Emily is fairly recent, he and I go not only all the way back to Iraq, but I was there the day Jason was injured so badly."

"Were you the only one injured, Jason?" Russo asked.

"No, there were three young men killed that afternoon and another injured," Jimmy volunteered. "Trayvon Johnson and Patrick Barnes were killed outright—dead at the scene——and Joey Delgado bled out ten minutes later. The fifth soldier, Hank Tomlinson, had burns but nothing like Jason and actually went on to do another tour before he left the reserves."

Both Agent Russo and the College Station officer wrote down the names. "Now we see if any of these men or their families has a connection to any of your campaign volunteers," Russo said. "I'll share these names with Russ Riley before I go." He glanced across the ICU to the cubicle where the Riley family was still clustered around Emily. "Mr. Adamcik, I guess I don't have to tell you that whoever this Chucky is, he's gotten about as close to Miss Riley as he can without actually attacking her. Unless he goes after the brother, which I don't think he will..."

"Yes, I know. You think she'll be next," Jimmy said flatly.

Agent Russo nodded. "You and Miss Riley are the two he's been threatening all along, and at this point he's running out of wounded warriors with a close connection to her. Yes, I seriously think that unless we can put something together from yours and Jason's tie to the past, it's highly likely that he will attempt an attack on Miss Riley in the very near future."

Jimmy looked across the ICU at Holly and his mouth tightened. He would be damned and then some if he let anything happened to the woman he loved. "Then the SOB will have to come through me to do it. Holly doesn't know it yet, but I'm not letting her out of my sight."

* * *

Chucky flexed his fingers on the steering wheel and blew out his breath, willing himself to relax as he drove down the patchwork of highways that would take him across the state from Verde to Midland. The sun shone weakly in the late afternoon sky and the temperature had dropped considerably. For the hundredth time since he'd gotten into the car Chucky asked himself if he could really do this one. The others hadn't been a problem; hell, he'd enjoyed beating the shit out of the gimp last night, and if the pizza boys hadn't arrived he would have bashed the bastard's head in with pleasure. But this...Chucky took a deep breath and let it out slowly. This one was going to be different. This one was going to hurt.

But he had to do it, and he had to do it today, before the gimp got to thinking and told the asshole deputy what Chucky said to him last night. The deputy wasn't stupid and it would be just a matter of time before he worked his way backward and came up with the old connection between Jason Donahue and Jimmy Adamcik. And it wouldn't take much after that to start connecting the dots, and the dots would lead them straight to him—or at least the man he used to be. So, if he was going to carry out the rest of his plan, he had to do this one now. Then it would be Adamcik's turn, his and the bitch's, at which point it would all be over and everything would be avenged.

Chucky pulled into Midland just as the sun was setting. When he trusted the dark of night to hide him, he headed toward the house, a sprawling ranch on the edge of town. He parked in the driveway as he inventoried the vehicles present. The late-model SUV was visible inside the garage but the impudent little Beamer convertible was nowhere to be seen. He wasn't sure how he felt about that, but there was nothing he could do to change things. He took a minute to pat the small loaded Walther he had zipped into the interior pocket of his oversized jacket—yes, he could get to it in an instant. Planting a big smile on his face, he walked boldly to the front door and rang the doorbell. He could see a light going on in the entry and suddenly the front door whooshed open. Annie stared at him for a moment before a huge smile lit her face and she opened her arms to him. "Tee, my God, is that really you?" she demanded. "You don't look like yourself anymore."

"Yes, Annie, it's me in the flesh," he said as he hugged the woman close. "How are you, darlin'?"

"As if you can't tell by looking," Annie laughed. "Come in, please." She grasped his hand and pulled him into the large family room, where a fire danced merrily in the fireplace. "What can I scare up for you to drink?"

"I would love a soda if you have it," he said sincerely. Annie brought in two sodas and curled up on the sofa while he took one of the side chairs. "So, how's your mom, Annie? And Arnold? Is she happy with him?"

"Yes, absolutely. They're off on a cruise right now, but they'll be back in time for Thanksgiving." Annie's bright smile faded. "And how are your mom and dad, Tee? Are they doing any better than they were in the spring?"

"About the same, I guess," he said. He hadn't seen his parents in over a year and had no idea how they were doing.

"So you have seen them," Annie pressed. "The last time I talked to them they weren't sure where you were."

"Well, they know now," he said. Or they would know when his dead body was identified.

Annie appeared satisfied with that answer. "So where have you been for the last little while?" she asked.

"Working on a ranch," he said. "Among other things."

"Far cry from fighting wars," Annie observed.

Maybe not as far as you think. "I like it," he said evenly. "I get to work outside and I love working with the animals."

Chucky spent the next half hour regaling Annie with stories from the ranch. It was almost like the old days, he thought as Annie howled with laughter at his mostly true stories. Almost, but not quite.

In the old days there would have been three of them sitting together, swapping stories and laughing at everything and nothing. The immensity of that loss grabbed at him suddenly and he couldn't keep the pain off his face. "I miss him, too," Annie volunteered as she looked across the space at him with concern. "So how are you really, Tee? Have you—can you—are you coping yet with losing Pat?"

Chucky could feel his face turning a dull shade of red as his agony swiftly morphed into a white-hot anger. "Funny you should ask that," he said quietly as he pulled the Walther from inside his jacket. He snickered as Annie froze and the blood drained from her face. "What do you mean by 'coping'? Am I coping with the fact that my baby brother was blown up in a hell-hole called Iraq?" He stood up and aimed the gun at Annie's forehead. "Am I coping with the fact that Pat died while the worthless gimp standing beside him is alive and well and selling cars? Am I coping with the fact that Adamcik and his bitch and all her friends survived and went on with their lives?"

"Oh my God, you're Chucky," Annie breathed, her voice shaking in terror. "You're the one who's been terrorizing all those soldiers. Damn it, Theo, how could you? How could you do the things you've done?"

"No, damn it, the question is how could *you*?" Chucky demanded. "How could you go to them, make them promises after what happened to Pat?" he demanded.

"But none of what happened to Pat was their fault, Tee," Annie protested weakly. "Not theirs, not Jimmy Adamcik's, and not mine. Please don't do this, no!"

"Yes, it is their fault," Chucky said implacably. "They lived and he died. Adamcik didn't save him. And you," he said as he cocked his weapon. "You went to them and gave them your support. You were disloyal, so you have to die."

"No, Tee," Annie protested as she dived to the floor. But Chucky's reflexes were faster and the bullet that tore into her skull found its mark before Annie even hit the carpet. Even though her eyes stared sightlessly up at him, he put two more bullets in her just to be sure. As the blood flowed from her lifeless body, he moistened his finger in the crimson flood and leaned over the glass-topped coffee table. He put the "Adamcik for Congress" brochure—ironic, in this house—on the coffee table and beside it in slashing letters wrote a single word: *traitor*.

Chucky started to wipe for fingerprints but remembered that he would be returning to his other persona for the short amount of time it would take to finish this up. Besides, there was at least one of his prints in the blood on the coffee table. *I'm sorry, Annie*, he thought as he took a picture of Annie's dead body to upload onto the Internet. *Really sorry*. He turned off the lights and locked the front door behind him and started on the long drive back to Verde. But she had been a traitor.

Leigh Anne had been disloyal to Patrick's memory, and now she had paid for it.

Chapter Twenty

Holly sat quietly in the hospital recliner across from Emily's bed and watched with tired eyes as Emily lay sleeping. Watery moonlight passed through the swaying branches of a tall oak tree to dance across the hospital room floor. A howling norther had blown in late in the afternoon, making Holly wish she had grabbed her coat in the mad dash to College Station. Thankfully she'd had the foresight to bring a couple of changes of clothes, and a gracious Jack Briscoe had assured her that her place right now was at Emily's side. Russ had been out most of the day working the case and Ben and Patsy and the Donahues had left for the evening. Jimmy had finally been convinced it was all right to make a late-night pizza run. Holly sighed as she peered out the door, nervous in spite of her assurances to Jimmy that she would be fine for a half-hour or so. As much as she hated to admit it, Holly was afraid that Jimmy was right, and that either she alone or the both of them together were Chucky's next target. And Chucky, knowing he had failed to kill Jason or Emily, would be just that much more determined that Holly, or Holly and Jimmy, would die.

Holly stepped across the hall and stuck her head in Jason's door. "Doing all right?" she asked softly as Jason looked up from a hand-held video game.

Jason turned stiffly toward Holly. "Damned ribs hurt," he admitted as he sat up and threw back the covers. "I want to see Emily."

Holly held up her hand as Jason started to get out of bed. "Only if you let me grab you a wheelchair," she protested.

"I don't need a damned wheelchair," Jason snapped. He stood up and immediately swayed back and forth.

"Yeah, right," she scoffed as she gently pushed him back down to the bed. "Sorry, soldier, it's a wheelchair or nothing. My bum leg can't support us both."

She found an abandoned wheelchair at the end of the hall and soon had Jason parked by Emily's bedside. "How close did I come to losing her?" he asked softly as he stroked Emily's arm.

"Too close," Holly admitted.

Emily blinked and turned sleepy eyes toward Jason. "Holly's hovering, and you shouldn't be out of bed," she said softly. "I'm fine now, honestly. My blood sugar's back up where it should be and the doctor said I can go home tomorrow." She turned frightened eyes toward Holly. "You're the one I'm worried about now."

"And Emily, you would be right," Jimmy said as he came through the door with a huge pizza carton and a big paper sack. "Holly's the logical next target."

"Or you and Holly together," Jason chimed in as he peered up at the pizza carton. "Is there enough of that for me to have a slice?"

"Yes, and I have no-sugar Buffalo wings for Emily," Jimmy volunteered as he set the food on Emily's tray cart. "And sugar-free sodas. I figured you two might be ready to eat some decent food with Holly and me."

"Amen to that," Emily said. Holly helped her sit up and Jimmy pulled up a second chair and the four of them dug into the food. Conversation was sparse but easy, and it occurred to Holly that if Jason and Emily married and she and Jimmy worked things out, this kind of camaraderie might very well be part of her future. And she wanted that, she thought fiercely. She desperately wanted a future with Emily and Jason loving one another and Russ as her neighbor and Jimmy as the man in her life. Her lips firmed as she looked at the beloved faces around Emily's bed. Chucky wasn't going to take this future from her, she vowed to herself as Jason and Jimmy shared a belly laugh. She would kill the bastard herself if she had to.

Jason was polishing off the last piece of pizza when Russ stuck his head in the door. "Jimmy, Holly, I need to see you out here for a minute," he said, his face even grimmer than it had been this morning.

The four clustered around the bed looked at one another. Holly and Jimmy started toward the door but Emily shook her head. "Russ, talk to them in here," the girl demanded. "Jason and I are involved in this now and whatever you have to tell them, it won't be any worse than sitting here wondering what you're out there talking about."

Russ stepped in the room. "There's been a murder," he said without preamble. "Leigh Anne Navarro's dead. Alex came home from a fundraiser in Odessa and found her about an hour ago. The usual brochure was found on her coffee table but there have been no pictures posted yet on your website."

Jimmy gasped and Holly put her hand to her mouth as Jason reached out and grasped Emily's hand. "Oh my God," Holly breathed in horror. "She was almost due to deliver. What about the baby?"

Russ shrugged. "You know as much as I do. Agent Russo's on his way to Midland and he'll call me when he gets there. And Jason, I'm glad you're here. We need to see if we can come up with any point of intersection between you, Emily, Holly and her soldiers, Jimmy, and Leigh Anne Navarro." Russ perched on the side of Emily's bed. "I know you tried and failed yesterday and now the murder of Leigh Anne makes it that much more confusing, but we need to try again. I'm going to assume that somehow Jimmy's at the heart of this." He picked up a napkin and wrote Jimmy's name in the center.

"The oldest relationship is between Jimmy and me," Jason said. "I was serving under his command when I was hurt in Iraq."

Russ wrote Jason's name and drew a line from him to Jimmy and wrote "Iraq" above the line. "It's my understanding that the two of you lost contact until the Fourth of July picnic this year."

"That's right," Jimmy said. "And then Jason started dating my girlfriend's sister."

"All right, let's put Holly on here and see where she and her wounded warrior friends fit in." He jotted Holly's name on the napkin. "I'm putting Emily down also." He wrote Emily's name and drew a line from Holly to Emily and another from Emily to Jason.

"My soldiers and I have been meeting for a while now," Holly said. "But nothing started happening to them until after I met Jimmy."

"And when was that?" Russ asked.

"Last May when I hired Holly to babysit Carrie for a couple of months," Jimmy said. "If my memory serves me correctly Tommy's barn was burned a couple of weeks after that."

"It was the night we went to San Angelo so Jimmy could meet mom's cronies," Holly added.

"But I didn't decide to accept their support until I saw the Navarros in action at the Fourth of July picnic," Jimmy clarified.

"That's right. You were all at that picnic that afternoon. So there is one point of intersection the five of you share—the Fourth of July Picnic." Russ jotted in Leigh Anne's name. "The other obvious connection is the war." He held up his hand when Emily started to protest. "I know you and Leigh Anne weren't part of it directly, but Holly and Jimmy and Jason were, and every other target of Chucky's ire is a combat veteran. A wounded or injured combat veteran. I need to talk to Alex Navarro. Maybe there's a tie-in with Leigh Anne that we aren't aware of."

Holly's eyes widened. "There is a tie-in," she said. "When Alex and Leigh Anne talked to the support group, Leigh Anne mentioned losing her cousin in Iraq and how his brother disappeared and his family fell apart. Could that possibly have drawn her into Chucky's twisted agenda?"

"It's worth checking out," Russ said. He checked a text message and tapped a few keys on his electronic pad. "Damn, the pictures just went up on your website," he said.

Holly peered over Russ's shoulder and flinched at the sight of Leigh Anne Navarro's sightless eyes staring vacantly into space. Blood and tissue caked one side of her head and darkened her hair and the carpet beneath her, and her left hand held the requisite campaign brochure. Beneath the grisly photograph Chucky had typed a message. "I've run out of family and friends. Adamcik, you and your bitch will definitely be next."

Holly pointed to a bloody smear on the coffee table. "What's that?" she asked Russ.

Russ zeroed in on the spot and sucked in his breath. "It says 'traitor,'" he said. "That makes it personal." He handed his pad to Holly. "I need to make a couple of calls," he said as he stepped from the room.

Holly handed the pad to Jimmy, who took a long look at the picture before handing the pad to Jason. Jason whistled under his breath. "I wonder how many nightmares that one's good for?"

Emily motioned and Jason handed her the pad. "Alex Navarro's the one who's going to have nightmares tonight," she said quietly as she gazed down at Leigh Anne's picture. "I hurt for him."

Russ was pocketing his phone as he came back into the room. "That was Agent Russo. They're processing the scene right now and have prints they're sure are the killer's, so if he's in any of the databases we should know who he is fairly quickly. Mr. Navarro's agreed to sit down with all of us, you four included," he said. "He's flying in tomorrow morning in his private plane."

"That's good of him," Jimmy said quietly. "Especially under the circumstances."

"He lost a wife and an unborn child tonight," Russ said flatly. "He wants this killer stopped as badly as you do." He looked at Jimmy and Holly. "Are either of you armed?"

Holly nodded. "Under my car seat," Jimmy said.

"Wade's on his way over to stay with the two of you tonight," Russ said to Jason and Emily. "It's a done deal, so save your breath. Besides, he's bringing more food," Russ added when Jason started to protest. "And I took the liberty of booking the three of us the deluxe suite at the hotel down the street. Safety in numbers and all that." He ran his hand down his tired face. "Come on, I'll walk you to your cars."

Holly supposed they were safe enough, the three of them soldiers and Chucky apparently on the other side of the state. But she didn't feel safe, not even locked in the third-story hotel suite with Russ and Jimmy and three pistols between them. Chucky had gotten to so many already, and he now had her and Jimmy firmly in his sights. Holly felt chilled in spite of the warmth of Jimmy's body curled tightly around hers. Would Chucky get to them, too? Would they be able to figure out who he was and stop him, or would she and Jimmy be the next targets of his unexplained, unreasonable hate?

* * *

The poor bastard's still in shock, Jimmy thought as Alex Navarro, his face blank and his eyes sunken, walked into the hospital waiting room commandeered for their meeting this morning. For once in his life at a loss for words, Jimmy nevertheless found himself moving toward Alex, Holly close beside him, both with arms outstretched toward the grieving man, who made a sound deep in his throat as he moved into their embrace. "Damn it, Alex, I am so, *so* sorry," Jimmy heard Holly murmur as Alex clung for a long moment to the both of them.

Then Russ put his arm around the stricken man and guided him toward the cracked vinyl sofa where Emily sat holding Jason's hand. Jason pushed himself from his wheelchair. "Emily and I are so sorry for your loss, Mr. Navarro," he said quietly as he and Alex shook hands. Alex murmured something incoherent and sat down. Agent Russo and officers from Midland, College Station, and Austin as well as Russ, Jimmy, and Holly found seats on other chairs and sofas and Jimmy shook his head inwardly. If they ever did catch the son of a bitch, he was wanted by four local police departments and the FBI. It would be interesting to see who got first crack at him.

Agent Russo turned compassionate eyes on Alex. "Mr. Navarro, thank you for flying out this morning." He gestured to Jason and Emily. "We needed Mr. Donahue in the meeting and it would have been very hard to get him to Midland."

Alex glanced over at Jason and nodded. "Yes, of course." His eyes flickered around the assembled circle. "I don't understand. Why did the individual who has been doing all of these things to Ms. Riley's friends and Mr. Adamcik's campaign suddenly"—he stopped and swallowed—"do what he did to Leigh Anne? What did *she* have to do with any of it?"

Russ motioned to the College Station detective, who handed him an easel and a cleaned-up version of the chart Russ had drawn last night on the paper napkin. "Mr. Navarro, this is a diagram of the interrelationships that exist between the people who have been attacked in some way by this Chucky individual. The only common point of intersection between Jimmy, Jason, Emily, Holly and her soldiers and your w—Leigh Anne—is the Heaven's Point picnic last summer, and the attacks on Holly's soldiers began before that. We were hoping that you might see something here that we didn't."

Alex stared at the diagram for a moment. "So you're saying the only time all four of them and Leigh Anne were actually together was that picnic?"

Jimmy and the others nodded. "But there may be some other way that they all come together," Russ said. "Holly said something last night about a tragedy in Leigh Anne's family involving a young soldier in Iraq. Leigh Anne talked about it the evening you all visited Holly's support group."

"Oh, yes, that cousin of hers," Alex said. "I don't know much about it. She told that story sometimes when she was visiting with soldiers."

"Was the story true?" Agent Russo asked.

"Of course it was true," Alex replied. "But she never talked about it with me, considering the blow up we had with that redneck uncle of hers before our wedding. Embarrassed the hell out of her father." His eyes flashed indignantly. "Let's see—how did the old bastard put it? 'I don't care if he can buy and sell China, Annie, no Barnes in their right mind would marry a damn Mexkin.' But what would—"

"Sir, did you say 'Barnes'?" Jason broke in as Jimmy jerked his head in Alex's direction.

Alex nodded. "Yes, Barnes. That was Leigh Anne's maiden name."

Good God Almighty, Jimmy thought. "Do you know her cousin's name?" he asked Alex.

Alex thought a minute. "I think the one who was killed went by 'Pat,'" he said finally.

Jason and Jimmy looked at each other, stunned. "Patrick Barnes was Leigh Anne's cousin," Jason breathed.

"Patrick Barnes was one of the three soldiers who were killed the afternoon Jason was burned so badly. I was their commanding officer," Jimmy said.

Everyone sat a minute, too stunned to speak. "Okay, that would be a major point of intersection between Jason, Jimmy, and Leigh Anne," Agent Russo said as Russ quickly updated the chart. "Let's keep going. Alex, Holly, what is the rest of that story?"

"Something about the parents separating and the brother falling off the face of the planet," Holly said.

Alex whipped out his phone and scrolled down the numbers. "Leigh Anne's father knows the whole story. Let me get it from him." He punched in a number. "Coop, Alex. I need to know everything that happened in your brother's family after their boy was killed. It may have a direct bearing on what happened to Leigh Anne." Alex listened for long moments and with a muttered "Thanks" punched off the phone. "Okay. My father-in-law doesn't know as much as I thought he did. According to Coop, before Pat died, his brother, Theo, was a model soldier—a Ranger, Special Forces, Airborne—you name it. But he developed a really sorry attitude after Patrick's death. There were constant run-ins with authority figures, he developed a serious resentment of injured veterans and there were even a couple of altercations involving wounded warriors, one leading to his arrest. And he made no secret of the fact that he blamed Patrick's death on the SOB who assigned his brother guard duty that afternoon."

"Which would be me," Jimmy murmured.

"Which would be you," Alex agreed. "Anyway, his attitude got him kicked out of the Army. Theo took himself out of the picture over a year ago and nobody knows where Theo is or what he's up to."

"Who he's bombing or raping," Holly murmured.

"Or who he's beating the shit out of," Emily snapped.

"Or who he's killing," Jason said quietly.

"Folks, let's not jump to conclusions," Agent Russo said.

"But you have to admit he looks good for it," Russ said. "He's demonstrated hostility toward wounded warriors in the past. He presumably resents the hell out of Jason for surviving when his brother didn't. Holly's a two-fer—she's a wounded warrior and Jimmy's girlfriend. And we know he blames Jimmy for what happened to his brother. And, thanks to the skills he learned from Uncle Sam, he can plan an assault, torch a building, make a bomb, tamper with things online, and disguise himself enough to fade into the woodwork. It even explains the nickname."

"Of course," Holly murmured. "He's an Eighteen-Charlie. A Special Forces demolition expert."

"And I just thought of something else," Jason said suddenly. "Remember when I said I thought I remembered my attacker's voice from somewhere in the past? His voice sounded just like Patrick's."

Agent Russo's fingers flew over the screen of his electronic pad. "Here's the most recent picture that I can find of Theodore Barnes." He handed the pad to Jason. "Does he look anything like your attacker?"

Jason stared for a moment at the picture, a five-year-old driver's license photograph. "It's hard to say. In this picture Theo Barnes has a round face and almost baby-like features and looks like he might be chubby. The man who attacked me is thin to the point of gaunt, and what I could see of his face under a scruffy beard is much thinner also. I honestly can't say it's the same man but I can't say it isn't either."

Jason showed the pad to Emily, who stared at the picture for long moments before shrugging her shoulders. They then handed the pad to Holly. "There's something about his eyes," she said. "Not the color, but the shape. I've seen them on somebody somewhere, but I'll be damned if I know who."

Holly handed the pad to Jimmy, who stared down for long moments at the image. He finally shook his head and handed the pad back to Agent Russo. "I'm sorry. Whoever he is, he's managed to change himself so much I don't recognize him."

"Or he's working in conjunction with someone else in your campaign." Agent Russo paused for a moment. "And we might be totally wrong, but Theodore Barnes, or whoever he's passing himself off as, is most likely our Chucky." He turned to Russ. "We'll get Theo Barnes's prints from the military database and start taking fingerprints from Jimmy's volunteers. If he's one of them we'll know it by the end of the day. Folks, I have a feeling this whole thing's about to come to a head." He turned to Alex. "Thank you again for flying in this morning. Your information was worth its weight in gold."

Alex stumbled to his feet. "Won't bring Leigh Anne or the baby back," he said a little bitterly. He turned to Jimmy and Holly. "For God's sake, be careful. I wouldn't wish this on my worst enemy." He nodded to the rest of the assembled group and left the room.

Their part in the meeting finished, Jimmy and Holly left the law officers conferring with one another and took Jason back to his room and delivered Emily to her anxious parents. What now? Jimmy wondered as he drove a tired-looking Holly to the hotel. Neither of them had slept much the night before and they had gotten no rest whatsoever the night before that. Jimmy figured that Holly was probably ready to drop. "Are you going to be all right driving back to Heaven's Point by yourself, or do you want to ride with me?" Jimmy asked.

Holly rubbed her forehead with the heel of her hand. "I'd take you up on that but I need the car. Oh, God, is that who I think it is?" she asked tiredly as Jimmy spotted Nadine Hightower getting out of her Escalade.

"Maybe she's just here to make sure you're okay," Jimmy said mildly.

"Oh, please, we both know better than that."

Jimmy admitted to himself that Holly was probably right and stifled a groan as Nadine made a beeline for the two of them. "Holly, Jimmy, I came as soon as I heard," she said as she eyed them.

"Heard what?" Holly asked. "That Jason and Emily almost died, that Leigh Anne did die, or that Chucky said Jimmy and I are next?"

"Why, all of it, I suppose," Nadine said. "Are you two all right?"

"For now," Jimmy said as Holly turned on her heel and headed into the hotel. "She's pretty badly strung out, Nadine," he added when Nadine shot a withering look at Holly's back. "We didn't know for hours if Emily was going to be okay or not, and then we heard about Leigh Anne, and then that SOB posted on my website that Holly and I are next. Has it even registered with you, Nadine, just how much danger your daughter is in right now?" he added softly.

"I'm well aware that she's in danger," Nadine said tartly. "And yes, I am worried about her, in spite of whatever you might think."

"Okay." Jimmy looked at Nadine critically. "But that's not what brought you chasing all the way to College Station, is it?"

Nadine had the grace to look embarrassed. "No, it isn't. Is there someplace we can speak privately?"

Jimmy nodded and followed after Holly. "The suite."

* * *

Holly took one look at the two of them coming in the suite and her eyes narrowed. "Do I need to give you two your privacy?" she asked as Jimmy offered Nadine bottled water and motioned for her to sit down on the couch.

"No, I don't have any secrets from you anymore and you know it," Jimmy said as he sat down in an easy chair across from Nadine. "So what can I do for you this morning, Nadine?" he asked. "Did Purcell Reynolds send you to complain about yet another black eye my campaign has suffered?"

"Actually, no," Nadine said. "He wanted me to come and talk to you about how you can use Leigh Anne Navarro's death to our benefit."

"You want me to do *what*?" Jimmy asked incredulously.

For the second time in ten minutes Nadine looked chagrined. "We want to talk to you about how to turn this around to your advantage. Not that the young woman's death isn't tragic," she added quickly. "But still, we're not doing all that well and we need to use every weapon at our disposal if we want to win this thing. And handled correctly, this could prove quite an advantage."

Jimmy shut his eyes and mentally counted to ten. "Let me see if I'm getting this correct. Leigh Anne Navarro is murdered, presumably by the same bastard who has bombed and raped Holly's soldiers, nearly killed her little sister, and threatened to kill her, and instead of being sick to your stomach at the senseless violence and scared to death about your own child, you're here to tell me to *take political advantage of it?* Good God, Nadine, just what kind of people are you folks?"

"The folks who win elections," Nadine snapped. "Look, Jimmy, of course we're horrified at the carnage and I'd be a fool if I weren't worried about my daughter, but damn it, we've had our first break in a long time and we'd be idiots if we didn't use it. You wouldn't have to be unkind-you could certainly express your horror and sadness, but leave the question out there—is a man distracted by grief the voter's best option? Besides," she added when Jimmy started to shake his head, "if my memory serves me correctly his campaign didn't hesitate to go after you when your PTSD became public."

"This is a different issue and you know it," Jimmy snapped. "That dealt as much with honesty as it did ability to serve, and if this were that kind of issue, you bet I'd use it. But for God's sake, the man's wife was *murdered.* I'm not going to use that against him in a political campaign, I don't care how many votes I could pick up. And, Nadine, I would like to remind you that his campaign said nothing, absolutely *nothing* all those times Chucky posted pictures of his handiwork on my website. If nothing else, I owe him for that. So not only no, but *hell no*, I will not use Leigh Anne Navarro's murder to gain an advantage over Alex in the campaign."

Nadine was silent for a moment. "Even if it costs you our financial support?" she asked softly.

Jimmy thought a minute and then nodded. "Even if it costs me your financial support," he said slowly. "Not that you delivered what you promised anyway."

Jimmy jumped when he felt Holly's hand on his shoulder. "Jimmy, are you sure you want to do this?" Holly asked softly. "If they pull their support your campaign is going to be broke."

Jimmy turned around and looked up into Holly's eyes. After all that had gone on between them, Holly was offering him her unconditional backing even though he knew she would loathe the thought of using Leigh Anne's death for a political advantage. Jimmy appreciated her support and loved her for it, but he had to do what he knew was right.

Jimmy reached out and grasped Holly's hand. "Yes, Holly, I'm sure." He turned back to Nadine. "If using a man's loss and his grief against him to win an election is the price of your money, then I am ready and willing to give it a pass. Nadine, I have to be able to look myself in the eye in the morning—otherwise, I'm going to cut myself shaving." He paused and took a deep breath. "Tell Reynolds and the rest of your gang that I do appreciate what they've done for me to this point and that I'm sorry it came to this."

"I'll let Purcell and the others know of your position." Nadine paused for a moment. "I guess this means that if we withdraw our support your position on a number of issues will be changing?"

"Am I going to push for increased support for soldiers and veterans and wounded warriors in particular? Am I going to insist that a quality education for the kids of Texas is more important than keeping taxes low? Am I—God forbid—going to expect the environment to take priority over the best interests of oil companies?" He grinned wickedly as Nadine shuddered. "You bet I am, Nadine. And am I going to lose this election to Alex Navarro? Probably. But you wouldn't have had much of a friend in me anyway. Oh, and if by some stretch of the imagination you decide to continue your support, those positions are going to be changing anyway. I'm tired of lying, Nadine, and I'm tired of dancing to the tune of a narrow-minded special-interest group with their own best interests at heart."

"I see," Nadine said stiffly. "Thank you for your honesty." She rose and was almost to the door when she turned around, a rueful expression on her face. "I told Purcell you'd never go along with the plan. You're a good man, Jimmy Adamcik. Too good for the likes of modern American politics. Go home to Verde and be a good husband to my daughter. You'll both be a lot happier that way."

"Well, that's a hell of a note," Jimmy said disgustedly as Nadine pulled the door shut behind her. "Too good for politics? What's that all about?" He pushed himself up off the sofa, irked and not even trying to hide it, his irritation growing when he saw Holly's grin. "What? You think she's right?"

Holly let out with a hoot of laughter. "If you could just see the look on your face. My mother calls you a good man and it pisses you off thoroughly. That's priceless."

Jimmy shot Holly a dirty look as he pulled his suitcase out of the closet. "She didn't mean it as a compliment, you know."

"Yes, I got that." Holly went in the bathroom and came out with Jimmy's clothes from yesterday. "And I sincerely hope mom's wrong. We need good men like you holding office." She reached out and squeezed Jimmy's hand. "I've never been as proud of anybody in my life as I was when you told mom off just now."

"Thanks. I'm not sure I deserve it, but thanks." He sat down on the bed and gently pulled Holly down in his lap. "Now, what about the rest of her suggestion to me? That I go home to Verde and be a good husband to you. I'd really like to do that, you know. I realize this is a hell of a time to propose, with my campaign in ruins and a homicidal maniac after us, but I really would like to marry you, Holly."

Holly put her arms around Jimmy. "That's a big step," she said seriously. "Do you think we're ready to take it yet?"

"I am," Jimmy said solemnly. "I love you and would love nothing more than to spend the rest of my life with you." He tipped her face toward his and gave her a long, lingering kiss. "Tell you what. Don't give me an answer right now. Spend a few days thinking about it." He framed her face in his hands. "Think about living with me in that big old house and sharing my king-size every night." He kissed her softly. "Think about being Carrie's mom—she loves you as much as I do." He kissed her again and rested his hand lightly on her stomach. "Think about having my babies and the two of us watching them grow up. And think about hitting the road with me someday when all those kids are grown and gone." He kissed her once more. "Just think about it."

Holly nodded. "Of course I'll think about it."

She was going to say yes, Jimmy thought as they packed their bags. It might take her a few days of thinking it over, but if the love in her eyes every time she looked at him was any indication, he wasn't going to have to wait too long to put a ring on her finger. But as he followed Holly back to Verde, sticking as close to her little car as the law allowed, his happy grin faded and gut-twisting fear took its place. He loved Holly, loved her more than life itself—*and*

Chucky knew it. Jimmy's breath hitched in his throat as he remembered the image of Leigh Anne Navarro, her beautiful blue eyes staring lifelessly into empty space and her blood dripping down into the carpet. "You're not going to do that to my woman," Jimmy vowed out loud as he stared at the woman in the little car in front of him. "I'll kill you or you'll kill me, but you're not going to do that to Holly."

Chapter Twenty-one

Holly glanced into the rearview mirror as she took the highway that ringed Lake Templeton. He was still sticking to her like glue, not close enough to be dangerous but still not letting her out of his sight. Not that she minded one little bit. Thoroughly shaken by the revelations of the morning, Holly welcomed Jimmy's presence and his protection, although she wondered if the two of them together made an even juicier target for Chucky. That was certainly possible, she thought as she glanced at the sparkling beauty of the wind-stirred water. But today even the sight and sound of the majestic lake waters did nothing to soothe Holly's anger or calm her fears.

The bottom line was that a vicious killer had both she and Jimmy in his sights, and she was both angry—no, furious—at all this bastard had done and terrified that he would succeed in his goal of killing her or Jimmy, or, God forbid, both of them.

Janelle had spirited Carrie all the way to Washington, D.C., and Holly's friends in personal security were on their way, but would they be enough? Russ had called just a few minutes ago and confirmed that the fingerprints of the killer matched the ones the Army had for Theo Barnes. Verde County deputies, armed with the new information, were once again cross-checking Jimmy's campaign workers one volunteer at a time, looking for some shred of a clue as to what identity Theo Barnes was now using. And they had to figure it out and soon, she thought as her fingers tightened on the steering wheel. Otherwise, either she or Jimmy or the both of them would be dead, and the exhilarating promise of a life and a future together with Jimmy Adamcik—a future that she wanted desperately—would never come to pass.

Jimmy's distinctive ringtone chimed as they pulled together into Heaven's Point. "We'll check out your house and then I have to go on home," he said, his irritation evident. "My damned alarm's screaming and Angie can't get it shut off."

"Want me to come with you?" Holly asked as she headed down the street that led to her house. She could already hear Jimmy's alarm screeching shrilly.

"No, I need for you to get packed as quickly as you can and get back to my place," Jimmy said as they pulled both cars into Holly's driveway. "Chucky's probably already back in town and if he's not he will be before long. It will be easier for the pros to do their jobs if they only have to guard one place."

Holly unlocked the door and she and Jimmy made swift work of going through her house. Jimmy drew her to him for a quick hug. "Get over to my place as quickly as you can."

Holly nodded. Jimmy bolted through the door and Holly quickly locked it behind him. She grabbed her suitcase and was packing panties and bras for the next several days when she heard a vehicle pull up and watched Hal Jackson pull himself slowly from his pickup truck. Remembering Dan's admonition to trust no one, Holly watched as Hal took a fishing pole and a bucket of bait from the bed and shuffled around the corner of the house, then shrugged inwardly and continued packing. She had thrown the last pair of underwear in the suitcase and was rummaging through a pile of clean clothes looking for her favorite jeans when she heard the distinctive hiss of a silenced pistol and the sound of splintering wood coming from her living room downstairs.

Damn, she thought as she looked around desperately for a weapon. She checked her nightstand and looked under her bed before remembering to her horror that since Carrie had become a regular visitor she had gathered them all up and locked them downstairs in the gun cabinet. *Okay, time for Plan B,* she thought as she fought down her terror. Swearing, she threw open a window. "Hal, I need some help," she yelled as she pushed out the screen, jumping outward into the grass and hoping she didn't screw up her good leg in the process. She landed on her stomach and quickly rolled to her back, and sat up to find herself staring into the barrel of a loaded, cocked Glock aimed point-blank at her forehead. Her eyes traveled up the arm holding the pistol and she stared in horror at the man calmly holding a weapon on her. "My God, it was you all along," she whispered as she stared into Hal Jackson's cold, reptilian eyes as he bent over her prostrate form. "You're Theo Barnes."

"In the flesh, Bitch," he said coldly as he reached out and hit her once in the head with the pistol. "In the flesh," he said again as Holly's unconscious form fell backward into the grass.

* * *

"Damn, Jimmy, that thing would wake the dead," Angie teased as Jimmy punched in his code and the screeching alarm came to a merciful silence. "I've tried for thirty minutes to shut the thing off but the code you gave me wouldn't work."

"My fault. I've been changing the code on a regular basis and didn't let you know. Can I offer you a soda or something for all your trouble? Holly will be here in a few minutes."

"Wouldn't mind if you did," Angie said. "And you can fill me in on how Jason and Emily are doing."

"They're going to be fine." Jimmy got them each a soda and they sat down at the kitchen table. "The ones I feel for are the Navarros; apparently Chucky is actually a relative of hers. And at this point Russ is more worried about Holly and me. He's certain we're the next targets."

"Cocky bastard's sure of that, huh?" Angie asked tartly.

"Uh-oh, haven't forgiven him for the 'hot babe' crack, have you?" Jimmy asked innocently, laughing out loud when Angie shot him a dirty look. "Yes, he's sure. Now the trick is going to be to figure out what identity Chucky is using at this point. Jason said his voice sounded like Patrick's and the more I think about it, I swear I've also heard a voice recently that sounds like that kid, but I'll be damned if I know where."

Angie finished off the rest of her soda. "I've got to run. Tell Holly I'll catch up with her in the next day or two. And you two be careful."

"We'll do that." Jimmy walked Angie to the door. He picked up his duffel in the foyer and was dumping his dirty clothes in the washer when he spotted the time and frowned. Damn it, Holly was sure taking a long time to pack for a few days. Alarmed, Jimmy went back to the front door and peered out and relaxed when he spotted Hal Jackson's beat-up old pickup in the driveway. She had probably stopped to reassure the anxious man that she was all right.

Jimmy hit the Wash button and smiled as he thought about Hal, how he had joined Holly in her support of Jimmy's candidacy when the other support group members shifted their support to Navarro. But his smile slowly faded as he replayed Hal's stuttered but passionately indignant diatribe against the rest of the support group members the next day at campaign headquarters. *Take away the stutter, the hesitation,* he said to himself, a cold spear of fear shooting down his spine. *Listen to the timbre, the cadence. Listen to the laugh. You remember that laugh. You remember that voice.*

"Good God damn!" Jimmy yelped, horrified, as the puzzle pieces clicked together. Swearing, he ran out of the laundry room and sprinted through the house. Yes, he had heard that voice before. He had heard it in Iraq on that horrible day everything had gone to shit. *He had heard it when Patrick Barnes uttered his last words before he was blown to hell.* Hal Jackson was Theo Barnes.

Jimmy grabbed his phone and scrolled down to Russ Riley's number. Cursing when it went to voice mail, he fired off a quick text—*TBarnes is Hal Jackson Holly in trouble go to her place*—and raced toward Holly's house, cursing when his phone rang and cursing even louder when he saw Holly's front curtain twitch and her number on his screen. With trembling fingers he held the phone to his ear. "I swear to God, Barnes, if you've harmed a hair on her head I'll kill you."

Jimmy heard a cold chuckle on the other end of the line. "Figured it out, have you? Throw the phone across the street and get your ass over here. If you let on to anybody else she dies."

"Hal—Theo—"Jimmy swore out loud when the connection broke. Thankful he'd already sent the text and hoping to hell Russ got it, Jimmy threw the phone across the street and marched up the sidewalk, trembling in fury as he slammed into Holly's house and skidding to a halt at the sight in front of him. Holly was sprawled, unconscious, on the rug in front of her easy chair, her hands and feet bound and a welt the diameter of a softball swelling her temple. Hal Jackson sat in Holly's easy chair, his feet almost touching Holly. His pistol was in one hand and he had a grenade dangling in the other. Hal gestured with the grenade. "Little souvenir from the war. Sneaked it home with me."

Jimmy made a show of shrugging. "You and every other soldier who served over there. No big deal."

"It is if I use it on you," Hal sneered. "Have a seat, Major Adamcik," he added coldly, gesturing to the sofa with the pistol. "We need to have a little talk before we all die. Nope, don't come near me," he said as Jimmy took a step forward. "I'll have the pin pulled and the fuse going before you can make it across the room. Now sit."

Jimmy edged across the room and sat down on the sofa. He stared across the room at the man who now held their lives in his hands. Gone was the shuffling, stuttering, war-wounded veteran. This man had no hesitation in his manner and his movements were strong and sure. His speech was clear and his eyes were cold and hard, and Jimmy had no doubt that the man sitting in front of him was a cold-blooded killer and that, if he had his way, none of the three of them would make it out of this room alive. But Theo Barnes apparently was in no big hurry to do the deed. Jimmy crossed his legs and hoped that the trembling in his hands did not show and that Theo could not detect his abject terror. If he could buy them some time, hopefully Russ would get the text and come get them out of this. "Am I to assume that you moved to Heaven's Point in search of me?" Jimmy asked almost conversationally.

Theo rolled his eyes. "Of course."

"So what happened to the real Hal Jackson?"

"Hal? What do you think happened to him?" Theo asked harshly. "I took him out awhile back. Couldn't have two of us running around, now could we? It was easy to slip into his identity. Height was close enough but losing the weight was a bitch. Injuries were easy enough to ape." He paused a minute. "Hardest part was retraining that damned dog. Raven was harder to fool than the people. You clowns in Heaven's Point are way, *way* too trusting." His laugh was cold as he looked down at Holly. "She sure as hell was easy enough to fool."

"Holly's a nice woman," Jimmy said calmly. "She wasn't looking for duplicity from someone in her support group."

Theo nudged Holly's inert body roughly with the toe of his shoe. "Stupid her. Stupid gimps, all of them. I ought to blow her away right now." He motioned toward her with the grenade.

"Why?" Jimmy asked quickly, hoping to distract Theo. "Why Holly? Why any of them?"

Resentment burned in Theo's eyes as he stared down at Holly's still form. "Because they *lived*. She and her gimps aren't worthy of living. They aren't worthy, them or any of the damn gimps who came back, and yet they lived while my brother's pushing daisies in a Round Rock cemetery." He stared down at Holly for a moment. "The barn and the house in Austin were kind of fun. Kind of like old home week, you know. That's what I did in the Army. Blew things up, mostly."

"But you obviously have other skills as well," Jimmy prompted him.

"Sure do," Theo said almost proudly. "Special Forces was really big on cross training. They taught me well, and as long as I worked alone, it pretty much went according to plan. It only started getting fucked when I got that punk to rape the ugly girl. Flores was supposed to die and Armbruster was supposed to go out there and find him." He laughed coldly. "Bastard I hired screwed it up big time. Can't get good help these days to save your life. Joke, get it?" He looked down at Holly. "But she's gonna die this afternoon and that's no joke."

Stall, stall, Jimmy thought. "Where did you build your bombs?"

Theo shrugged. "A deserted trailer out on the Wilcox place. Couldn't build them here on the Point."

"What about Jason and Emily? Were they supposed to die, too?"

"Hell, yes," Theo snapped. "And they would have if those yahoos with the pizza hadn't shown up. That shit Donahue—damn it, he was standing right next to Pat when the bomb went off. He should have died. *He should have died instead of Patrick.*" His eyes flashed and the hand with the grenade trembled.

Jimmy glanced down at Holly. Was it his imagination or had Holly's eyelid just twitched a little? Jimmy caught Theo's eyes. "What about Leigh Anne? She was your flesh and blood."

"Yes, she was, and I took no pleasure in killing her." Theo's face hardened. "But she was also a fucking traitor to Pat's memory and for that she had to die."

"How did you get all the log-ins?" Jimmy asked. No, it wasn't his imagination, he thought as he caught another flicker of Holly's eyelid out of the corner of his eye. She was starting to come around.

Theo shrugged. "Shoulder surfing, how else? Why be careful around someone like Hal? None of you ever thought of the stupid, stuttering Hal Jackson as a threat."

Theo stopped for a minute. Jimmy could feel the change in Holly but continued to hold Theo's gaze. "Why me?" Jimmy pressed, even though he already knew the answer. "I'm not a gimp."

"You are, actually," Theo reminded him. "But that's not why I came after you." He stood up on two steady legs and stared at Jimmy with smoldering fury. "You killed my brother. You singled him out. You ordered him to stand guard just because he was big. It was *you*, Jimmy Adamcik, who sent my brother to his death. And now by God I'm sending you and the bitch to yours and I'm going with you." Theo put down the pistol and stared across the room as Jimmy rose from his chair. "Bye, bye," Theo said as he reached for the pin.

There was a flash of movement on the floor and Jimmy leapt across the room. Theo jumped and screeched as Holly sunk her teeth into the tendons behind his ankle and jerked her head back, yanking Theo off his feet back into the chair. Theo immediately started back up but Jimmy threw himself on top of the man and even with Theo kicking at her viciously Holly refused to let go, biting and pulling at his leg. Jimmy smashed his fist into Theo's face twice, grimacing a little at the sound of his nose breaking before turning his attention to the grenade still clutched in Theo's fist.

Fighting like the mad man he was, Theo arched and threw his body up and landed both of them on the floor, his body sprawled on top of Jimmy. He tried to reach again for the pin but Jimmy, with a strength borne of adrenaline-fueled terror, rolled them over so that Theo was beneath him but still clutching the grenade tightly in his fist. Theo bucked Jimmy off and yanked the pin from the grenade. "Checkmate," he whispered as he let go of the safety lever, starting the grenade's five second fuse. He clung to the grenade for precious seconds then let the grenade slip from his fingers.

"Not," Jimmy said as he snatched up the falling grenade and threw it through Holly's living room window above the easy chair, shattering the glass. Jimmy dove to the floor, ramming Holly up against the bottom of the easy chair and covering her body with his own as the grenade exploded in a burst of heat and light. The glass window exploded inward and shrapnel ripped through the window and glass rained into the room. Although the easy chair provided a modicum of protection, Jimmy screamed as he felt the pain of flying glass and shards of something much worse rip into his back and his legs.

Theo let out a single blood-curdling yell of anguish as the worst of the onslaught rained down on him and then he went silent.

Shaking with pain, Jimmy tried to pull himself from Holly but cried out in agony and collapsed on top of her instead. "Are you all right?" he gasped as he stared into her glazed eyes.

Holly shook her head, her eyes glassy. "I don't think so," she said. "There are two of you and you both look like hell." She eased out from under him, careful to avoid the glass and shrapnel littering the floor, and Jimmy heard her gasp. "Oh, God, Jimmy, you're hurt," she said. "You're hurt bad. We've got to get you to a doctor."

"I'll live," Jimmy gasped painfully as Russ Riley burst through the door with his weapon drawn. He slowly raised himself up on his elbows and looked across the room and sucked in his breath at the sight of Theo Barnes' bloody, mangled body. Without even the flimsy shelter the back of the easy chair had provided, Theo had taken the brunt of the mid-air explosion. He was still alive, but the entire front of his body was covered with burns and pitted with shrapnel wounds, several of them deep enough to expose bone, and there was a particularly large hole in his abdomen. His face looked like hamburger meat and one of his eyes was damaged, probably permanently.

Russ scooped up Theo's pistol from the floor and rushed to their side, quickly untied Holly and whipped out his radio. "Get three ambulances out to Heaven's Point, to Holly Riley's residence, as quickly as you can. Put in a call to Caroline Briscoe to get over here. One head injury and two with shrapnel and glass. And get Russo and Sheriff Waller here. One of the injured is Theo Barnes. We have Chucky."

He thumbed off his radio and moved across the room to stand over Theo, a satisfied grin teasing his mouth. "The cocky asshole has you, Chucky."

Amazingly, Theo turned his head and stared malevolently across the room at Jimmy even as Russ snapped a pair of cuffs on him. "Fuck you," he said hoarsely. "Fuck you, Adamcik. Fuck you, bitch. Fuck you and the rest of your gimps."

Jimmy looked across the room and in spite of the excruciating pain of the glass and the shrapnel he barked out a laugh. "No, you're the one that's fucked now. Can you feel the pain? Can you smell the burns? Can you see anything out of the mangled eye? You're going to be months in the hospital, Chucky. You're going to have surgeries and skin grafts and scars. You're going to have a hole in your gut. You're going to have to function with only one eye and you're going to look like a monster."

Theo glared at him out of his remaining eye. "So?"

Holly shakily pushed herself to her feet and stared down at Theo before throwing her head back and laughing out loud. "Jimmy's right. God, you don't get it, do you, Theo? You know all us gimps you hold in such contempt? Well, look down at yourself, chum. Now you're one of us."

* * *

Holly blinked her eyes in the quiet bedroom, coming to instant wakefulness when she heard the faint sound coming from the other side of Jimmy's king-sized bed. Moonlight shone through the open drapes, illuminating both her and the man mumbling and stirring restlessly in his sleep beside her. She turned over and slid across the mattress, careful not to jostle her still-tender head, and took Jimmy's hand. "Wake up, Jimmy," she crooned softly as she gave his hand a reassuring squeeze. "Wake up, love. We're safe. It's all right now."

Jimmy's eyes popped open and he stared for a moment before a rueful smile touched his lips. "Sorry," he said softly as he shifted slowly on the bed, his movements obviously causing pain. "I was dreaming."

"I can imagine," she said softly. She leaned down and touched his lips with her own. "Same song, second verse. I can't remember most of what happened that afternoon with Chucky and you're having nightmares." Holly's memories were fuzzy, much to the frustration of both Russ and the federal agents, who wanted her testimony to corroborate Jimmy's. Theo, recuperating under armed guard at BAMC, was the subject of a lively tug-of-war between the FBI and the four jurisdictions in which he committed his crimes, and he had gone so far off the deep end that absolutely nothing he said, even a confession, would hold up in court. As far as Holly was concerned she was just as glad she couldn't remember the traumatic events that were now haunting Jimmy, who had added them to his roster of nightmares. She looked at him with worry in her eyes. "Is this going to set you back?" she asked. "Is it going to make the PTSD worse?"

Jimmy shrugged and rolled onto his stomach, the exhaustion and pain etched into his face more painful to her than the angry wounds covering his back and his butt and the backs of his legs.

Some of his wounds were going to leave lasting scars, not that either of them gave a damn, but she was worried about the PTSD.

"Holly, quit fretting," he told her. "It's only my first night home. Besides, you woke me up before it got that bad. And you're going to stay right here and keep waking me up like you did just now. Okay?" He shifted onto his side and held out his arm. "Come here. I want to hold you."

"Are you sure?" sbe asked. "I don't want to roll over in my sleep and hurt you."

"I'll be fine," he said. "Come on, Holly. I've missed being close to you."

Holly scooted closer and turned so that she was spooned up against his chest. "Wish we could do more," she said wistfully.

"Well, we could—"

"Don't even go there," she snickered softly. "Damn, even laughing makes my head hurt. And you're in no shape either."

The doctors had warned them that Jimmy was looking at a recovery time of several months and strongly suggested that he abandon his run for Congress and concentrate on getting well. He had taken their advice with good grace and Misty issued a press release announcing his withdrawal just one day after the Navarro campaign announced Alex's withdrawal. "I'm sorry about the campaign," Holly said softly as Jimmy tucked his arm around her and rested his chin on the top of her head. "I don't care what mom thinks, you would have made a damn good congressman. Maybe you can run again next time."

"Thanks, Holly. That means a lot." Jimmy ran his hand up and down her arm. "But another proposal was put to me this week that frankly has a lot more appeal."

"Oh, really? And what proposal was that?" Holly asked.

"Remember when Judge Riley came to see me in the hospital? He had more on his mind that afternoon than just checking on his favorite niece's sweetie. Your uncle's thinking about retiring. He and the Verde County party committee asked if I would consider running for his position next fall."

Holly turned over and looked at Jimmy. "Retiring? Uncle Willis? Why would he do that?"

Jimmy chuckled at the surprise on her face. "Maybe because he's over seventy years old and getting tired? Anyway, I told him I really liked the idea. I could announce but wouldn't have to start campaigning until later in the spring, which would give me time to get better. It wouldn't be as grueling as a congressional race and money wouldn't be that much of an issue. Besides, I think I'd really like being a judge." He was quiet for a moment. "Do you think I'd be any good at it?"

"Can you give a tirade from the bench?" She asked with a smile in her voice.

"Bet I can try," he said. "I hope your mom and her cronies won't be too disappointed by my defection."

"Oh. That," Holly said flatly.

"That, what?" He asked curiously.

"They already found somebody else. Some rabid conservative out of Big Spring. She makes mom and her buddies look like flaming liberals. Oh come on, it's not that funny," she groused when he let out a hoot of laughter.

"Sorry," Jimmy sputtered.

"By the way, I had a proposal put to me, too," she said as she bent down and brushed his lips with her own. "Something about you and me and marriage. I really liked that proposal, Jimmy. I liked it very much, in fact. I had planned to accept that proposal with a little fanfare and make you really glad you came to the party, but under the circumstances will a simple 'yes' suffice?"

Jimmy reached around and gently pulled her lips down to his own. "Considering the fact that one of your parties might kill me at this point, a simple 'yes' will do just fine." His kiss was long and lingering. "I love you, Holly. I love you and want to marry you and spend the rest of my life with you. And I want to be the kind of husband you can be proud of. I maybe got sidetracked for a while, but I swear I'll try my damnedest to be the kind of politician—hell, the kind of man—you can be proud of."

"I love you, too, Jimmy," Holly said as she gazed at him. "And as far as being proud of you? I already am."

ABOUT THE AUTHOR

The author of twenty romance novels, Emily Mims combined her writing career with a career in public education until leaving the classroom to write full time. The mother of two sons, now she and her husband Charles split their time between central Texas and eastern Tennessee. For relaxation she plays the piano, organ, dulcimer, and ukulele. She says, "I love to write romances because I believe in them. Romance happened to me and it can happen to any woman—if she'll just let it."

Did you enjoy this book? Drop us a line and say so! We love to hear from readers, and so do our authors. To connect, visit www.boroughspublishinggroup.com online, send comments directly to info@boroughspublishinggroup.com, or friend us on Facebook and Twitter. And be sure to check back regularly for contests and new releases in your favorite subgenres of romance!

Are you an aspiring writer? Check out www.boroughspublishinggroup.com/submit and see if we can help you make your dreams come true.

www.ingramcontent.com/pod-product-compliance
Lightning Source LLC
Chambersburg PA
CBHW071136170626
46809CB00002B/641